EXTRAORDINARY PORTRAITS BY EXTRAORDINARY WOMEN

Rich girls—poor wives . . .

A divorcee on Fifth Avenue—a black woman in Harlem . . .

Mabel, Virginia Woolf's lower-class Londoner—Laura, Katherine Mansfield's mansion-dweller . . .

Women in the city, suburb, country, ghetto . . .

Working-class Jewish, celibate Catholic, Irish, English, American, Canadian, French . . .

Women who choose husbands over personal fulfillment—women who choose women over men . . .

Women who know themselves—women too oppressed or weak to know or choose anything . . .

Here are twenty-six stories about women—their lives as mysterious and individual as the human personality itself—as perceived by the finest modern women writers, women who often lived these lives themselves.

SUSAN CAHILL has taught literature and writing at several universities in the New York area. She is the editor of Women and Fiction, Volume II; *the coeditor of a number of anthologies, and the author of* Earth Angels *and* A Literary Guide to Ireland *(with Thomas Cahill).*

WOMEN AND FICTION

Short Stories by and about Women

EDITED BY

Susan Cahill

A MENTOR BOOK

NEW AMERICAN LIBRARY

NEW YORK AND SCARBOROUGH, ONTARIO

Library of Congress Catalog Card Number: 75-21588

ACKNOWLEDGMENTS

"The Other Two" by Edith Wharton is reprinted with the permission of Charles Scribner's Sons from *The Descent of Man* by Edith Wharton. Copyright 1904 Charles Scribner's Sons, renewal copyright 1932 Edith Wharton.

"A Wagner Matinee" by Willa Cather. Reprinted from *Youth and the Bright Medusa*, by Willa Cather, courtesy of Alfred A. Knopf, Inc.

"The Secret Woman" by Colette. From *The Other Woman* by Colette, translated by Margaret Crosland, copyright © 1972 by The Bobbs-Merrill Company, Inc., reprinted by permission of the publisher and Peter Owen Ltd.

"Miss Furr and Miss Skeene" by Gertrude Stein. Copyright 1922 by The Four Seasons Co. Reprinted from *Selected Writings of Gertrude Stein* by permission of Random House, Inc. and the Estate of Gertrude Stein.

"The New Dress" by Virginia Woolf. From *A Haunted House and Other Stories* by Virginia Woolf, copyright, 1944, 1972, by Harcourt Brace Jovanovich, Inc. and reprinted by permission of Harcourt Brace Jovanovich, the Hogarth Press, and the Author's Literary Estate.

"The Garden Party" by Katherine Mansfield. Copyright 1922 by Alfred A. Knopf, Inc. and renewed 1950 by J. Middleton Murry. Reprinted from *The Short Stories of Katherine Mansfield* by permission of the publisher.

"Rope" by Katherine Anne Porter. Copyright, 1930, 1958, by Katherine Anne Porter. Reprinted from her volume *Flowering Judas and Other Stories* by permission of Harcourt Brace Jovanovich, Inc.

(The following pages constitute an extension of this copyright page.)

SIGNET, SIGNET CLASSIC, MENTOR, PLUME, MERIDIAN AND NAL BOOKS are published *in the United States* by
New American Library,
1633 Broadway, New York, New York 10019,
in Canada by The New American Library of Canada Limited,
81 Mack Avenue, Scarborough, Ontario M1L 1M8

First Printing, December, 1975

9 10 11 12 13 14 15 16 17

PRINTED IN THE UNITED STATES OF AMERICA

For my sisters,
Elizabeth Ann and Mary Florence

[illegible] now as I think a man is entitled to rights he

Contents

Introduction

Virginia Woolf believed that women were better suited to write fiction than poetry. In *Granite and Rainbow* she wrote:

> . . . living as she did in the common sitting-room, surrounded by people, a woman was trained to use her mind in observation and upon the analysis of character. She was trained to be a novelist and not to be a poet.

A poet was one who indulged "that romantic intensity which is connected with a sense of one's individuality." A poet thought the world existed to serve the needs of one's imagination, but a novelist desired to express the world more fully than oneself. A novelist existed to serve the world as its dispassionate observer. Woman, destined to watch and wait in the parlors of her father and husband, was thus better equipped for writing fiction than poetry.

In support of Virginia Woolf's theory we have the unforgettable picture of Jane Austen, hiding away her manuscript as the floorboards on the other side of the sitting-room door creaked to announce another visit from nieces and brothers and Chawton neighbors. One imagines those visits: dear Aunt Jane sitting poised, perhaps embroidering, a dispassionate audience to whichever duplicitous Fanny or awkward Mr. Collins was displaying the newest ruffle. Sly Aunt Jane. She watched, she waited, and after they all left, she scratched away again, making it clear in six great novels that on her nothing had been lost.

Novelists and poets, however, may divide their time between the sitting rooms in the house of fiction and Parnassus. The biography and art of the next great woman novelist show the imaginative writer as a member of a world larger than the one to which Mrs. Woolf's theory assigns her. The year after Jane Austen was buried beneath the civilized arches of Winchester Cathedral, Emily Brontë was born on the edge of the Yorkshire moors. She was a great poet as well as, for many readers, the writer of the greatest English novel. She got her training by walking the windswept mountainy moors, alone, or in the company of a brother or sister or two rather than by surrounding herself with people in the common sitting room of the Haworth parsonage. To avoid the need to go out from the blessed isolation of her father's house to earn her living as a governess in strange sitting rooms, she sat uninterrupted in a corner of her father's garden writing *Wuthering Heights*. She was most admired, perhaps, for "that romantic intensity" which Mrs. Woolf attributes to the imagination of the poet. For resisting classification by literary historians and critics alike, Emily Brontë has gone down in literary history as something of a "freak."

After Jane Austen lived her so-called uneventful life in the genteel south, and Emily Brontë spent her life writing in the rugged North Country, George Eliot arrived from the newly evangelized Midlands to "live in sin" in agnostic, intellectual London. Clearly, the three early mistresses of the house of fiction lived in varied and multiple environments.

Twenty-six of their most worthy descendants are represented in this collection. All are women who have chosen the writing of fiction as a lifetime vocation. Reflecting the varieties of human experience that people today, especially women, are examining from often unconventional points of view, their fictions show that among artists there is no one orthodoxy about how to live. Stories of marriage and motherhood and growing up female that are told from points of view as different as those represented here call to mind the wisdom of Thoreau: "This is the only way, we say, but there are as many ways as there can be drawn radii from one centre." The stories in this collection do not illustrate anyone's fixed ideas; rather they reflect the ambiguities of human experience. The women in the stories cannot be classified as either victims or agents of their destiny. The mother in the story by Margaret Drabble, for instance, is at once a victim and a woman possessed of her soul. She is pathetic, she is magnificent; she suffers, and yet she is no stranger at life's feast. The stories in *Women and Fiction* point up the impoverished imaginations behind all one-dimensional views of the lives women have lived to both limit and create themselves. Surely, a collection of fiction that exposes the tyranny of theoretical views—whether sociological, psychological, theological—in the light of fiction's own complex honesty serves to truly liberate its readers' consciousness.

The house of fiction has never been a comfortable place for ideologues. Because this collection shows the fiction writer in her habit of admitting the mysteriousness and complexity of our condition—especially with regard to relationships between women and men, between women and women, between women and their children—it is a useful contribution to the current dialectic about women. Too often the argument is a dreary one because it takes place in an atmosphere in which ideology is in control and imagination struggles to survive. Art, however, has not yet yielded her seat of wisdom. Within her radiance is still to be found the truth of paradox rather than the rote answers of doctrine. The art of fiction, says Mrs. Woolf, exists to "express character," not to "preach doctrine." In each story in this collection an artist expresses with realistic compassion the consciousness of an individual woman. To label any of the writers "feminist" would be to force that writer into an easy category, to insist her home is not the house of fiction but a smaller place. Yet it is no error to see these fictions as feminism's sacred texts, their authors as the movement's greatest prophets, for they tell us more about what it feels like to be a woman than all the gray abstractions about Women heard on the talk shows or read in gray reviews about gray books on sexual stereotypes. In a world whose future may be rationalized by the abstractions of *realpolitic,* anything that takes us closer to the heart, that makes us respond seriously and sympathetically to the individual human being is to be revered. "In the end, our technique is sensitivity," Eudora Welty writes about the crafting of the short story.

A sense of the humanistic value of writing fiction emerges again and again from Katherine Mansfield's *Journal,* Katherine Anne Porter's *Notes on Writing,* Flannery O'Connor's essays, Carson McCullers's journalism, and Doris Lessing's interviews. Through them all runs a common theme, a vision of their art as a moral imperative, as an act of faith. The focus of the stories in this collection is on the lives of girls and women. It is time to see how these lives—the growing up, the marrying, the vowing virginity, the longing, the being poor, the going crazy and carrying on, the loving the children—how these experiences have been perceived by some of the best modern writers who happen to have lived these lives themselves.

The journals and prose of women writers reveal how difficult it has often been for them to both live and reflect on their living in their art. Faith is one thing. Practicing it wholeheartedly is quite another. "I have like most women," writes Rebecca West, "written only a quarter of what I might have written owing to my family responsibilities." Tillie Olsen in her article "Silences: When Writers Don't Write" has given perhaps the fullest exposition to the subject of the practical difficulties—the impossibility?—of being a great writer as well as a mother/wife/daughter/lover, who must also teach, type, or translate for a living, and then, at the end of the day, stand there ironing. Those who know firsthand the endless distractions for the writer without a room of her own and the economic pressures on those without a secure income will find especially convincing the story included here by the Canadian writer Alice Munro. In "The Office" a young wife and mother, unable to write at home, rents a room in town to write in, only to be constantly interrupted there and finally driven out by her new landlord.

And yet, paradoxically, the woman in Alice Munro's story feels herself enlarged by this failure to survive in a room of her own. Not every woman who writes would agree entirely with Tillie Olsen that the quotidian maze and, in particular, the demands of children make the creative writer impotent. It is interesting to find in the biographies of the writers in this collection that fourteen have had children and have still managed to write. Joyce Carol Oates, an amazingly prolific writer, is also a teacher and housewife. Housework, she says, "is like Zen meditation." She would feel "alienated" from her own life if she had a maid. Is it possible that the necessity of living in many worlds at once actually disciplines a woman in a way that enriches her writing?

In the preface to her *Selected Stories,* Mary Lavin writes:

> There was a time after I first started to write when I resented having so little time for stories. I used to think, with some bitterness, that if I were to cease writing altogether it would be months, even years, before anyone in my household would notice that this had happened—if they ever did! But now all that resentment has gone from me, and I believe that the things that took up my time, and even used up creative energy that might have gone into writing, have served me well. They imposed a selectivity that I might not otherwise have been strong enough to impose upon my often feverish, overfertile imagination. So if my life has set limits to my writing I am glad of it. I do not get a chance to write more stories than I ought; or put more into them than ought to be there.

Carson McCullers, a great writer despite a lifetime of physical suffering, once asked Hortense Calisher if she had wanted her children, saying that she herself had felt children would interfere with her work. Hortense Calisher answered, "Yes, I did want them, and yes, they did interfere—but everything does. And everything contributes. Writers know this instinctively."

Everything contributes. Such a consciousness has much to do with the psychological authority of the stories in this collection. For they are the fruits of rich experience like that of Mary Lavin and Kay Boyle and Grace Paley, people who have always lived simultaneously in multiple environments—farm, campus, city, labor room, slum, church, Europe, jail, kitchen, playground, office, nursery, picket line—and have thereby come to what Pauline Kael, writing of Joyce, has called "a love of the supreme juices of everyday life." This catholic sense of the extraordinariness of the ordinary is felt in some of the finest stories in this book. In "A Worn Path" by Eudora Welty, "Everyday Use" by Alice Walker, and "The Gifts of War" by Margaret Drabble, we meet an ordinary woman who does nothing more than be her everyday self. Each woman is an extraordinary human being. In "Winter Night" Kay Boyle sees in a rather commonplace situation involving a babysitter, a mother, and a child the unearthly pathos of human experience and brings it to life with the lyric power of a great artist.

The twenty-six stories in this book have been selected because they are extraordinarily moving and convincing portraits of women and their lives by extraordinary writers. Many of the stories are masterpieces. Many of the writers have not been widely anthologized, but, then, the poor representation of fiction by women in standard anthologies is universal. There is a recent collection of approximately forty stories about "The American Experience" that contains not one story by a woman writer, a ratio that tells a lot about the making and breaking of American literature. Each of the selections here is introduced by a sketch of the writer's background; most of the sketches include a few of the writer's ideas about her craft. No story has been included because it either illustrates or disputes a currently popular theory about Women. Vision and great craft have been the criteria of selection.

The work of some writers has had to be omitted for a number of reasons: an editorial decision about the number of stories that could be published (Sarah Orne Jewett, Isak Dinesen, Caroline Gordon, Tess Slesinger, Olivia Manning, to name a few, were dropped from the original table of contents); and Jean Stafford's refusal to have her work included in anthologies devoted exclusively to writing by women. And there are many women writers whose understanding of the lives of women is best expressed in their novels or whose stories are already widely anthologized or are too long to print here. Elizabeth Bowen, Cynthia Ozick, Paule Marshall, Jean Rhys, Mary McCarthy, Jane Bowles, Iris Murdoch, Selma Lagerlof, Siegrid Undset, Joan Didion, Nadine Gordimer, Alison Lurie, and Shirley Jackson fall into one or all of these categories. Knowing the work of these artists, one wonders when their names will be added to the litany of literary saints. It is Bellow, Roth, Malamud, Wolfe, Mailer, Styron, Updike, and Vonnegut, we read again and again, who, prophetlike (and career-wise) have forced us to respond with heightened vision to the upheaval of our times. How much longer before the hierarchy of the literary marketplace updates this litany to acknowledge Joan Didion, Joyce Carol Oates, Flannery O'Connor, Cynthia Ozick, and Tillie Olsen for their sense of moral rot in the waning twentieth century?

Those who would use this book in an educational setting will find it eminently teachable. Many of the stories can be compared and contrasted with one another on a number of levels.

A consideration of the differences between the woman in Doris Lessing's "To Room Nineteen," her classic story about a woman's boredom, and Grace Paley's large-spirited protagonist in "An Interest in Life" can lead to a sense of the differences between English sensibility and American sense, or, for that matter, between cerebration and celebration as two contrasting modes of consciousness.

Joyce Carol Oates's "In a Region of Ice" and Alice Munro's "The Office" have to do with virginity, real and symbolic, as ways of both preserving and losing one's humanity. Celibacy and human intercourse emerge as two ways of being to be evaluated by the reader.

For all the hours spent in the common sitting-room and for all the gadding-about in multiple environments, women have written great stories about loneliness. It is a theme explored here in several stories that are deeply and permanently moving: for the married woman in Willa Cather's "A Wagner Matinee" loneliness has been a way of life; in "The Scream on Fifty-Seventh Street" Hortense Calisher writes about a widow's growing old alone in New York City; Mary Lavin's widow in "In a Café" spends a lonely afternoon in Dublin, the world's largest village.

The growing up of a romantic, aspiring girl is treated with brilliant sensitivity by Carson McCullers and Katherine Mansfield, but it is illuminating to contrast each writer's view of the forces that crush the spirit rather than encourage it to grow.

Money is seen as one of the forces that determines both the growth and loss of identity. Economic poverty becomes symbolic—but in significantly different ways—of the experience of the women characters in the stories by Tillie Olsen, Virginia Woolf, and Alice Walker.

Kate Chopin in "The Story of an Hour" and Mary Lavin in "In a Café" bring to life the experience of losing a husband, but for Chopin's protagonist, widowhood, in its first moments, is an exhilarating expectation of freedom; for Mary Lavin's character, life without the beloved is experienced as a state of loss that time does not heal. Both writers achieve powerful effects through very different uses of language. Chopin's style is restrained. There is an appropriate sense of information withheld, for Mrs. Mallard, after all, has always kept her own soul's counsel. Lavin's tone, on the other hand, is ruminative, full of eager life, like the widow Mary herself.

Marriage is seen in an economic and political context in "Like a Winding Sheet" by Ann Petry and in "Rope" by Katherine Anne Porter against a modern psychological backdrop—human beings presented as inextricably confused, flawed, streaked. In neither context does it seem possible that the marriage can survive in one case the racism or in the other the confusion that strangle them unless the partners make extraordinary acts of self-transcendence. In Willa Cather's "A Wagner Matinee" a marriage has endured, but Cather makes the woman's self-abnegation a matter for tears.

The happy wife, like successful romantic love, is not a common fictional theme. More often, mothering is treated as a source of self-knowledge, even when it demands great self-sacrifice. The mother in "The Gifts of War" by Margaret Drabble and the grandmother in Eudora Welty's "A Worn Path" have already been mentioned as extraordinary characters, heroines of a kind; yet there are important differences in the way these women are perceived by their authors. Drabble shows a mother's love in an economic and social context, amid broken glass and shouting sidewalk ideologues, and her story is, therefore, also about injustice. But Welty's Old Phoenix is almost outside of time: her world is southern rural, the only possible context for this beautiful and harmonious character who is often compared with Dilsey in *The Sound and the Fury*. The social differences between the women in the stories by Maeve Brennan and Julie Hayden are significant, too, but both the Irish mother who has lost her first baby in Brennan's "The Eldest Child" and the young woman who has had an abortion in Hayden's "Day-Old Baby Rats" are defined by a sense of loss.

In "Miss Furr and Miss Skeene" by Gertrude Stein, in "Cousin Lewis" by Jean Stubbs, and in Colette's "The Secret Woman," each writer is concerned in different ways with the mystery of sexual definition. Stein and Colette treat the subject of their characters' sexuality with a playful elusiveness. Jean Stubbs's story, however, unfolded against a more complex psychological background, arrives at a more profound truth.

Rich girls, poor wives, loss and hope, consciousness and ignorance, Edith Wharton's divorcée on brownstoned Fifth Avenue and Ann Petry's black couple up in Harlem, Virginia Woolf's lower-class Londoner, Mabel Waring, and

Katherine Mansfield's big-house Laura, women in the city, suburb, country, ghetto, working-class Jewish, celibate Catholic, Irish, English, American, Canadian, and a few secret French women. Women who choose women over men, women who choose husband over personal fulfillment, women who know self, women who are too oppressed or too weak to know or choose anything. The twenty-six stories in this anthology show that a woman's destiny is as mysterious and individual and various as the human personality itself. They represent exciting moments in the house of fiction, ones their ancestors would be proud to share. For in the great tradition of Jane Austen, Emily Brontë, and George Eliot, these fictions from the twentieth century unfold a deep understanding of what Stephen Daedalus's mother in *A Portrait of the Artist as a Young Man* prayed her son would someday learn:

"What the heart is and what it feels."

KATE CHOPIN was born Katherine O'Flaherty in St. Louis in 1851; her father was a prosperous emigrant from County Galway and her mother was of French descent. When she entered the Academy of the Sacred Heart at the age of nine, she was fluent in both English and French. As a girl she preferred "her dear reading and writing" to the "fiddle-scraping, flute tooting, and horn blowing" of St. Louis society. At twenty she married and moved to Cloutierville in the fertile Cane River region of Natchitoches Parish, the setting and inspiration of many of her stories about her Creole and Cajun neighbors. After her husband died suddenly of swamp fever in 1882, she moved back to St. Louis with her six children and began to write seriously. Tradition says that a doctor suggested she write about her life in Louisiana as therapy for the loneliness she experienced as a widow.

She studied the French writers she most admired, Flaubert and Maupassant. Her first novel, *At Fault*, was published in 1890 at her own expense; her short stories, which Jean Stafford has compared to those of Maupassant, began to appear in *Vogue* and *Century*. After the publication in 1899 of *The Awakening*, her novel about miscegenation and a wife's love for a man other than her husband, she was ostracized by St. Louis society, and editors and publishers boycotted her work. The novel, quite frankly about sex, was deemed "too strong drink for moral babes" by the *St. Louis Republic*— "it should be labelled poison." Later critics pronounced the book beautifully written and praised it for its treatment of infidelity and sexual happiness as a forerunner of the work of D. H. Lawrence and Simone de Beauvoir. Chopin's heroine Edna Pontellier, the mother of two children who falls in love with a younger man, has been compared with Hester Prynne, Emma Bovary, and Isabel Archer.

After the outrage provoked by her novel, Kate Chopin published nothing. She died suddenly of a cerebral hemorrhage after a hot day at the St. Louis Exposition in 1904.

Kate Chopin (1851–1904)

THE STORY OF AN HOUR

Knowing that Mrs. Mallard was afflicted with a heart trouble, great care was taken to break to her as gently as possible the news of her husband's death.

It was her sister Josephine who told her, in broken sentences, veiled hints that revealed in half concealing. Her husband's friend Richards was there, too, near her. It was he who had been in the newspaper office when intelligence of the railroad disaster was received, with Brently Mallard's name leading the list of "killed." He had only taken the time to assure himself of its truth by a second telegram, and had hastened to forestall any less careful, less tender friend in bearing the sad message.

She did not hear the story as many women have heard the same, with a paralyzed inability to accept its significance. She wept at once, with sudden, wild abandonment, in her sister's arms. When the storm of grief had spent itself she went away to her room alone. She would have no one follow her.

There stood, facing the open window, a comfortable, roomy armchair. Into this she sank, pressed down by a physical exhaustion that haunted her body and seemed to reach into her soul.

She could see in the open square before her house the tops of trees that were all aquiver with the new spring life. The delicious breath of rain was in the air. In the street below a peddler was crying his wares. The notes of a distant song which some one was singing reached her faintly, and countless sparrows were twittering in the eaves.

There were patches of blue sky showing here and there through the clouds that had met and piled above the other in the west facing her window.

She sat with her head thrown back upon the cushion of the chair quite motionless, except when a sob came up into her throat and shook her, as a child who has cried itself to sleep continues to sob in its dreams.

She was young, with a fair, calm face, whose lines bespoke repression and even a certain strength. But now there was a dull stare in her eyes, whose gaze was fixed away off yonder on one of those patches of blue sky. It was not a glance of reflection, but rather indicated a suspension of intelligent thought.

There was something coming to her and she was waiting for it, fearfully. What was it? She did not know; it was too subtle and elusive to name. But she felt it, creeping out of the sky, reaching toward her through the sounds, the scents, the color that filled the air.

Now her bosom rose and fell tumultuously. She was beginning to recognize this thing that was approaching to possess her, and she was striving to beat it back with her will—as powerless as her two white slender hands would have been.

When she abandoned herself a little whispered word escaped her slightly parted lips. She said it over and over under her breath: "Free, free, free!" The vacant stare and the look of terror that had followed it went from her eyes. They stayed keen and bright. Her pulses beat fast, and the coursing blood warmed and relaxed every inch of her body.

She did not stop to ask if it were not a monstrous joy that held her. A clear and exalted perception enabled her to dismiss the suggestion as trivial.

She knew that she would weep again when she saw the kind, tender hands folded in death; the face that had never looked save with love upon her, fixed and gray and dead. But she saw beyond that bitter moment a long procession of years to come that would belong to her absolutely. And she opened and spread her arms out to them in welcome.

There would be no one to live for during those coming years; she would live for herself. There would be no powerful will bending her in that blind persistence with which men and women believe they have a right to impose a private will upon a fellow-creature. A kind intention or a cruel intention made the act seem no less a crime as she looked upon it in that brief moment of illumination.

And yet she had loved him—sometimes. Often she had not. What did it matter! What could love, the unsolved mystery, count for in face of this possession of self-assertion which she suddenly recognized as the strongest impulse of her being!

"Free! Body and soul free!" she kept whispering.

Josephine was kneeling before the closed door with her lips to the keyhole, imploring for admission. "Louise, open the door! I beg; open the door—you will make yourself ill. What are you doing, Louise? For heaven's sake open the door."

"Go away. I am not making myself ill." No; she was drinking in a very elixir of life through that open window.

Her fancy was running riot along those days ahead of her. Spring days, and summer days, and all sorts of days that would be her own. She breathed a quick prayer that life might be long. It was only yesterday she had thought with a shudder that life might be long.

She arose at length and opened the door to her sister's importunities. There was a feverish triumph in her eyes, and she carried herself unwittingly like a goddess of Victory. She clasped her sister's waist, and together they descended the stairs. Richards stood waiting for them at the bottom.

Some one was opening the front door with a latchkey. It was Brently Mallard who entered, a little travel-stained, composedly carrying his grip-sack and umbrella. He had been far from the scene of accident, and did not even know there had been one. He stood amazed at Josephine's piercing cry; at Richards' quick motion to screen him from the view of his wife.

But Richards was too late.

When the doctors came they said she had died of heart disease—of joy that kills.

EDITH WHARTON was born Edith Newbold Jones in 1862 in New York City. She was a true daughter of the American Revolution, descended on her mother's side from a Revolutionary patriot. The youngest in a socially prominent and wealthy family, she spent a lonely childhood in her father's brownstone on West Twenty-Third Street. Educated at home by tutors, she liked to read, and wrote "make-up" stories on pieces of brown wrapping paper. In 1885 she married Edward Wharton ("Teddy"), an amiable Bostonian who did not share her intellectual and literary passions. The couple was divorced in 1912.

Mrs. Wharton began writing during her marriage—short stories at first, a form of writing in which she had always excelled; she then went on to write novels and travel books, becoming recognized as one of the most prominent writers in America following the publication of her novel *The House of Mirth*. F. Scott Ftizgerald describes his meeting with her, when as a young, unknown writer he came upon her in the office of Charles Scribner, their mutual publisher, and was reduced to stuttering by the great lady of letters. In her autobiography she said she turned to art as a way of enduring the "moral solitude" imposed by life with Teddy. According to Edmund Wilson, she began to write fiction on the advice of Dr. S. Weir Mitchell, her husband's psychiatrist and a specialist in female neurosis. But in his recent biography of Edith Warton, R. W. B. Lewis calls this one of the many minor legends that have surrounded her reputation. The theme of the affluent society as a moral wasteland runs through many of her novels and short stories. It is in her stories about marriage and divorce that her vision of that wasteland is most penetrating.

Edith Wharton
(1862–1937)

THE OTHER TWO

Waythorn, on the drawing-room hearth, waited for his wife to come down to dinner.

It was their first night under his own roof, and he was surprised at his thrill of boyish agitation. He was not so old, to be sure—his glass gave him little more than the five-and-thirty years to which his wife confessed—but he had fancied himself already in the temperate zone; yet here he was listening for her step with a tender sense of all it symbolized, with some old trail of verse about the garlanded nuptial doorposts floating through his enjoyment of the pleasant room and the good dinner just beyond it.

They had been hastily recalled from their honeymoon by the illness of Lily Haskett, the child of Mrs. Waythorn's first marriage. The little girl, at Waythorn's desire, had been transferred to his house on the day of her mother's wedding, and the doctor, on their arrival, broke the news that she was ill with typhoid, but declared that all the symptoms were favorable. Lily could show twelve years of unblemished health, and the case promised to be a light one. The nurse spoke as reassuringly, and after a moment of alarm Mrs. Waythorn had adjusted herself to the situation. She was very fond of Lily—her affection for the child had perhaps been her decisive charm in Waythorn's eyes—but she had the perfectly balanced nerves which her little girl had inherited, and no woman ever wasted less tissue in unproductive worry. Waythorn was therefore quite prepared to see her come in presently, a little late because of a last look at Lily, but as serene and well-appointed as if her good-night kiss had been laid on the brow of health. Her composure was restful to him; it acted as ballast to his somewhat unstable sensibilities. As he pictured her bending over the child's bed he thought how soothing her presence must be in illness: her very step would prognosticate recovery.

His own life had been a gray one, from temperament rather than circumstance, and he had been drawn to her by the unperturbed gaiety which kept her fresh and elastic at an age when most women's activities are growing either slack or febrile. He knew what was said about her; for, popular as she was, there had always been a faint undercurrent of detraction. When she had appeared in New York, nine or ten years earlier, as the pretty Mrs. Haskett whom Gus Varick had unearthed somewhere—was it in Pittsburgh or Utica?—society, while promptly accepting her, had reserved the right to cast a doubt on its own indiscrimination. Inquiry, however, established her undoubted connection with a socially reigning family, and explained her recent divorce as the natural result of a runaway match at seventeen; and as nothing was known of Mr. Haskett it was easy to believe the worst of him.

Alice Haskett's remarriage with Gus Varick was a passport to the set whose recognition she coveted, and for a few years the Varicks were the most popular couple in town. Unfortunately the alliance was brief and stormy, and this time the husband had his champions. Still, even Varick's stanchest supporters admitted that he was not meant for matrimony, and Mrs. Varick's grievances were of a nature to bear the inspection of the New York courts. A New York divorce is in itself a diploma of virtue, and in the semiwidowhood of this second separation Mrs. Varick took on an air of sanctity, and was allowed to confide her wrongs to some of the most scrupulous ears in town. But when it was known that she was to marry Waythorn there was a momentary reaction. Her best friends would have preferred to see her remain in the role of the injured wife, which was as becoming to her as crepe to a rosy complexion. True, a decent time had elapsed, and it was not even suggested that Waythorn had supplanted his predecessor. People shook their heads over him, however, and one grudging friend, to whom he affirmed that he took the step with his eyes open, replied oracularly: "Yes—and with your ears shut."

Waythorn could afford to smile at these innuendoes. In the Wall Street phrase, he had "discounted" them. He knew that society has not yet adapted itself to the consequences of divorce, and that till the adaptation takes place every woman who uses the freedom the law accords her must be her own social justification. Waythorn had an amused confidence in his wife's ability to justify herself. His expectations were fulfilled, and before the wedding took place Alice Varick's group had rallied openly to her support. She took it all imperturbably: she had a way of surmounting obstacles without seeming to be aware of them, and Waythorn looked back with wonder at the trivialities over which he had worn his nerves thin. He had the sense of having found refuge in a richer, warmer nature than his own, and his satisfaction, at the moment, was humorously summed up in the thought that his wife, when she had done all she could for Lily, would not be ashamed to come down and enjoy a good dinner.

The anticipation of such enjoyment was not, however, the sentiment expressed by Mrs. Waythorn's charming face when she presently joined him. Though she had put on her most engaging tea gown she had neglected to assume the smile that went with it, and Waythorn thought he had never seen her look so nearly worried.

"What is it?" he asked. "Is anything wrong with Lily?"

"No; I've just been in and she's still sleeping." Mrs. Waythorn hesitated. "But something tiresome has happened."

He had taken her two hands, and now perceived that he was crushing a paper between them.

"This letter?"

"Yes—Mr. Haskett has written—I mean his lawyer has written."

Waythorn felt himself flush uncomfortably. He dropped his wife's hands.

"What about?"

"About seeing Lily. You know the courts——"

"Yes, yes," he interrupted nervously.

Nothing was known about Haskett in New York. He was vaguely supposed to have remained in the outer darkness from which his wife had been rescued, and Waythorn was one of the few who were aware that he had given up his business in Utica and followed her to New York in order to be near his little girl. In the days of his wooing, Waythorn had often met Lily on the doorstep, rosy and smiling, on her way "to see papa."

"I am so sorry," Mrs. Waythorn murmured.

He roused himself. "What does he want?"

"He wants to see her. You know she goes to him once a week."

"Well—he doesn't expect her to go to him now, does he?"

"No—he has heard of her illness; but he expects to come here."

"*Here?*"

Mrs. Waythorn reddened under his gaze. They looked away from each other.

"I'm afraid he has the right. . . . You'll see. . . ." She made a proffer of the letter.

Waythorn moved away with a gesture of refusal. He stood staring about the softly-lighted room, which a moment before had seemed so full of bridal intimacy.

"I'm so sorry," she repeated. "If Lily could have been moved—"

"That's out of the question," he returned impatiently.

"I suppose so."

Her lip was beginning to tremble, and he felt himself a brute.

"He must come, of course," he said. "When is—his day?"

"I'm afraid—tomorrow."

"Very well. Send a note in the morning."

The butler entered to announce dinner.

Waythorn turned to his wife. "Come—you must be tired. It's beastly, but try to forget about it," he said, drawing her hand through his arm.

"You're so good, dear. I'll try," she whispered back.

Her face cleared at once, and as she looked at him across the flowers, between the rosy candleshades, he saw her lips waver back into a smile.

"How pretty everything is!" she sighed luxuriously.

He turned to the butler. "The champagne at once, please. Mrs. Waythorn is tired."

In a moment or two their eyes met above the sparkling glasses. Her own were quite clear and untroubled: he saw that she had obeyed his injunction and forgotten.

II

Waythorn, the next morning, went downtown earlier than usual. Haskett was not likely to come till the afternoon, but the instinct of flight drove him forth. He meant to stay away all day—he had thoughts of dining at his club. As his door closed behind him he reflected that before he opened it again it would have admitted another man who had as much right to enter it as himself, and the thought filled him with a physical repugnance.

He caught the elevated at the employees' hour, and found himself crushed between two layers of pendulous humanity. At Eighth Street the man facing him wriggled out, and another took his place. Waythorn glanced up and saw that it was Gus Varick. The men were so close together that it was impossible to ignore the smile of recognition on Varick's handsome overblown face. And after all—why not? They had always been on good terms, and Varick had been divorced before Waythorn's attentions to his wife began. The two exchanged a word on the perennial grievance of the congested trains, and when a seat at their side was miraculously left empty the instinct of self-preservation made Waythorn slip into it after Varick.

The latter drew the stout man's breath of relief. "Lord—I was beginning to feel like a pressed flower." He leaned back, looking unconcernedly at Waythorn. "Sorry to hear that Sellers is knocked out again."

"Sellers?" echoed Waythorn, starting at his partner's name.

Varick looked surprised. "You didn't know he was laid up with the gout?"

"No. I've been away—I only got back last night." Waythorn felt himself reddening in anticipation of the other's smile.

"Ah—yes; to be sure. And Sellers' attack came on two days ago. I'm afraid he's pretty bad. Very awkward for me, as it happens, because he was just putting through a rather important thing for me."

"Ah?" Waythorn wondered vaguely since when Varick had been dealing in "important things." Hitherto he had dabbled only in the shallow pools of speculation, with which Waythorn's office did not usually concern itself.

It occurred to him that Varick might be talking at random, to relieve the strain of their propinquity. That strain was becoming momentarily more apparent to Waythorn, and when, at Cortlandt Street, he caught sight of an acquaintance and had a sudden vision of the picture he and Varick must present to an initiated eye, he jumped up with a muttered excuse.

"I hope you'll find Sellers better," said Varick civilly, and he stammered back: "If I can be of any use to you—"

and let the departing crowd sweep him to the platform.

At his office he heard that Sellers was in fact ill with the gout, and would probably not be able to leave the house for some weeks.

"I'm sorry it should have happened so, Mr. Waythorn," the senior clerk said with affable significance. "Mr. Sellers was very much upset at the idea of giving you such a lot of extra work just now."

"Oh, that's no matter," said Waythorn hastily. He secretly welcomed the pressure of additional business, and was glad to think that, when the day's work was over, he would have to call at his partner's on the way home.

He was late for luncheon, and turned in at the nearest restaurant instead of going to his club. The place was full, and the waiter hurried him to the back of the room to capture the only vacant table. In the cloud of cigar smoke Waythorn did not at once distinguish his neighbors: but presently, looking about him, he saw Varick seated a few feet off. This time, luckily, they were too far apart for conversation, and Varick, who faced another way, had probably not even seen him; but there was an irony in their renewed nearness.

Varick was said to be fond of good living, and as Waythorn sat dispatching his hurried luncheon he looked across half enviously at the other's leisurely degustation of his meal. When Waythorn first saw him he had been helping himself with critical deliberation to a bit of Camembert at the ideal point of liquefaction, and now, the cheese removed, he was just pouring his *café double* from its little two-storied earthen pot. He poured slowly, his ruddy profile bent over the task, and one beringed white hand steadying the lid of the coffeepot; then he stretched his other hand to the decanter of cognac at his elbow, filled a liqueur glass, took a tentative sip, and poured the brandy into his coffee cup.

Waythorn watched him in a kind of fascination. What was he thinking of—only of the flavor of the coffee and the liqueur? Had the morning's meeting left no more trace in his thoughts than on his face? Had his wife so completely passed out of his life that even this odd encounter with her present husband, within a week after her remarriage, was no more than an incident in his day? And as Waythorn mused, another idea struck him: had Haskett ever met Varick as Varick and he had just met? The recollection of

Haskett perturbed him, and he rose and left the restaurant, taking a circuitous way out to escape the placid irony of Varick's nod.

It was after seven when Waythorn reached home. He thought the footman who opened the door looked at him oddly.

"How is Miss Lily?" he asked in haste.

"Doing very well, sir. A gentleman——"

"Tell Barlow to put off dinner for half an hour," Waythorn cut him off, hurrying upstairs.

He went straight to his room and dressed without seeing his wife. When he reached the drawing room she was there, fresh and radiant. Lily's day had been good; the doctor was not coming back that evening.

At dinner Waythorn told her of Sellers' illness and of the resulting complications. She listened sympathetically, adjuring him not to let himself be overworked, and asking vague feminine questions about the routine of the office. Then she gave him the chronicle of Lily's day; quoted the nurse and doctor, and told him who had called to inquire. He had never seen her more serene and unruffled. It struck him with a curious pang, that she was very happy in being with him, so happy that she found a childish pleasure in rehearsing the trivial incidents of her day.

After dinner they went to the library, and the servant put the coffee and liqueurs on a low table before her and left the room. She looked singularly soft and girlish in her rosy-pale dress, against the dark leather of one of his bachelor armchairs. A day earlier the contrast would have charmed him.

He turned away now, choosing a cigar with affected deliberation.

"Did Haskett come?" he asked, with his back to her.

"Oh, yes—he came."

"You didn't see him, of course?"

She hesitated a moment. "I let the nurse see him."

That was all. There was nothing more to ask. He swung round toward her, applying a match to his cigar. Well, the thing was over for a week, at any rate. He would try not to think of it. She looked up at him, a trifle rosier than usual, with a smile in her eyes.

"Ready for your coffee, dear?"

He leaned against the mantelpiece, watching her as she lifted the coffeepot. The lamplight struck a gleam from her bracelets and tipped her soft hair with brightness. How light and slender she was, and how each gesture flowed into the next! She seemed a creature all compact of harmonies. As the thought of Haskett receded, Waythorn felt himself yielding again to the joy of possessorship. They were his, those white hands with their flitting motions, his the light haze of hair, the lips and eyes....

She set down the coffeepot, and reaching for the decanter of cognac, measured off a liqueur glass and poured it into his cup.

Waythorn uttered a sudden exclamation.

"What is the matter?" she said, startled.

"Nothing; only—I don't take cognac in my coffee."

"Oh, how stupid of me," she cried.

Their eyes met, and she blushed a sudden agonized red.

III

Ten days later, Mr. Sellers, still housebound, asked Waythorn to call on his way downtown.

The senior partner, with his swaddled foot propped up by the fire, greeted his associate with an air of embarrassment.

"I'm sorry, my dear fellow; I've got to ask you to do an awkward thing for me."

Waythorn waited, and the other went on, after a pause apparently given to the arrangement of his phrases: "The fact is, when I was knocked out I had just gone into a rather complicated piece of business for—Gus Varick."

"Well?" said Waythorn, with an attempt to put him at his ease.

"Well—it's this way: Varick came to me the day before my attack. He had evidently had an inside tip from somebody, and had made about a hundred thousand. He came to me for advice, and I suggested his going in with Vanderlyn."

"Oh, the deuce!" Waythorn exclaimed. He saw in a flash what had happened. The investment was an alluring one, but required negotiation. He listened quietly while Sellers put the case before him, and the statement ended, he said: "You think I ought to see Varick?"

"I'm afraid I can't as yet. The doctor is obdurate. And this thing can't wait. I hate to ask you, but no one else in the office knows the ins and outs of it."

Waythorn stood silent. He did not care a farthing for the success of Varick's venture, but the honor of the office was to be considered, and he could hardly refuse to oblige his partner.

"Very well," he said, "I'll do it."

That afternoon, apprised by telephone, Varick called at the office. Waythorn, waiting in his private room, wondered what the others thought of it. The newspapers, at the time of Mrs. Waythorn's marriage, had acquainted their readers with every detail of her previous matrimonial ventures, and Waythorn could fancy the clerks smiling behind Varick's back as he was ushered in.

Varick bore himself admirably. He was easy without being undignified, and Waythorn was conscious of cutting a much less impressive figure. Varick had no experience of business, and the talk prolonged itself for nearly an hour while Waythorn set forth with scrupulous precision the details of the proposed transaction.

"I'm awfully obliged to you," Varick said as he rose. "The fact is I'm not used to having much money to look after, and I don't want to make an ass of myself—" He smiled, and Waythorn could not help noticing that there was something pleasant about his smile. "It feels uncommonly queer to have enough cash to pay one's bills. I'd have sold my soul for it a few years ago!"

Waythorn winced at the allusion. He had heard it rumored that a lack of funds had been one of the determining causes of the Varick separation, but it did not occur to him that Varick's words were intentional. It seemed more likely that the desire to keep clear of embarrassing topics had fatally drawn him into one. Waythorn did not wish to be outdone in civility.

"We'll do the best we can for you," he said. "I think this is a good thing you're in."

"Oh, I'm sure it's immense. It's awfully good of you—" Varick broke off, embarrassed. "I suppose the thing's settled now—but if—"

"If anything happens before Sellers is about, I'll see you again," said Waythorn quietly. He was glad, in the end, to appear the more self-possessed of the two.

The course of Lily's illness ran smooth, and as the days passed Waythorn grew used to the idea of Haskett's weekly visit. The first time the day came round, he stayed out late, and questioned his wife as to the visit on his return. She replied at once that Haskett had merely seen the nurse downstairs, as the doctor did not wish anyone in the child's sickroom till after the crisis.

The following week Waythorn was again conscious of the recurrence of the day, but had forgotten it by the time he came home to dinner. The crisis of the disease came a few days later, with a rapid decline of fever, and the little girl was pronounced out of danger. In the rejoicing which ensued the thought of Haskett passed out of Waythorn's mind, and one afternoon, letting himself into the house with a latchkey, he went straight to his library without noticing a shabby hat and umbrella in the hall.

In the library he found a small effaced-looking man with a thinnish gray beard sitting on the edge of a chair. The stranger might have been a piano tuner, or one of those mysteriously efficient persons who are summoned in emergencies to adjust some detail of the domestic machinery. He blinked at Waythorn through a pair of gold-rimmed spectacles and said mildly: "Mr. Waythorn, I presume? I am Lily's father."

Waythorn flushed. "Oh—" he stammered uncomfortably. He broke off, disliking to appear rude. Inwardly he was trying to adjust the actual Haskett to the image of him projected by his wife's reminiscences. Waythorn had been allowed to infer that Alice's first husband was a brute.

"I am sorry to intrude," said Haskett, with his over-the-counter politeness.

"Don't mention it," returned Waythorn, collecting himself. "I suppose the nurse has been told?"

"I presume so. I can wait," said Haskett. He had a resigned way of speaking, as though life had worn down his natural powers of resistance.

Waythorn stood on the threshold, nervously pulling off his gloves.

"I'm sorry you've been detained. I will send for the nurse," he said; and as he opened the door he added with an effort: "I'm glad we can give you a good report of Lily." He winced as the *we* slipped out, but Haskett seemed not to notice it.

"Thank you, Mr. Waythorn, it's been an anxious time for me."

"Ah, well, that's past. Soon she'll be able to go to you." Waythorn nodded and passed out.

In his own room he flung himself down with a groan. He hated the womanish sensibility which made him suffer so acutely from the grotesque chances of life. He had known when he married that his wife's former husbands were both living, and that amid the multiplied contacts of modern existence there were a thousand chances to one that he would run against one or the other, yet he found himself as much disturbed by his brief encounter with Haskett as though the law had not obligingly removed all difficulties in the way of their meeting.

Waythorn sprang up and began to pace the room nervously. He had not suffered half as much from his two meetings with Varick. It was Haskett's presence in his own house that made the situation so intolerable. He stood still, hearing steps in the passage.

"This way, please," he heard the nurse say. Haskett was being taken upstairs, then: not a corner of the house but was open to him. Waythorn dropped into another chair, staring vaguely ahead of him. On his dressing table stood a photograph of Alice, taken when he had first known her. She was Alice Varick then—how fine and exquisite he had thought her! Those were Varick's pearls about her neck. At Waythorn's instance they had been returned before her marriage. Had Haskett ever given her any trinkets—and what had become of them, Waythorn wondered? He realized suddenly that he knew very little of Haskett's past or present situation; but from the man's appearance and manner of speech he could reconstruct with curious precision the surroundings of Alice's first marriage. And it startled him to think that she had, in the background of her life, a phase of existence so different from anything with which he had connected her. Varick, whatever his faults, was a gentleman, in the conventional, traditional sense of the term: the sense which at that moment seemed, oddly enough, to have most meaning to Waythorn. He and Varick had the same social habits, spoke the same language, understood the same allusions. But this other man . . . it was grotesquely uppermost in Waythorn's mind that Haskett had worn a made-up tie attached with an elastic. Why should that ridiculous detail symbolize the whole man? Waythorn was exasperated by his own paltriness, but the fact of the tie expanded, forced itself on him, became as it were the key to Alice's past. He could see her, as Mrs. Haskett, sitting in a "front parlor" furnished in plush, with a pianola, and copy of *Ben Hur* on the center table. He could see her going to the theater with Haskett—or perhaps even to a "Church Sociable"—she in a "picture hat" and Haskett in a black frock coat, a little creased, with the made-up tie on an elastic. On the way home they would stop and look at the illuminated shop windows, lingering over the photographs of New York actresses. On Sunday afternoons Haskett would take her for a walk, pushing Lily ahead of them in a white enameled perambulator, and Waythorn had a vision of the people they would stop and talk to. He could fancy how pretty Alice must have looked, in a dress adriotly constructed from the hints of a New York fashion paper, and how she must have looked down on the other women, chafing at her life, and secretly feeling that she belonged in a bigger place.

For the moment his foremost thought was one of wonder at the way in which she had shed the phase of existence which her marriage with Haskett implied. It was as if her whole aspect, every gesture, every inflection, every allusion, were a studied negation of that period of her life. If she had denied being married to Haskett she could hardly have stood more convicted of duplicity than in this obliteration of the self which had been his wife.

Waythorn started up, checking himself in the analysis of her motives. What right had he to create a fantastic effigy of her and then pass judgment on it? She had spoken vaguely of her first marriage as unhappy, had hinted, with becoming reticence, that Haskett had wrought havoc among her young illusions. . . . It was a pity for Waythorn's peace of mind that Haskett's very inoffensiveness shed a new light on the nature of those illusions. A man would rather think that his wife has been brutalized by her first husband than that the process has been reversed.

IV

"Mr. Waythorn, I don't like that French governess of Lily's."

Haskett, subdued and apologetic, stood before Waythorn in the library, revolving his shabby hat in his hand.

Waythorn, surprised in his armchair over the evening paper, stared back perplexedly at his visitor.

"You'll excuse my asking to see you," Haskett continued. "But this is my last visit, and I thought if I could have a word with you it would be a better way than writing to Mrs. Waythorn's lawyer."

Waythorn rose uneasily. He did not like the French governess either; but that was irrelevant.

"I am not so sure of that," he returned stiffly; "but since you wish it I will give your message to—my wife." He always hesitated over the possessive pronoun in addressing Haskett.

The latter sighed. "I don't know as that will help much. She didn't like it when I spoke to her."

Waythorn turned red. "When did you see her?" he asked.

"Not since the first day I came to see Lily—right after she was taken sick. I remarked to her then that I didn't like the governess."

Waythorn made no answer. He remembered distinctly that, after that first visit, he had asked his wife if she had seen Haskett. She had lied to him then, but she had respected his wishes since; and the incident cast a curious light on her character. He was sure she would not have seen Haskett that first day if she had divined that Waythorn would object, and the fact that she did not divine it was almost as disagreeable to the latter as the discovery that she had lied to him.

"I don't like the woman," Haskett was repeating with mild persistency. "She ain't straight, Mr. Waythorn—she'll teach the child to be underhand. I've noticed a change in Lily—she's too anxious to please—and she don't always tell the truth. She used to be the straightest child. Mr. Waythorn—" He broke off, his voice a little thick. "Not but what I want her to have a stylish education," he ended.

Waythorn was touched. "I'm sorry, Mr. Haskett; but frankly, I don't quite see what I can do."

Haskett hesitated. Then he laid his hat on the table, and advanced to the hearthrug, on which Waythorn was standing. There was nothing aggressive in his manner, but he had the solemnity of a timid man resolved on a decisive measure.

"There's just one thing you can do, Mr. Waythorn," he said. "You can remind Mrs. Waythorn that, by the decree of the courts, I am entitled to have a voice in Lily's bringing-up." He paused, and went on more deprecatingly: "I'm not the kind to talk about enforcing my rights, Mr. Waythorn. I don't know as I think a man is entitled to rights he hasn't known how to hold on to; but this business of the child is different. I've never let go there—and I never mean to."

The scene left Waythorn deeply shaken. Shamefacedly, in indirect ways, he had been finding out about Haskett; and all that he had learned was favorable. The little man, in order to be near his daughter, had sold out his share in a profitable business in Utica, and accepted a modest clerkship in a New York manufacturing house. He boarded in a shabby street and had few acquaintances. His passion for Lily filled his life. Waythorn felt that this exploration of Haskett was like groping about with a dark lantern in his wife's past; but he saw now that there were recesses his lantern had not explored. He had never inquired into the exact circumstances of his wife's first matrimonial rupture. On the surface all had been fair. It was she who had obtained the divorce, and the court had given her the child. But Waythorn knew how many ambiguities such a verdict might cover. The mere fact that Haskett retained a right over his daughter implied an unsuspected compromise. Waythorn was an idealist. He always refused to recognize unpleasant contingencies till he found himself confronted with them, and then he saw them followed by a spectral train of consequences. His next days were thus haunted, and he determined to try to lay the ghosts by conjuring them up in his wife's presence.

When he repeated Haskett's request a flame of anger passed over her face; but she subdued it instantly and spoke with a slight quiver of outraged motherhood.

"It is very ungentlemanly of him," she said.

The word grated on Waythorn. "That is neither here nor there. It's a bare question of rights."

She murmured: "It's not as if he could ever be a help to Lily—"

Waythorn flushed. This was even less to his taste. "The question is," he repeated, "what authority has he over her?"

She looked downward, twisting herself a little in her seat. "I am willing to see him—I thought you objected," she faltered.

In a flash he understood that she knew the extent of

Haskett's claims. Perhaps it was not the first time she had resisted them.

"My objecting has nothing to do with it," he said coldly; "if Haskett has a right to be consulted you must consult him."

She burst into tears, and he saw that she expected him to regard her as a victim.

Haskett did not abuse his rights. Waythorn had felt miserably sure that he would not. But the governess was dismissed, and from time to time the little man demanded an interview with Alice. After the first outburst she accepted the situation with her usual adaptability. Haskett had once reminded Waythorn of the piano tuner, and Mrs. Waythorn, after a month or two, appeared to class him with that domestic familiar. Waythorn could not but respect the father's tenacity. At first he had tried to cultivate the suspicion that Haskett might be "up to" something, that he had an object in securing a foothold in the house. But in his heart Waythorn was sure of Haskett's single-mindedness; he even guessed in the latter a mild contempt for such advantages as his relation with the Waythorns might offer. Haskett's sincerity of purpose made him invulnerable, and his successor had to accept him as a lien on the property.

Mr. Sellers was sent to Europe to recover from his gout, and Varick's affairs hung on Waythorn's hands. The negotiations were prolonged and complicated; they necessitated frequent conferences between the two men, and the interests of the firm forbade Waythorn's suggesting that his client should transfer his business to another office.

Varick appeared well in the transaction. In moments of relaxation his coarse streak appeared, and Waythorn dreaded his geniality; but in the office he was concise and clear-headed, with a flattering deference to Waythorn's judgment. Their business relations being so affably established, it would have been absurd for the two men to ignore each other in society. The first time they met in a drawing room, Varick took up their intercourse in the same easy key, and his hostess' grateful glance obliged Waythorn to respond to it. After that they ran across each other frequently, and one evening at a ball Waythorn, wandering through the remoter rooms, came upon Varick seated beside his wife. She colored a little, and faltered in what she was saying; but Varick nodded to Waythorn without rising, and the latter strolled on.

In the carriage, on the way home, he broke out nervously: "I didn't know you spoke to Varick."

Her voice trembled a little. "It's the first time—he happened to be standing near me; I didn't know what to do. It's so awkward, meeting everywhere—and he said you had been very kind about some business."

"That's different," said Waythorn.

She paused a moment. "I'll do just as you wish," she returned pliantly. "I thought it would be less awkward to speak to him when we meet."

Her pliancy was beginning to sicken him. Had she really no will of her own—no theory about her relation to these men? She had accepted Haskett—did she mean to accept Varick? It was "less awkward," as she had said, and her instinct was to evade difficulties or to circumvent them. With sudden vividness Waythorn saw how the instinct had developed. She was "as easy as an old shoe"—a shoe that too many feet had worn. Her elasticity was the result of tension in too many different directions. Alice Haskett—Alice Varick—Alice Waythorn—she had been each in turn, and had left hanging to each name a little of her privacy, a little of her personality, a little of the inmost self where the unknown god abides.

"Yes—it's better to speak to Varick," said Waythorn wearily.

V

The winter wore on, and society took advantage of the Waythorns' acceptance of Varick. Harassed hostesses were grateful to them for bridging over a social difficulty, and Mrs. Waythorn was held up as a miracle of good taste. Some experimental spirits could not resist the diversion of throwing Varick and his former wife together, and there were those who thought he found a zest in the propinquity. But Mrs. Waythorn's conduct remained irreproachable. She neither avoided Varick nor sought him out. Even Waythorn could not but admit that she had discovered the solution of the newest social problem.

He had married her without giving much thought to that problem. He had fancied that a woman can shed her past like a man. But now he saw that Alice was bound to hers both by the circumstances which forced her into continued relation with it, and by the traces it had left on her nature. With grim irony Waythorn compared himself to a member of a syndicate. He held so many shares in his wife's personality and his predecessors were his partners in the business. If there had been any element of passion in the transaction he would have felt less deteriorated by it. The fact that Alice took her change of husbands like a change of weather reduced the situation to mediocrity. He could have forgiven her for blunders, for excesses; for resisting Haskett, for yielding to Varick; for anything but her acquiescence and her tact. She reminded him of a juggler tossing knives; but the knives were blunt and she knew they would never cut her.

And then, gradually, habit formed a protecting surface for his sensibilities. If he paid for each day's comfort with the small change of his illusions, he grew daily to value the comfort more and set less store upon the coin. He had drifted into a dulling propinquity with Haskett and Varick and he took refuge in the cheap revenge of satirizing the situation. He even began to reckon up the advantages which accrued from it, to ask himself if it were not better to own a third of a wife who knew how to make a man happy than a whole one who had lacked opportunity to acquire the art. For it *was* an art, and made up, like all others, of concessions, eliminations and embellishments; of lights judiciously thrown and shadows skillfully softened. His wife knew exactly how to manage the lights, and he knew exactly to what training she owed her skill. He even tried to trace the source of his obligations, to discriminate between the influences which had combined to produce his domestic happiness: he perceived that Haskett's commonness had made Alice worship good breeding, while Varick's liberal construction of the marriage bond had taught her to value the conjugal virtues; so that he was directly indebted to his predecessors for the devotion which made his life easy if not inspiring.

From this phase he passed into that of complete acceptance. He ceased to satirize himself because time dulled the irony of the situation and the joke lost its humor with its sting. Even the sight of Haskett's hat on the hall table had ceased to touch the springs of epigram. The hat was often seen there now, for it had been decided that it was better for Lily's father to visit her than for the little girl to go to his boardinghouse. Waythorn, having acquiesced in this arrangement, had been surprised to find how little difference it made. Haskett was never obtrusive, and the few visitors who met him on the stairs were unaware of his identity. Waythorn did not know how often he saw Alice, but with himself Haskett was seldom in contact.

One afternoon, however, he learned on entering that Lily's father was waiting to see him. In the library he found Haskett occupying a chair in his usual provisional way. Waythorn always felt grateful to him for not leaning back.

"I hope you'll excuse me, Mr. Waythorn," he said rising. "I wanted to see Mrs. Waythorn about Lily, and your man asked me to wait here till she came in."

"Of course," said Waythorn, remembering that a sudden leak had that morning given over the drawing room to the plumbers.

He opened his cigar case and held it out to his visitor, and Haskett's acceptance seemed to mark a fresh stage in their intercourse. The spring evening was chilly, and Waythorn invited his guest to draw up his chair to the fire. He meant to find an excuse to leave Haskett in a moment; but he was tired and cold, and after all the little man no longer jarred on him.

The two were enclosed in the intimacy of their blended cigar smoke when the door opened and Varick walked into the room. Waythorn rose abruptly. It was the first time that Varick had come to the house, and the surprise of seeing him, combined with the singular inopportuneness of his arrival, gave a new edge to Waythorn's blunted sensibilities. He stared at his visitor without speaking.

Varick seemed too preoccupied to notice his host's embarrassment.

"My dear fellow," he exclaimed in his most expansive tone, "I must apologize for tumbling in on you in this way, but I was too late to catch you downtown, and so I thought—"

He stopped short, catching sight of Haskett, and his sanguine color deepened to a flush which spread vividly under his scant blond hair. But in a moment he recovered himself and nodded slightly. Haskett returned the bow in silence, and Waythorn was still groping for speech when the footman came in carrying a tea table.

The intrusion offered a welcome vent to Waythorn's

nerves. "What the deuce are you bringing this here for?" he said sharply.

"I beg your pardon, sir, but the plumbers are still in the drawing room, and Mrs. Waythorn said she would have tea in the library." The footman's perfectly respectful tone implied a reflection on Waythorn's reasonableness.

"Oh, very well," said the latter resignedly, and the footman proceeded to open the folding tea table and set out its complicated appointments. While this interminable process continued the three men stood motionless, watching it with a fascinated stare, till Waythorn, to break the silence, said to Varick, "Won't you have a cigar?"

He held out the case he had just tendered to Haskett, and Varick helped himself with a smile. Waythorn looked about for a match, and finding none, proffered a light from his own cigar. Haskett, in the background, held his ground mildly, examining his cigar tip now and then, and stepping forward at the right moment to knock its ashes into the fire.

The footman at last withdrew, and Varick immediately began: "If I could just say half a word to you about this business—"

"Certainly," stammered Waythorn; "in the dining room—"

But as he placed his hand on the door it opened from without, and his wife appeared on the threshold.

She came in fresh and smiling, in her street dress and hat, shedding a fragrance from the boa which she loosened in advancing.

"Shall we have tea in here, dear?" she began; and then she caught sight of Varick. Her smile deepened, veiling a slight tremor of surprise.

"Why, how do you do?" she said with a distinct note of pleasure.

As she shook hands with Varick she saw Haskett standing behind him. Her smile faded for a moment, but she recalled it quickly, with a scarcely perceptible side glance at Waythorn.

"How do you do, Mr. Haskett?" she said, and shook hands with him a shade less cordially.

The three men stood awkwardly before her, till Varick, always the most self-possessed, dashed into an explanatory phrase.

"We—I had to see Waythorn a moment on business," he stammered, brick-red from chin to nape.

Haskett stepped forward with his air of mild obstinacy. "I am sorry to intrude; but you appointed five o'clock—" he directed his resigned glance to the timepiece on the mantel.

She swept aside their embarrassment with a charming gesture of hospitality.

"I'm so sorry—I'm always late; but the afternoon was so lovely." She stood drawing off her gloves, propitiatory and graceful, diffusing about her a sense of ease and familiarity in which the situation lost its grotesqueness. "But before talking business," she added brightly, "I'm sure everyone wants a cup of tea."

She dropped into her low chair by the tea table, and the two visitors, as if drawn by her smile, advanced to receive the cups she held out.

She glanced about for Waythorn, and he took the third cup with a laugh.

WILLA CATHER was born near Winchester, Virginia, in 1873 and at the age of eight moved to Nebraska, then still pioneer territory. She spent her girlhood riding the prairie, learning how to kill rattlesnakes and getting to know the children of the other ranchers, most of them the foreign-born and second-generation Americans she later brought to life in her fiction. She was educated at home by her grandmothers who schooled her in the English classics and Latin. She worked her way through the University of Nebraska as a newspaper correspondent. After graduation she went to Pittsburgh where she worked as drama critic for the *Leader* and then as an English teacher at Allegheny High School. In 1905, after her first volume of short stories was published to excellent reviews, she moved to New York and went to work as managing editor for *McClure's Magazine.* By 1912 she had saved enough money to quit her job and become a full-time writer. She never cared to analyze her reasons for wanting to be a writer. She once remarked that "anyone who ever has experienced the delight of living with people and in places which are beautiful and which he loves, throughout the long months required to get them down on paper, would never waste a minute drawing up lists of rules or tracing down reasons why."

In her best fiction she writes about her native place (the prairie country between the Little Blue and Republican rivers in south-central Nebraska) with a simplicity and integrity that have won her art the praise of other creative writers. At the Cather Centenary celebration held in 1973 at the University of Nebraska, Eudora Welty observed that Willa Cather's landscapes are always brought home in an artistic way. "Her focus is always on human values, not on geography for its own sake. Her characters possess the passion of the young to surpass, the achieve, to gain self-discovery." The poet Louise Bogan, in an essay entitled

"Willa Cather, American Classic," writes: "She would be the first person to admit her limitations. She has admitted them, in each successive novel by working more and more closely within them, by letting what she could not do alone. She is not a profound or subtle psychologist. Madame Colette's minute dissections of intimate personal relationships are not in her line. She lacks the broad canvas of Sigrid Undset. But she is a writer who can conjure up from the look of a place and the actions of people a narrative as solid as a house, written in prose as surely counterpointed as music." And, in one of his letters, Wallace Stevens says that though it is easy to miss her quality, "We have nothing better than she is."

Willa Cather
(1873–1947)

A WAGNER MATINÉE

I received one morning a letter, written in pale ink on glassy, blue-lined note-paper, and bearing the postmark of a little Nebraska village. This communication, worn and rubbed, looking as if it had been carried for some days in a coat pocket that was none too clean, was from my uncle Howard, and informed me that his wife had been left a small legacy by a bachelor relative, and that it would be necessary for her to go to Boston to attend to the settling of the estate. He requested me to meet her at the station and render her whatever services might be necessary. On examining the date indicated as that of her arrival, I found it to be no later than tomorrow. He had characteristically delayed writing until, had I been away from home for a day, I must have missed my aunt altogether.

The name of my Aunt Georgiana opened before me a gulf of recollection so wide and deep that, as the letter dropped from my hand, I felt suddenly a stranger to all the present conditions of my existence, wholly ill at ease and out of place amid the familiar surroundings of my study. I became, in short, the gangling farmer-boy my aunt had known, scourged with chilblains and bashfulness, my hands cracked and sore from the corn husking. I sat again before her parlour organ, fumbling the scales with my stiff, red fingers, while she, beside me, made canvas mittens for the huskers.

The next morning, after preparing my landlady for a visitor, I set out for the station. When the train arrived I had some difficulty finding my aunt. She was the last of the passengers to alight, and it was not until I got her into the carriage that she seemed really to recognize me. She had come all the way in a day coach; her linen duster had become black with soot and her black bonnet grey with dust during her journey. When we arrived at my boarding-house the landlady put her to bed at once and I did not see her again until the next morning.

Whatever shock Mrs. Springer experienced at my aunt's appearance, she considerately concealed. As for myself, I saw my aunt's battered figure with that feeling of awe and respect with which we behold explorers who have left their ears and fingers north of Franz-Joseph-Land, or their health somewhere along the Upper Congo. My Aunt Georgiana had been a music teacher at the Boston Conservatory, somewhere back in the latter sixties. One summer, while visiting in the little village among the Green Mountains where her ancestors had dwelt for generations, she had kindled the callow fancy of my uncle, Howard Carpenter, then an idle, shiftless boy of twenty-one. When she returned to her duties in Boston, Howard followed her, and the upshot of this infatuation was that she eloped with him, eluding the reproaches of her family and the criticism of her friends by going with him to the Nebraska frontier. Carpenter, who, of course, had no money, took up a homestead in Red Willow County, fifty miles from the railroad. There they had measured off their land themselves, driving across the prairie in a wagon, to the wheel of which they had tied a red cotton handkerchief, and counting its revolutions. They built a dug-out in the red hillside, one of those cave dwellings whose inmates so often reverted to primitive conditions. Their water they got from the lagoons where the buffalo drank, and their slender stock of provisions was always at the mercy of bands of roving Indians. For thirty years my aunt had not been farther than fifty miles from the homestead.

I owed to this woman most of the good that ever came my way in my boyhood, and had a reverential affection for her. During the years when I was riding herd for my uncle, my aunt, after cooking the three meals—the first of which was ready at six o'clock in the morning—and putting the six children to bed, would often stand until midnight at her ironing-board, with me at the kitchen table beside her, hearing me recite Latin declensions and conjugations, gently shaking me when my drowsy head sank down over a page of irregular verbs. It was to her, at her ironing or mending, that I read my first Shakespeare, and her old textbook on mythology was the first that ever came into my empty hands. She taught me my scales and exercises on the little parlour organ which her husband had bought her after fifteen years during which she had not so much as seen a musical instrument. She would sit beside me by the hour, darning and counting, while I struggled with the "Joyous Farmer." She seldom talked to me about music, and I understood why. Once when I had been doggedly beating out some easy passages from an old score of *Euryanthe* I had found among her music books, she came up to me and, putting her hands over my eyes, gently drew my head back upon her shoulder, saying tremulously, "Don't love it so well, Clark, or it may be taken from you."

When my aunt appeared on the morning after her arrival in Boston, she was still in a semi-somnambulant state. She seemed not to realize that she was in the city where she had spent her youth, the place longed for hungrily half a lifetime. She had been so wretchedly trainsick throughout the journey that she had no recollection of anything but her discomfort, and, to all intents and purposes, there were but a few hours of nightmare between the farm in Red Willow County and my study on Newbury Street. I had planned a little pleasure for her that afternoon, to repay her for some of the glorious moments she had given me when we used to milk together in the straw-thatched cowshed and she, because I was more than usually tired, or because her husband had spoken sharply to me, would tell me of the splendid performance of the *Huguenots* she had seen in Paris, in her youth.

At two o'clock the Symphony Orchestra was to give a Wagner program, and I intended to take my aunt; though, as I conversed with her, I grew doubtful about her enjoyment of it. I suggested our visiting the Conservatory and the Common before lunch, but she seemed altogether too timid to wish to venture out. She questioned me absently about various changes in the city, but she was chiefly concerned that she had forgotten to leave instructions about feeding half-skimmed milk to a certain weakling calf, "old Maggie's calf, you know, Clark," she explained, evidently having forgotten how long I had been away. She was further troubled because she had neglected to tell her daughter about the freshly-opened kit of mackerel in the cellar, which would spoil if it were not used directly.

I asked her whether she had ever heard any of the Wagnerian operas, and found that she had not, though she was perfectly familiar with their respective situations, and had once possessed the piano score of *The Flying Dutchman*. I began to think it would be best to get her back to Red Willow County without waking her, and regretted having suggested the concert.

From the time we entered the concert hall, however, she was a trifle less passive and inert, and for the first time seemed to perceive her surroundings. I had felt some trepidation lest she might become aware of her queer, country clothes, or might experience some painful embarrassment at stepping suddenly into the world to which she had been dead for a quarter of a century. But, again, I found how superficially I had judged her. She sat looking about her with eyes as impersonal, almost as stony, as those with which the granite Rameses in a museum watches the froth and fret that ebbs and flows about his pedestal. I have seen this same aloofness in old miners who drift into the Brown hotel at Denver, their pockets full of bullion, their linen soiled, their haggard faces unshaven; standing in the thronged corridors as solitary as though they were still in a frozen camp on the Yukon.

The matinée audience was made up chiefly of women. One lost the contour of faces and figures, indeed any effect of line whatever, and there was only the colour of bodices past counting, the shimmer of fabrics soft and firm, silky and sheer; red, mauve, pink, blue, lilac, purple, écru, rose, yellow, cream, and white, all the colours that an impressionist finds in a sunlit landscape, with here and there the dead shadow of a frock coat. My Aunt Georgiana regarded them as though they had been so many daubs of tube-paint on a palette.

When the musicians came out and took their places, she gave a little stir of anticipation, and looked with quickening interest down over the rail at that invariable grouping, perhaps the first wholly familiar thing that had greeted her eye since she had left old Maggie and her weakling calf. I could feel how all those details sank into her soul, for I had not forgotten how they had sunk into mine when I came fresh from ploughing forever and forever between green aisles of corn, where, as in a treadmill, one might walk from daybreak to dusk without perceiving a shadow of change. The clean profiles of the musicians, the gloss of their linen, the dull black of their coats, the beloved shapes of the instruments, the patches of yellow light on the smooth, varnished bellies of the 'cellos and the bass viols in the rear, the restless, wind-tossed forest of fiddle necks and bows—I recalled how, in the first orchestra I ever heard, those long bow-strokes seemed to draw the heart out of me, as a conjurer's stick reels out yards of paper ribbon from a hat.

The first number was the *Tannhäuser* overture. When the horns drew out the first strain of the Pilgrim's chorus, Aunt Georgiana clutched my coat sleeve. Then it was I first realized that for her this broke a silence of thirty years. With the battle between the two motives, with the frenzy of the Venusberg theme and its ripping of strings, there came to me an overwhelming sense of the waste and wear we are so powerless to combat; and I saw again the tall, naked house on the prairie, black and grim as a wooden fortress; the black pond where I had learned to swim, its margin pitted with sun-dried cattle tracks; the rain-gullied clay banks about the naked house, the four dwarf-ash seedlings where the dish-cloths were always hung to dry before the kitchen door. The world there was the flat world of the ancients; to the east, a cornfield that stretched to daybreak; to the west, a corral that reached to sunset; between, the conquests of peace, dearer-bought than those of war.

The overture closed, my aunt released my coat sleeve, but she said nothing. She sat staring dully at the orchestra. What, I wondered, did she get from it? She had been a good pianist in her day, I knew, and her musical education had been broader than that of most music teachers of a quarter of a century ago. She had often told me of Mozart's operas and Meyerbeer's, and I could remember hearing her sing, years ago, certain melodies of Verdi. When I had fallen ill with a fever in her house she used to sit by my cot in the evening—when the cool, night wind blew in through the faded mosquito netting tacked over the window and I lay watching a certain bright star that burned red above the cornfield—and sing "Home to our mountains, O, let us return!" in a way fit to break the heart of a Vermont boy near dead of homesickness already.

I watched her closely through the prelude to *Tristan and Isolde*, trying vainly to conjecture what that seething turmoil of strings and winds might mean to her, but she sat mutely staring at the violin bows that drove obliquely downward, like the pelting streaks of rain in a summer shower. Had this music any message for her? Had she enough left to at all comprehend this power which had kindled the world since she had left it? I was in a fever of curiosity, but Aunt Georgiana sat silent upon her peak in Darien. She preserved this utter immobility throughout the number from *The Flying Dutchman,* though her fingers worked mechanically upon her black dress, as if, of themselves, they were recalling the piano score they had once played. Poor hands! They had been stretched and twisted into mere tentacles to hold and lift and knead with;—on one of them a thin, worn band that had once been a wedding ring. As I pressed and gently quieted one of those groping hands, I remembered with quivering eyelids their services for me in other days.

Soon after the tenor began the "Prize Song," I heard a quick drawn breath and turned to my aunt. Her eyes were closed, but the tears were glistening on her cheeks, and I think, in a moment more, they were in my eyes as well. It never really died, then—the soul which can suffer so excruciatingly and so interminably; it withers to the outward eye only; like that strange moss which can lie on a dusty shelf half a century and yet, if placed in water, grows green again. She wept so throughout the development and elaboration of the melody.

During the intermission before the second half, I questioned my aunt and found that the "Prize Song" was not new to her. Some years before there had drifted to the farm in Red Willow County a young German, a tramp cow-puncher, who had sung in the chorus at Bayreuth when he was a boy, along with the other peasant boys and girls. Of a Sunday morning he used to sit on his gingham-sheeted bed in the hands' bedroom which opened off the kitchen, cleaning the leather of his boots and saddle, singing the "Prize Song," while my aunt went about her work in the kitchen. She had hovered over him until she had prevailed upon him to join the country church, though his sole fitness for this step, in so far as I could gather, lay in his boyish face and his possession of this divine melody. Shortly afterward, he had gone to town on the Fourth of July, been drunk for several days, lost his money at a faro table, ridden a saddled Texas steer on a bet, and disappeared with a fractured collar-bone. All this my aunt told me huskily, wanderingly, as though she were talking in the weak lapses of illness.

"Well, we have come to better things than the old *Tro-*

vatore at any rate, Aunt Georgie?" I queried, with a well-mean effort at jocularity.

Her lip quivered and she hastily put her handkerchief up to her mouth. From behind it she murmured, "And you have been hearing this ever since you left me, Clark?" Her question was the gentlest and saddest of reproaches.

The second half of the program consisted of four numbers from the *Ring*, and closed with Siegfried's funeral march. My aunt wept quietly, but almost continuously, as a shallow vessel overflows in a rain-storm. From time to time her dim eyes looked up at the lights, burning softly under their dull glass globes.

The deluge of sound poured on and on; I never knew what she found in the shining current of it; I never knew how far it bore her, or past what happy islands. From the trembling of her face I could well believe that before the last number she had been carried out where the myriad graves are, into the grey, nameless burying grounds of the sea; or into some world of death vaster yet, where, from the beginning of the world, hope has lain down with hope and dream with dream and, renouncing, slept.

The concert was over; the people filed out of the hall chattering and laughing, glad to relax and find the living level again, but my kinswoman made no effort to rise. The harpist slipped the green felt cover over his instrument; the flute-players shook the water from their mouth-pieces; the men of the orchestra went out one by one, leaving the stage to the chairs and music stands, empty as a winter cornfield.

I spoke to my aunt. She burst into tears and sobbed pleadingly. "I don't want to go, Clark, I don't want to go!"

I understood. For her, just outside the concert hall, lay the black pond with the cattle-tracked bluffs; the tall, unpainted house, with weather-curled boards, naked as a tower; the crook-backed ash seedlings where the dishcloths hung to dry; the gaunt, moulting turkeys picking up refuse about the kitchen door.

SIDONIE-GABRIELLE COLETTE was born in 1873 in Saint-Sauveur-en-Puisaye in Burgundy. Her mother, the chief love of her life and the greatest influence on her, is described as a lovable woman, fond of animals and books, and attuned to nature—an avid reader, who, during Mass, read the plays of Corneille cached inside her prayerbook. By the time Colette was eight she was reading Labiche, Daudet, and Mérimée. She was the local school's prodigy, especially in composition class.

The tales of her youth that she told her first husband, Gauthier-Villars, ("Willy"), a writer of light novels, became the Claudine series of novels (1900–1903). In 1906 she divorced Willy and became a music-hall dancer. Between 1900 and 1954, the year she died in Paris, she published over fifty books and more have appeared since her death. They include novels, short stories, and what her biographer Margaret Crosland calls "that subtle blend of autobiographical narrative and fiction so characteristic of Colette." Colette also wrote for *Figaro, Vogue, Femina,* and *Le Matin* as drama critic, fashion columnist, book reviewer, feature writer, and woman's page editor.

In her introduction to *The Other Woman,* the collection of short stories from which the following selection is taken, Margaret Crosland describes Colette's treatment of women in fiction: "Most of Colette's writing reveals her to be more interested in women than in men. Her male characters are not the cardboard creations produced by so many women novelists, but they are seldom of a very admirable breed and they make the women characters unhappy. Often they remain off-stage, as though the women, realizing their own vulnerability, want to keep them on the fringes of their life. The women observe men with a certain curiosity—which lasts longer than love—but most of all they relish that world of femininity which they have created for themselves and from which no man can banish them. This world is not necessarily peopled by lesbians, but it is self-sufficient. Women can do as they wish there—it is pleasing to watch other women dressing and making up, pleasing to remember the dream-world of one's girlhood. Colette does not take sides in any obvious sex war, but few women have written about it as she did—she remains feminine, never feminist, while in the famous book *The Pure and the Impure* she wrote about homosexual relationships with friendly but uncommitted impartiality."

Colette
(1873–1954)

THE SECRET WOMAN

He had been looking for a long time at the sea of masks in front of him, suffering vaguely from their mixture of colours and from the synchronization of two orchestras which were too close. His hood constricted his temples; a nervous headache was coming on between his eyes. But he relished, without impatience, a state of malaise and pleasure which permitted the imperceptible passing of the hours. He had wandered along all the corridors of the Opéra, drunk the silvery dust of the dance-floor, recognized bored friends and placed round his neck the indifferent arms of a very plump girl who was disguised as though humorously as a sylph.

This hooded doctor was embarrassed by his fancy-dress and staggered about like a man in skirts, but he dared not remove either his costume or his hood, because of his school-boy lie:

"I'll be spending tomorrow night at Nogent," he had said to his wife the day before. "They've just telephoned me, and I'm very much afraid that my patient, you know, the poor old lady.... Just imagine, I was looking forward to this ball like any kid. Isn't it ridiculous, a man of my age who's never been to the Opéra ball?"

"Utterly ridiculous, darling, utterly! If I'd known, perhaps I wouldn't have married you...."

She laughed, and he admired her narrow face, pink, matt and long, like a delicate sugared almond.

"Don't you want to go to the green and purple ball? Even without me, if it amuses you, darling...."

She had trembled, there passed through her one of those long shudders of disgust which brought a tremble to her hair, her delicate hands and her bosom beneath her white dress whenever she saw a slug or a filthy passer-by:

"As for me.... Can you see me in a crowd, at the mercy of all those hands.... What do you think, I'm not straitlaced, I'm . . . I'm put out! There's nothing to be done about it!"

Leaning against the loggia balustrade, above the great staircase, he thought of this trembling hand, as he contemplated before him two enormous square hands, with black nails, clasped round the bare back of a sultana. Emerging from the braided sleeves of a Venetian lord they dug into the white female flesh as though it were dough. . . . Because he was thinking of her he jumped violently as he heard beside him a little uh-hum, a kind of cough typical of his wife. . . . He turned round and saw someone sitting astride the balustrade, wearing a long and impenetrable disguise, looking like Pierrot because of the smock with vast sleeves, the loose trousers, the headband and the plaster-white colour which covered the small area of skin visible below the fluffy lace of the mask. The fluid fabric of the costume and the cap, woven of dark purple and silver, shone like the conger-eels that you fish for at night with iron hooks from boats lit by lamps burning resin. Overwhelmed with astonishment he awaited the recurrence of the little uh-hum, which did not come. . . . The eel-like Pierrot remained seated in nonchalant fashion and its heel tapped against the marble baluster, revealing only two satin slippers, while a black-gloved hand lay folded at one hip. The two oblique slits in the mask, carefully meshed over with tulle, revealed only a subdued glint of indeterminate colour.

He almost called out "Irène!" And restrained himself, remembering his own lie. Since he was clumsy at play-acting he also rejected the idea of disguising his voice. The Pierrot scratched its thigh, with a free, proletarian gesture, and the anxious husband breathed again.

"Ah! It's not her."

But the Pierrot pulled out of a pocket a flat gold box, opened it and took out a lipstick, and the anxious husband recognized an antique snuff-box fitted with a mirror inside, the last birthday gift. . . . He placed his left hand over the painful area of his heart with such a brusque and involuntary gesture that the eel-like Pierrot noticed him.

"Is that a declaration, purple Domino?"

He did not reply, for he was half stifled with surprise, waiting and nightmare, and listened for a long moment to the barely disguised voice—the voice of his wife. The Eel looked at him, as it sat in cavalier fashion, its head on one side like a bird; it shrugged its shoulders, jumped to the ground and moved away. Its movement liberated the anxious husband who, restored to a state of active and normal jealousy, began to think again and rose without haste to follow his wife.

"She's here for someone, with someone. In less than an hour I'll know everything."

A hundred hoods, purple and green, guaranteed that he would be neither noticed nor recognized. Irène walked in front of him, nonchalantly; he was astonished to find that she rolled her hips softly and dragged her feet a little as though she were wearing Turkish slippers. A Byzantine figure, wearing emerald green, embroidered with gold, seized her as she went by, and her body bent in his arms; she looked thinner, as though the embrace would cut her in two. Her husband ran a few steps and reached the couple just as Irène was crying flatteringly "You big brute!"

She moved away, with the same relaxed and quiet step, stopping often, musing at the doors to the open boxes, hardly ever looking round. She hesitated at the foot of the steps, turned off to the side, came back towards the entrance of the orchestra stalls, joined a noisy, closely packed crowd with a skillful gliding movement like the blade of a knife fitting neatly into its sheath. Ten arms imprisoned her, an almost naked wrestler pinned her firmly against the edge of the ground-floor boxes and held her there. She gave way beneath the weight of the naked man, threw back her head in laughter that was drowned by other laughter, and the man in the purple hood saw her teeth gleam beneath the lace of the mask. Then she escaped easily and sat down on the steps which led to the dance-floor. Her husband, standing two paces behind her, looked at her. She readjusted her mask and her crumpled smock, then tightened the headband. She seemed as calm as if she had been alone, and moved away again after a few moments' rest. She went down the steps, placed her hand on the shoulders of a warrior who asked her, silently, to dance, and she danced, clinging to him.

"That's the man," the husband said to himself.

But she did not say a word to the dancer encased in iron, whose skin was damp, and left him quietly after the dance. She went off to drink a glass of champagne at the buffet, then a second glass, paid, stood by motionless and curious as two men began to fight among screaming women. She also amused herself by placing her little satanic hands, which were entirely black, on the white bosom of a Dutch woman wearing a gold head-dress, who cried out nervously.

At last the anxious man who was following her saw her stop, as though bumping against him on the way, close to a young man who had collapsed on a bench, out of breath, and was fanning himself with his mask. She bent down, disdainfully held the savage, handsome young face, and kissed the panting, half-open mouth. . . .

But her husband, instead of rushing forward and forcing the two mouths apart, disappeared into the crowd. In his consternation he no longer feared, no longer hoped for betrayal. He was sure now that Irène did not know the young man, drunk with dancing, whom she was kissing, nor the Hercules; he was sure that she was neither waiting nor looking for anyone, and that abandoning the lips she held beneath her own like an empty grape, she was going to leave again the next moment, wander about once more, collect some other passer-by, forget him, and simply enjoy, until she felt tired and went back home, the monstrous pleasure of being alone, free, honest in her crude, native state, of being the unknown woman, eternally solitary and shameless, restored to her irremediable solitude and immodest innocence by a little mask and a concealing costume.

GERTRUDE STEIN was born in 1874 in Allegheny, Pennsylvania, spent her infancy in Vienna and Paris, and an unhappy girlhood in Oakland, California. "I wish I had died when I was a little baby and had not any feeling, I would not then have to be always suffering . . . ," she later wrote of her adolescence in *The Making of Americans*. She read voraciously in Shakespeare, Defoe, and Trollope, but she knew the time was coming when she would be expected to marry and be "willing to take everything and be satisfied to live in Belmont in a large house with a view and plenty of flowers and neighbors who were cousins and some friends who did not say anything." She deferred the entombment in house and garden by going to college, which she later referred to as "freedom physical and mental freedom." At Radcliffe she was a favorite student of William James. After college she studied medicine at Johns Hopkins in Baltimore, but left without taking a degree. In 1903 she went to live in Paris. A few years later she was joined by Alice B. Toklas who became Miss Stein's companion and secretary until her death in 1946. Their home at 27 rue de Fleurus was the legendary meeting-place of painters and writers and many of the so-called Lost Generation who lived in Paris after World War I. *The Autobiography of Alice B. Toklas* (1933) pretends to be about Gertrude Stein's secretary and companion, but it is really her own life story.

Stein's use of language has been described by some critics as mere experimentation and eccentricity. But John Hersey in *The Writer's Craft* explains that as a writer Gertrude Stein is a Cubist. "She played incessant games with words, her sentences spun and spiraled with deliberated repetitions and onrushing rhythms." Her advice about how to write prose was quite straightforward. "Sentences must not have bad plumbing—they must not leak," she remarked to F. Scott Fitzgerald. Her book *Three Lives,* which contains the beautiful portraits of the Gentle Lena, the Good Anna, and Melanctha, is perhaps her most accessible writing and the best example of her great relish for human beings. "Everybody's life is full of stories," she once wrote. "Your life is full of stories; my life is full of stories. They are very occupying, but they are not really interesting. What is interesting is the way everyone tells their stories."

Gertrude Stein (1874–1946)

MISS FURR AND MISS SKEENE

Helen Furr had quite a pleasant home. Mrs. Furr was quite a pleasant woman. Mr. Furr was quite a pleasant man. Helen Furr had quite a pleasant voice quite worth cultivating. She did not mind working. She worked to cultivate her voice. She did not find it gay living in the same place where she had always been living. She went to a place where some were cultivating something, voices and other things needing cultivating. She met Georgine Skeene there who was cultivating her voice which some thought was quite a pleasant one. Helen Furr and Georgine Skeene lived together then. Georgine Skeene liked travelling. Helen Furr did not care about travelling, she liked to stay in one place and be gay there. They were together then and travelled to another place and stayed there and were gay there.

They stayed there and were gay there, not very gay there, just gay there. They were both gay there, they were regularly working there both of them cultivating their voices there, they were both gay there. Georgine Skeene was gay there and she was regular, regular in being gay, regular in not being gay, regular in being a gay one who was not being gay longer than was needed to be one being quite a gay one. They were both gay then there and both working there then.

They were in a way both gay there where there were many cultivating something. They were both regular in being gay there. Helen Furr was gay there, she was gayer and gayer there and really she was just gay there, she was gayer and gayer there, that is to say she found ways of being gay there that she was using in being gay there. She was gay there, not gayer and gayer, just gay there, that is to say she was not gayer by using the things she found there that were gay things, she was gay there.

They were quite regularly gay there, Helen Furr and

Georgine Skeene, they were regularly gay there where they were gay. They were very regularly gay.

To be regularly gay was to do every day the gay thing that they did every day. To be regularly gay was to end every day at the same time after they had been regularly gay. They were regularly gay. They were gay every day. They ended every day in the same way, at the same time, and they had been every day regularly gay.

The voice Helen Furr was cultivating was quite a pleasant one. The voice Georgine Skeene was cultivating was, some said, a better one. The voice Helen Furr was cultivating she cultivated and it was quite completely a pleasant enough one then, a cultivated enough one then. The voice Georgine Skeene was cultivating she did not cultivate too much. She cultivated it quite some. She cultivated and she would sometime go on cultivating it and it was not then an unpleasant one, it would not be then an unpleasant one, it would be a quite richly cultivated one, it would be quite richly enough to be a pleasant enough one.

They were gay where there were many cultivating something. The two were gay there, were regularly gay there. Georgine Skeene would have liked to do more travelling. They did some travelling, not very much travelling, Georgine Skeene would have liked to do more travelling, Helen Furr did not care about doing travelling, she liked to stay in a place and be gay there.

They stayed in a place and were gay there, both of them stayed there, they stayed together there, they were gay there, they were regularly gay there.

They went quite often, not very often, but they did go back to where Helen Furr had a pleasant enough home and then Georgine Skeene went to a place where her brother had quite some distinction. They both went, every few years, went visiting to where Helen Furr had quite a pleasant home. Certainly Helen Furr would not find it gay to stay, she did not find it gay, she said she would not stay, she said she did not find it gay, she said she would not stay where she did not find it gay, she said she found it gay where she did stay and she did stay there where very many were cultivating something. She did stay there. She always did find it gay there.

She went to see them where she had always been living and where she did not find it gay. She had a pleasant home there, Mrs. Furr was a pleasant enough woman, Mr. Furr was a pleasant enough man, Helen told them and they were not worrying, that she did not find it gay living where she had always been living.

Georgine Skeene and Helen Furr were living where they were both cultivating their voices and they were gay there. They visited where Helen Furr had come from and then they went to where they were living where they were then regularly living.

There were some dark and heavy men there then. There were some who were not so heavy and some who were not so dark. Helen Furr and Georgine Skeene sat regularly with them. They sat regularly with the ones who were dark and heavy. They sat regularly with the ones who were not so dark. They sat regularly with the ones that were not so heavy. They sat with them regularly, sat with some of them. They went with them regularly went with them. They were regular then, they were gay then, they were where they wanted to be then where it was gay to be then, they were regularly gay then. There were men there then who were dark and heavy and they sat with them with Helen Furr and Georgine Skeene and they went with them with Miss Furr and Miss Skeene, and they went with the heavy and dark men Miss Furr and Miss Skeene went with them, and they sat with them, Miss Furr and Miss Skeene sat with them, and there were other men, some were not heavy men and they sat with Miss Furr and Miss Skeene and Miss Furr and Miss Skeene sat with them, and there were other men who were not dark men and they sat with Miss Furr and Miss Skeene and Miss Furr and Miss Skeene sat with them. Miss Furr and Miss Skeene went with them and they went with Miss Furr and Miss Skeene, some who were not heavy men, some who were not dark men. Miss Furr and Miss Skeene sat regularly, they sat with some men. Miss Furr and Miss Skeene went and there were some men with them. There were men and Miss Furr and Miss Skeene went with them, went somewhere with them, went with some of them.

Helen Furr and Georgine Skeene were regularly living where very many were living and cultivating in themselves something. Helen Furr and Georgine Skeene were living very regularly then, being very regular then in being gay then. They did then learn many ways to be gay and they were then being gay being quite regular in being gay, being gay and they were learning little things, little things in ways of being gay, they were very regular then, they were learning very many little things in ways of being gay, they were being gay and using these little things they were learning to have to be gay with regularly gay with then and they were gay the same amount they had been gay. They were quite gay, they were quite regular, they were learning little things, gay little things, they were gay inside them the same amount they had been gay, they were gay the same length of time they had been gay every day.

They were regular in being gay, they learned little things that are things in being gay, they learned many little things that are things in being gay, they were gay every day, they were regular, they were gay, they were gay the same length of time every day, they were gay, they were quite regularly gay.

Georgine Skeene went away to stay two months with her brother. Helen Furr did not go then to stay with her father and her mother. Helen Furr stayed there where they had been regularly living the two of them and she would then certainly not be lonesome, she would go on being gay. She did go on being gay. She was not any more gay but she was gay longer every day than they had been being gay when they were together being gay. She was gay then quite exactly the same way. She learned a few more little ways of being gay. She was quite gay and in the same way, the same way she had been gay and she was gay a little longer in the day, more of each day she was gay. She was gay longer every day than when the two of them had been being gay. She was gay quite in the way they had been gay, quite in the same way.

She was not lonesome then, she was not at all feeling any need of having Georgine Skeene. She was not astonished at this thing. She would have been a little astonished by this thing but she knew she was not astonished at anything and so she was not astonished at this thing not astonished at not feeling any need of having Georgine Skeene.

Helen Furr had quite a completely pleasant voice and it was quite well enough cultivated and she could use it and she did use it but then there was not any way of working at cultivating a completely pleasant voice when it has become a quite completely well enough cultivated one, and there was not much use in using it when one was not wanting it to be helping to make one a gay one. Helen Furr was not needing using her voice to be a gay one. She was gay then and sometimes she used her voice and she was not using it very often. It was quite completely enough cultivated and it was quite completely a pleasant one and she did not use it very often. She was then, she was quite exactly as gay as she had been, she was gay a little longer in the day than she had been.

She was gay exactly the same way. She was never tired of being gay that way. She had learned very many little ways to use in being gay. Very many were telling about using other ways in being gay. She was gay enough, she was always gay exactly the same way, she was always learning little things to use in being gay, she was telling about using other ways in being gay, she was telling about learning other ways in being gay, she was learning other ways in being gay, she would be using other ways in being gay, she would always be gay in the same way, when Georgine Skeene was there not so long each day as when Georgine Skeene was away.

She came to using many ways in being gay, she came to use every way in being gay. She went on living where many were cultivating something and she was gay, she had used every way to be gay.

They did not live together then Helen Furr and Georgine Skeene. Helen Furr lived there the longer where they had been living regularly together. Then neither of them were living there any longer. Helen Furr was living somewhere else then and telling some about being gay and she was gay then and she was living quite regularly then. She was regularly gay then. She was quite regular in being gay then. She remembered all the little ways of being gay. She used all the little ways of being gay. She was quite regularly gay. She told many then the way of being gay, she taught very many then little ways they could use in being gay. She was living very well, she was gay then, she went on living then, she was regular in being gay, she always was living very well and was gay very well and was telling about little ways one could be learning to use in being gay, and later was telling them quite often, telling them again and again.

VIRGINIA WOOLF was born in London in 1882. Her father, Sir Leslie Stephen, at one time editor of the monumental *Dictionary of National Biography*, was a famous figure in nineteenth-century British letters. Mrs. Woolf's education took place at home where she had the freedom of her father's magnificent library and the acquaintance of his friends, who included Thomas Hardy, Robert Louis Stevenson, and John Ruskin. The family spent their summers in St. Ives, a coastal village in Cornwall, which later became the background of her novel *To the Lighthouse*. In 1912 she married Leonard Woolf—"the wisest decision of her life." Their home in Bloomsbury near the British Museum became the meeting-place of the "Bloomsbury Group" which included E. M. Forster, Lytton Strachey, Victoria Sackville-West, J. M. Keynes, and T. S. Eliot. In 1917 the Woolfs started the Hogarth Press. Their intention was to publish on their old handpress the "best and most original" works of young, unknown writers. (The press on which Virginia Woolf set the type for *The Waste Land* is still preserved in V. Sackville-West's tower at Sissinghurst.) In 1941, fearing a mental breakdown, Mrs. Woolf committed suicide by drowning herself in the river Ouse near her home in Rodmell, Sussex.

In her diary and critical works she had much to say about women and fiction. In *A Room of One's Own* she observes that literary history contains the names of so few women because of economic and social circumstances. "A woman must have money and a room of her own if she is to write fiction." In her own fiction she often explores the interior consciousness of women. In *Collected Impressions*, Elizabeth Bowen notes that the point about women that Virginia Woolf's novels most emphasize "is not that they despise truth but that they see something beyond truth, which we may call reality; and they see other roads of approach to this reality than the path of verbal logic. If verbal logic (which is what men generally mean by 'truth') gets in the way of kindness, or vision, it has to be given up; the human values are worth more than the purely intellectual."

Virginia Woolf
(1882–1941)

THE NEW DRESS

Mabel had her first serious suspicion that something was wrong as she took her cloak off and Mrs. Barnet, while handing her the mirror and touching the brushes and thus drawing her attention, perhaps rather markedly, to all the appliances for tidying and improving hair, complexion, clothes, which existed on the dressing table, confirmed the suspicion—that it was not right, not quite right, which growing stronger as she went upstairs and springing at her, with conviction as she greeted Clarissa Dalloway, she went straight to the far end of the room, to a shaded corner where a looking-glass hung and looked. No! It was not *right.* And at once the misery which she always tried to hide, the profound dissatisfaction—the sense she had had, ever since she was a child, of being inferior to other people—set upon her, relentlessly, remorselessly, with an intensity which she could not beat off, as she would when she woke at night at home, by reading Borrow or Scott; for oh these men, oh these women, all were thinking—"What's Mabel wearing? What a fright she looks! What a hideous new dress!"—their eyelids flickering as they came up and then their lids shutting rather tight. It was her own appalling inadequacy; her cowardice; her mean, water-sprinkled blood that depressed her. And at once the whole of the room where, for ever so many hours, she had planned with the little dressmaker how it was to go, seemed sordid, repulsive; and her own drawing-room so shabby, and herself, going out, puffed up with vanity as she touched the letters on the hall table and said: "How dull!" to show off—all this now seemed unutterably silly, paltry, and provincial. All this had been absolutely destroyed, shown up, exploded, the moment she came into Mrs. Dalloway's drawing-room.

What she had thought that evening when, sitting over the teacups, Mrs. Dalloway's invitation came, was that, of course, she could not be fashionable. It was absurd to pretend it even—fashion meant cut, meant style, meant thirty guineas at least—but why not be original? Why not be herself, anyhow? And, getting up, she had taken that old fashion book of her mother's, a Paris fashion book of the time of the Empire, and had thought how much prettier, more dignified, and more womanly they were then, and so set herself—oh, it was foolish—trying to be like them, pluming herself in fact, upon being modest and old-fashioned, and very charming, giving herself up, no doubt about it, to an orgy of self-love, which deserved to be chastised, and so rigged herself out like this.

But she dared not look in the glass. She could not face the whole horror—the pale yellow, idiotically old-fashioned silk dress with its long skirt and its high sleeves and its waist and all the things that looked so charming in the fashion book, but not on her, not among all these ordinary people. She felt like a dressmaker's dummy standing there, for young people to stick pins into.

"But, my dear, it's perfectly charming!" Rose Shaw said, looking her up and down with that little satirical pucker of the lips which she expected—Rose herself being dressed in the height of fashion, precisely like everybody else, always.

We are all like flies trying to crawl over the edge of the saucer, Mabel thought, and repeated the phrase as if she were crossing herself, as if she were trying to find some spell to annul this pain, to make this agony endurable. Tags of Shakespeare, lines from books she had read ages ago, suddenly came to her when she was in agony, and she repeated them over and over again. "Flies trying to crawl," she repeated. If she could say that over often enough and make herself see the flies, she would become numb, chill, frozen, dumb. Now she could see flies crawling slowly out of a saucer of milk with their wings stuck together; and she strained and strained (standing in front of the looking-glass, listening to Rose Shaw) to make herself see Rose Shaw and all the other people as flies, trying to hoist themselves out of something, or into something, meagre, insignificant, toiling flies. But she could not see them like that, not other people. She saw herself like that—she was a fly, but the others were dragonflies, butterflies, beautiful insects, dancing, fluttering, skimming, while she alone dragged herself up out of the saucer. (Envy and spite, the most detestable of the vices, were her chief faults.)

"I feel like some dowdy, decrepit, horribly dingy old fly," she said, making Robert Haydon stop just to hear her say that, just to reassure herself by furbishing up a poor weak-kneed phrase and so showing how detached she was, how witty, that she did not feel in the least out of anything. And, of course, Robert Haydon answered something, quite polite, quite insincere, which she saw through instantly, and said to herself, directly he went (again from some book), "Lies, lies, lies!" For a party makes things either much more real, or much less real, she thought; she saw in a flash to the bottom of Robert Haydon's heart; she saw through everything. She saw the truth. *This* was true, this drawing-room, this self, and the other false. Miss Milan's little workroom was really terribly hot, stuffy, sordid. It smelt of clothes and cabbage cooking; and yet, when Miss Milan put the glass in her hand, and she looked at herself with the dress on, finished, an extraordinary bliss shot through her heart. Suffused with light, she sprang into existence. Rid of cares and wrinkles, what she had dreamed of herself was there—a beautiful woman. Just for a second (she had not dared look longer, Miss Milan wanted to know about the length of the skirt), there looked at her, framed in the scrolloping mahogany, a grey-white, mysteriously smiling, charming girl, the core of herself, the soul of herself; and it was not vanity only, not only self-love that made her think it good, tender, and true. Miss Milan said that the skirt could not well be longer; if anything the skirt, said Miss Milan, puckering her forehead, considering with all her wits about her, must be shorter; and she felt, suddenly, honestly, full of love for Miss Milan, much, much fonder of Miss Milan than of any one in the whole world, and could have cried for pity that she should be crawling on the floor with her mouth full of pins, and her face red and her eyes bulging—that one human being should be doing this for another, and she saw them all as human beings merely, and herself going off to her party, and Miss Milan pulling the cover over the canary's cage, or letting him pick a hempseed from between her lips, and the thought of it, of this side of human nature and its patience and its endurance and its being content with such miserable, scanty, sordid, little pleasures filled her eyes with tears.

And now the whole thing had vanished. The dress, the room, the love, the pity, the scrolloping looking-glass, and the canary's cage—all had vanished, and here she was in a corner of Mrs. Dalloway's drawing-room, suffering tortures, woken wide awake to reality.

But it was all so paltry, weak-blooded, and petty-minded to care so much at her age with two children, to be still so utterly dependent on people's opinions and not have principles or convictions, not to be able to say as other people did, "There's Shakespeare! There's death! We're all weevils in a captain's biscuit"—or whatever it was that people did say.

She faced herself straight in the glass; she pecked at her left shoulder; she issued out into the room, as if spears were thrown at her yellow dress from all sides. But instead of looking fierce or tragic, as Rose Shaw would have done—Rose would have looked like Boadicea—she looked foolish and self-conscious, and simpered like a schoolgirl and slouched across the room, positively slinking, as if she were a beaten mongrel, and looked at a picture, an engraving. As if one went to a party to look at a picture! Everybody knew why she did it—it was from shame, from humiliation.

"Now the fly's in the saucer," she said to herself, "right in the middle, and can't get out, and the milk," she thought, rigidly staring at the picture, "is sticking its wings together."

"It's so old-fashioned," she said to Charles Burt, making him stop (which by itself he hated) on his way to talk to some one else.

She meant, or she tried to make herself think that she meant, that it was the picture and not her dress, that was old-fashioned. And one word of praise, one word of affection from Charles would have made all the difference to her at the moment. If he had only said, "Mabel, you're looking charming tonight!" it would have changed her life. But then she ought to have been truthful and direct. Charles said nothing of the kind, of course. He was malice itself. He always saw through one, especially if one were feeling particularly mean, paltry, or feeble-minded.

"Mabel's got a new dress!" he said, and the poor fly was absolutely shoved into the middle of the saucer. Really, he would like her to drown, she believed. He had no heart, no fundamental kindness, only a veneer of friendliness. Miss Milan was much more real, much kinder. If only one could feel that and stick to it, always. "Why," she asked herself—replying to Charles much too pertly, letting him see that she was out of temper, or "ruffled" as he called it. ("Rather ruffled?" he said and went on to laugh at her with some woman over there)—"Why," she asked herself, "can't I feel one thing always, feel quite sure that Miss Milan is right, and Charles wrong and stick to it, feel sure about the canary and pity and love and not be whipped all round in a second by coming into a room full of people?" It was her odious, weak, vacillating character again, always giving at the critical moment and not being seriously interested in conchology, etymology, botany, archaeology, cutting up potatoes and watching them fructify like Mary Dennis, like Violet Searle.

Then Mrs. Holman, seeing her standing there, bore down upon her. Of course a thing like a dress was beneath Mrs. Holman's notice, with her family always tumbling downstairs or having the scarlet fever. Could Mabel tell her if Elmthorpe was ever let for August and September? Oh, it was a conversation that bored her unutterably!—it made her furious to be treated like a house agent or a messenger boy, to be made use of. Not to have value, that was it, she thought, trying to grasp something hard, something real, while she tried to answer sensibly about the bathroom and the south aspect and the hot water to the top of the house; and all the time she could see little bits of her yellow dress in the round looking-glass which made them all the size of boot-buttons or tadpoles; and it was amazing to think how much humiliation and agony and self-loathing and effort and passionate ups and downs of feeling were contained in a thing the size of a threepenny bit. And what was still odder, this thing, this Mabel Waring, was separate, quite disconnected: and though Mrs. Holman (the black button) was leaning forward and telling her how her eldest boy had strained his heart running, she could see her, too, quite detached in the looking-glass, and it was impossible that the black dot, leaning forward, gesticulating, should make the yellow dot, sitting solitary, self-centred, feel what the black dot was feeling, yet they pretended.

"So impossible to keep boys quiet"—that was the kind of thing one said.

And Mrs. Holman, who could never get enough sympathy and snatched what little there was greedily, as if it were her right (but she deserved much more for, there was her little girl who had come down this morning with a swollen knee-joint), took this miserable offering and looked at it suspiciously, grudgingly, as if it were a half-penny when it ought to have been a pound and put it away in her purse, must put up with it, mean and miserly though it was, times being hard, so very hard; and on she went, creaking, injured Mrs. Holman, about the girl with the swollen joints. Ah, it was tragic, this greed, this clamour of human beings, like a row of cormorants, barking and flapping their wings for sympathy—it was tragic, could one have felt it and not merely pretended to feel it!

But in her yellow dress to-night she could not wring out one drop more; she wanted it all, all for herself. She knew (she kept on looking into the glass, dipping into that dreadfully showing-up blue pool) that she was condemned, despised, left like this in a backwater, because of her being like this a feeble, vacillating creature; and it seemed to her that the yellow dress was a penance which she had deserved, and if she had been dressed like Rose Shaw, in lovely, clinging green with a ruffle of swansdown, she would have deserved that; and she thought that there was no escape for her—none whatever. But it was not her fault altogether, after all. It was being one of a family of ten; never having money enough, always skimping and paring; and her mother carrying great cans, and the linoleum worn on the stair edges, and one sordid little domestic tragedy after another—nothing catastrophic, the sheep farm failing, but not utterly; her eldest brother marrying beneath him but not very much—there was no romance, nothing extreme about them all. They petered out respectably in seaside resorts; every watering-place had one of her aunts even now asleep in some lodging with the front windows not quite facing the sea. That was so like them—they had to squint at things always. And she had done the same—she was just like her aunts. For all her dreams of living in India, married to some hero like Sir Henry Lawrence, some empire builder (still the sight of a native in a turban filled her with romance), she had failed utterly. She had married Hubert, with his safe, permanent underling's job in the Law Courts, and they managed tolerably in a smallish house, without proper maids, and hash when she was alone or just bread and butter, but now and then—Mrs. Holman was off, thinking her the most dried-up, unsympathetic twig she had ever met, absurdly dressed, too, and would tell every one about Mabel's fantastic appearance—now and then, thought Mabel Waring, left alone on the blue sofa, punching the cushion in order to look occupied, for she would not join Charles Burt and Rose Shaw, chattering like magpies and perhaps laughing at her by the fireplace—now and then, there did come to her delicious moments, reading the other night in bed, for instance, or down by the sea on the sand in the sun, at Easter—let her recall it—a great tuft of pale sand-grass standing all twisted like a shock of spears against the sky, which was blue like a smooth china egg, so firm, so hard, and then the melody of the waves—"Hush, hush," they said, and the children's shouts paddling—yes, it was a divine moment, and there she lay, she felt, in the hand of the Goddess who was the world; rather a hard-hearted, but very beautiful Goddess, a little lamb laid on the altar (one did think these silly things, and it didn't matter so long as one never said them). And also with Hubert sometimes she had quite unexpectedly—carving the mutton for Sunday lunch, for no reason, opening a letter, coming into a room—divine moments, when she said to herself (for she would never say this to anybody else), "This is it. This has happened. This is it!" And the other way about it was equally surprising—that is, when everything was arranged—music, weather, holidays, every reason for happiness was there—then nothing happened at all. One wasn't happy. It was flat, just flat, that was all.

Her wretched self again, no doubt! She had always been a fretful, weak, unsatisfactory mother, a wobbly wife, lolling about in a kind of twilight existence with nothing very clear or very bold, or more one thing than another, like all her brothers and sisters, except perhaps Herbert—they were all the same poor water-veined creatures who did nothing. Then in the midst of this creeping, crawling life, suddenly she was on the crest of a wave. That wretched fly—where had she read the story that kept coming into her mind about the fly and the saucer?—struggled out. Yes, she had those moments. But now that she was forty, they might come more and more seldom. By degrees she would cease to struggle any more. But that was deplorable! That was not to be endured! That made her feel ashamed of herself!

She would go to the London Library tomorrow. She would find some wonderful, helpful, astonishing book, quite by chance, a book by a clergyman, by an American no one had ever heard of; or she would walk down the Strand and drop, accidentally, into a hall where a miner was telling about the life in the pit, and suddenly she would become a new person. She would be absolutely transformed. She would wear a uniform; she would be called Sister Somebody; she would never give a thought to clothes again. And for ever after she would be perfectly clear about Charles Burt and Miss Milan and this room and that room; and it would be always, day after day, as if she were lying in the sun or carving the mutton. It would be it!

So she got up from the blue sofa, and the yellow button in the looking-glass got up too, and she waved her hand to Charles and Rose to show them she did not depend on them one scrap, and the yellow button moved out of the looking-glass, and all the spears were gathered into her breast as she walked towards Mrs. Dalloway and said, "Good night."

"But it's too early to go," said Mrs. Dalloway, who was always so charming.

"I'm afraid I must," said Mabel Waring. "But," she added in her weak, wobbly voice which only sounded ridiculous when she tried to strengthen it, "I have enjoyed myself enormously."

"I have enjoyed myself," she said to Mr. Dalloway, whom she met on the stairs.

"Lies, lies, lies!" she said to herself, going downstairs, and "Right in the saucer!" she said to herself as she thanked Mrs. Barnet for helping her and wrapped herself, round and round and round, in the Chinese cloak she had worn these twenty years.

KATHERINE MANSFIELD was born Kathleen Mansfield Beauchamp in 1888 in New Zealand. She grew up in the village of Karori, near Wellington, where she had the ordinary education of other local children. When she was nine her first story was published in a magazine called *The Lone Hand*. In 1903 she went to London to study music at Queen's College in Harley Street. After graduation she returned to New Zealand, but after two very unhappy years she left home again, this time for good. Her father, a successful banker, gave her an annual allowance of one hundred pounds on which she was meant to survive in London. In her fiction the recurring character of the self-centered family man who drains the life of the family women is said to mirror her resentment of her father. In 1909 she married George Bowden, but left him after a few days. Her life with the critic John Middleton Murray began in 1911. They traveled extensively, living for a time in France and Germany, always in search of a mild climate because of Katherine Mansfield's chronic poor health. During the First World War they spent several years living in Cornwall with D. H. Lawrence and his wife Frieda. Katherine Mansfield died of consumption in 1923 at the age of thirty-four. Murray subsequently edited her *Journal* (1927), *Letters* (1928), and *Scrapbook* (1940).

Her *Journal* is an extraordinary document of a writer's mind and heart and soul. It is the best record of a woman's passionate commitment to being a writer. "I really only ask for time to write it all—time to write my books. Then I don't mind dying. I live to write. . . ." In a vein that suggests the spiritual tension of the story that follows, she writes of her dissatisfaction with the idea "that Life must be a lesser thing than we were capable of imagining it to be. I had the feeling that the same thing happened to nearly everybody whom I knew and whom I did not know. No sooner was their youth, with the little force and impetus characteristic of youth, done, than they stopped growing. At the very moment that one felt that now was the time to gather oneself together, to use one's whole strength, to take control, to be an adult, in fact, they seemed content to swop the darling wish of their hearts for innumerable little wishes. . . ."

Katherine Mansfield (1888–1923)

THE GARDEN PARTY

And after all the weather was ideal. They could not have had a more perfect day for a garden-party if they had ordered it. Windless, warm, the sky without a cloud. Only the blue was veiled with a haze of light gold, as it is sometimes in early summer. The gardener had been up since dawn, mowing the lawns and sweeping them, until the grass and the dark flat rosettes where the daisy plants had been seemed to shine. As for the roses, you could not help feeling they understood that roses are the only flowers that impress people at garden-parties; the only flowers that everybody is certain of knowing. Hundreds, yes, literally hundreds, had come out in a single night; the green bushes bowed down as though they had been visited by archangels.

Breakfast was not yet over before the men came to put up the marquee.

"Where do you want the marquee put, mother?"

"My dear child, it's no use asking me. I'm determined to leave everything to you children this year. Forget I am your mother. Treat me as an honoured guest."

But Meg could not possibly go and supervise the men. She had washed her hair before breakfast, and she sat drinking coffee in a green turban, with a dark wet curl stamped on each cheek. Jose, the butterfly, always came down in a silk petticoat and a kimono jacket.

"You'll have to go, Laura; you're the artistic one."

Away Laura flew, still holding her piece of bread-and-butter. It's so delicious to have an excuse for eating out of doors, and besides, she loved having to arrange things; she always felt she could do it so much better than anybody else.

Four men in their shirt-sleeves stood grouped together on the garden path. They carried staves covered with rolls of canvas, and they had big tool-bags slung on their backs.

They looked impressive. Laura wished now that she had not got the bread-and-butter, but there was nowhere to put it, and she couldn't possibly throw it away. She blushed and tried to look severe and even a little bit short-sighted as she came up to them.

"Good morning," she said, copying her mother's voice. But that sounded so fearfully affected that she was ashamed, and stammered like a little girl, "Oh—er—have you come—is it about the marquee?"

"That's right, miss," said the tallest of the men, a lanky, freckled fellow, and he shifted his tool-bag, knocked back his straw hat and smiled down at her. "That's about it."

His smile was so easy, so friendly that Laura recovered. What nice eyes he had, small, but such a dark blue! And now she looked at the others, they were smiling too. "Cheer up, we won't bite," their smile seemed to say. How very nice workmen were! And what a beautiful morning! She mustn't mention the morning; she must be businesslike. The marquee.

"Well, what about the lily-lawn? Would that do?"

And she pointed to the lily-lawn with the hand that didn't hold the bread-and-butter. They turned, they stared in the direction. A little fat chap thrust out his under-lip, and the tall fellow frowned.

"I don't fancy it," said he. "Not conspicuous enough. You see, with a thing like a marquee," and he turned to Laura in his easy way, "you want to put it somewhere where it'll give you a bang slap in the eye, if you follow me."

Laura's upbringing made her wonder for a moment whether it was quite respectful of a workman to talk to her of bangs slap in the eye. But she did quite follow him.

"A corner of the tennis-court," she suggested. "But the band's going to be in one corner."

"H'm, going to have a band, are you?" said another of the workmen. He was pale. He had a haggard look as his dark eyes scanned the tennis-court. What was he thinking?

"Only a very small band," said Laura gently. Perhaps he wouldn't mind so much if the band was quite small. But the tall fellow interrupted.

"Look here, miss, that's the place. Against those trees, over there. That'll do fine."

Against the karakas. Then the karakas-trees would be hidden. And they were so lovely, with their broad, gleaming leaves, and their clusters of yellow fruit. They were like trees you imagined growing on a desert island, proud, solitary, lifting their leaves and fruits to the sun in a kind of silent splendour. Must they be hidden by a marquee?

They must. Already the men had shouldered their staves and were making for the place. Only the tall fellow was left. He bent down, pinched a sprig of lavender, put his thumb and forefinger to his nose and snuffed up the smell. When Laura saw that gesture she forgot all about the karakas in her wonder at him caring for things like that—caring for the smell of lavender. How many men that she knew would have done such a thing? Oh, how extraordinarily nice workmen were, she thought. Why couldn't she have workmen for friends rather than the silly boys she danced with and who came to Sunday night supper? She would get on much better with men like these.

It's all the fault, she decided, as the tall fellow drew something on the back of an envelope, something that was to be looped up or left to hang, of these absurd class distinctions. Well, for her part, she didn't feel them. Not a bit, not an atom. . . . And now there came the chock-chock of wooden hammers. Some one whistled, some one sang out, "Are you right there, matey?" "Matey!" The friendliness of it, the—the— Just to prove how happy she was, just to show the tall fellow how at home she felt, and how she despised stupid conventions, Laura took a big bite of her bread-and-butter as she stared at the little drawing. She felt just like a work-girl.

"Laura, Laura, where are you? Telephone, Laura!" a voice cried from the house.

"Coming!" Away she skimmed, over the lawn, up the path, up the steps, across the veranda, and into the porch. In the hall her father and Laurie were brushing their hats ready to go to the office.

"I say, Laura," said Laurie very fast, "you might just give a squiz at my coat before this afternoon. See if it wants pressing."

"I will," said she. Suddenly she couldn't stop herself. She ran at Laurie and gave him a small, quick squeeze. "Oh, I do love parties, don't you?" gasped Laura.

"Ra-ther," said Laurie's warm, boyish voice, and he squeezed his sister too, and gave her a gentle push. "Dash off to the telephone, old girl."

The telephone. "Yes, yes; oh yes. Kitty? Good morning,

dear. Come to lunch? Do, dear. Delighted of course. It will only be a very scratch meal—just the sandwich crusts and broken meringue-shells and what's left over. Yes, isn't it a perfect morning? Your white? Oh, I certainly should. One moment—hold the line. Mother's calling." And Laura sat back. "What, mother? Can't hear."

Mrs. Sheridan's voice floated down the stairs. "Tell her to wear that sweet hat she had on last Sunday."

"Mother says you're to wear that *sweet* hat you had on last Sunday. Good. One o'clock. Bye-bye."

Laura put back the receiver, flung her arms over her head, took a deep breath, stretched and let them fall. "Huh," she sighed, and the moment after the sigh sat up quickly. She was still, listening. All the doors in the house seemed to be open. The house was alive with soft, quick steps and running voices. The green baize door that led to the kitchen regions swung open and shut with a muffled thud. And now there came a long, chuckling absurd sound. It was the heavy piano being moved on its stiff castors. But the air! If you stopped to notice, was the air always like this? Little faint winds were playing chase, in at the tops of the windows, out at the doors. And there were two tiny spots of sun, one on the inkpot, one on a silver photograph frame, playing too. Darling little spots. Especially the one on the inkpot lid. It was quite warm. A warm little silver star. She could have kissed it.

The front door bell pealed, and there sounded the rustle of Sadie's print skirt on the stairs. A man's voice murmured; Sadie answered, careless, "I'm sure I don't know. Wait. I'll ask Mrs. Sheridan."

"What is it, Sadie?" Laura came into the hall.

"It's the florist, Miss Laura."

It was, indeed. There, just inside the door, stood a wide, shallow tray full of pots of pink lilies. No other kind. Nothing but lilies—canna lilies, big pink flowers, wide open, radiant, almost frighteningly alive on bright crimson stems.

"O-oh, Sadie!" said Laura, and the sound was like a little moan. She crouched down as if to warm herself at that blaze of lilies; she felt they were in her fingers, on her lips, growing in her breast.

"It's some mistake," she said faintly. "Nobody ever ordered so many. Sadie, go and find mother."

But at that moment Mrs. Sheridan joined them.

"It's quite right," she said calmly. "Yes, I ordered them. Aren't they lovely?" She pressed Laura's arm. "I was passing the shop yesterday, and I saw them in the window. And I suddenly thought for once in my life I shall have enough canna lilies. The garden-party will be a good excuse."

"But I thought you said you didn't mean to interfere," said Laura. Sadie had gone. The florist's man was still outside at his van. She put her arm round her mother's neck and gently, very gently, she bit her mother's ear.

"My darling child, you wouldn't like a logical mother, would you? Don't do that. Here's the man."

He carried more lilies still, another whole tray.

"Bank them up, just inside the door, on both sides of the porch, please," said Mrs. Sheridan. "Don't you agree, Laura?"

"Oh, I *do*, mother."

In the drawing-room Meg, Jose and good little Hans had at last succeeded in moving the piano.

"Now, if we put this chesterfield against the wall and move everything out of the room except the chairs, don't you think?"

"Quite."

"Hans, move these tables into the smoking-room, and bring a sweeper to take these marks off the carpet and—one moment, Hans—" Jose loved giving orders to the servants, and they loved obeying her. She always made them feel they were taking part in some drama. "Tell mother and Miss Laura to come here at once."

"Very good, Miss Jose."

She turned to Meg. "I want to hear what the piano sounds like, just in case I'm asked to sing this afternoon. Let's try over 'This Life is Weary.'"

Pom! Ta-ta-ta *Tee*-ta! The piano burst out so passionately that Jose's face changed. She clasped her hands. She looked mournfully and enigmatically at her mother and Laura as they came in.

This Life is *Wee*-ary,
A Tear—A Sigh.
A Love that *Chan-ges*,
This Life is *Wee*-ary,
A Tear—a Sigh.

A Love that *Chan*-ges,
And then . . . Good-bye!

But at the word "Good-bye," and although the piano sounded more desperate than ever, her face broke into a brilliant, dreadfully unsympathetic smile.

"Aren't I in good voice, mummy?" she beamed.

This Life is *Wee*-ary,
Hope comes to Die.
A Dream—a *Wa*-kening.

But now Sadie interrupted them. "What is it, Sadie?"

"If you please, m'm, cook says have you got the flags for the sandwiches?"

"The flags for the sandwiches, Sadie?" echoed Mrs. Sheridan dreamily. And the children knew by her face that she hadn't got them. "Let me see." And she said to Sadie firmly, "Tell cook I'll let her have them in ten minutes."

Sadie went.

"Now, Laura," said her mother quickly. "Come with me into the smoking-room. I've got the names somewhere on the back of an envelope. You'll have to write them out for me. Meg, go upstairs this minute and take that wet thing off your head. Jose, run and finish dressing this instant. Do you hear me, children, or shall I have to tell your father when he comes home to-night? And—and, Jose, pacify cook if you do go into the kitchen, will you? I'm terrified of her this morning."

The envelope was found at last behind the dining-room clock, though how it had got there Mrs. Sheridan could not imagine.

"One of you children must have stolen it out of my bag, because I remember vividly—cream cheese and lemon-curd. Have you done that?"

"Yes."

"Egg and—" Mrs. Sheridan held the envelope away from her. "It looks like mice. It can't be mice, can it?"

"Olive, pet," said Laura, looking over her shoulder.

"Yes, of course, olive. What a horrible combination it sounds. Egg and olive."

They were finished at last, and Laura took them off to the kitchen. She found Jose there pacifying the cook, who did not look at all terrifying.

"I have never seen such exquisite sandwiches," said Jose's rapturous voice. "How many kinds did you say there were, cook? Fifteen?"

"Fifteen, Miss Jose."

"Well, cook, I congratulate you."

Cook swept up crusts with the long sandwich knife, and smiled broadly.

"Godber's has come," announced Sadie, issuing out of the pantry. She had seen the man pass the window.

That meant the cream puffs had come. Godber's were famous for their cream puffs. Nobody ever thought of making them at home.

"Bring them in and put them on the table, my girl," ordered cook.

Sadie brought them in and went back to the door. Of course Laura and Jose were far too grown-up to really care about such things. All the same, they couldn't help agreeing that the puffs looked very attractive. Very. Cook began arranging them, shaking off the extra icing sugar.

"Don't they carry one back to all one's parties?" said Laura.

"I suppose they do," said practical Jose, who never liked to be carried back. "They look beautifully light and feathery, I must say."

"Have one each, my dears," said cook in her comfortable voice. "Yer ma won't know."

Oh, impossible. Fancy cream puffs so soon after breakfast. The very idea made one shudder. All the same, two minutes later Jose and Laura were licking their fingers with that absorbed inward look that only comes from whipped cream.

"Let's go into the garden, out by the back way," suggested Laura. "I want to see how the men are getting on with the marquee. They're such awfully nice men."

But the back door was blocked by cook, Sadie, Godber's man and Hans.

Something had happened.

"Tuk-tuk-tuk," clucked cook like an agitated hen. Sadie had her hand clapped to her cheek as though she had toothache. Hans's face was screwed up in the effort to understand. Only Godber's man seemed to be enjoying himself; it was his story.

"What's the matter? What's happened?"

"There's been a horrible accident," said cook. "A man killed."

"A man killed! Where? How? When?"

But Godber's man wasn't going to have his story snatched from under his very nose.

"Know those little cottages just below here, miss?" Know them? Of course, she knew them. "Well, there's a young chap living there, name of Scott, a carter. His horse shied at a traction-engine, corner of Hawke Street this morning, and he was thrown out on the back of his head. Killed."

"Dead!" Laura stared at Godber's man.

"Dead when they picked him up," said Godber's man with relish. "They were taking the body home as I come up here." And he said to the cook, "He's left a wife and five little ones."

"Jose, come here." Laura caught hold of her sister's sleeve and dragged her through the kitchen to the other side of the green baize door. There she paused and leaned against it. "Jose!" she said, horrified, "however are we going to stop everything?"

"Stop everything, Laura!" cried Jose in astonishment. "What do you mean?"

"Stop the garden-party, of course." Why did Jose pretend?

But Jose was still more amazed. "Stop the garden-party? My dear Laura, don't be so absurd. Of course we can't do anything of the kind. Nobody expects us to. Don't be so extravagant."

"But we can't possibly have a garden-party with a man dead just outside the front gate."

That really was extravagant, for the little cottages were in a lane to themselves at the very bottom of a steep rise that led up to the house. A broad road ran between. True, they were far too near. They were the greatest possible eyesore, and they had no right to be in that neighbourhood at all. They were little mean dwellings painted a chocolate brown. In the garden patches there was nothing but cabbage stalks, sick hens and tomato cans. The very smoke coming out of their chimneys was poverty-stricken. Little rags and shreds of smoke, so unlike the great silvery plumes that uncurled from the Sheridans' chimneys. Washer-women lived in the lane and sweeps and a cobbler, and a man whose house-front was studded all over with minute bird-cages. Children swarmed. When the Sheridans were little they were forbidden to set foot there because of the revolting language and of what they might catch. But since they were grown up, Laura and Laurie on their prowls sometimes walked through. It was disgusting and sordid. They came out with a shudder. But still one must go everywhere; one must see everything. So through they went.

"And just think of what the band would sound like to that poor woman," said Laura.

"Oh, Laura!" Jose began to be seriously annoyed. "If you're going to stop a band playing every time some one has an accident, you'll lead a very strenuous life. I'm every bit as sorry about it as you. I feel just as sympathetic." Her eyes hardened. She looked at her sister just as she used to when they were little and fighting together. "You won't bring a drunken workman back to life by being sentimental," she said softly.

"Drunk! Who said he was drunk?" Laura turned furiously on Jose. She said, just as they had used to say on those occasions, "I'm going straight up to tell mother."

"Do, dear," cooed Jose.

"Mother, can I come into your room?" Laura turned the big glass door-knob.

"Of course, child. Why, what's the matter? What's given you such a colour?" And Mrs. Sheridan turned round from her dressing-table. She was trying on a new hat.

"Mother, a man's been killed," began Laura.

"*Not* in the garden?" interrupted her mother.

"No, no!"

"Oh, what a fright you gave me!" Mrs. Sheridan sighed with relief, and took off the big hat and held it on her knees.

"But listen, mother," said Laura. Breathless, half-choking, she told the dreadful story. "Of course, we can't have our party, can we?" she pleaded. "The band and everybody arriving. They'd hear us, mother; they're nearly neighbours!"

To Laura's astonishment her mother behaved just like Jose; it was harder to bear because she seemed amused. She refused to take Laura seriously.

"But, my dear child, use your common sense. It's only by accident we've heard of it. If some one had died there normally—and I can't understand how they keep alive in those poky little holes—we should still be having our party, shouldn't we?"

Laura had to say "yes" to that, but she felt it was all wrong. She sat down on her mother's sofa and pinched the cushion frill.

"Mother, isn't it really terribly heartless of us?" she asked.

"Darling!" Mrs. Sheridan got up and came over to her, carrying the hat. Before Laura could stop her she had popped it on. "My child!" said her mother, "the hat is yours. It's made for you. It's much too young for me. I have never seen you look such a picture. Look at yourself!" And she held up her hand-mirror.

"But, mother," Laura began again. She couldn't look at herself; she turned aside.

This time Mrs. Sheridan lost patience just as Jose had done.

"You are being very absurd, Laura," she said coldly. "People like that don't expect sacrifices from us. And it's not very sympathetic to spoil everybody's enjoyment as you're doing now."

"I don't understand," said Laura, and she walked quickly out of the room into her own bedroom. There, quite by chance, the first thing she saw was this charming girl in the mirror, in her black hat trimmed with gold daisies, and a long black velvet ribbon. Never had she imagined she could look like that. Is mother right? she thought. And now she hoped her mother was right. Am I being extravagant? Perhaps it was extravagant. Just for a moment she had another glimpse of that poor woman and those little children, and the body being carried into the house. But it all seemed blurred, unreal, like a picture in the newspaper. I'll remember it again after the party's over, she decided. And somehow that seemed quite the best plan. . . .

Lunch was over by half-past one. By half-past two they were all ready for the fray. The green-coated band had arrived and was established in a corner of the tennis-court.

"My dear!" trilled Kitty Maitland, "aren't they too like frogs for words? You ought to have arranged them round the pond with the conductor in the middle on a leaf."

Laurie arrived and hailed them on his way to dress. At the sight of him Laura remembered the accident again. She wanted to tell him. If Laurie agreed with the others, then it was bound to be all right. And she followed him into the hall.

"Laurie!"

"Hallo!" He was half-way upstairs, but when he turned round and saw Laura he suddenly puffed out his cheeks and goggled his eyes at her. "My word, Laura! You do look stunning," said Laurie. "What an absolutely topping hat!"

Laura said faintly "Is it?" and smiled up at Laurie, and didn't tell him after all.

Soon after that people began coming in streams. The band struck up; the hired waiters ran from the house to the marquee. Wherever you looked there were couples strolling, bending to the flowers, greeting, moving on over the lawn. They were like bright birds that had alighted in the Sheridans' garden for this one afternoon, on their way to—where? Ah, what happiness it is to be with people who all are happy, to press hands, press cheeks, smile into eyes.

"Darling Laura, how well you look!"

"What a becoming hat, child!"

"Laura, you look quite Spanish. I've never seen you look so striking."

And Laura, glowing, answered softly, "Have you had tea? Won't you have an ice? The passion-fruit ices really are rather special." She ran to her father and begged him. "Daddy darling, can't the band have something to drink?"

And the perfect afternoon slowly ripened, slowly faded, slowly its petals closed.

"Never a more delightful garden-party . . ." "The greatest success . . ." "Quite the most . . ."

Laura helped her mother with the good-byes. They stood side by side in the porch till it was all over.

"All over, all over, thank heaven," said Mrs. Sheridan. "Round up the others, Laura. Let's go and have some fresh coffee. I'm exhausted. Yes, it's been very successful. But oh, these parties, these parties! Why will you children insist on giving parties!" And they all of them sat down in the deserted marquee.

"Have a sandwich, daddy dear. I wrote the flag."

"Thanks." Mr. Sheridan took a bite and the sandwich was gone. He took another. "I suppose you didn't hear of a beastly accident that happened to-day?" he said.

"My dear," said Mrs. Sheridan, holding up her hand,

"we did. It nearly ruined the party. Laura insisted we should put it off."

"Oh, mother!" Laura didn't want to be teased about it.

"It was a horrible affair all the same," said Mr. Sheridan. "The chap was married too. Lived just below in the lane, and leaves a wife and half a dozen kiddies, so they say."

An awkward little silence fell. Mrs. Sheridan fidgeted with her cup. Really, it was very tactless of father . . .

Suddenly she looked up. There on the table were all those sandwiches, cakes, puffs, all uneaten, all going to be wasted. She had one of her brilliant ideas.

"I know," she said. "Let's make up a basket. Let's send that poor creature some of this perfectly good food. At any rate, it will be the greatest treat for the children. Don't you agree? And she's sure to have neighbours calling in and so on. What a point to have it all ready prepared. Laura!" She jumped up. "Get me the big basket out of the stairs cupboard."

"But, mother, do you really think it's a good idea?" said Laura.

Again, how curious, she seemed to be different from them all. To take scraps from their party. Would the poor woman really like that?

"Of course! What's the matter with you to-day? An hour or two ago you were insisting on us being sympathetic, and now—"

Oh, well! Laura ran for the basket. It was filled, it was heaped by her mother.

"Take it yourself, darling," said she. "Run down just as you are. No, wait, take the arum lilies too. People of that class are so impressed by arum lilies."

"The stems will ruin her lace frock," said practical Jose.

So they would. Just in time. "Only the basket, then. And, Laura!"—her mother followed her out of the marquee—"don't on any account—"

"What, mother?"

No, better not put such ideas into the child's head! "Nothing! Run along."

It was just growing dusky as Laura shut their garden gates. A big dog ran by like a shadow. The road gleamed white, and down below in the hollow the little cottages were in deep shade. How quiet it seemed after the afternoon. Here she was going down the hill to somewhere where a man lay dead, and she couldn't realize it. Why couldn't she? She stopped a minute. And it seemed to her that kisses, voices, tinkling spoons, laughter, the smell of crushed grass were somehow inside her. She had no room for anything else. How strange! She looked up at the pale sky, and all she thought was, "Yes, it was the most successful party."

Now the broad road was crossed. The lane began, smoky and dark. Women in shawls and men's tweed caps hurried by. Men hung over the palings; the children played in the doorways. A low hum came from the mean little cottages. In some of them there was a flicker of light, and a shadow, crab-like, moved across the window. Laura bent her head and hurried on. She wished now she had put on a coat. How her frock shone! And the big hat with the velvet streamer—if only it was another hat! Were the people looking at her? They must be. It was a mistake to have come; she knew all along it was a mistake. Should she go back even now?

No, too late. This was the house. It must be. A dark knot of people stood outside. Beside the gate an old, old woman with a crutch sat in a chair, watching. She had her feet on a newspaper. The voices stopped as Laura drew near. The group parted. It was as though she was expected, as though they had known she was coming here.

Laura was terribly nervous. Tossing the velvet ribbon over her shoulder, she said to a woman standing by, "Is this Mrs. Scott's house?" and the woman, smiling queerly, said, "It is, my lass."

Oh, to be away from this! She actually said, "Help me, God," as she walked up the tiny path and knocked. To be away from those staring eyes, or to be covered up in anything, one of those women's shawls even. I'll just leave the basket and go, she decided. I shan't even wait for it to be emptied.

Then the door opened. A little woman in black showed in the gloom.

Laura said, "Are you Mrs. Scott?" But to her horror the woman answered, "Walk in please, miss," and she was shut in the passage.

"No," said Laura, "I don't want to come in. I only want to leave this basket. Mother sent—"

The little woman in the gloomy passage seemed not to have heard her. "Step this way, please, miss," she said in an oily voice, and Laura followed her.

She found herself in a wretched little low kitchen, lighted by a smoky lamp. There was a woman sitting before the fire.

"Em," said the little creature who had let her in. "Em! It's a young lady." She turned to Laura. She said meaningly, "I'm 'er sister, miss. You'll excuse 'er, wont you?"

"Oh, but of course!" said Laura. "Please, please don't disturb her. I—I only want to leave—"

But at that moment the woman at the fire turned round. Her face, puffed up, red, with swollen eyes and swollen lips, looked terrible. She seemed as though she couldn't understand why Laura was there. What did it mean? Why was this stranger standing in the kitchen with a basket? What was it all about? And the poor face puckered up again.

"All right, my dear," said the other. "I'll thenk the young lady."

And again she began, "You'll excuse her, miss, I'm sure," and her face, swollen too, tried an oily smile.

Laura only wanted to get out, to get away. She was back in the passage. The door opened. She walked straight through into the bedroom, where the dead man was lying.

"You'd like a look at 'im, wouldn't you?" said Em's sister, and she brushed past Laura over to the bed. "Don't be afraid, my lass—" and now her voice sounded fond and sly, and fondly she drew down the sheet—" 'e looks a picture. There's nothing to show. Come along, my dear."

Laura came.

There lay a young man, fast asleep—sleeping so soundly, so deeply, that he was far, far away from them both. Oh, so remote, so peaceful. He was dreaming. Never wake him up again. His head was sunk in the pillow, his eyes were closed; they were blind under the closed eyelids. He was given up to his dream. What did garden-parties and baskets and lace frocks matter to him? He was far from all those things. He was wonderful, beautiful. While they were laughing and while the band was playing, this marvel had come to the lane. Happy . . . happy. . . . All is well, said that sleeping face. This is just as it should be. I am content.

But all the same you had to cry, and she couldn't go out of the room without saying something to him. Laura gave a loud childish sob.

"Forgive my hat," she said.

And this time she didn't wait for Em's sister. She found

her way out of the door, down the path, past all those dark people. At the corner of the lane she met Laurie.

He stepped out of the shadow. "Is that you, Laura?"

"Yes."

"Mother was getting anxious. Was it all right?"

"Yes, quite. Oh, Laurie!" She took his arm, she pressed up against him.

"I say, you're not crying, are you?" asked her brother.

Laura shook her head. She was.

Laurie put his arm round her shoulder. "Don't cry," he said in his warm, loving voice. "Was it awful?"

"No," sobbed Laura. "It was simply marvellous. But, Laurie—" She stopped, she looked at her brother. "Isn't life," she stammered, "isn't life—" But what life was she couldn't explain. No matter. He quite understood.

"*Isn't* it, darling?" said Laurie.

KATHERINE ANNE PORTER was born in 1894 in Indian Creek, Texas. She was educated at Catholic convent schools and at home. In an interview with the *Paris Review*, she said that the books of her early youth included Shakespeare's sonnets, Dante, Homer, Ronsard, and Montaigne. When she was fourteen, her father introduced her to Voltaire's philosophical dictionary with notes by Smollett, saying, "Why don't you read this? It'll knock some of the nonsense out of you!" "And, of course," she continues in the same interview, "we read all the eighteenth-century novelists, though Jane Austen, like Turgenev, didn't really engage me until I was quite mature. I read them both when I was very young, but I was grown up before I really took them in. And I discovered for myself *Wuthering Heights*—I think I read that book every year of my life for fifteen years. I simply adored it. Henry James and Thomas Hardy were really my introduction to modern literature: Grandmother didn't much approve of it—she thought Dickens might do, but she was a little against Mr. Thackeray; she thought he was too trivial. So that was as far as I got into the modern world until I left home."

When she was thirty her first story "Maria Concepcion" was published. Before that, she had destroyed masses of manuscripts because they did not satisfy her high standards. Maria Concepcion, the main character in the story of the same name, "the very type of unevolved femaleness" in the words of one critic, is the first of the many rich psychological studies of women that are to be found in her short stories. Her short stories, universally regarded as among the best in the English language, have won her a place among the other classical moderns, Yeats, Joyce, James, Eliot, and Pound. When asked about the importance of her southern background in her evolution as a writer, she said her family explained her more than the South: "I think it's something in the blood. We've always had great letter writers, readers, great story-tellers in our family. I've listened all my life to articulate people. They were all great story-tellers, and every story had shape and meaning and point." In 1973, at the age of seventy-nine, she spoke at the Poetry Center in New York City on the topic, "Life, Love, and Literature." Her advice to her audience was "Find out what you're good for, and then do that."

Katherine Anne Porter
(1894–   )

ROPE

On the third day after they moved to the country he came walking back from the village carrying a basket of groceries and a twenty-four-yard coil of rope. She came out to meet him, wiping her hands on her green smock. Her hair was tumbled, her nose was scarlet with sunburn; he told her that already she looked like a born country woman. His gray flannel shirt stuck to him, his heavy shoes were dusty. She assured him he looked like a rural character in a play.

Had he brought the coffee? She had been waiting all day long for coffee. They had forgot it when they ordered at the store the first day.

Gosh, no, he hadn't. Lord, now he'd have to go back. Yes, he would if it killed him. He thought, though, he had everything else. She reminded him it was only because he didn't drink coffee himself. If he did he would remember it quick enough. Suppose they ran out of cigarettes? Then she saw the rope. What was that for? Well, he thought it might do to hang clothes on, or something. Naturally she asked him if he thought they were going to run a laundry? They already had a fifty-foot line hanging right before his eyes? Why, hadn't he noticed it, really? It was a blot on the landscape to her.

He thought there were a lot of things a rope might come in handy for. She wanted to know what, for instance. He thought a few seconds, but nothing occurred. They could wait and see, couldn't they? You need all sorts of strange odds and ends around a place in the country. She said, yes, that was so; but she thought just at that time when every penny counted, it seemed funny to buy more rope. That was all. She hadn't meant anything else. She hadn't just seen, not at first, why he felt it was necessary.

Well, thunder, he had bought it because he wanted to, and that was all there was to it. She thought that was reason enough, and couldn't understand why he hadn't said so, at first. Undoubtedly it would be useful, twenty-four yards of rope, there were hundreds of things, she couldn't think of any at the moment, but it would come in. Of course. As he had said, things always did in the country.

But she was a little disappointed about the coffee, and oh, look, look, look at the eggs! Oh, my, they're all running! What had he put on top of them? Hadn't he known eggs mustn't be squeezed? Squeezed, who had squeezed them, he wanted to know. What a silly thing to say. He had simply brought them along in the basket with the other things. If they got broke it was the grocer's fault. He should know better than to put heavy things on top of eggs.

She believed it was the rope. That was the heaviest thing in the pack, she saw him plainly when he came in from the road, the rope was a big package on top of everything. He desired the whole wide world to witness that this was not a fact. He had carried the rope in one hand and the basket in the other, and what was the use of her having eyes if that was the best they could do for her?

Well, anyhow, she could see one thing plain: no eggs for breakfast. They'd have to scramble them now, for supper. It was too damned bad. She had planned to have steak for supper. No ice, meat wouldn't keep. He wanted to know why she couldn't finish breaking the eggs in a bowl and set them in a cool place.

Cool place! If he could find one for her, she'd be glad to set them there. Well, then, it seemed to him they might very well cook the meat at the same time they cooked the eggs and then warm up the meat for tomorrow. The idea simply choked her. Warmed-over meat, when they might as well have had it fresh. Second best and scraps and makeshifts, even to the meat! He rubbed her shoulder a little. It doesn't really matter so much, does it, darling? Sometimes when they were playful, he would rub her shoulder and she would arch and purr. This time she hissed and almost clawed. He was getting ready to say that they could surely manage somehow when she turned on him and said, if he told her they could manage somehow she would certainly slap his face.

He swallowed the words red hot, his face burned. He picked up the rope and started to put it on the top shelf. She would not have it on the top shelf, the jars and tins belonged there; positively she would not have the top shelf cluttered up with a lot of rope. She had borne all the clutter she meant to bear in the flat in town, there was space here at least and she meant to keep things in order.

Well, in that case, he wanted to know what the hammer and nails were doing up there? And why had she put them there when she knew very well he needed that hammer and those nails upstairs to fix the window sashes? She simply slowed down everything and made double work on the place with her insane habit of changing things around and hiding them.

She was sure she begged his pardon, and if she had had any reason to believe he was going to fix the sashes this summer she would have left the hammer and nails right where he put them; in the middle of the bedroom floor where they could step on them in the dark. And now if he didn't clear the whole mess out of there she would throw them down the well.

Oh, all right, all right—could he put them in the closet? Naturally not, there were brooms and mops and dustpans in the closet, and why couldn't he find a place for his rope outside her kitchen? Had he stopped to consider there were seven God-forsaken rooms in the house, and only one kitchen?

He wanted to know what of it? And did she realize she was making a complete fool of herself? And what did she take him for, a three-year-old idiot? The whole trouble with her was she needed something weaker than she was to heckle and tyrannize over. He wished to God now they had a couple of children she could take it out on. Maybe he'd get some rest.

Her face changed at this, she reminded him he had forgot the coffee and had bought a worthless piece of rope. And when she thought of all the things they actually needed to make the place even decently fit to live in, well, she could cry, that was all. She looked so forlorn, so lost and despairing he couldn't believe it was only a piece of rope that was causing all the racket. What *was* the matter, for God's sake?

Oh, would he please hush and go away, and *stay* away, if he could, for five minutes? By all means, yes, he would. He'd stay away indefinitely if she wished. Lord, yes, there was nothing he'd like better than to clear out and never come back. She couldn't for the life of her see what was holding him, then. It was a swell time. Here she was, stuck, miles from a railroad, with a half-empty house on her hands, and not a penny in her pocket, and everything on earth to do; it seemed the God-sent moment for him to get out from under. She was surprised he hadn't stayed in town as it was until she had come out and done the work and got things straightened out. It was his usual trick.

It appeared to him that this was going a little far. Just a touch out of bounds, if she didn't mind his saying so. Why the hell had he stayed in town the summer before? To do a half-dozen extra jobs to get the money he had sent her. That was it. She knew perfectly well they couldn't have done it otherwise. She had agreed with him at the time. And that was the only time so help him he had ever left her to do anything by herself.

Oh, he could tell that to his great-grandmother. She had her notion of what had kept him in town. Considerably more than a notion, if he wanted to know. So, she was going to bring all that up again, was she? Well, she could just think what she pleased. He was tired of explaining. It may have looked funny but he had simply got hooked in, and what could he do? It was impossible to believe that she was going to take it seriously. Yes, yes, she knew how it was with a man: if he was left by himself a minute, some woman was certain to kidnap him. And naturally he couldn't hurt her feelings by refusing!

Well, what was she raving about? Did she forget she had told him those two weeks alone in the country were the happiest she had known for four years? And how long had they been married when she said that? All right, shut up! If she thought that hadn't stuck in his craw.

She hadn't meant she was happy because she was away from him. She meant she was happy getting the devilish house nice and ready for him. That was what she had meant, and now look! Bringing up something she had said a year ago simply to justify himself for forgetting her coffee and breaking the eggs and buying a wretched piece of rope they couldn't afford. She really thought it was time to drop the subject, and now she wanted only two things in the world. She wanted him to get that rope from underfoot, and go back to the village and get her coffee, and if he could remember it, he might bring a metal mitt for the skillets, and two more curtain rods, and if there were any rubber gloves in the village, her hands were simply raw, and a bottle of milk of magnesia from the drugstore.

He looked out at the dark blue afternoon sweltering on the slopes, and mopped his forehead and sighed heavily and said, if only she could wait a minute for *anything*, he was going back. He had said so, hadn't he, the very instant they found he had overlooked it?

Oh, yes, well . . . run along. She was going to wash windows. The country was so beautiful! She doubted they'd have a moment to enjoy it. He meant to go, but he could not until he had said that if she wasn't such a hopeless melancholiac she might see that this was only for a few days. Couldn't she remember anything pleasant about the other summers? Hadn't they ever had any fun? She hadn't time to talk about it, and now would he please not leave that rope lying around for her to trip on? He picked it up, somehow it had toppled off the table, and walked out with it under his arm.

Was he going this minute? He certainly was. She thought so. Sometimes it seemed to her he had second sight about the precisely perfect moment to leave her ditched. She had meant to put the mattresses out to sun, if they put them out this minute they would get at least three hours, he must have heard her say that morning she meant to put them out. So of course he would walk off and leave her to it. She supposed he thought the exercise would do her good.

Well, he was merely going to get her coffee. A four-mile walk for two pounds of coffee was ridiculous, but he was perfectly willing to do it. The habit was making a wreck of her, but if she wanted to wreck herself there was nothing he could so about it. If he thought it was coffee that was making a wreck of her, she congratulated him: he must have a damned easy conscience.

Conscience or no conscience, he didn't see why the mattresses couldn't very well wait until tomorrow. And anyhow, for God's sake, were they living in the house, or were they going to let the house ride them to death? She paled at this, her face grew livid about the mouth, she looked quite dangerous, and reminded him that housekeeping was no more her work than it was his: she had other work to do as well, and when did he think she was going to find time to do it at this rate?

Was she going to start on that again? She knew as well as he did that his work brought in the regular money, hers was only occasional, if they depended on what *she* made—and she might as well get straight on this question once for all!

That was positively not the point. The question was, when both of them were working on their own time, was there going to be a division of the housework, or wasn't there? She merely wanted to know, she had to make her plans. Why, he thought that was all arranged. It was understood that he was to help. Hadn't he always, in summers?

Hadn't he, though? Oh, just hadn't he? And when, and where, and doing what? Lord, what an uproarious joke!

It was such a very uproarious joke that her face turned slightly purple, and she screamed with laughter. She laughed so hard she had to sit down, and finally a rush of tears spurted from her eyes and poured down into the lifted corners of her mouth. He dashed towards her and dragged her up to her feet and tried to pour water on her head. The dipper hung by a string on a nail and he broke it loose. Then he tried to pump water with one hand while she struggled in the other. So he gave it up and shook her instead.

She wrenched away, crying out for him to take his rope and go to hell, she had simply given him up: and ran. He heard her high-heeled bedroom slippers clattering and stumbling on the stairs.

He went out around the house and into the lane; he suddenly realized he had a blister on his heel and his shirt felt as if it were on fire. Things broke so suddenly you didn't know where you were. She could work herself into a fury about simply nothing. She was terrible, damn it: not an ounce of reason. You might as well talk to a sieve as that woman when she got going. Damned if he'd spend his life humoring her. Well, what to do now? He would take back the rope and exchange it for something else. Things accumulated, things were mountainous, you couldn't move them or sort them out or get rid of them. They just lay and rotted around. He'd take it back. Hell, why should he? He wanted it. What was it anyhow? A piece of rope. Imagine anybody caring more about a piece of rope than about a man's feelings. What earthly right had she to say a word about it? He remembered all the useless, meaningless things she bought for herself: Why? Because I wanted it, that's why! He stopped and selected a large stone by the road. He would put the rope behind it. He would put it in the toolbox when he got back. He'd heard enough about it to last him a life-time.

When he came back she was leaning against the post box beside the road waiting. It was pretty late, the smell of broiled steak floated nose high in the cooling air. Her face was young and smooth and freshlooking. Her unmanageable funny black hair was all on end. She waved to him from a distance, and he speeded up. She called out that supper was ready and waiting, was he starved?

You bet he was starved. Here was the coffee. He waved it at her. She looked at his other hand. What was that he had there?

Well, it was the rope again. He stopped short. He had meant to exchange it but forgot. She wanted to know why he should exchange it, if it was something he really wanted. Wasn't the air sweet now, and wasn't it fine to be here?

She walked beside him with one hand hooked into his leather belt. She pulled and jostled him a little as he walked, and leaned against him. He put his arm clear around her and patted her stomach. They exchanged wary smiles. Coffee, coffee for the Ootsum-Wootsums! He felt as if he were bringing her a beautiful present.

He was a love, she firmly believed, and if she had had her coffee in the morning, she wouldn't have behaved so funny. . . . There was a whippoorwill still coming back, imagine, clear out of season, sitting in the crab-apple tree calling all by himself. Maybe his girl stood him up. Maybe she did. She hoped to hear him once more, she loved whippoorwills. . . . He knew how she was, didn't he?

Sure, he knew how she was.

KAY BOYLE was born in St. Paul, Minnesota, in 1903. She has been a student of music and architecture, lived a good part of her life in Europe, worked as foreign correspondent for *The New Yorker*, won two Guggenheim Fellowships and two O. Henry Awards for the best short story of 1934 ("The White Horses of Vienna") and 1941 ("Defeat"), lectured and taught in various universities, married three times and mothered six children, written, edited, translated, and ghost-written a total of more than forty books. Her bibliography includes novels, short stories, poetry, juvenile literature, essays, a memoir, and anthologies.

In 1963 she was appointed Professor of English at San Francisco State where she took an active part in the demonstrations held to protest the administration of President S. I. Hayakawa, in particular his summoning of armed police to suppress campus unrest. Kay Boyle has always believed that a writer has a responsibility to make his opposition to tyranny public by participating in the political movements of his time and place. She comments: "Thomas Mann once said that if the writers of Germany through their vision and their expression of that vision had made richer and more impelling promises than those Hitler made, it would have been Hitler, and not the writers of Germany, who would have been forced into exile. It is *always* the intellectuals, however we may shrink from the chilling sound of that word, and, above all, it is *always* the writers who must bear the full weight of moral responsibility. Frenchmen will tell you that the decision to speak out is the vocation and life-long peril by which the intellectual must live. I remember the days in Paris when we who were writers, or painters, or composers wrote pamphlets and distributed them in the streets and cafés. . . . For we considered ourselves a portion of the contemporary conscience, and we had no pity on the compromiser or the poor in spirit of our time. . . ."

Kay Boyle *(1903–   )*

WINTER NIGHT

There is a time of apprehension which begins with the beginning of darkness, and to which only the speech of love can lend security. It is there, in abeyance, at the end of every day, not urgent enough to be given the name of fear but rather of concern for how the hours are to be reprieved from fear, and those who have forgotten how it was when they were children can remember nothing of this. It may begin around five o'clock on a winter afternoon when the light outside is dying in the windows. At that hour the New York apartment in which Felicia lived was filled with shadows, and the little girl would wait alone in the living room, looking out at the winter-stripped trees that stood black in the park against the isolated ovals of unclean snow. Now it was January, and the day had been a cold one; the water of the artificial lake was frozen fast, but because of the cold and the coming darkness, the skaters had ceased to move across its surface. The street that lay between the park and the apartment house was wide, and the two-way streams of cars and busses, some with their headlamps already shining, advanced and halted, halted and poured swiftly on to the tempo of the traffic signals' altering lights. The time of apprehension had set in, and Felicia, who was seven, stood at the window in the evening and waited before she asked the question. When the signals below would change from red to green again, or when the double-decker bus would turn the corner below, she would ask it. The words of it were already there, tentative in her mouth, when the answer came from the far end of the hall.

"Your mother," said the voice among the sound of kitchen things, "she telephoned up before you came in from nursery school. She won't be back in time for supper. I was to tell you a sitter was coming in from the sitting parents' place."

Felicia turned back from the window into the obscurity

of the living room, and she looked toward the open door, and into the hall beyond it where the light from the kitchen fell in a clear yellow angle across the wall and onto the strip of carpet. Her hands were cold, and she put them in her jacket pockets as she walked carefully across the living-room rug and stopped at the edge of light.

"Will she be home late?" she said.

For a moment there was the sound of water running in the kitchen, a long way away, and then the sound of the water ceased, and the high, Southern voice went on:

"She'll come home when she gets ready to come home. That's all I have to say. If she wants to spend two dollars and fifty cents and ten cents' carfare on top of that three or four nights out of the week for a sitting parent to come in here and sit, it's her own business. It certainly ain't nothing to do with you or me. She makes her money, just like the rest of us does. She works all day down there in the office, or whatever it is, just like the rest of us works, and she's entitled to spend her money like she wants to spend it. There's no law in the world against buying your own freedom. Your mother and me, we're just buying our own freedom, that's all we're doing. And we're not doing nobody no harm."

"Do you know who she's having supper with?" said Felicia from the edge of dark. There was one more step to take, and then she would be standing in the light that fell on the strip of carpet, but she did not take the step.

"Do I know who she's having supper with?" the voice cried out in what might have been derision, and there was the sound of dishes striking the metal ribs of the drainboard by the sink. "Maybe it's Mr. Van Johnson, or Mr. Frank Sinatra, or maybe it's just the Duke of Wincers for the evening. All I know is you're having soft-boiled egg and spinach and applesauce for supper, and you're going to have it quick now because the time is getting away."

The voice from the kitchen had no name. It was as variable as the faces and figures of the women who came and sat in the evenings. Month by month the voice in the kitchen altered to another voice, and the sitting parents were no more than lonely aunts of an evening or two who sometimes returned and sometimes did not to this apartment in which they had sat before. Nobody stayed anywhere very long any more, Felicia's mother told her. It was part of the time in which you lived, and part of the life of the city, but when the fathers came back, all this would be miraculously changed. Perhaps you would live in a house again, a small one, with fir trees on either side of the short brick walk, and Father would drive up every night from the station just after darkness set in. When Felicia thought of this, she stepped quickly into the clear angle of light, and she left the dark of the living room behind her and ran softly down the hall.

The drop-leaf table stood in the kitchen between the refrigerator and the sink, and Felicia sat down at the place that was set. The voice at the sink was speaking still, and while Felicia ate it did not cease to speak until the bell of the front door rang abruptly. The girl walked around the table and went down the hall, wiping her dark palms in her apron, and, from the drop-leaf table, Felicia watched her step from the angle of light into darkness and open the door.

"You put in an early appearance," the girl said, and the woman who had rung the bell came into the hall. The door closed behind her, and the girl showed her into the living room, and lit the lamp on the bookcase, and the shadows were suddenly bleached away. But when the girl turned, the woman turned from the living room too and followed her, humbly and in silence, to the threshold of the kitchen. "Sometimes they keep me standing around waiting after it's time for me to be getting on home, the sitting parents do," the girl said, and she picked up the last two dishes from the table and put them in the sink. The woman who stood in the doorway was a small woman, and when she undid the white silk scarf from around her head, Felicia saw that her hair was black. She wore it parted in the middle, and it had not been cut, but was drawn back loosely into a knot behind her head. She had very clean white gloves on, and her face was pale, and there was a look of sorrow in her soft black eyes. "Sometimes I have to stand out there in the hall with my hat and coat on, waiting for the sitting parents to turn up," the girl said, and, as she turned on the water in the sink, the contempt she had for them hung on the kitchen air. "But you're ahead of time," she said, and she held the dishes, first one and then the other, under the flow of steaming water.

The woman in the doorway wore a neat black coat, not a new-looking coat, and it had no fur on it, but it had a smooth velvet collar and velvet lapels. She did not move, or smile, and she gave no sign that she had heard the girl speaking above the sound of water at the sink. She simply stood looking at Felicia, who sat at the table with the milk in her glass not finished yet.

"Are you the child?" she said at last, and her voice was low, and the pronunciation of the words a little strange.

"Yes, this here's Felicia," the girl said, and the dark hands dried the dishes and put them away. "You drink up your milk quick now, Felicia, so's I can rinse your glass."

"I will wash the glass," said the woman. "I would like to wash the glass for her," and Felicia sat looking across the table at the face in the doorway that was filled with such unspoken grief. "I will wash the glass for her and clean off the table," the woman was saying quietly. "When the child is finished, she will show me where her night things are."

"The others, they wouldn't do anything like that," the girl said, and she hung the dishcloth over the rack. "They wouldn't put their hand to housework, the sitting parents. That's where they got the name for them," she said.

Whenever the front door closed behind the girl in the evening, it would usually be that the sitting parent who was there would take up a book of fairy stories and read aloud for a while to Felicia; or else would settle herself in the big chair in the living room and begin to tell the words of a story in drowsiness to her, while Felicia took off her clothes in the bedroom, and folded them, and put her pajamas on, and brushed her teeth, and did her hair. But this time, that was not the way it happened. Instead, the woman sat down on the other chair at the kitchen table, and she began at once to speak, not of good fairies or bad, or of animals endowed with human speech, but to speak quietly, in spite of the eagerness behind her words, of a thing that seemed of singular importance to her.

"It is strange that I should have been sent here tonight," she said, her eyes moving slowly from feature to feature of Felicia's face, "for you look like a child that I knew once, and this is the anniversary of that child."

"Did she have hair like mine?" Felicia asked quickly, and she did not keep her eyes fixed on the unfinished glass of milk in shyness any more.

"Yes, she did. She had hair like yours," said the woman, and her glance paused for a moment on the locks which fell straight and thick on the shoulders of Felicia's dress. It may have been that she thought to stretch out her hand

and touch the ends of Felicia's hair, for her fingers stirred as they lay clasped together on the table, and then they relapsed into passivity again. "But it is not the hair alone, it is the delicacy of your face, too, and your eyes the same, filled with the same spring lilac color," the woman said, pronouncing the words carefully. "She had little coats of golden fur on her arms and legs," she said, "and when we were closed up there, the lot of us in the cold, I used to make her laugh when I told her that the fur that was so pretty, like a little fawn's skin on her arms, would always help to keep her warm."

"And did it keep her warm?" asked Felicia, and she gave a little jerk of laughter as she looked down at her own legs hanging under the table, with the bare calves thin and covered with a down of hair.

"It did not keep her warm enough," the woman said, and now the mask of grief had come back upon her face. "So we used to take everything we could spare from ourselves, and we would sew them into cloaks and other kinds of garments for her and for the other children. . . ."

"Was it a school?" said Felicia when the woman's voice had ceased to speak.

"No," said the woman softly, "it was not a school, but still there were a lot of children there. It was a camp—that was the name the place had; it was a camp. It was a place where they put people until they could decide what was to be done with them." She sat with her hands clasped, silent a moment, looking at Felicia. "That little dress you have on," she said, not saying the words to anybody, scarcely saying them aloud. "Oh, she would have liked that little dress, the little buttons shaped like hearts, and the white collar—"

"I have four school dresses," Felicia said. "I'll show them to you. How many dresses did she have?"

"Well, there, you see, there in the camp," said the woman, "she did not have any dresses except the little skirt and the pullover. That was all she had. She had brought just a handkerchief of her belongings with her, like everybody else—just enough for three days away from home was what they told us, so she did not have enough to last the winter. But she had her ballet slippers," the woman said, and her clasped fingers did not move. "She had brought them because she thought during her three days away from home she would have the time to practice her ballet."

"I've been to the ballet," Felicia said suddenly, and she said it so eagerly that she stuttered a little as the words came out of her mouth. She slipped quickly down from the chair and went around the table to where the woman sat. Then she took one of the woman's hands away from the other that held it fast, and she pulled her toward the door. "Come into the living room and I'll do a pirouette for you," she said, and then she stopped speaking, her eyes halted on the woman's face. "Did she—did the little girl—could she do a pirouette very well?" she said.

"Yes, she could. At first she could," said the woman, and Felicia felt uneasy now at the sound of sorrow in her words. "But after that she was hungry. She was hungry all winter," she said in a low voice. "We were all hungry, but the children were the hungriest. Even now," she said, and her voice went suddenly savage, "when I see milk like that, clean, fresh milk standing in a glass, I want to cry out loud, I want to beat my hands on the table, because it did not have to be . . ." She had drawn her fingers abruptly away from Felicia now, and Felicia stood before her, cast off, forlorn, alone again in the time of apprehension. "That was three years ago," the woman was saying, and one hand was lifted, as in wariness, to shade her face. "It was somewhere else, it was in another country," she said, and behind her hand her eyes were turned upon the substance of a world in which Felicia had played no part.

"Did—did the little girl cry when she was hungry?" Felicia asked, and the woman shook her head.

"Sometimes she cried," she said, "but not very much. She was very quiet. One night when she heard the other children crying, she said to me, 'You know, they are not crying because they want something to eat. They are crying because their mothers have gone away.'"

"Did the mothers have to go out to supper?" Felicia asked, and she watched the woman's face for the answer.

"No," said the woman. She stood up from her chair, and now that she put her hand on the little girl's shoulder, Felicia was taken into the sphere of love and intimacy again. "Shall we go into the other room, and you will do your pirouette for me?" the woman said, and they went from the kitchen and down the strip of carpet on which the clear light fell. In the front room, they paused hand in hand in the glow of the shaded lamp, and the woman looked about her, at the books, the low tables with the magazines and ash trays on them, the vase of roses on the piano, looking with dark, scarcely seeing eyes at these things that had no reality at all. It was only when she saw the little white clock on the mantelpiece that she gave any sign, and then she said quickly: "What time does your mother put you to bed?"

Felicia waited a moment, and in the interval of waiting the woman lifted one hand and, as if in reverence, touched Felicia's hair.

"What time did the little girl you knew in the other place go to bed?" Felicia asked.

"Ah, God, I do not know, I do not remember," the woman said.

"Was she your little girl?" said Felicia softly, stubbornly.

"No," said the woman. "She was not mine. At least, at first she was not mine. She had a mother, a real mother, but the mother had to go away."

"Did she come back late?" asked Felicia.

"No, ah, no, she could not come back, she never came back," the woman said, and now she turned, her arm around Felicia's shoulders, and she sat down in the low soft chair. "Why am I saying all this to you, why am I doing it?" she cried out in grief, and she held Felicia close against her. "I had thought to speak of the anniversary to you, and that was all, and now I am saying these other things to you. Three years ago today, exactly, the little girl became my little girl because her mother went away. That is all there is to it. There is nothing more."

Felicia waited another moment, held close against the woman, and listening to the swift, strong heartbeats in the woman's breast.

"But the mother," she said then in the small, persistent voice, "did she take a taxi when she went?"

"This is the way it used to happen," said the woman, speaking in hopelessness and bitterness in the softly lighted room. "Every week they used to come into the place where we were and they would read a list of names out. Sometimes it would be the names of children they would read out, and then a little later they would have to go away. And sometimes it would be the grown people's names, the names of the mothers or big sisters, or other women's names. The men were not with us. The fathers were somewhere else, in another place."

"Yes," Felicia said. "I know."

"We had been there only a little while, maybe ten days or maybe not so long," the woman went on, holding Felicia against her still, "when they read the name of the little girl's mother out, and that afternoon they took her away."

"What did the little girl do?" Felicia said.

"She wanted to think up the best way of getting out so that she could go find her mother," said the woman, "but she could not think of anything good enough until the third or fourth day. And then she tied her ballet slippers up in the handkerchief again, and she went up to the guard standing at the door." The woman's voice was gentle, controlled now. "She asked the guard please to open the door so that she could go out. 'This is Thursday,' she said, 'and every Tuesday and Thursday I have my ballet lessons. If I miss a ballet lesson, they do not count the money off, so my mother would be just paying for nothing, and she cannot afford to pay for nothing. I missed my ballet lesson on Tuesday,' she said to the guard, 'and I must not miss it again today.' "

Felicia lifted her head from the woman's shoulder, and she shook her hair back and looked in question and wonder at the woman's face.

"And did the man let her go?" she said.

"No, he did not. He could not do that," said the woman. "He was a soldier and he had to do what he was told. So every evening after her mother went, I used to brush the little girl's hair for her," the woman went on saying. "And while I brushed it, I used to tell her the stories of the ballets. Sometimes I would begin with *Narcissus*," the woman said, and she parted Felicia's locks with her fingers, "so if you will go and get your brush now, I will tell it while I brush your hair."

"Oh, yes," said Felicia, and she made two whirls as she went quickly to the bedroom. On the way back, she stopped and held on to the piano with the fingers of one hand while she went up on her toes. "Did you see me? Did you see me standing on my toes?" she called the woman, and the woman sat smiling in love and contentment at her.

"Yes, wonderful, really wonderful," she said. "I am sure I have never seen anyone do it so well." Felicia came spinning toward her, whirling in pirouette after pirouette, and she flung herself down in the chair close to her, with her thin bones pressed against the woman's soft, wide hip. The woman took the silver-backed, monogrammed brush and the tortoise-shell comb in her hands, and now she began to brush Felicia's hair. "We did not have any soap at all and not very much water to wash in, so I never could fix her as nicely and prettily as I wanted to," she said, and the brush stroked regularly, carefully down, caressing the shape of Felicia's head.

"If there wasn't very much water, then how did she do her teeth?" Felicia said.

"She did not do her teeth," said the woman, and she drew the comb through Felicia's hair. "There were not any toothbrushes or tooth paste, or anything like that."

Felicia waited a moment, constructing the unfamiliar scene of it in silence, and then she asked the tentative question.

"Do I have to do my teeth tonight?" she said.

"No," said the woman, and she was thinking of something else, "you do not have to do your teeth."

"If I am your little girl tonight, can I pretend there isn't enough water to wash?" said Felicia.

"Yes," said the woman, "you can pretend that if you like. You do not have to wash," she said, and the comb passed lightly through Felicia's hair.

"Will you tell me the story of the ballet?" said Felicia, and the rhythm of the brushing was like the soft, slow rocking of sleep.

"Yes," said the woman. "In the first one, the place is a forest glade with little pale birches growing in it, and they have green veils over their faces and green veils drifting from their fingers, because it is the springtime. There is the music of a flute," said the woman's voice softly, softly, "and creatures of the wood are dancing—"

"But the mother," Felicia said as suddenly as if she had been awaked from sleep. "What did the little girl's mother say when she didn't do her teeth and didn't wash at night?"

"The mother was not there, you remember," said the woman, and the brush moved steadily in her hand. "But she did send one little letter back. Sometimes the people who went away were able to do that. The mother wrote it in a train, standing up in a car that had no seats," she said, and she might have been telling the story of the ballet still, for her voice was gentle and the brush did not falter on Felicia's hair. "There were perhaps a great many other people standing up in the train with her, perhaps all trying to write their little letters on the bits of paper they had managed to hide on them, or that they had found in forgotten corners as they traveled. When they had written their letters, then they must try to slip them out through the boards of the car in which they journeyed, standing up," said the woman, "and these letters fell down on the tracks under the train, or they were blown into the fields or onto the country roads, and if it was a kind person who picked them up, he would seal them in envelopes and send them to where they were addressed to go. So a letter came back like this from the little girl's mother," the woman said, and the brush followed the comb, the comb the brush in steady pursuit through Felicia's hair. "It said good-by to the little girl, and it said please to take care of her. It said: 'Whoever reads this letter in the camp, please take good care of my little girl for me, and please have her tonsils looked at by a doctor if this is possible to do."

"And then," said Felicia softly, persistently, "what happened to the little girl?"

"I do not know. I cannot say," the woman said. But now the brush and comb had ceased to move, and in the silence Felicia turned her thin, small body on the chair, and she and the woman suddenly put their arms around each other. "They must all be asleep now, all of them," the woman said, and in the silence that fell on them again, they held each other closer. "They must be quietly asleep somewhere, and not crying all night because they are hungry and because they are cold. For three years I have been saying 'They must all be asleep, and the cold and the hunger and the seasons or night or day or nothing matters to them—' "

It was after midnight when Felicia's mother put her key in the lock of the front door, and pushed it open, and stepped into the hallway. She walked quickly to the living room, and just across the threshold she slipped the three blue foxskins from her shoulders and dropped them, with her little velvet bag, upon the chair. The room was quiet, so quiet that she could hear the sound of breathing in it, and no one spoke to her in greeting as she crossed toward the bedroom door. And then, as startling as a slap across her delicately tinted face, she saw the woman lying sleeping on the divan, and Felicia, in her school dress still, asleep within the woman's arms.

EUDORA WELTY was born in 1909 in Jackson, Mississippi. Except for time spent at the University of Wisconsin and Columbia University, she has lived most of her life in Mississippi. During the Depression she earned her living as a "Junior Publicity Agent" with the WPA, in which capacity she traveled the length and breadth of her native state, taking photographs, writing newspaper copy, interviewing "everybody from farmers to the Key Brothers who stayed up in an airplane longer than anybody else up to then." All the time, she was writing stories about the people she was meeting. But first she tried to sell her photographs of rural Mississippi Negroes, thinking that if a publisher liked her pictures, "they might be inclined to take my stories, . . . but they weren't decoyed. Once a year for three or four years I carried around the two bundles under arm on my two-weeks' trip to New York, and carried them home again—not much downcast, perhaps because all the time I simply loved writing, and was going to do it anyway." Her career as a writer was successfully launched after Diarmuid Russell, son of Irish poet George Russell—AE—became her literary agent and sold "A Worn Path" and "Why I Live at the P.O." to the *Atlantic* and her first collection of short stories was published a year later with a preface by Katherine Anne Porter.

Commenting on her life, she strikes the tone of disarming simplicity that makes her fiction so elusive. "Except for what's personal, there is really so little to tell, and that little lacking in excitement and drama in the way of the world." In the same vein she talks about how she writes: "I certainly never think of who is going to read it. I don't think of myself either—at least, I don't believe I do. I just think of what it is that I'm writing, that's enough to do." Critics have found numerous affinities between her fiction and other writers: her projection of the hidden inner life suggests Virginia Woolf, Dorothy Richardson, and James Joyce; her method of indirection Katherine Mansfield; her pictorial quality Elizabeth Bowen. And the words of Allen Tate help to explain the connection between her native place and her art: "How could the most backward state in the Union produce not only William Faulkner but Stark Young, Roark Bradford, and Eudora Welty—all very different from one another but all very Mississippi? Yeats gave the best answer to this question when he was asked how Ireland could have had a literary renascence in the first decade of this century. He said, in effect, that poverty and ignorance had made it possible. There is no real paradox in giving Yeats' answer to the same question about Mississippi after 1919. Poverty, and the ignorance that attends poverty, had isolated the common people—the Snopeses, the Varners, the Bundrens—with the result that their language retained an *illiterate* purity, uncorrupted by the 'correct' English of the half-educated schoolteachers, or by sociological jargon, or by the conditioned reflex language of advertising; while at the same time a small minority in Mississippi (and in other Southern states) maintained at a high level of sophistication a *literate* purity of diction based upon the old traditions of classical humanism." In Eudora Welty's novel *Delta Wedding* is sounded the wisdom that makes all her fiction radiant: "How deep were the complexities of the everyday, of the family, what caves were in the mountains, what blocked chambers and what crystal rivers that had not yet seen light."

Eudora Welty
(1909–   )

THE WORN PATH

It was December—a bright frozen day in the early morning. Far out in the country there was an old Negro woman with her head tied in a red rag, coming along a path through the pinewoods. Her name was Phoenix Jackson. She was very old and small and she walked slowly in the dark pine shadows, moving a little from side to side in her steps, with the balanced heaviness and lightness of a pendulum in a grandfather clock. She carried a thin, small cane made from an umbrella, and with this she kept tapping the frozen earth in front of her. This made a grave and persistent noise in the still air, that seemed meditative, like the chirping of a solitary little bird.

She wore a dark striped dress reaching down to her shoetops, and an equally long apron of bleached sugar sacks, with a full pocket; all neat and tidy, but every time she took a step she might have fallen over her shoelaces, which dragged from her unlaced shoes. She looked straight ahead. Her eyes were blue with age. Her skin had a pattern all its own of numberless branching wrinkles and as though a whole little tree stood in the middle of her forehead, but a golden colour ran underneath, and the two knobs of her cheeks were illuminated by a yellow burning under the dark. Under the red rag her hair came down on her neck in the frailest of ringlets, still black, and with an odor like copper.

Now and then there was a quivering in the thicket. Old Phoenix said, "Out of my way, all you foxes, owls, beetles, jack rabbits, coons, and wild animals! . . . Keep out from under these feet, little bobwhites. . . . Keep the big wild hogs out of my path. Don't let none of those come running my direction. I got a long way." Under her small black-freckled hand her cane, limber as a buggy whip, would switch at the brush as if to rouse up any hiding things.

On she went. The woods were deep and still. The sun made the pine needles almost too bright to look at, up where the wind rocked. The cones dropped as light as feathers. Down in the hollow was the mourning dove—it was not too late for him.

The path ran up a hill. "Seem like there is chains about my feet, time I get this far," she said, in the voice of argument old people keep to use with themselves. "Something always take a hold on this hill—pleads I should stay."

After she got to the top she turned and gave a full, severe look behind her where she had come. "Up through pines," she said at length. "Now down through oaks."

Her eyes opened their widest and she stared down gently. But before she got to the bottom of the hill a bush caught her dress.

Her fingers were busy and intent, but her skirts were full and long, so that before she could pull them free in one place they were caught in another. It was not possible to allow the dress to tear. "I in the thorny bush," she said. "Thorns, you doing your appointed work. Never want to let folks pass—no sir. Old eyes thought you was a pretty little *green* bush."

Finally, trembling all over, she stood free, and after a moment dared to stoop for her cane.

"Sun so high!" she cried, leaning back and looking, while the thick tears went over her eyes. "The time getting all gone here."

At the foot of this hill was a place where a log was laid across the creek.

"Now comes the trial," said Phoenix.

Putting her right foot out, she mounted the log and shut her eyes. Lifting her skirt, levelling her cane fiercely before her, like a festival figure in some parade, she began to march across. Then she opened her eyes and she was safe on the other side.

"I wasn't as old as I thought," she said.

But she sat down to rest. She spread her skirts on the bank around her and folded her hands over her knees. Up above her was a tree in a pearly cloud of mistletoe. She did not dare to close her eyes, and when a little boy brought her a little plate with a slice of marble-cake on it she spoke to him. "That would be acceptable," she said. But when she went to take it there was just her own hand in the air.

So she left that tree, and had to go through a barbed-wire fence. There she had to creep and crawl, spreading her knees and stretching her fingers like a baby trying to climb the steps. But she talked loudly to herself: she could not let her dress be torn now, so late in the day, and she could not pay for having her arm or leg sawed off if she got caught fast where she was.

At last she was safe through the fence and risen up out in the clearing. Big dead trees, like black men with one arm, were standing in the purple stalks of the withered cotton field. There sat a buzzard.

"Who you watching?"

In the furrow she made her way along.

"Glad this not the season for bulls," she said, looking sideways, "and the good Lord made his snakes to curl up and sleep in the winter. A pleasure I don't see no two-headed snake coming around that tree, where it come once. It took a while to get by him, back in the summer."

She passed through the old cotton and went into a field of dead corn. It whispered and shook, and was taller than her head. "Through the maze now," she said, for there was no path.

Then there was something tall, black, and skinny there, moving before her.

At first she took it for a man. It could have been a man dancing in the field. But she stood still and listened, and it did not make a sound. It was as silent as a ghost.

"Ghost," she said sharply, "who be you the ghost of? For I have heard of nary death close by."

But there was no answer, only the ragged dancing in the wind.

She shut her eyes, reached out her hand, and touched a sleeve. She found a coat and inside that an emptiness, cold as ice.

"You scarecrow," she said. Her face lighted. "I ought to be shut up for good," she said with laughter. "My senses is gone. I too old. I the oldest people I ever know. Dance, old scarecrow," she said, "while I dancing with you."

She kicked her foot over the furrow, and with mouth drawn down shook her head once or twice in a little strutting way. Some husks blew down and whirled in streamers about her skirts.

Then she went on, parting her way from side to side with the cane, through the whispering field. At last she came to the end, to a wagon track, where the silver grass blew between the red ruts. The quail were walking around like pullets, seeming all dainty and unseen.

"Walk pretty," she said. "This the easy place. This the easy going."

She followed the track, swaying through the quiet bare fields, through the little strings of trees silver in their dead leaves, past cabins silver from weather, with the doors and windows boarded shut, all like old women under a spell sitting there. "I walking in their sleep," she said, nodding her head vigorously.

In a ravine she went where a spring was silently flowing through a hollow log. Old Phoenix bent and drank. "Sweetgum makes the water sweet," she said, and drank more. "Nobody knows who made this well, for it was here when I was born."

The track crossed a swampy part where the moss hung as white as lace from every limb. "Sleep on, alligators, and blow your bubbles." Then the track went into the road.

Deep, deep the road went down between the high green-coloured banks. Overhead the live-oaks met, and it was as dark as a cave.

A black dog with a lolling tongue came up out of the weeds by the ditch. She was meditating, and not ready, and when he came at her she only hit him a little with her cane. Over she went in the ditch, like a little puff of milk-weed.

Down there, her senses drifted away. A dream visited her, and she reached her hand up, but nothing reached down and gave her a pull. So she lay there and presently went to talking. "Old woman," she said to herself, "that black dog came up out of the weeds to stall you off, and now there he sitting on his fine tail, smiling at you."

A white man finally came along and found her—a hunter, a young man, with his dog on a chain.

"Well, Granny!" he laughed. "What are you doing there?"

"Lying on my back like a June-bug waiting to be turned over, mister," she said, reaching up her hand.

He lifted her up, gave her a swing in the air, and set her down, "Anything broken, Granny?"

"No, sir, them old dead weeds is springy enough," said Phoenix, when she had got her breath. "I thank you for your trouble."

"Where do you live, Granny?" he asked, while the two dogs were growling at each other.

"Away back yonder, sir, behind the ridge. You can't even see it from here."

"On your way home?"

"No, sir, I going to town."

"Why, that's too far! That's as far as I walk when I come out myself, and I get something for my trouble." He patted the stuffed bag he carried, and there hung down a little closed claw. It was one of the bobwhites, with its beak hooked bitterly to show it was dead. "Now you go on home, Granny!"

"I bound to go to town, mister," said Phoenix. "The time come around."

He gave another laugh, filling the whole landscape. "I know you colored people! Wouldn't miss going to town to see Santa Claus!"

But something held Old Phoenix very still. The deep lines in her face went into a fierce and different radiation. Without warning she had seen with her own eyes a flashing nickel fall out of the man's pocket on to the ground.

"How old are you, Granny?" he was saying.

"There's is no telling, mister," she said, "no telling."

Then she gave a little cry and clapped her hands, and said, "Git on away from here, dog! Look! Look at that dog!" She laughed as if in admiration. "He ain't scared of nobody. He a big black dog." She whispered, "Sick him!"

"Watch me get rid of that cur," said the man. "Sick him, Pete! Sick him!"

Phoenix heard the dogs fighting and heard the man running and throwing sticks. She even heard a gunshot. But she was slowly bending forward by that time, further and further forward, the lids stretched down over her eyes, as if she were doing this in her sleep. Her chin was lowered almost to her knees. The yellow palm of her hand came out from the fold of her apron. Her fingers slid down and along the ground under the piece of money with the grace and care they would have in lifting an egg from under a sitting hen. Then she slowly straightened up, she stood erect, and the nickel was in her apron pocket. A bird flew by. Her lips moved. "God watching me the whole time. I come to stealing."

The man came back, and his own dog panted about then. "Well, I scared him off that time," he said, and then he laughed and lifted his gun and pointed it at Phoenix.

She stood straight and faced him.

"Doesn't the gun scare you?" he said, still pointing it.

"No, sir, I seen plenty go off closer by, in my day, and

for less than what I done," she said, holding utterly still.

He smiled, and shouldered the gun. "Well, Granny," he said, "you must be a hundred years old, and scared of nothing. I'd give you a dime if I had any money with me. But you take my advice and stay home, and nothing will happen to you."

"I bound to go on my way, mister," said Phoenix. She inclined her head in the red rag. Then they went in different directions, but she could hear the gun shooting again and again over the hill.

She walked on. The shadows hung from the oak trees to the road like curtains. Then she smelled wood-smoke, and smelled the river, and she saw a steeple and the cabins on their steep steps. Dozens of little black children whirled around her. There ahead was Natchez shining. Bells were ringing. She walked on.

In the paved city it was Christmas time. There were red and green electric lights strung and crisscrossed everywhere, and all turned on in the daytime. Old Phoenix would have been lost if she had not distrusted her eyesight and depended on her feet to know where to take her.

She paused quietly on the sidewalk, where people were passing by. A lady came along in the crowd, carrying an armful of red-, green-, and silver-wrapped presents; she gave off perfume like the red roses in hot summer, and Phoenix stopped her.

"Please, missy, will you lace up my shoe?" She held up her foot.

"What do you want, Grandma?"

"See my shoe," said Phoenix. "Do all right for out in the country, but wouldn't look right to go in a big building."

"Stand still then, Grandma," said the lady. She put her packages down carefully on the sidewalk beside her and laced and tied both shoes tightly.

"Can't lace 'em with a cane," said Phoenix. "Thank you, missy. I doesn't mind asking a nice lady to tie up my shoe when I gets out on the street."

Moving slowly and from side to side, she went into the stone building and into a tower of steps, where she walked up and around and around until her feet knew to stop.

She entered a door, and there she saw nailed up on the wall the document that had been stamped with the gold seal and framed in the gold frame which matched the dream that was hung up in her head.

"Here I be," she said. There was a fixed and ceremonial stiffness over her body.

"A charity case, I suppose," said an attendant who sat at the desk before her.

But Phoenix only looked above her head. There was sweat on her face; the wrinkles shone like a bright net.

"Speak up, Grandma," the woman said. "What's your name? We must have your history, you know. Have you been here before? What seems to be the trouble with you?"

Old Phoenix only gave a twitch to her face as if a fly were bothering her.

"Are you deaf?" cried the attendant.

But then the nurse came in.

"Oh, that's just old Aunt Phoenix," she said. "She doesn't come for herself—she has a little grandson. She makes these trips just as regular as clockwork. She lives away back off the Old Natchez Trace." She bent down. "Well, Aunt Phoenix, why don't you just take a seat? We won't keep you standing after your long trip." She pointed.

The old woman sat down, bolt upright in the chair.

"Now, how is the boy?" asked the nurse.

Old Phoenix did not speak.

"I said, how is the boy?"

But Phoenix only waited and stared straight ahead, her face very solemn and withdrawn into rigidity.

"Is his throat any better?" asked the nurse. "Aunt Phoenix, don't you hear me? Is your grandson's throat any better since the last time you came for medicine?"

With her hand on her knees, the old woman waited, silent, erect and motionless, just as if she were in armour.

"You mustn't take up our time this way, Aunt Phoenix," the nurse said. "Tell us quickly about your grandson, and get it over. He isn't dead, is he?"

At last there came a flicker and then a flame of comprehension across her face, and she spoke.

"My grandson. It was my memory had left me. There I sat and forgot why I made my long trip."

"Forgot?" the nurse frowned. "After you came so far?"

Then Phoenix was like an old woman begging a dignified forgiveness for waking up frightened in the night. "I never did go to school—I was too old at the Surrender," she said in a soft voice. "I'm an old woman without an education. It was my memory fail me. My little grandson, he is just the same, and I forgot it in the coming."

"Throat never heals, does it?" said the nurse, speaking in a loud, sure voice to Old Phoenix. By now she had a card with something written on it, a little list. "Yes. Swallowed lye. When was it—January—two–three years ago—"

Phoenix spoke unasked now. "No, missy, he not dead, he just the same. Every little while his throat begin to close up again, and he not able to swallow. He not get his breath. He not able to help himself. So the time come around, and I go on another trip for the soothing medicine."

"All right. The doctor said as long as you came to get it you could have it," said the nurse. "But it's an obstinate case."

"My little grandson, he sit up there in the house all wrapped up, waiting by himself," Phoenix went on. "We is the only two left in the world. He suffer and it don't seem to put him back at all. He got a sweet look. He going to last. He wear a little patch quilt and peep out, holding his mouth open like a little bird. I remembers so plain now. I not going to forget him again, no, the whole enduring time. I could tell him from all the others in creation."

"All right." The nurse was trying to hush her now. She brought her a bottle of medicine. "Charity," she said, making a check mark in a book.

Old Phoenix held the bottle close to her eyes and then carefully put it into her pocket.

"I thank you," she said.

"It's Christmas time, Grandma," said the attendant. "Could I give you a few pennies out of my purse?"

"Five pennies is a nickel," said Phoenix stiffly.

"Here's a nickel," said the attendant.

Phoenix rose carefully and held out her hand. She received the nickel and then fished the other nickel out of her pocket and laid it beside the new one. She stared at her palm closely, with her head on one side.

Then she gave a tap with her cane on the floor.

"This is what come to me to do," she said. "I going to the store and buy my child a little windmill they sells, made out of paper. He going to find it hard to believe there such a thing in the world. I'll march myself back where he waiting, holding it straight in this hand."

She lifted her free hand, gave a little nod, turning round, and walked out of the doctor's office. Then her slow step began on the stairs, going down.

HORTENSE CALISHER was born in New York City in 1911. She writes: "My mother came . . . from Oberelsbach to family already residents of Yorkville, the German community in New York. My father, old enough to be hers, was born in Richmond, Virginia, during the Civil War. They were middle-class German Jews. . . . There were thus many influences in the household. The combination was odd all round, volcanic to meditative to fruitfully dull, bound to produce someone interested in character, society and time." After graduating from Barnard College she worked in a department store, as a social worker, married and had two children, published a few stories, taught, did editorial work on a girls' magazine. "This was all experience, of course," writes Emily Hahn, "but it hardly contributed to the tranquility one should have for sustained writing. When awarded a Guggenheim Fellowship on the strength of her published stories she was asked what she intended to do as a project, she replied that she wanted to go to England, sit there for a year, and just think." With the help of numerous fellowships and grants she has had published seven novels, several collections of short stories, and an autobiography in a little more than a decade. She has also taught literature on the faculties of several universities. In an essay in *The American Scholar*, entitled "The Writer: Being and Doing," she gives a witty defense of writers who teach: "Much needless worry has been expended over the possible destruction of writers by teaching. If a man is sucked into scholasticism, or silenced, it seems more likely that his stamina for that aloneness which should be part of his gifts has never been strong. Teaching is hard. But every man spends part of his life-energy away from his most personal work. Fashionably considered, the university is not a part of going 'life' at all, as against the pursuit of homosexuality in Algiers, or strong drink in Connecticut. But I find it impossible to exclude from at least tentative reality any place where so many people are. . . ."

Hortense Calisher
(1911–   )

THE SCREAM ON FIFTY-SEVENTH STREET

When the scream came, from downstairs in the street five flights below her bedroom window, Mrs. Hazlitt, who in her month's tenancy of the flat had become the lightest of sleepers, stumbled up, groped her way past the empty second twin bed that stood nearer the window, and looked out. There was nothing to be seen of course—the apartment house she was in, though smartly kept up to the standards of the neighborhood, dated from the era of front fire escapes, and the sound, if it had come at all, had come from directly beneath them. From other half-insomniac nights she knew that the hour must be somewhere between three and four in the morning. The "all-night" doorman who guarded the huge façade of the apartment house opposite had retired, per custom, to some region behind its canopy; the one down the block at the corner of First, who blew his taxi-whistle so incessantly that she had for some nights mistaken it for a traffic policeman's, had been quiet for a long time. Even the white-shaded lamp that burned all day and most of the night on the top floor of the little gray town house sandwiched between the tall buildings across the way—an invalid's light perhaps—had been quenched. At this hour the wide expanse of the avenue, Fifty-Seventh Street at its easternmost end, looked calm, reassuring and amazingly silent for one of the main arteries of the city. The cross-town bus service had long since ceased; the truck traffic over on First made only an occasional dim rumble. If she went into the next room, where there was a French window opening like a double door, and leaned out, absurd idea, in her nightgown, she would see, far down to the right, the lamps of a portion of the Queensboro Bridge, quietly necklaced on the night. In the blur beneath them, out of range but comfortable to imagine, the beautiful cul-de-sac of Sutton Square must be musing, Edwardian in the starlight, its one antique bow-front jutting over the river shimmering below. And in the façades opposite her, lights were still spotted here and there, as was always the case, even in the small hours, in New York. Other consciousnesses were awake, a vigil of anonymous neighbors whom she would never know, that still gave one the hive-sense of never being utterly alone.

All was silent. No, she must have dreamed it, reinterpreted in her doze some routine sound, perhaps the siren of the police car that often keened through this street but never stopped, no doubt on its way to the more tumultuous West Side. Until the death of her husband, companion of twenty years, eight months ago, her ability to sleep had always been healthy and immediate; since then it had gradually, not unnaturally deteriorated, but this was the worst; she had never done this before. For she could still hear very clearly the character of the sound, or rather its lack of one—a long, oddly sustained note, then a shorter one, both perfectly even, not discernible as a man's or a woman's, and without—yes, without the color of any emotion—surely the sound that one heard in dreams. Never a woman of small midnight fears in either city or country, as a girl she had done settlement work on some of this city's blackest streets, as a mining engineer's wife had nestled peacefully within the shrieking velvet of an Andes night. Not to give herself special marks for this, it was still all the more reason why what she had heard, or thought she had heard, must have been hallucinatory. A harsh word, but she must be stern with herself at the very beginnings of any such, of what could presage the sort of disintegrating widowhood, full of the mouse-fears and softening self-indulgences of the manless, that she could not, would not abide. Scarcely a second or two could have elapsed between that long—yes, that was it, soulless—cry, and her arrival at the window. And look, down there on the street and upward, everything remained motionless. Not a soul, in answer, had erupted from a doorway. All the fanlights of the lobbies shone serenely. Up above, no one leaned, not a window had flapped wide. After twenty years of living outside of the city, she could still flatter herself that she knew New York down to the ground—she had been born here, and raised. Secretly mourning it, missing it through all the happiest suburban years, she had kept up with it like a scholar, building a red-book of it for herself even through all its savage, incontinent rebuilding. She still knew all its neighborhoods. She knew. And this was one in which such a sound would be policed at once, such a cry serviced at once, if only by doormen running. No, the fault, the disturbance, must be hers.

Reaching into the pretty, built-in wardrobe on her right—the flat, with so many features that made it more like a house, fireplace, high ceilings, had attracted her from the first for this reason—she took out a warm dressing gown and sat down on the bed to put on her slippers. The window was wide open and she meant to leave it that way; country living had made unbearable the steam heat of her youth. There was no point to winter otherwise, and she—she and Sam—had always been ones to enjoy the weather as it came. Perhaps she had been unwise to give up the dog, excuse for walks early and late, outlet for talking aloud—the city was full of them. Unwise too, in the self-denuding impulse of loss, to have made herself that solitary in readiness for a city where she would have to remake friends, and no longer had kin. And charming as this flat was, wooed as she increasingly was by the delicately winning personality of its unknown, absent owner, Mrs. Berry, by her bric-a-brac, her cookbooks, even by her widowhood, almost as recent as Mrs. Hazlitt's own—perhaps it would be best to do something about getting the empty second twin bed removed from this room. No doubt Mrs. Berry, fled to London, possibly even residing in the rooms of yet a third woman in search of recommended change, would understand. Mrs. Hazlitt stretched her arms, able to smile at this imagined procession of women inhabiting each other's rooms, fallen one against the other like a pack of playing cards. How could she have forgotten what anyone who had reached middle age through the normal amount of trouble should know, that the very horizontal position itself of sleep, when one could not, laid one open to every attack from within, on a couch with no psychiatrist to listen but oneself. The best way to meet the horrors was on two feet, vertical. What she meant to do now was to fix herself a sensible hot drink, not coffee, reminiscent of shared midnight snacks, not even tea, but a nursery drink, cocoa. In a lifetime, she thought, there are probably two eras of the sleep that is utterly sound: the nursery sleep (if one had the lucky kind of childhood I did) and the sleep next or near the heart and body of the one permanently loved and loving, if one has been lucky enough for that too. I must learn from within, as well as without, that both are over. She stood up, tying her sash more firmly. And at that moment the scream came again.

She listened, rigid. It came exactly as remembered, one shrilled long note, then the shorter second, like a cut-off Amen to the first and of the same timbre, dreadful in its cool, a madness expanded almost with calm, near the edge of joy. No wonder she had thought of the siren; this had the same note of terror controlled. One could not tell whether it sped toward a victim or from one. As before, it seemed to come from directly below.

Shaking, she leaned out, could see nothing because of the high sill, ran into the next room, opened the French window and all but stood on the fire escape. As she did so, the sound, certainly human, had just ceased; at the same moment a cab, going slowly down the middle of the avenue, its toplight up, veered directly toward her, as if the driver too had heard, poised there beneath her with its nose pointed toward the curb, then veered sharply back to the center of the street, gathered speed, and drove on. Immediately behind it another cab, toplight off, slowed up, performed exactly the same orbit, then it too, with a hasty squeal of brakes, made for the center street and sped away. In the confusion of noises she thought she heard the grind of a window-sash coming down, then a slam—perhaps the downstairs door of the adjoining set of flats, or of this one. Dropping to her knees, she leaned both palms on the floor-level lintel of the window and peered down through the iron slats of her fire escape and the successive ones below. Crouched that way, she could see straight back to the building line. To the left, a streetlamp cast a pale, even glow on empty sidewalk and the free space of curb either side of a hydrant; to the right, the shadows were obscure, but motionless. She saw nothing to conjure into a half-expected human bundle lying still, heard no footfall staggering or slipping away. Not more than a minute or two could have elapsed since she had heard the cry. Tilting her head up at the façades opposite, she saw that their simple pattern of lit windows seemed the same. While she stared, one of the squares blotted out, then another, both on floors not too high to have heard. Would no one, having heard, attend? Would she?

Standing up, her hand on the hasp of the French window, she felt herself still shaking, not with fear, but with the effort to keep herself from in some way heeding that cry. Again she told herself that she had been born here, knew the city's ways, had not the *auslander's* incredulity about some of them. These ways had hardened since her day, people had warned her, to an indifference beyond that of any civilized city; there were no "good" neighborhoods now, none of any kind really, except the half-hostile enclosure that each family must build for itself. She had discounted this, knowing unsentimentally what city life was; even in the tender version of it that was her childhood there had been noises, human ones, that the most responsible people, the kindest, had shrugged away, saying, "Nothing, dear. Something outside." What she had not taken into account was her own twenty years of living elsewhere, where such a cry in the night would be succored at once if only for gossip's sake, if only because one gave up privacy—anonymity—forever, when one went to live in a house on a road. If only, she thought, holding herself rigid to stop her trembling, because it would be the cry of someone one knew. Nevertheless, it took all her strength not to rush downstairs, to hang on to the handle, while in her mind's eye she ran out of her apartment door, remembering to take the key, pressed the elevator button and waited, went down at the car's deliberate pace. After that there would be the inner, buzzer door to open, then at last the door to the outside. No, it would take too long, and it was already too late for the phone, by the time police could come or she could find the number of the superintendent in his back basement—and when either answered, what would she say? She looked at the fire escape. Not counting hers, there must be three others between herself and the street. Whether there was a ladder extending from the lowest one she could not remember; possibly one hung by one's hands and dropped to the ground. Years ago there had been more of them, even the better houses had had them in their rear areaways, but she had never in her life seen one used. And this one fronted direct on the avenue. It was this that brought her to her senses—the vision of herself in her blue robe creeping down the front of a building on Fifty-Seventh Street, hanging by her hands until she dropped to the ground. She shut the long window quickly, leaning her weight against it to help the slightly swollen frame into place, and turned the handle counterclockwise, shooting the long vertical bolt. The bolt fell into place with a thump she had never noticed before but already seemed familiar. Probably, she thought, sighing, it was the kind of sound—old hardware on old wood—that more often went with a house.

In the kitchen, over her cocoa, she shook herself with a reminiscent tremble, in the way one did after a narrow escape. It was a gesture made more often to a companion, an auditor. Easy enough to make the larger gestures involved in cutting down one's life to the pattern of the single; the selling of a house, the arranging of income or new occupation. Even the abnegation of sex had a drama that lent one strength, made one hold up one's head as one saw oneself traveling a clear, melancholy line. It was the small gestures for which there was no possible sublimation, the sudden phrase, posture—to no auditor, the constant clueing of identity in another's—its cessation. "Dear me," she would have said—they would have come to town for the winter months as they had often planned, and he would have just returned from an overnight business trip—"what do you suppose I'd have done, Sam, if I'd gone all the way, in my housecoat, really found myself outside? Funny how the distinction between outdoors and in breaks down in the country. I'd forgotten how absolute it is here—with so many barriers between." Of course, she thought, that's the simple reason why here, in the city, the sense of responsibility has to weaken. Who could maintain it, through a door, an elevator, a door and a door, toward everyone, anyone, who screamed? Perhaps that was the real reason she had come here, she thought, washing the cup under the faucet. Where the walls are soundproofed there are no more "people next door" with their ready "casserole" pity, at worst with the harbored glow of their own family life peering from their averted eyelids like the lamplight from under their eaves. Perhaps she had known all along that the best way to learn how to live alone was to come to the place where people really were.

She set the cup out for the morning and added a plate and a spoon. It was wiser not to let herself deteriorate to the utterly casual; besides, the sight of them always gave her a certain pleasure, like a greeting, if only from herself of the night before. Tomorrow she had a meeting, of one of the two hospital boards on which, luckily for now, she had served for years. There was plenty more of that kind of useful occupation available and no one would care a hoot whether what once she had done for conscience' sake she now did for her own. The meeting was not scheduled until two. Before that she would manage to inquire very discreetly, careful not to appear either eccentric or too friendly, both of which made city people uneasy, as to whether anyone else in the building had heard what she had. This too she would do for discipline's sake. There was no longer any doubt that the sound had been real.

The next morning at eight-thirty, dressed to go out except for her coat, she waited just inside her door for one or the other of the tenants on her floor to emerge. Her heart pounded at the very queerness of what she was doing, but she overruled it; if she did feel somewhat too interested, too much as if she were embarking on a chase, then let her get it out of her system at once, and have done. How to do so was precisely what she had considered while dressing. The problem was not to make too many inquiries, too earnest ones, and not to seem to be making any personal overture, from which people would naturally withdraw. One did not make inconvenient, hothouse friendships in the place one lived in, here. Therefore she had decided to limit her approaches to three—the first to the girl who lived in the adjacent apartment, who could usually be encountered at this hour and was the only tenant she knew for sure lived in the front of the building—back tenants were less likely to have heard. For the rest, she must trust to luck. And whatever the outcome, she would not let herself pursue the matter beyond today.

She opened the door a crack and listened. Still too early. Actually the place, being small—six floors of four or five flats each—had a more intimate feeling than most. According to the super's wife, Mrs. Stump, with whom she had had a chat or two in the hall, many of the tenants, clinging to ceiling rents in what had become a fancier district, had been here for years, a few for the thirty since the place had been built. This would account for so many middle-aged and elderly, seemingly either single or the remnants of families—besides various quiet, well-mannered women who, like herself, did not work, she had noticed at times two men who were obviously father and son, two others who, from their ages and nameplate, noticed at mailtime, might be brothers, and a mother with the only child in the place—a subdued little girl of about eight. As soon as a tenant of long standing vacated or died, Mrs. Stump had added, the larger units were converted to smaller, and this would account for the substratum of slightly showier or younger occupants: two modish blondes, a couple of homburged "decorator" types—all more in keeping with the newly sub-theatrical, antique-shop character of the neighborhood—as well as for the "career girl" on her floor. Mrs. Berry, who from evidences in the flat should be something past forty like herself, belonged to the first group, having been here, with her husband of course until recently, since just after the war. A pity that she, Mrs. Berry, who from her books, her one charming letter, her own situation, might have been just the person to understand, even share Mrs. Hazlitt's reaction to the event of last night, was not here. But this was nonsense; if she were, then she, Mrs. Hazlitt, would not be. She thought again of the chain of women, sighed, and immediately chid herself for this new habit of sighing, as well as for this alarming mound of gratuitous information she seemed to have acquired, in less than a month, about people with whom she was in no way concerned. At that moment she heard the door next hers creak open. Quickly she put on her coat, opened her door and bent to pick up the morning paper. The girl coming out stepped back, dropping one of a pile of boxes she was carrying. Mrs. Hazlitt returned it to her, pressed the button for the elevator, and when it came, held the door. It was the girl she had seen twice before; for the first time they had a nice exchange of smiles.

"Whoops, I'm late," said the girl, craning to look at her watch.

"Me too," said Mrs. Hazlitt, as the cage slid slowly down. She drew breath. "Overslept, once I did get to sleep. Rather a noisy night outside—did you hear all that fuss, must have been around three or four?" She waited hopefully for the answer: Why yes indeed, what on earth was it, did you?

"Uh-uh," said the girl, shaking her head serenely. " 'Fraid the three of us sleep like a log, that's the trouble. My roommates are still at it, lucky stiffs." She checked her watch again, was first out of the elevator, nodded her thanks when Mrs. Hazlitt hurried to hold the buzzer door for her because of the boxes, managed the outer door herself, and departed.

Mrs. Hazlitt walked briskly around the corner to the bakery, came back with her bag of two brioches, and reentered. Imagine, there are three of them, she thought, and I never knew. Well, I envy them their log. The inner door, usually locked, was propped open. Mrs. Stump was on her knees just behind it, washing the marble floor, as she did every day. It was certainly a tidy house, not luxurious but up to a firmly well-bred standard, just the sort a woman like Mrs. Berry would have, that she herself, when the sublease was over, would like to find. Nodding to Mrs. Stump, she went past her to the row of brass mail slots, pretending to search her own although she knew it was too early, weighing whether she ought to risk wasting one of her three chances on her.

"Mail don't come till ten," said Mrs. Stump from behind her.

"Yes, I know," said Mrs. Hazlitt, recalling suddenly that they had had this exchange before. "But I forgot to check yesterday."

"Yesterday vass holiday."

"Oh, so it was." Guiltily Mrs. Hazlitt entered the elevator and faced the door, relieved when it closed. The truth was that she had known yesterday was a holiday and had checked the mail anyway. The truth was that she often did this even on Sundays here, often even more than once. It made an errand in the long expanse of a day when she either flinched from the daily walk that was too dreary to do alone on Sunday, or had not provided herself with a ticket to something. One had to tidy one's hair, spruce a bit for the possible regard of someone in the hall, and when she did see someone, although of course they never spoke, she always returned feeling refreshed, reaffirmed.

Upstairs again, she felt that way now; her day had begun in the eyes of others, as a day should. She made a few phone calls to laundry and bank, and felt even better. Curious how, when one lived alone, one began to feel that only one's own consciousness held up the world, and at the very same time that only an incursion into the world, or a recognition from it, made one continue to exist at all. There was another phone call she might make, to a friend up in the country, who had broken an ankle, but she would save that for a time when she needed it more. This was yet another discipline—not to become a phone bore. The era when she herself had been a victim of such, had often thought of the phone as a nuisance, now seemed as distant as China. She looked at the clock—time enough to make another pot of coffee. With it she ate a brioche slowly, then with the pleasant sense of hurry she now had so seldom, another.

At ten sharp she went downstairs again, resolving to take her chance with whoever might be there. As she emerged from the elevator she saw that she was in luck; the owner of a big brown poodle—a tall, well set up man of sixty or so—was bent over his mail slot while the dog stood by. It was the simplest of matters to make an overture to the poodle, who was already politely nosing the palm she offered him, to expose her own love of the breed, remarking on this one's exceptional manners, to skip lightly on from the question of barking to noise in general, to a particular noise.

"Ah well, Coco's had stage training," said his owner, in answer to her compliments. She guessed that his owner might have had the same; he had that fine, bravura face which aging actors of another generation often had, a trifle shallow for its years perhaps but very fine, and he inclined toward her with the same majestic politeness as his dog, looking into her face very intently as she spoke, answering her in the slender, semi-British accent she recalled from matinee idols of her youth. She had to repeat her question on the noise. This time she firmly gave the sound its name—a scream, really rather an unusual scream.

"A scream?" The man straightened. She thought that for a moment he looked dismayed. Then he pursed his lips very judiciously, in almost an acting-out of that kind of repose. "Come to think of it, ye-es, I may have heard something." He squared his shoulders. "But no doubt I just turned over. And Coco's a city dog, very blasé fellow. Rather imagine he did too." He tipped his excellent homburg. "Good morning," he added, with sudden reserve, and turned away, giving a flick to the dog's leash that started the animal off with his master behind him.

"Good morning," she called after them, "and thanks for the tip on where to get one like Coco." Coco looked back at her; but his master, back turned, disentangling the leash from the doorknob, did not, and went out without answering.

So I've done it after all, she thought. Too friendly. Especially too friendly since I'm a woman. Her face grew hot at this probable estimate of her—gushy woman chattering over-brightly, lingering in the hall. Bore of a woman who heard things at night, no doubt looked under the bed before she got into it. No, she thought, there was something—when I mentioned the scream. At the aural memory of that latter, still clear, she felt her resolve stiffen. Also—what a dunce she was being—there were the taxis. Taxis, one of them occupied, did not veer, one after the other, on an empty street, without reason. Emboldened, she bent to look at the man's mailbox. The name, Reginald Warwick, certainly fitted her imaginary dossier, but that was not what gave her pause. Apartment 3A. Hers was 5A. He lived in the front, two floors beneath her, where he must have heard.

As she inserted the key in her apartment door, she heard the telephone ringing, fumbled the key and dropped it, then had to open the double lock up above. All part of the city picture, she thought resentfully, remembering their four doors, never locked, in the country—utterly foolhardy, never to be dreamed of here. Even if she had, there were Mrs. Berry's possessions to be considered, nothing extraordinary, but rather like the modest, crotchety bits of treasure she had inherited or acquired herself—in the matter of bric-a-brac alone there was really quite a kinship between them. The phone was still ringing as she entered. She raced toward it eagerly. It was the secretary of the hospital board, telling her that this afternoon's meeting was put off.

"Oh . . . oh dear," said Mrs. Hazlitt. "I mean—I'm so sorry to hear about Mrs. Levin. Hope it's nothing serious."

"I really couldn't say," said the secretary. "But we've enough for a quorum the week after." She rang off.

Mrs. Hazlitt put down the phone, alarmed at the sudden sinking of her heart over such a minor reversal. She had looked forward to seeing people of course, but particularly to spending an afternoon in the brightly capable impersonality of the boardroom, among men and women who brought with them a sense of indefinable swathes of well-being extending behind them, of such a superfluity of it, from lives as full as their checkbooks, that they were met in that efficient room to dispense what overflowed. The meeting would have been an antidote to that dark, anarchic version of the city which had been obsessing her; it would have been a reminder that everywhere, on flight after flight of the city's high, brilliant floors, similar groups of the responsible were convening, could always be applied to, were in command. The phone gave a reminiscent tinkle as she pushed it aside, and she waited, but there was no further ring. She looked at her calendar, scribbled with domestic markings—the hairdresser on Tuesday, a fitting for her spring suit, the date when she must appear at the lawyer's for the closing on the sale of the house. Beyond that she had a dinner party with old acquaintances on the following Thursday, tickets with a woman friend for the Philharmonic on Saturday week. Certainly she was not destitute of either company or activity. But the facts were that within the next two weeks, she could look forward to only two occasions when she would be communicating on any terms of intimacy with people who, within limits, knew "who" she was. A default on either would be felt keenly—much more than the collapse of this afternoon's little—prop. Absently she twiddled the dial back and forth. Proportion was what went first "in solitary"; circling one's own small platform in space, the need for speech mute in one's own throat, one developed an abnormal concern over the night-cries of others. No, she thought, remembering the board meeting, those high convocations of the responsible, I've promised—Lord knows who, myself, somebody. She stood up and gave herself a smart slap on the buttock. "Come on, Millie," she said, using the nickname her husband always had. "Get on with it." She started to leave the room, then remained in its center, hand at her mouth, wondering. Talking aloud to oneself was more common than admitted; almost everyone did. It was merely that she could not decide whether or not she had.

Around eleven o'clock, making up a bundle of lingerie, she went down to the basement where there was a community washing machine, set the machine's cycle, and went back upstairs. Forty minutes later she went through the same routine, shifting the wet clothes to the dryer. At one o'clock she returned for the finished clothes and carried them up. This made six trips in all, but at no time had she met anyone en route; it was Saturday afternoon, perhaps a bad time. At two she went out to do her weekend shopping. The streets were buzzing, the women in the supermarket evidently laying in enough stores for a visitation of giants. Outside the market, a few kids from Third Avenue always waited in the hope of tips for carrying, and on impulse, although her load was small, she engaged a boy of about ten. On the way home, promising him extra for waiting, she stopped at the patisserie where she always lingered for the sheer gilt-and-chocolate gaiety of the place, bought her brioches for the morning, and, again on impulse, an éclair for the boy. Going up in the elevator they encountered the mother and small girl, but she had never found any pretext for addressing that glum pair, the mother engaged as usual in a low, toneless tongue-lashing of the child. Divorcée, Mrs. Hazlitt fancied, and no man in the offing, an inconvenient child. In the kitchen, she tipped the boy and offered him the pastry. After an astonished glance, he wolfed it with a practical air, peering at her furtively between bites, and darted off at once, looking askance over his shoulder at her "See you next Saturday, maybe." Obviously he had been brought up to believe that only witches dispensed free gingerbread. In front of the bathroom mirror, Mrs. Hazlitt, tidying up before her walk, almost ritual now, to Sutton Square, regarded her image, not yet a witch's but certainly a fool's, a country-cookie-jar fool's. "Oh well, you're company," she said, quite consciously aloud this time, and for some reason this cheered her. Before leaving, she went over face and costume with the laborious attention she always gave them nowadays before going anywhere outside.

Again, when she rode down, she met no one, but she walked with bracing step, making herself take a circuitous route for health's sake, all the way to Bloomingdale's, then on to Park and around again, along the Fifty-Eighth Street bridge pass, the dejectedly frivolous shops that lurked near it, before she let herself approach the house with the niche with the little statue of Dante in it, then the Square. Sitting in the Square, the air rapidly blueing now, lapping her like reverie, she wondered whether any of the residents of the windows surrounding her had noticed her almost daily presence, half hoped they had. Before it became too much of a habit, of course, she would stop coming. Meanwhile, if she took off her distance glasses, the scene before her, seen through the tender, Whistlerian blur of myopia—misted gray bridge, blue and green lights of a barge going at its tranced pace downriver—was the very likeness of a corner of the Chelsea embankment, glimpsed throughout a winter of happy teatime windows seven years ago, from a certain angle below Battersea Bridge. Surely it was blameless to remember past happiness if one did so without self-pity, better still, of course, to be able to speak of it to someone in an even, healing voice. Idly she wondered where Mrs. Berry was living in London. The flat in Cheyne Walk would have just suited her. "Just the thing for you," she would have said to her had she known her. "The Sebrings still let it every season. We always meant to go back." Her watch said five and the air was chilling. She walked rapidly home through the evening scurry, the hour of appointments, catching its excitement as she too hurried, half-persuaded of her own appointment, mythical but still possible, with someone as yet unknown. Outside her own building she paused. All day long she had been entering it from the westerly side. Now, approaching from the east, she saw that the fire escape on this side of the entrance did end in a ladder, about four feet above her. Anyone moderately tall, like herself, would have had an easy drop of it, as she would have done last night. Shaking her head at that crazy image, she looked up at the brilliant hives all around her. Lights were cramming in, crowding on, but she knew too much now about their nighttime progression, their gradual decline to a single indifferent string on that rising, insomniac silence in which she might lie until morning, dreading to hear again what no one else would appear to have heard. Scaring myself to death, she thought (or muttered?), and in the same instant resolved to drop all limits, go down to the basement and interrogate the Stumps, sit on the bench in the lobby and accost anyone who came in, ring doorbells if necessary, until she had confirmation—and not go upstairs until she had. "Excuse me," said someone. She turned. A small, frail, elderly woman, smiling timidly, waited to get past her through the outer door.

"Oh—sorry," said Mrs. Hazlitt. "Why—good evening!" she added with a rush, an enormous rush of relief. "Here—let me," she said more quietly, opening the door with a numb sense of gratitude for having been tugged back from the brink of what she saw now, at the touch of a voice, had been panic. For here was a tenant, unaccountably forgotten, with whom she was almost on speaking terms, a gentle old sort, badly crippled with arthritis, for whom Mrs. Hazlitt had once or twice unlocked the inner door. She did so now.

"Thank you, my dear—my hands are that knobbly." There was the trace of brogue that Mrs. Hazlitt had noticed before. The old woman, her gray hair sparse from the disease but freshly done in the artfully messy arrangements used to conceal the skulls of old ladies, her broadtail coat not new but excellently maintained, gave off the comfortable essence, pleasing as rosewater, of one who had been serenely protected all her life. Unmarried, for she had that strangely deducible aura about her even before one noted the lack of ring, she had also a certain simpleness, now almost bygone, of those household women who had never gone to business—Mrs. Hazlitt had put her down as perhaps the relict sister of a contractor, or of a school superintendent of the days when the system had been Irish from top to bottom, at the top, of Irish of just this class. The old lady fumbled now with the minute key to her mailbox.

"May I?"

"Ah, if you would now. Couldn't manage it when I came down. The fingers don't seem to warm up until evening. It's 2B."

Mrs. Hazlitt, inserting the key, barely noticed the name—Finan. 2B would be a front apartment also, in the line adjacent to the A's.

"And you would be the lady in Mrs. Berry's. Such a nicely spoken woman, she was."

"Oh yes, isn't she," said Mrs. Hazlitt. "I mean . . . I just came through the agent. But when you live in a person's house—do you know her?"

"Just to speak. Half as long as me, they'd lived here. Fifteen years." The old lady took the one letter Mrs. Hazlitt passed her, the yellow-fronted rent bill whose duplicate she herself had received this morning. "Ah well, we're always sure of this one, aren't we?" Nodding her thanks, she shuffled toward the elevator on built-up shoes shaped like hods. "Still, it's a nice, quiet building, and lucky we are to be in it these days."

There was such a rickety bravery about her, of neat habit long overborne by the imprecisions of age, of dowager hat set slightly askew by fingers unable to deal with a key yet living alone, that Mrs. Hazlitt, reluctant to shake the poor, tottery dear further, had to remind herself of the moment before their encounter.

"Last night?" The old blue eyes looked blank, then brightened. "Ah no, I must have taken one of my Seconals. Otherwise I'd have heard it surely. 'Auntie,' my niece always says—'what if there should be a fire, and you there sleeping away?' Do what she says, I do sometimes, only to hear every pin drop till morning." She shook her head, entering the elevator. "Going up?"

"N-no," said Mrs. Hazlitt. "I—have to wait here for a minute." She sat down on the bench, the token bench that she had never seen anybody sitting on, and watched the car door close on the little figure still shaking its head, borne upward like a fairy godmother, willing but unable to oblige. The car's hum stopped, then its light glowed on again. Someone else was coming down. No, this is the nadir, Mrs. Hazlitt thought. Whether I heard it or not, I'm obviously no longer myself. Sleeping pills for me too, though I've never—and no more nonsense. And no more questioning, no matter who.

The car door opened. "Wssht!" said Miss Finan, scuttling out again. "I've just remembered. Not last night, but two weeks ago. And once before that. A scream, you said?"

Mrs. Hazlitt stood up. Almost unable to speak, for the tears that suddenly wrenched her throat, she described it.

"That's it, just what I told my niece on the phone next morning. Like nothing human, and yet it was. I'd taken my Seconal too early, so there I was wide awake again, lying there just thinking, when it came. 'Auntie,' she tried to tell me, 'it was just one of the sireens. Or hoodlums maybe.'" Miss Finan reached up very slowly and settled her hat. "The city's gone down, you know. Not what it was," she said in a reduced voice, casting a glance over her shoulder, as if whatever the city now was loomed behind her. "But I've laid awake on this street too many years, I said, not to know what I hear." She leaned forward. "But—she ... they think I'm getting old, you know," she said, in the whisper used to confide the unimaginable. "So ... well ... when I heard it again I just didn't tell her."

Mrs. Hazlitt grubbed for her handkerchief, found it and blew her nose. Breaking down, she thought—I never knew what a literal phrase it is. For she felt as if all the muscles that usually held her up, knee to ankle, had slipped their knots and were melting her, unless she could stop them, to the floor. "I'm not normally such a nervous woman," she managed to say. "But it was just that no one else seemed to—why, there were people with lights on, but they just seemed to ignore."

The old lady nodded absently. "Well, thank God my

hearing's as good as ever. Hmm. Wait till I tell Jennie that!" She began making her painful way back to the car.

Mrs. Hazlitt put out a hand to delay her. "In case it—I mean, in case somebody ought to be notified—do you have any idea what it was?"

"Oh, I don't know. And what could we—?" Miss Finan shrugged, eager to get along. Still, gossip was tempting. "I did think—" She paused, lowering her voice uneasily. "Like somebody in a fit, it was. We'd a sexton at church taken that way with epilepsy once. And it stopped short like that, just as if somebody'd clapped a hand over its mouth, poor devil. Then the next time I thought—no, more like a signal, like somebody calling. You know the things you'll think at night." She turned, clearly eager to get away.

"But, oughtn't we to inquire?" Mrs. Hazlitt thought of the taxis. "In case it came from this building?"

"This build—" For a moment Miss Finan looked scared, her chin trembling, eyes rounded in the misty, affronted stare that the old gave, not to physical danger, but to a new idea swum too late into their ken. Then she drew herself up, all five feet of her bowed backbone. "Not from here it wouldn't. Across from that big place, maybe. Lots of riff-raff there, not used to their money. Or from Third Avenue, maybe. That's always been tenements there." She looked at Mrs. Hazlitt with an obtuse patronage that reminded her of an old nurse who had first instructed her on the social order, blandly mixing up all first causes—disease, money, poverty, snobbery—with a firm illogic that had still seemed somehow in possession—far more firmly so than her own good-hearted parents—of the crude facts. "New to the city, are you," she said, more kindly. "It takes a while."

This time they rode up together. "Now you remember," Miss Finan said, on leaving. "You've two locks on your door, one downstairs. Get a telephone put in by your bed. Snug as a bug in a rug you are then. Nothing to get at you but what's there already. That's what I always tell myself when I'm wakeful. Nothing to get at you then but the Old Nick."

The door closed on her. Watching her go, Mrs. Hazlitt envied her the simplicity, even the spinsterhood that had barred her from imagination as it had from experience. Even the narrowing-in of age would have its compensations, tenderly constricting the horizon as it cramped the fingers, adding the best of locks to Miss Finan's snugness, on her way by now to the triumphant phone call to Jennie.

But that was sinful, to wish for that too soon, what's more it was sentimental, in just the way she had vowed to avoid. Mrs. Hazlitt pushed the button for Down. Emerging from the building, she looked back at it from the corner, back at her day of contrived exits and entrances, abortive conversations. People were hurrying in and out now at a great rate. An invisible glass separated her from them; she was no longer in the fold.

Later that night, Mrs. Hazlitt, once more preparing for bed, peered down at the streets through the slats of the Venetian blind. Catching herself in the attitude of peering made her uneasy. Darkening the room behind her, she raised the blind. After dinner in one of the good French restaurants on Third Avenue and a Tati movie afterward—the French were such competent dispensers of gaiety—she could review her day more as a convalescent does his delirium—"Did I really say—do—that?" And even here she was addressing a vis-à-vis, so deeply was the habit ingrained. But she could see her self-imposed project now for what it was—only a hysterical seeking after conversation, the final breaking-point, like the old-fashioned "crisis" in pneumonia, of the long, low fever of loneliness unexpressed. Even the city, gazed at squarely, was really no anarchy. only a huge diffuseness that returned to the eye of the beholder, to the walker in its streets, even to the closed dream of its sleeper, his own mood, dark or light. Dozens of the solitary must be looking down at it with her, most of them with some *modus vivendi,* many of them booking themselves into life with the same painful intentness, the way the middle-aged sometimes set themselves to learning the tango. And a queer booking you gave yourself today, she told herself, the words lilting with Miss Finan's Irish, this being the last exchange of speech she had had. Testing the words aloud, she found her way with accents, always such a delight to Sam, as good as ever. Well, she had heard a scream, had discovered someone else who had heard it. And now to forget it as promised; the day was done. Prowling the room a bit, she took up her robe, draped it over her shoulders, still more providently put it on. "Oh Millie," she said, tossing the dark mirror a look of scorn as she passed it "you're such a sensible woman."

Wear out Mrs. Berry's carpet you will, Millie, she

thought, twenty minutes later by the bedroom clock, but the accent, adulterated now by Sam's, had escaped her. Had the scream had an accent? The trouble was that the mind had its own discipline; one could remember, even with a smile, the story of the man promised all the gold in the world if he could but go for two minutes not thinking of the word "hippopotamus." She stopped in front of the mirror, seeking her smile, but it too had escaped. "Hippopotamus," she said, to her dark image. The knuckles of one hand rose, somnambulist, as she watched, and pressed against her teeth. She forced the hand, hers, down again. I will say it again, aloud, she thought, and while I am saying it I will be sure to say to myself that I am saying it aloud. She did so. "Hippopotamus." For a long moment she remained there, staring into the mirror. Then she turned and snapped on every light in the room.

Across from her, in another mirror, the full-length one, herself regarded her. She went forward to it, to that image so irritatingly familiar, so constant as life changed it, so necessarily dear. Fair hair, if maintained too late in life, too brightly, always made the most sensible of women look foolish. There was hers, allowed to gray gently, disordered no more than was natural in the boudoir, framing a face still rational, if strained. "Dear me," she said to it. "All you need is somebody to talk to, get it out of your system. Somebody like yourself." As if prodded, she turned and surveyed the room.

Even in the glare of the lights, the naked black projected from the window, the room sent out to her, in half a dozen pleasant little touches, the same sense of its compatible owner that she had had from the beginning. There, flung down, was Mrs. Berry's copy of *The Eustace Diamonds*, a book that she had always meant to read and had been delighted to find here, along with many others of its ilk and still others she herself owned. How many people knew good bisque and how cheaply it might still be collected, or could let it hobnob so amiably with grandmotherly bits of Tiffanyware, even with the chipped Quimper ashtrays that Mrs. Berry, like Mrs. Hazlitt at the time of her own marriage, must once have thought the cutest in the world. There were the white walls, with the silly, strawberry-mouthed Marie Laurencin just above the Beerbohm, the presence of good faded colors, the absence of the new or fauve. On the night table were the scissors, placed, like everything in the house, where Mrs. Hazlitt would have had them, near them a relic that winked of her own childhood—and kept on, she would wager, for the same reason—a magnifiying glass exactly like her father's. Above them, the only floor lamp in the house, least offensive of its kind, towered above all the table ones, sign of a struggle between practicality and grace that she knew well, whose end she could applaud. Everywhere indeed there were the same signs of the struggles toward taste, the decline of taste into the prejudices of comfort, that went with a whole milieu and a generation—both hers. And over there was, even more personally, the second bed.

Mrs. Hazlitt sat down on it. If it were moved, into the study say, a few things out of storage with it, how sympathetically this flat might be shared. Nonsense, sheer fantasy to go on like this, to fancy herself embarking on the pitiable twin-life of leftover women, much less with a stranger. But was a woman a stranger if you happened to know that on her twelfth birthday she had received a copy of *Dr. Doolittle*, inscribed to Helena Nelson from her loving father, if you knew the secret, packrat place in the linen closet where she stuffed the neglected mending, of another, in a kitchen drawer, full of broken Mexican terrines and clipped recipes as shamefully grimy as your own cherished ones; if you knew that on 2/11/58 and on 7/25/57 a Dr. Burke had prescribed what looked to be sulfa pills, never used, that must have cured her at the point of purchase, as had embarrassingly happened time and again to yourself? If, in short, you knew almost every endearing thing about her, except her face?

Mrs. Hazlitt, blinking in the excessive light, looked sideways. She knew where there was a photograph album, tumbled once by accident from its shunted place in the bookshelf, and at once honorably replaced. She had seen enough to know that the snapshots, not pasted in separately, would have to be exhumed, one by one, from their packets. No, she told herself, she already knew more than enough of Mrs. Berry from all that had been so trustfully exposed here—enough to know that this was the sort of prying to which Mrs. Berry, like herself, would never stoop. Somehow this clinched it—their understanding. She could see them exchanging notes at some future meeting, Mrs. Berry saying, "Why, do you know—one night, when I was in London—" —herself, the vis-à-vis, nodding, their perfect rapprochement. Then what would be wrong in using, when so handily provided, so graciously awaiting her, such a comforting vis-à-vis, now?

Mrs. Hazlitt found herself standing, the room's glare pressing on her as if she were arraigned in a police line-up, as if, she reminded herself irritably, it were not self-imposed. She forced herself to make a circuit of the room, turning out each lamp with the crisp, no-nonsense flick of the wrist that nurses employed. At the one lamp still burning she hesitated, reluctant to cross over that last shadow-line. Then, with a shrug, she turned it out and sat down in the darkness, in one of the two opposing boudoir chairs. For long minutes she sat there. Once or twice she trembled on the verge of speech, covered it with a swallow. The conventions that guarded the mind in its strict relationship with the tongue were the hardest to flaunt. But this was the century of talk, of the long talk, in which all were healthily urged to confide. Even the children were encouraged toward, praised for, the imaginary companion. Why should the grown person, who for circumstance beyond his control had no other, be denied? As she watched the window, the light in the small gray house was extinguished. Some minutes later the doorman across the way disappeared. Without looking at the luminous dial of the clock, she could feel the silence aging, ripening. At last she bent forward to the opposite chair.

"Helena?" she said.

Her voice, clear-cut, surprised her. There was nothing so strange about it. The walls remained walls. No one could hear her, or cared to, and now, tucking her feet up, she could remember how cozy this could be, with someone opposite. "Helena," she said. "Wait till I tell you what happened while you were away."

She told her everything. At first she stumbled, went back, as if she were rehearsing in front of a mirror. Several times she froze, unsure whether a sentence had been spoken aloud entirely, or had begun, or terminated, unspoken, in the mind. But as she went on, this wavering borderline seemed only to resemble the clued conversation, meshed with silences, between two people who knew each other well. By the time she had finished her account she was almost at ease, settling back into the comfortably shared midnight post-mortem that always restored balance to the world—so nearly could she imagine the face, not unlike her own, in the chair opposite, smiling ruefully at her over the boy and his gingerbread fears, wondering mischievously with her as to in which of the shapes of temptation the Old Nick visited Miss Finan.

"That girl and her *log!*" said Mrs. Hazlitt. "You know how, when they're that young, you want to smash in the smugness. And yet, when you think of all they've got to go through, you feel so maternal. Even if—" Even if, came the nod, imperceptibly—you've never had children, like us.

For a while they were silent. "Warwick!" said Mrs. Hazlitt then. "Years ago there was an actor—Robert Warwick. I was in love with him—at about the age of eight." Then she smiled, bridling slightly, at the dark chair opposite, whose occupant would know her age. "Oh, all right then—twelve. But what is it, do you suppose, always makes old actors look seedy, even when they're not? Daylight maybe. Or all the pretenses." She ruminated. "Why . . . do you know," she said slowly, "I think I've got it. The way he looked in my face when I was speaking, and the way the dog turned back and he didn't. He was lip-reading. Why, the poor old boy is deaf!" She settled back, dropping her slippers one by one to the floor. "Of course, that's it. And he wouldn't want to admit that he couldn't have heard it. Probably doesn't dare wear an aid. Poor old boy, pretty dreary for him if he is an actor, and I'll bet he is." She sighed, a luxury permitted now. "Ah, well. Frail reed—Miss Finan. Lucky for me, though, that I stumbled on her." And on you.

A police siren sounded, muffled less and less by distance, approaching. She was at the window in time to see the car's red dome light streak by as it always did, its alarum dying behind it. Nothing else was on the road. "And there were the taxis," she said, looking down. "I don't know why I keep forgetting them. Veering to the side like that, one right after the other, and one had his light out, so it wasn't for a fare. Nothing on the curb either. Then they both shot away, almost as if they'd caught sight of something up here. And wanted no part of it—the way people do in this town. Wish you could've seen them—it was eerie." There was no response from behind her.

She sat down again. Yes, there was a response, for the first time faintly contrary.

"No," she said. "It certainly was *not* the siren. I was up in a flash. I'd have seen it." She found herself clenching the arms of the chair. "Besides," she said, in a quieter voice, "don't you remember? I heard it twice."

There was no answer. Glancing sideways, she saw the string of lights opposite, not quite of last night's pattern. But the silence was the same, opened to its perfect hour like a century plant, multiple-rooted, that came of age every night. The silence was in full bloom, and it had its own sound. Hark hark, no dogs do bark. And there is nobody in the chair.

Never was, never had been. It was sad to be up at this hour and sane. For now is the hour, now is the hour when all good men are asleep. Her hand smoothed the rim of the wastebasket, about the height from the floor of a dog's collar. Get one tomorrow. But how to manage until then, with all this silence speaking?

She made herself stretch out on the bed, close her eyes. "Sam," she said at last, as she had sworn never to do in thought or word, "I'm lonely." Listening vainly, she thought how wise her resolve had been. Too late, now she had tested his loss to the full, knew him for the void he was—far more of a one than Mrs. Berry, who, though unknown, was still somewhere. By using the name of love, when she had been ready to settle for anybody, she had sent him into the void forever. Opening her eyes, adjusted now to the sourceless city light that never ceased trickling on ceiling, lancing from mirrors, she turned her head right to left, left to right on the pillow, in a gesture to the one auditor who remained.

"No," she said, in the dry voice of correction. "I'm not lonely. I'm alone."

Almost at once she raised herself on her elbow, her head cocked. No, she had heard nothing from outside. But in her mind's ear she could hear the sound of the word she had just spoken, its final syllable twanging like a tuning fork, infinitely receding to octaves above itself, infinitely returning. In what seemed scarcely a stride, she was in the next room, at the French window, brought there by that thin, directional vibration which not necessarily even the blind would hear. For she had recognized it. She had identified the accent of the scream.

The long window frame, its swollen wood shoved tight by her the night before, at first would not budge; then, as she put both hands on the hasp and braced her knees, it gave slowly, grinding inward, the heavy man-high bolt thumping down. Both sounds, too, fell into their proper places. That's what I heard before, she thought, the noise of a window opening or closing, exactly like mine. Two lines of them, down the six floors of the building, made twelve possibles. But that was of no importance now. Stepping up on the lintel, she spread the casements wide.

Yes, there was the bridge, one small arc of it, sheering off into the mist, beautiful against the night, as all bridges were. Now that she was outside, past all barriers, she could hear, with her ordinary ear, faint nickings that marred the silence, but these were only the surface scratches on a record that still revolved one low, continuous tone. No dogs do bark. That was the key to it, that her own hand, smoothing a remembered dog-collar, had been trying to give her. There were certain dog-whistles, to be bought anywhere—one had hung, with the unused leash, on a hook near a door in the country—which blew a summons so high above the human range that only a dog could hear it. What had summoned her last night would have been that much higher, audible only to those tuned in by necessity—the thin, soaring decibel of those who were no longer in the fold. Alone-oh. Alone-oh. That would have been the shape of it, of silence expelled from the mouth in one long relieving note, cool, irrepressible, the second one clapped short by the hand. No dog would have heard it. No animal but one was ever that alone.

She stepped out onto the fire escape. There must be legions of them, of us, she thought, in the dim alleyways, the high, flashing terraces—each one of them come to the end of his bookings, circling his small platform in space. And who would hear such a person? Not the log-girls, not for years and years. None of any age who, body to body, bed to bed, either in love or in the mutual pluck-pluck of hate—like the little girl and her mother—were still nested down. Reginald Warwick, stoppered in his special quiet, might hear it, turn to his Coco for confirmation which did not come, and persuade himself once again that it was only his affliction. Others lying awake snug as a bug, listening for that Old Nick, death, would hear the thin, sororal signal and not know what they had heard. But an endless assemblage of others all over the city would be waiting for it—all those sitting in the dark void of the one lamp quenched, the one syllable spoken—who would start up, some from sleep, to their windows . . . or were already there.

A car passed below. Instinctively, she flattened against the casement, but the car traveled on. Last night someone, man or woman, would have been standing in one of the line of niches above and beneath hers—perhaps even a woman in a blue robe like her own. But literal distance or person would not matter; in that audience all would be the same. Looking up, she could see the tired, heated lavender of the mid-town sky, behind which lay that real imperial into which some men were already hurling their exquisitely signaling spheres. But this sound would come from breast to breast, at an altitude higher than any of those. She brought her fist to her mouth, in savage pride at having heard it, at belonging to a race some of whom could never adapt to any range less than that. *Some of us*, she thought, *are still responsible.*

Stepping forward, she leaned on the iron railing. At that moment, another car, traveling slowly by, hesitated opposite, its red dome light blinking. Mrs. Hazlitt stood very still. She watched until the police car went on again, inching ahead slowly, as if somebody inside were looking back. The two men inside there would never understand what she was waiting for. Hand clapped to her mouth, she herself had just understood. She was waiting for it—for its company. She was waiting for a second chance—to answer it. She was waiting for the scream to come again.

ANN PETRY was born in Old Saybrook, Connecticut, in 1912. She was educated at the University of Connecticut, Storrs, and Columbia University. After working as a pharmacist in Old Saybrook and Lyme, she married in 1938 and went to work as a reporter for *The Amsterdam News* and later for *The People's Voice*. She covered the Harlem riot of 1943, on which her novella "In Darkness" is based. Her first novel, *The Street* (1946), completed on a Houghton Mifflin Literary Fellowship, drew upon her life in Harlem. It established her literary reputation as an outstanding young writer of fiction. In the same year the story that is printed here, "Like a Winding Sheet," was chosen for Martha Foley's *The Best American Short Stories of 1946*.

Mrs. Petry says that everything she writes—short stories, novels, books for children, a biography of Harriet Tubman—deals with race relations in the United States. Her stories show her ability to deal with human relationships in their political and economic contexts without losing the sense of their mysterious psychological complexity. Whether her characters live in middle-class Connecticut or an urban slum, Mrs. Petry never fails to make her readers share her sympathy for their oppression or her vision of man's inhumanity to man.

Ann Petry
(1912–)

LIKE A WINDING SHEET

He had planned to get up before Mae did and surprise her by fixing breakfast. Instead he went back to sleep and she got out of bed so quietly he didn't know she wasn't there beside him until he woke up and heard the queer soft gurgle of water running out of the sink in the bathroom.

He knew he ought to get up but instead he put his arms across his forehead to shut the afternoon sunlight out of his eyes, pulled his legs up close to his body, testing them to see if the ache was still in them.

Mae had finished in the bathroom. He could tell because she never closed the door when she was in there and now the sweet smell of talcum powder was drifting down the hall and into the bedroom. Then he heard her coming down the hall.

"Hi, babe," she said affectionately.

"Hum," he grunted, and moved his arms away from his head, opened one eye.

"It's a nice morning."

"Yeah." He rolled over and the sheet twisted around him, outlining his thighs, his chest. "You mean afternoon, don't ya?"

Mae looked at the twisted sheet and giggled. "Looks like a winding sheet," she said. "A shroud—" Laughter tangled with her words and she had to pause for a moment before she could continue. "You look like a huckleberry—in a winding sheet—"

"That's no way to talk. Early in the day like this," he protested.

He looked at his arms silhouetted against the white of the sheets. They were inky black by contrast and he had to smile in spite of himself and he lay there smiling and savoring the sweet sound of Mae's giggling.

"Early?" She pointed a finger at the alarm clock on the table near the bed and giggled again. "It's almost four o'clock. And if you don't spring up out of there, you're going to be late again."

"What do you mean 'again'?"

"Twice last week. Three times the week before. And once the week before and—"

"I can't get used to sleeping in the daytime," he said fretfully. He pushed his legs out from under the covers experimentally. Some of the ache had gone out of them but they weren't really rested yet. "It's too light for good sleeping. And all that standing beats the hell out of my legs."

"After two years you oughta be used to it," Mae said.

He watched her as she fixed her hair, powdered her face, slipped into a pair of blue denim overalls. She moved quickly and yet she didn't seem to hurry.

"You look like you'd had plenty of sleep," he said lazily. He had to get up but he kept putting the moment off, not wanting to move, yet he didn't dare let his legs go completely limp because if he did he'd go back to sleep. It was getting later and later but the thought of putting his weight on his legs kept him lying there.

When he finally got up he had to hurry, and he gulped his breakfast so fast that he wondered if his stomach could possibly use food thrown at it at such a rate of speed. He was still wondering about it as he and Mae were putting their coats on in the hall.

Mae paused to look at the calendar. "It's the thirteenth," she said. Then a faint excitement in her voice, "Why, it's Friday the thirteenth." She had one arm in her coat sleeve and she held it there while she stared at the calendar. "I oughta stay home," she said. "I shouldn't go outa the house."

"Aw, don't be a fool," he said. "Today's payday. And payday is a good luck day everywhere, any way you look at it." And as she stood hesitating he said, "Aw, come on."

And he was late for work again because they spent fifteen minutes arguing before he could convince her she ought to go to work just the same. He had to talk persuasively, urging her gently, and it took time. But he couldn't bring himself to talk to her roughly or threaten to strike her like a lot of men might have done. He wasn't made that way.

So when he reached the plant he was late and he had to wait to punch the time clock because the day-shift workers were streaming out in long lines, in groups and bunches that impeded his progress.

Even now just starting his workday his legs ached. He had to force himself to struggle past the outgoing workers, punch the time clock, and get the little cart he pushed around all night, because he kept toying with the idea of going home and getting back in bed.

He pushed the cart out on the concrete floor, thinking that if this was his plant he'd make a lot of changes in it. There were too many standing-up jobs for one thing. He'd figure out some way most of 'em could be done sitting down and he'd put a lot more benches around. And this job he had—this job that forced him to walk ten hours a night, pushing this little cart, well, he'd turn it into a sitting-down job. One of those little trucks they used around railroad stations would be good for a job like this. Guys sat on a seat and the thing moved easily, taking up little room and turning in hardly any space at all, like on a dime.

He pushed the cart near the foreman. He never could remember to refer to her as the forelady even in his mind. It was funny to have a white woman for a boss in a plant like this one.

She was sore about something. He could tell by the way her face was red and her eyes were half-shut until they were slits. Probably been out late and didn't get enough sleep. He avoided looking at her and hurried a little, head down, as he passed her though he couldn't resist stealing a glance at her out of the corner of his eye. He saw the edge of the light-colored slacks she wore and the tip end of a big tan shoe.

"Hey, Johnson!" the woman said.

The machines had started full blast. The whirr and the grinding made the building shake, made it impossible to hear conversations. The men and women at the machines talked to each other but looking at them from just a little distance away, they appeared to be simply moving their lips because you couldn't hear what they were saying. Yet the woman's voice cut across the machine sounds—harsh, angry.

He turned his head slowly. "Good evenin', Mrs. Scott," he said, and waited.

"You're late again."

"That's right. My legs were bothering me."

The woman's face grew redder, angrier looking. "Half this shift comes in late," she said. "And you're the worst one of all. You're always late. Whatsa matter with ya?"

"It's my legs," he said. "Somehow they don't ever get rested. I don't seem to get used to sleeping days. And I just can't get started."

"Excuses. You guys always got excuses," her anger grew and spread. "Every guy comes in here late always has an excuse. His wife's sick or his grandmother died or somebody in the family had to go to the hospital," she paused, drew a deep breath. "And the niggers is the worse. I don't care what's wrong with your legs. You get in here on time. I'm sick of you niggers—"

"You got the right to get mad," he interrupted softly. "You got the right to cuss me four ways to Sunday but I ain't letting nobody call me a nigger."

He stepped closer to her. His fists were doubled. His lips were drawn back in a thin narrow line. A vein in his forehead stood out swollen, thick.

And the woman backed away from him, not hurriedly but slowly—two, three steps back.

"Aw, forget it," she said. "I didn't mean nothing by it. It slipped out. It was an accident." The red of her face deepened until the small blood vessels in her cheeks were purple. "Go on and get to work," she urged. And she took three more slow backward steps.

He stood motionless for a moment and then turned away from the sight of the red lipstick on her mouth that made him remember that the foreman was a woman. And he couldn't bring himself to hit a woman. He felt a curious tingling in his fingers and he looked down at his hands. They were clenched tight, hard, ready to smash some of those small purple veins in her face.

He pushed the cart ahead of him, walking slowly. When he turned his head, she was staring in his direction, mopping her forehead with a dark blue handkerchief. Their eyes met and then they both looked away.

He didn't glance in her direction again but moved past the long work benches, carefully collecting the finished parts, going slowly and steadily up and down, and back and forth the length of the building, and as he walked he forced himself to swallow his anger, get rid of it.

And he succeeded so that he was able to think about what had happened without getting upset about it. An hour went by but the tension stayed in his hands. They were clenched and knotted on the handles of the cart as though ready to aim a blow.

And he thought he should have hit her anyway, smacked her hard in the face, felt the soft flesh of her face give under the hardness of his hands. He tried to make his hands relax by offering them a description of what it would have been like to strike her because he had the queer feeling that his hands were not exactly a part of him anymore—they had developed a separate life of their own over which he had no control. So he dwelt on the pleasure his hands would have felt—both of them cracking at her, first one and then the other. If he had done that his hands would have felt good now—relaxed, rested.

And he decided that even if he'd lost his job for it, he should have let her have it and it would have been a long time, maybe the rest of her life, before she called anybody else a nigger.

The only trouble was he couldn't hit a woman. A woman couldn't hit back the same way a man did. But it would have been a deeply satisfying thing to have cracked her narrow lips wide open with just one blow, beautifully timed and with all his weight in back of it. That way he would have gotten rid of all the energy and tension his anger had created in him. He kept remembering how his heart had started pumping blood so fast he had felt it tingle even in the tips of his fingers.

With the approach of night, fatigue nibbled at him. The corners of his mouth drooped, the frown between his eyes deepened, his shoulders sagged; but his hands stayed tight and tense. As the hours dragged by he noticed that the women workers had started to snap and snarl at each other. He couldn't hear what they said because of the sound of machines but he could see the quick lip movements that sent words tumbling from the sides of their mouths. They gestured irritably with their hands and scowled as their mouths moved.

Their violent jerky motions told him that it was getting close on to quitting time but somehow he felt that the night still stretched ahead of him, composed of endless hours of steady walking on his aching legs. When the whistle finally blew he went on pushing the cart, unable to believe that it had sounded. The whirring of the machines died away to a murmur and he knew then that he'd really heard the whistle. He stood still for a moment, filled with a relief that made him sigh.

Then he moved briskly, putting the cart in the storeroom, hurrying to take his place in the line forming before the paymaster. That was another thing he'd change, he thought. He'd have the pay envelopes handed to the people right at their benches so there wouldn't be ten or fifteen minutes lost waiting for the pay. He always got home about fifteen minutes late on payday. They did it better in the plant where Mae worked, brought the money right to them at their benches.

He stuck his pay envelope in his pants' pocket and followed the line of workers heading for the subway in a slow-moving stream. He glanced up at the sky. It was a nice night, the sky looked packed full to running over with stars. And he thought if he and Mae would go right to bed when they got home from work they'd catch a few hours of darkness for sleeping. But they never did. They fooled around—cooking and eating and listening to the radio and he always stayed in a big chair in the living room and went almost but not quite to sleep and when they finally got to bed it was five or six in the morning and daylight was already seeping around the edges of the sky.

He walked slowly, putting off the moment when he would have to plunge into the crowd hurrying toward the subway. It was a long ride to Harlem and tonight the thought of it appalled him. He paused outside an all-night restaurant to kill time, so that some of the first rush of workers would be gone when he reached the subway.

The lights in the restaurant were brilliant, enticing. There was life and motion inside. And as he looked through the window he thought that everything within range of his eyes gleamed—the long imitation marble counter, the tall stools, the white porcelain-topped tables and especially the big metal coffee urn right near the window. Steam issued from its top and a gas flame flickered under it—a lively, dancing, blue flame.

A lot of the workers from his shift—men and women—were lining up near the coffee urn. He watched them walk to the porcelain-topped tables carrying steaming cups of coffee and he saw that just the smell of the coffee lessened the fatigue lines in their faces. After the first sip their faces softened, they smiled, they began to talk and laugh.

On a sudden impulse he shoved the door open and

joined the line in front of the coffee urn. The line moved slowly. And as he stood there the smell of the coffee, the sound of the laughter and of the voices, helped dull the sharp ache in his legs.

He didn't pay any attention to the white girl who was serving the coffee at the urn. He kept looking at the cups in the hands of the men who had been ahead of him. Each time a man stepped out of the line with one of the thick white cups the fragrant steam got in his nostrils. He saw that they walked carefully so as not to spill a single drop. There was a froth of bubbles at the top of each cup and he thought about how he would let the bubbles break against his lips before he actually took a big deep swallow.

Then it was his turn. "A cup of coffee," he said, just as he had heard the others say.

The white girl looked past him, put her hands up to her head and gently lifted her hair away from the back of her neck, tossing her head back a little. "No more coffee for a while," she said.

He wasn't certain he'd heard her correctly and he said "What?" blankly.

"No more coffee for a while," she repeated.

There was silence behind him and then uneasy movement. He thought someone would say something, ask why or protest, but there was only silence and then a faint shuffling sound as though the men standing behind him had simultaneously shifted their weight from one foot to the other.

He looked at the girl without saying anything. He felt his hands begin to tingle and the tingling went all the way down to his finger tips so that he glanced down at them. They were clenched tight, hard, into fists. Then he looked at the girl again. What he wanted to do was hit her so hard that the scarlet lipstick on her mouth would smear and spread over her nose, her chin, out toward her cheeks, so hard that she would never toss her head again and refuse a man a cup of coffee because he was black.

He estimated the distance across the counter and reached forward, balancing his weight on the balls of his feet, ready to let the blow go. And then his hands fell back down to his sides because he forced himself to lower them, to unclench them and make them dangle loose. The effort took his breath away because his hands fought against him. But he couldn't hit her. He couldn't even now bring himself to hit a woman, not even this one, who had refused him a cup of coffee with a toss of her head. He kept seeing the gesture with which she had lifted the length of her blond hair from the back of her neck as expressive of her contempt for him.

When he went out the door he didn't look back. If he had he would have seen the flickering blue flame under the shiny coffee urn being extinguished. The line of men who had stood behind him lingered a moment to watch the people drinking coffee at the tables and then they left just as he had without having had the coffee they wanted so badly. The girl behind the counter poured water in the urn and swabbed it out and as she waited for the water to run out, she lifted her hair gently from the back of her neck and tossed her head before she began making a fresh lot of coffee.

But he had walked away without a backward look, his head down, his hands in his pockets, raging at himself and whatever it was inside of him that had forced him to stand quiet and still when he wanted to strike out.

The subway was crowded and he had to stand. He tried grasping an overhead strap and his hands were too tense to grip it. So he moved near the train door and stood there swaying back and forth with the rocking of the train. The roar of the train beat inside his head, making it ache and throb, and the pain in his legs clawed up into his groin so that he seemed to be bursting with pain and he told himself that it was due to all that anger-born energy that had piled up in him and not been used and so it had spread through him like a poison—from his feet and legs all the way up to his head.

Mae was in the house before he was. He knew she was home before he put the key in the door of the apartment. The radio was going. She had it tuned up loud and she was singing along with it.

"Hello, babe," she called out, as soon as he opened the door.

He tried to say "hello" and it came out half grunt and half sigh.

"You sure sound cheerful," she said.

She was in the bedroom and he went and leaned against the doorjamb. The denim overalls she wore to work were carefully draped over the back of a chair by the bed. She was standing in front of the dresser, tying the sash of a yellow housecoat around her waist and chewing gum vigorously as she admired her reflection in the mirror over the dresser.

"Whatsa matter?" she said. "You get bawled out by the boss or somep'n?"

"Just tired," he said slowly. "For God's sake, do you have to crack that gum like that?"

"You don't have to lissen to me," she said complacently. She patted a curl in place near the side of her head and then lifted her hair away from the back of her neck, ducking her head forward and then back.

He winced away from the gesture. "What you got to be always fooling with your hair for?" he protested.

"Say, what's the matter with you anyway?" She turned away from the mirror to face him, put her hands on her hips. "You ain't been in the house two minutes and you're picking on me."

He didn't answer her because her eyes were angry and he didn't want to quarrel with her. They'd been married too long and got along too well and so he walked all the way into the room and sat down in the chair by the bed and stretched his legs out in front of him, putting his weight on the heels of his shoes, leaning way back in the chair, not saying anything.

"Lissen," she said sharply. "I've got to wear those overalls again tomorrow. You're going to get them all wrinkled up leaning against them like that."

He didn't move. He was too tired and his legs were throbbing now that he had sat down. Besides the overalls were already wrinkled and dirty, he thought. They couldn't help but be for she'd worn them all week. He leaned farther back in the chair.

"Come on, get up," she ordered.

"Oh, what the hell," he said wearily, and got up from the chair. "I'd just as soon live in a subway. There'd be just as much place to sit down."

He saw that her sense of humor was struggling with her anger. But her sense of humor won because she giggled.

"Aw, come on and eat," she said. There was a coaxing note in her voice. "You're nothing but an old hungry nigger trying to act tough and—" she paused to giggle and then continued, "You—"

He had always found her giggling pleasant and deliberately said things that might amuse her and then waited, listening for the delicate sound to emerge from her throat. This time he didn't even hear the giggle. He didn't let her finish what she was saying. She was standing close to him and that funny tingling started in his finger tips, went fast up his arms and sent his fist shooting straight for her face.

There was the smacking sound of soft flesh being struck by a hard object and it wasn't until she screamed that he realized he had hit her in the mouth—so hard that the dark red lipstick had blurred and spread over her full lips, reaching up toward the tip of her nose, down toward her chin, out toward her cheeks.

The knowledge that he had struck her seeped through him slowly and he was appalled but he couldn't drag his hands away from her face. He kept striking her and he thought with horror that something inside him was holding him, binding him to this act, wrapping and twisting about him so that he had to continue it. He had lost all control over his hands. And he groped for a phrase, a word, something to describe what this thing was like that was happening to him and he thought it was like being enmeshed in a winding sheet—that was it—like a winding sheet. And even as the thought formed in his mind, his hands reached for her face again and yet again.

MARY LAVIN was born in East Walpole, Massachusetts, in 1912 and has lived in Ireland since childhood. She did undergraduate and graduate work at the National University in Dublin, married, and then was left a widow with three children and a farm to take care of.

She wrote her first short story in the middle of writing her doctoral dissertation on Virginia Woolf. Since receiving the Tait Black Memorial Prize for her first book of short stories, *Tales from Bective Bridge* (1943), she has produced twelve more collections. In the Preface to her *Selected Stories* she writes: "I . . . wish that I could break up the two long novels I have published into the few short stories they ought to have been in the first place. For in spite of these two novels, and in spite of the fact that I may write other novels, I feel that it is in the short story that a writer distills the essence of his thought. I believe this because the short story, shape as well as matter, is determined by the writer's own character. Both are one. Short-story writing—for me—is only looking closer than normal into the human heart. . . ."

Kay Boyle has recognized her uniqueness as well as her affinity with James Joyce, against whom all twentieth-century Irish writers are inevitably measured: "I am very much moved by her writing. Her stories speak to us from a far, green world—a world whose freshness we have desperate need of at this time. Mary Lavin's characters are living people, all of them, who speak directly from the spiritual setting of Joyce's Dubliners. But this time it is a woman's voice telling us with eloquence and compassion of other women's love, and pride, and courage, and despair. Mary Lavin has given us in these stories an entire country, and surely there is no greater gift a writer can make to his time."

Mary Lavin (1912—   )

IN A CAFÉ

The café was in a back street. Mary's ankles ached and she was glad Maudie had not got there before her. She sat down at a table near the door.

It was a place she had only recently found, and she dropped in often, whenever she came up to Dublin. She hated to go anywhere else now. For one thing, she knew that she would be unlikely ever to have set foot in it if Richard were still alive. And this knowledge helped to give her back a semblance of the identity she lost willingly in marriage, but lost doubly, and unwillingly, in widowhood.

Not that Richard would have disliked the café. It was the kind of place they went to when they were students. Too much water had gone under the bridge since those days, though. Say what you liked, there was something faintly snobby about a farm in Meath, and together she and Richard would have been out of place here. But it was a different matter to come here alone. There could be nothing—oh, nothing—snobby about a widow. Just by being one, she fitted into this kind of café. It was an unusual little place. She looked around.

The walls were distempered red above and the lower part was boarded, with the boards painted white. It was probably the boarded walls that gave it the peculiarly functional look you get in the snuggery of a public house or in the confessional of a small and poor parish church. For furniture there were only deal tables and chairs, with black-and-white checked tablecloths that were either unironed or badly ironed. But there was a decided feeling that money was not so much in short supply as dedicated to other purposes—as witness the paintings on the walls, and a notice over the fire-grate to say that there were others on view in a studio overhead, in rather the same way as pictures in an exhibition. The paintings were for the most part experimental in their technique.

The café was run by two students from the Art College. They often went out and left the place quite empty—as now—while they had a cup of coffee in another café—across the street. Regular clients sometimes helped themselves to coffee from the pot on the gas-ring, behind a curtain at the back; or, if they only came in for company and found none, merely warmed themselves at the big fire always blazing in the little black grate that was the original grate when the café was a warehouse office. Today, the fire was banked up with coke. The coffee was spitting on the gas-ring.

Would Maudie like the place? That it might not be exactly the right place to have arranged to meet her, above all under the present circumstances, occurred vaguely to Mary, but there was nothing that could be done about it now. When Maudie got there, if she didn't like it, they could go somewhere else. On the other hand, perhaps she might like it? Or perhaps she would be too upset to take notice of her surroundings? The paintings might interest her. They were certainly stimulating. There were two new ones today, which Mary herself had not seen before: two flower paintings, just inside the door. From where she sat she could read the signature, Johann van Stiegler. Or at least they suggested flowers. They were nameable as roses surely in spite of being a bit angular. She knew what Richard would have said about them. But she and Richard were no longer one. So what would *she* say about them? She would say—she would say—

But what was keeping Maudie? It was all very well to be glad of a few minutes' time in which to gather herself together; it was a different thing altogether to be kept a quarter of an hour.

Mary leaned back against the boarding. She was less tired than when she came in, but she was still in no way prepared for the encounter in front of her.

What had she to say to a young widow recently bereaved? Why on earth had she arranged to meet her? The incongruity of their both being widowed came forcibly upon her. Would Maudie, too, be in black with touches of white? Two widows! It was like two magpies: one for sorrow, two for joy. The absurdity of it was all at once so great she had an impulse to get up and make off out of the place. She felt herself vibrating all over with resentment at being coupled with anyone, and urgently she began to sever them, seeking out their disparities.

Maudie was only a year married! And her parents had been only too ready to take care of her child, greedily possessing themselves of it. Maudie was as free as a girl. Then—if it mattered—?—she had a nice little income in her own right too, apart from all Michael had left her. So?

But what was keeping her? Was she not coming at all?

Ah! the little iron bell that was over the door—it too, since the warehouse days—tinkled to tell there was another customer coming into the café.

It wasn't Maudie though. It was a young man—youngish anyway—and Mary would say that he was an artist. Yet his hands at which, when he sat down, he began to stare, were not like the hands of an artist. They were peculiarly plump soft-skinned hands, and there was something touching in the relaxed way in which, lightly clasped one in the other, they rested on the table. Had they a womanish look perhaps? No; that was not the word, but she couldn't for the life of her find the right word to describe them. And her mind was teased by trying to find it. Fascinated, her eyes were drawn to those hands, time and again, no matter how resolutely she tore them away. It was almost as if it was by touch, not sight, that she knew their warm fleshiness.

Even when she closed her eyes—as she did—she could still see them. And so, innocent of where she was being led, she made no real effort to free her thoughts from them, and not until it was too late did she see before her the familiar shape of her recurring nightmare. All at once it was Richard's hands she saw, so different from those others, wiry, supple, thin. There they were for an instant in her mind, limned by love and anguish, before they vanished.

It happened so often. In her mind she would see a part of him, his hand—his arm, his foot perhaps, in the finely worked leather shoes he always wore—and from it, frantically, she would try to build up the whole man. Sometimes she succeeded better than others, built him up from foot to shoulder, seeing his hands, his grey suit, his tie, knotted always in a slightly special way, his neck, even his chin that was rather sharp, a little less attractive than his other features—

—But always at that point she would be defeated. Never

once voluntarily since the day he died had she been able to see his face again.

And if she could not remember him, at will, what meaning had time at all? What use was it to have lived the past, if behind us it fell away so sheer?

In the hour of his death, for her it was part of the pain that she knew this would happen. She was standing beside him, and at once the roar died down in her mind. She with a sweet, clear whistle, and hearing it she knew that he was dead, because not for years had she really heard bird-song or bird-call, so loud was the noise of their love in her ears. When she looked down it was a strange face, the look of death itself, that lay on the pillow. And after that brief moment of silence that let in the bird-song for an instant, a new noise started in her head; the noise of a nameless panic that did not always roar, but never altogether died down.

And now—here in the little café—she caught at the table-edge—for the conflagration had started again and her mind was a roaring furnace.

It was just then the man at the end of the table stood up and reached for the menu-card on which, as a matter of fact, she was leaning—breasts and elbows—with her face in her hands. Hastily, apologetically, she pushed it towards him, and at once the roar died down in her mind. She looked at him. Could he have known? Her heart was filled with gratitude, and she saw that his eyes were soft and gentle. But she had to admit that he didn't look as if he were much aware of her. No matter! She still was grateful to him.

"Don't you want this too?" she cried, thankful, warm, as she saw that the small slip of paper with the specialty for the day that had been clipped to the menu card with a paper-pin, had come off and remained under the elbow, caught on the rough sleeve of her jacket. She stood up and leant over the table with it.

"Ah! thank you!" he said, and bowed. She smiled. There was such gallantry in a bow. He was a foreigner, of course. And then, before she sat down again she saw that he had been sketching, making little pencil sketches all over a newspaper on the table, in the margins and in the spaces between the newsprint. Such intricate minutely involuted little figures—she was fascinated, but of course she could not stare.

Yet, when she sat down, she watched him covertly, and every now and then she saw that he made a particular flourish: it was his signature, she felt sure, and she tried to make it out from where she sat. A disproportionate, a ridiculous excitement rushed through her, when she realized it was Johann van Stiegler, the name on the new flower paintings that had preoccupied her when she first came into the place.

But it's impossible, she thought. The sketches were so meticulous; the paintings so—

But the little bell tinkled again.

"Ah! Maudie!"

For all her waiting, taken by surprise in the end, she got to her feet in her embarrassment, like a man.

"Maudie, my dear!" She had to stare fixedly at her in an effort to convey the sympathy, which, tongue-tied, she could express in no other way.

They shook hands, wordlessly.

"I'm deliberately refraining from expressing sympathy —you know that?" said Mary then, as they sat down at the checkered table.

"Oh, I do!" cried Maudie. And she seemed genuinely appreciative. "It's so awful trying to think of something to say back!—Isn't it? It has to come right out of yourself, and sometimes what comes is something you can't even say out loud when you do think of it!"

It was so true. Mary looked at her in surprise. Her mind ran back over the things people had said to her, and the replies.

Them: It's a good thing it wasn't one of the children.

Her: I'd give them all for him.

Them: Time is a great healer.

Her: Thief would be more like: taking away even my memory of him.

Them: God's ways are wonderful. Some day you'll see His plan in all this.

Her: Do you mean, some day I'll be glad he's dead?

So Maudie apprehended these subtleties too? Mary looked hard at her. "I know, I know," she said. "In the end you have to say what is expected of you—and you feel so cheapened by it."

"Worse still, you cheapen the dead!" said Maudie.

Mary looked really hard at her now. Was it possible for a young girl—a simple person at that—to have wrung from one single experience so much bitter knowledge? In spite of herself, she felt she was being drawn into complicity with her. She drew back resolutely.

"Of course, you were more or less expecting it, weren't you?" she said, spitefully.

Unrepulsed, Maudie looked back at her. "Does that matter?" she asked, and then, unexpectedly, she herself put a rift between them. "You have the children, of course!" she said, and then, hastily, before Mary could say anything, she rushed on. "Oh, I know I have my baby, but there seems so little link between him and his father! I just can't believe that it's me, sometimes, wheeling him around the park in his pram: it's like as if he was illegitimate. No! I mean it really, I'm not just trying to be shocking. It must be so different when there has been time for a relationship to be started between children and their father, like there was in your case."

"Oh, I don't know that that matters," said Mary. "And you'll be glad to have him some day." This time she spoke with deliberate malice, for she knew so well how those same words had lacerated her. She knew what they were meant to say: the children would be better than nothing.

But the poison of her words did not penetrate Maudie. And with another stab she knew why this was so. Maudie was so young; so beautiful. Looking at her, it seemed quite inaccurate to say that she had lost her husband: it was Michael who had lost her, fallen out, as it were, while she perforce went outward. She didn't even look like a widow. There was nothing about her to suggest that she was in any way bereft or maimed.

"You'll marry again, Maudie," she said, impulsively. "Don't mind my saying it," she added quickly, hastily. "It's not a criticism. It's because I know how you're suffering that I say it. Don't take offence."

Maudie didn't really look offended though, she only looked on the defensive. Then she relaxed.

"Not coming from you," she said. "You know what it's like." Mary saw she was trying to cover up the fact that she simply could not violently refute the suggestion. "Not that I think I will," she added, but weakly, "After all, you didn't!"

It was Mary who was put upon the defensive now.

"After all, it's only two years—less even," she said stiffly.

"Oh, it's not altogether a matter of time," said Maudie,

seeing she had erred, but not clear how or where. "It's the kind of person you are, I think. I admire you so much! It's what I'd want to be like myself if I had the strength. With remarriage it is largely the effect on oneself that matters I think, don't you? I don't think it really matters to—to the dead! Do you? I'm sure Michael would want me to marry again if he were able to express a wish. After all, people say it's a compliment to a man if his widow marries again, did you ever hear that?"

"I did," said Mary, curtly. "But I wouldn't pay much heed to it. A fat lot the dead care about compliments."

So Maudie *was* already thinking about remarriage? Mary's irritation was succeeded by a vague feeling of envy, and then the irritation returned tenfold.

How easily it was accepted that *she* would not marry again. This girl regards me as too old, of course. And she's right—or she ought to be right! She remembered the way, even two years ago, people had said she "had" her children. They meant, even then, that it was unlikely, unlooked for, that she'd remarry.

Other things that had been said crowded back into her mind as well. So many people had spoken of the special quality of her marriage—hers and Richard's—their remarkable suitability one for the other, and the uniqueness of the bond between them. She was avid to hear this said at the time.

But suddenly, in this little café, the light that had played over those words flickered and went out. Did they perhaps mean that if Richard had not appeared when he did, no one else would have been interested in her?

Whereas Maudie—! If she looked so attractive now, when she must still be suffering from shock, what would she be like a year from now, when she would be "out of mourning," as it would be put? Why, right now, she was so fresh and—looking at her there was no other word for it—virginal. Of course she was only a year married. A year! You could hardly call it being married at all.

But Maudie knew a thing or two about men for all that. There was no denying it. And in her eyes at that moment there was a strange expression. Seeing it, Mary remembered at once that they were not alone in the café. She wondered urgently how much the man at the other end of the table had heard and could hear of what they were saying. But it was too late to stop Maudie.

"Oh Mary," cried Maudie, leaning forward, "it's not what they give us—I've got over wanting things like a child—it's what we have to give them! It's something—" and she pressed her hands suddenly to her breasts, "something in here!"

"Maudie!"

Sharply, urgently, Mary tried to make her lower her voice, and with a quick movement of her head she did manage at last to convey some caution to her.

"In case you might say something," she said, in a low voice.

"Oh, there was no fear," said Maudie. "I was aware all the time." She didn't speak quite so low as Mary, but did lower her voice. "I was aware of him *all the time*," she said. "It was *him* that put it into my mind—about what we have to give." She pressed her hands to her breasts again. "He looks so lonely, don't you think? He is a foreigner, isn't he? I always think it's sad for them; they don't have many friends, and even when they do, there is always a barrier, don't you agree?"

But Mary was too embarrassed to let her go on. Almost frantically she made a diversion.

"What are you going to have, Maudie?" she said, loudly. "Coffee? Tea? And is there no one to take an order?"

Immediately she felt a fool. To whom had she spoken? She looked across at Johann van Stiegler. As if he were waiting to meet her glance, his mild and patient eyes looked into hers.

"There is no one there," he said, nodding at the curtained gas-ring, "but one can serve oneself. Perhaps you would wish that I—"

"Oh, not at all," cried Mary. "Please don't trouble! We're in absolutely no hurry! Please don't trouble yourself," she said, "not on our account."

But she saw at once that he was very much a foreigner, and that he was at a disadvantage, not knowing if he had not perhaps made a gaffe. "I have perhaps intruded?" he said, miserably.

"Oh, not at all," cried Mary, and he was so serious she had to laugh.

The laugh was another mistake though. His face took on a look of despair that could come upon a foreigner, it seemed, at the slightest provocation, as if suddenly everything was obscure to him—everything.

"Please," she murmured, and then vaguely, "—your work," meaning that she did not wish to interrupt his sketching.

"Ah, you know my work?" he said, brightening immediately, pleased and with a small and quite endearing vanity. "We have met before? Yes?"

"Oh no, we haven't met," she said, quickly, and she sat down, but of course after that it was impossible to go on acting as if he were a complete stranger. She turned to see what Maudie would make of the situation. It was then she felt the full force of her irritation with Maudie. She could have given her a slap in the face. Yes: a slap right in the face! For there she sat, remotely, her face indeed partly averted from them.

Maudie was waiting to be introduced! To be *introduced*, as if she, Mary, did not need any conventional preliminaries. As if it was all right that she, Mary, should begin an unprefaced conversation with a strange man in a café because—and of course that was what was so infuriating, that she knew Maudie's unconscious thought—it was all right for a woman of *her* age to strike up a conversation like that, but that it wouldn't have done for a young woman. Yet, on her still partly averted face, Mary could see the quickened look of interest. She had a good mind not to make any gesture to draw her into the conversation at all, but she had the young man to consider. She had to bring them together whether she liked it or not.

"Maudie, this is—" she turned back and smiled at van Stiegler, "this is—" But she was confused and she had to abandon the introduction altogether. Instead, she broke into a direct question.

"Those are your flower pictures, aren't they?" she asked.

It was enough for Maudie—more than enough you might say.

She turned to the young man, obviously greatly impressed; her lips apart, her eyes shining. My God, how attractive she was!

"Oh no, not really?" she cried. "How marvellous of you!"

But Johann van Stiegler was looking at Mary.

"You are sure we have not met before?"

"Oh no, but you were scribbling your signature all over that newspaper," she looked around to show it to him, but it had fallen on to the floor.

"Ah yes," he said, and—she couldn't be certain, of course —but she thought he was disappointed.

"Ah yes, you saw my signature," he said, flatly. He looked dejected. Mary felt helpless. She turned to Maudie. It was up to her to say something now.

Just then the little warehouse bell tinkled again, and this time it was one of the proprietors who came in, casually, like a client.

"Ah good!" said van Stiegler. "Coffee," he called out. Then he turned to Mary. "Coffee for you too?"

"Oh yes, coffee for us," said Mary, but she couldn't help wondering who was going to pay for it, and simultaneously she couldn't help noticing the shabbiness of his jacket. Well —they'd see! Meanwhile, she determined to ignore the plate of cakes that was put down with the coffee. And she hoped Maudie would too. She pushed the plate aside as a kind of hint to her, but Maudie leaned across and took a large bun filled with cream.

"Do you mind my asking you something—about your work—?" said Mary.

But Maudie interrupted.

"You are living in Ireland? I mean, you are not just here on a visit?"

There was intimacy and intimacy, and Mary felt nervous in case the young man might resent this question.

"I teach art in a college here," he said, and he did seem a little surprised, but Mary could see, too, that he was not at all displeased. He seemed to settle more comfortably into the conversation.

"It is very good for a while to go to another country," he said, "and this country is cheap. I have a flat in the next street to here, and it is very private. If I hang myself from the ceiling, it is all right—nobody knows; nobody cares. That is a good way to live when you paint."

Mary was prepared to ponder. "Do you think so?"

Maudie was not prepared to ponder. "How odd," she said, shortly, and then she looked at her watch. "I'll have to go," she said inexplicably.

They had finished the coffee. Immediately Mary's thoughts returned to the problem of who was to pay for it. It was a small affair for which to call up all one's spiritual resources, but she felt enormously courageous and determined when she heard herself ask in a loud voice for her bill.

"My bill, please," she called out, over the sound of spitting coffee on the gas stove.

Johann van Stiegler made no move to ask for his bill, and yet he was buttoning his jacket and folding his newspaper as if to leave too. Would his coffee go on her bill? Mary wondered.

It was all settled, however, in a second. The bill was for two eight-penny coffees, and one bun, and there was no charge for van Stiegler's coffee. He had some understanding with the owners, she supposed. Or perhaps he was not really going to leave then at all?

As they stood up, however, gloved and ready to depart, the young man bowed.

"Perhaps we go the same way?" They could see he was anxious to be polite.

"Oh, not at all," they said together, as if he had offered to escort them, and Maudie even laughed openly.

Then there was, of course, another ridiculous situation. Van Stiegler sat down again. Had they been too brusque? Had they hurt his feelings?

Oh, if only he wasn't a foreigner, thought Mary, and she hesitated. Maudie already had her hand on the door.

"I hope I will see some more of your work sometime," said Mary. It was not a question, merely a compliment.

But van Stiegler sprung to his feet again.

"Tonight after my classes I am bringing another picture to hang here," he said. "You would like to see it? I would be here—" he pulled out a large, old-fashioned watch, "—at ten minutes past nine."

"Oh, not tonight—I couldn't come back tonight," said Mary. "I live in the country, you see," she said, explaining and excusing herself. "Another time perhaps? It will be here for how long?"

She wasn't really listening to what he said. She was thinking that he had not asked if Maudie could come. Perhaps it was that, of the two of them, she looked the most likely to buy a picture, whereas Maudie, although in actual fact more likely to do so, looked less so. Or was it that he coupled them so that he thought if one came, both came. Or was it really Maudie he'd like to see again, and that he regarded her as a chaperone? Or was it—?

There was no knowing, however, and so she said goodbye again, and the next minute the little bell had tinkled over the door and they were in the street. In the street they looked at each other.

"Well! if ever there was—" began Maudie, but she didn't get time to finish her sentence. Behind them the little bell tinkled yet again, and their painter was out in the street with them.

"I forgot to give you the address of my flat—it is also my studio," he said. "I would be glad to show you my paintings at any time." He pulled out a notebook and tore out a sheet. "I will write it down," he said, concisely. And he did. But when he went to hand it to them, it was Maudie who took it. "I am nearly always there, except when I am at my classes," he said. And bowing, he turned and went back into the café.

They dared not laugh until they had walked some distance away, until they turned into the next street in fact.

"Well, I never!" said Maudie, and she handed the paper to Mary.

"Chatham Row," Mary read, "number 8."

"Will you go to see them?" asked Maudie.

Mary felt outraged.

"What do you take me for?" she asked. "I may be a bit unconventional, but can you see me presenting myself at his place? Would *you* go?"

"Oh, it's different for me," said Maudie, enigmatically. "And anyway, it was you he asked. But I see your point—it's a pity. Poor fellow!—he must be very lonely. I wish there was something we could do for him—someone to whom we could introduce him."

Mary looked at her. It had never occurred to her that he might be lonely! How was it that the obvious always escaped her?

They were in Grafton Street by this time.

"Well, I have some shopping to do. I suppose it's the same with you," said Maudie. "I am glad I had that talk with you. We must have another chat soon."

"Oh yes," said Mary, over-readily, replying to her adieux though, and not to the suggestion of their meeting again! She was anxious all at once to be rid of Maudie.

And yet, as she watched her walk away from her, making her passage quickly and expertly through the crowds in the street, Mary felt a sudden terrible aimlessness descend upon herself like a physical paralysis. She walked along, pausing to look in at the shop windows.

It was the evening hour when everyone in the streets was hurrying home, purposeful and intent. Even those who paused to look into the shop windows did so with direction and aim, darting their bright glances keenly, like birds. Their minds were all intent upon substantives; tangibles, while her mind was straying back to the student café, and the strange flower pictures on the walls; to the young man who was so vulnerable in his vanity: the legitimate vanity of his art.

It was so like Maudie to laugh at him. What did she know of an artist's mind? If Maudie had not been with her, it would have been so different. She might, for one thing, have got him to talk about his work, to explain the discrepancy between the loose style of the pictures on the wall and the exact, small sketches he'd been drawing on the margins of the paper.

She might even have taken up his invitation to go and see his paintings. Why had that seemed so unconventional—so laughable? Because of Maudie, that was why.

How ridiculous their scruples would have seemed to the young man. She could only hope he had not guessed them. She looked up at a clock. Supposing, right now, she were to slip back to the café and suggest that after all she found she would have time for a quick visit to his studio? Or would he have left the café? Better perhaps to call around to the studio? He would surely be back there now!

For a moment she stood debating the arguments for and against going back. Would it seem odd to him? Would he be surprised? But as if it were Maudie who put the questions, she frowned them down and all at once purposeful as anyone in the street, began to go back, headlong, you might say, towards Chatham Street.

At the point where two small streets crossed each other she had to pause, while a team of Guinness's dray horses turned with difficulty in the narrow cube of the intersection. And, while she waited impatiently, she caught sight of herself in the gilded mirror of a public house. For a second, the familiar sight gave her a misgiving of her mission, but as the dray horses moved out of the way, she told herself that her dowdy, lumpish, and unromantic figure vouched for her spiritual integrity. She pulled herself away from the face in the glass and hurried across the street.

Between two lock-up shops, down a short alley—roofed by the second story of the premises overhead, till it was like a tunnel—was his door. Away at the end of the tunnel the door could clearly be seen even from the middle of the street, for it was painted bright yellow. Odd that she had never seen it in the times she had passed that way. She crossed the street.

Once across the street, she ran down the tunnel, her footsteps echoing loud in her ears. And there on the door, tied to the latchet of the letter-box, was a piece of white cardboard with his name on it. Grabbing the knocker, she gave three clear hammer-strokes on the door.

The little alley was a sort of cul-de-sac; except for the street behind her and the door in front of her, it had no outlet. There was not even a skylight or an aperture of any kind. As for the premises into which the door led, there was no way of telling its size or its extent, or anything at all about it, until the door was opened.

Irresponsibly, she giggled. It was like the mystifying doors in the trunks of trees that beguiled her as a child in fairy tales and fantasies. Did this door, too, like those fairy doors, lead into rooms of possible amplitude, or would it be a cramped and poky place?

As she pondered upon what was within, seemingly so mysteriously sealed, she saw that—just as in a fairy tale—after all there was an aperture. The letter-box had lost its shutter, or lid, and it gaped open, a vacant hole in the wood, reminding her of a sleeping doll whose eyeballs had been poked back in its head, and creating an expression of vacancy and emptiness.

Impulsively, going down on one knee, she peered in through the slit.

At first she could see only segments of the objects within, but by moving her head, she was able to identify things; an unfinished canvas up against the splattered white wainscot, a bicycle-pump flat on the floor, the leg of a table, black iron bed-legs and, to her amusement, dangling down by the leg of the table, dripping their moisture in a pool on the floor, a pair of elongated, grey wool socks. It was, of course, only possible to see the lower portion of the room, but it seemed enough to infer conclusively that this was indeed a little room in a tree, no bigger than the bulk of the outer trunk, leading nowhere, and—sufficient or no—itself its own end.

There was just one break in the wainscot, where a door ran down to the floor, but this was so narrow and made of roughly jointed boards, that she took it to be the door of a press. And then, as she started moving, she saw something else, an intricate segment of fine wire spokes. It was a second before she realized it was the wheel of a bicycle.

So, a bicycle, too, lived here, in this little room in a tree-trunk!

Oh, poor young man, poor painter; poor foreigner, inept at finding the good lodgings in a strange city. Her heart went out to him.

It was just then that the boarded door—it couldn't have been a press after all—opened into the room, and she found herself staring at two feet. They were large feet, shoved into unlaced shoes, and they were bare to the white ankles. For, of course, she thought wildly, focusing her thoughts, his socks are washed! But her power to think clearly only lasted an instant. She sprang to her feet.

"Who iss that?" asked a voice. "Did someone knock?"

It was the voice of the man in the café. But where was she to find a voice with which to reply? And who was she to say what she was? Who—to this stranger—was she?

And if he opened the door, what then? All the thoughts and words that had, like a wind, blown her down this tunnel, subsided suddenly, and she stood, appalled, at where they had brought her.

"Who iss that?" came the voice within, troubled.

Staring at those white feet, thrust into the unlaced shoes, she felt that she would die on the spot if they moved an inch. She turned.

Ahead of her, bright, shining and clear, as if it were at the end of a powerful telescope, was the street. Not caring if her feet were heard, volleying and echoing as if she ran through a mighty drain-pipe, she kept running till she reached the street, kept running even then, jostling surprised shoppers, hitting her ankles off the wheel-knobs of push-cars and prams. Only when she came to the junction of the streets again, did she stop, as in the pub mirror she caught sight again of her familiar face. That face steadied her. How absurd to think that anyone would sinisterly follow this middle-age woman?

But suppose he had been in the outer room when she knocked! If he had opened the door? What would have happened then? What would she have said? A flush spread over her face. The only true words that she could have uttered were those that had sunk into her mind in the café; put there by Maudie.

"I'm lonely!" That was all she could have said. "I'm lonely. Are you?"

A deep shame came over her with this admission and, guiltily, she began to walk quickly onward again, towards Grafton Street. If anyone had seen her, there in that dark alleyway! If anyone could have looked into her mind, her heart!

And yet, was it so unnatural? Was it so hard to understand? So unforgivable?

As she passed the open door of the Carmelite Church she paused. Could she rid herself of her feeling of shame in the dark of the confessional? To the sin-accustomed ears of the wise old fathers her story would be lightweight; a tedious tale of scrupulosity. Was there no one, no one who'd understand?

She had reached Grafton Street once more, and stepped into its crowded thoroughfare. It was only a few minutes since she left it, but in the street the evasion of light had begun. Only the bustle of people, and the activity of traffic, made it seem that it was yet day. Away at the top of the street, in Stephen's Green, to which she turned, although the tops of the trees were still clear, branch for branch, in the last of the light, mist muted the outline of the bushes. If one were to put a hand between the railings now, it would be with a slight shock that the fingers would feel the little branches, like fine bones, under the feathers of mist. And in their secret nests the smaller birds were making faint avowals in the last of the day. It was the time at which she used to meet Richard.

"Oh Richard!" she cried, almost out loud, as she walked along by the railings to where the car was parked. "Oh Richard! it's you I want."

And as she cried out, her mind presented him to her, as she so often saw him, coming towards her: tall, handsome, and with his curious air of apartness from those around him. He had his hat in his hand, down by his side, as on a summer day he might trail a hand in water from the side of a boat. She wanted to preserve that picture of him for ever in an image, and only as she struggled to hold on to it did she realize there was no urgency in the search. She had a sense of having all the time in the world to look and look and look at him. That was the very way he used to come to meet her—indolently trailing the old felt hat, glad to be done with the day; and when they got nearer to each other she used to take such joy in his unsmiling face, with its happiness integral to it in all its features. It was the first time in the two years he'd been gone from her that she'd seen his face.

Not till she had taken out the key of the car, and gone straight around to the driver's side, not stupidly, as so often, to the passenger seat—not till then did she realize what she had achieved. Yet she had no more than got back her rights. No more. It was not a subject for amazement. By what means exactly had she got them back though—in that little café? That was the wonder.

TILLIE OLSEN was born in Omaha, Nebraska, in 1913. She is married and has raised four daughters in San Francisco. In her article entitled "Silences: When Writers Don't Write" (adapted from a talk "Death of the Creative Process" given at the Radcliffe Institute for Independent Study), she describes, out of deep personal experience, the distractions and pressures that keep a writer from her work. For twenty years or so, Tillie Olsen led what she calls "the triple life" of mothering and housewifery, of working full-time as a transcriber in a dairy equipment company and part-time as a Kelly Girl typist and Western Agency Girl secretary, and of trying to be a writer—on the bus going back and forth to work and in "the deep night hours for as long as I could stay awake, after the kids were in bed, after the household tasks were done, sometimes during. It is no accident that the first work I considered publishable began. " 'I stand here ironing, and what you asked me moves tormented back and forth with the iron.' "

Her writing life was saved by a Stanford University creative writing fellowship in 1955 and a Ford grant in 1959. In 1961 she won the O. Henry Award for the best American short story of the year with "Tell Me a Riddle," the title story in the collection of four stories that was published in the same year. Critic Irving Howe praised the collection in his review but remarked upon Mrs. Olsen's "narrowness of experience," a comment supremely ironic to those familiar with the wide-ranging, free-wheeling resourcefulness demanded by "the triple life." Novelist Richard Elman came closer to the source of Mrs. Olsen's disturbing power in his review in *Commonweal*: "With a faultless accuracy, her stories treat the very young, the mature, the dying—poor people without the means to buy or invent lies about their situations. . . ." Since 1961 Tillie Olsen's reputation as one of the most profound (though not prolific) writers of contemporary fiction has grown. "Tell Me a Riddle" was included in the anthology *Twelve from the Sixties,* subtitled, *The Decade's Most Provocative and Significant Writers.* She has lectured at the Poetry Center in New York City, been resident scholar at the Radcliffe Institute for Independent Study, and finished a novel she began before she started raising a family. Reading her fiction to one informal audience of writers in San Francisco she said that women who write must continue to "voice the unvoiced, to pass on to our children the experience of our world, what we know and believe."

But her success does not cancel out the burden of her article about the writer's unnatural silences. She would still affirm that women writers who must hold a job, who mother children, and who cannot afford household help, cannot keep what Henry James has called the terrible law of the artist, the law of fructification and fertilization: "the old, old lesson of the art of meditation. To woo combinations and inspirations into being by a depth and continuity of attention and meditation."

I STAND HERE IRONING

I stand here ironing, and what you asked me moves tormented back and forth with the iron.

"I wish you would manage the time to come in and talk with me about your daughter. I'm sure you can help me understand her. She's a youngster who needs help and whom I'm deeply interested in helping."

"Who needs help." . . . Even if I came, what good would it do? You think because I am her mother I have a key, or that in some way you could use me as a key? She has lived for nineteen years. There is all that life that has happened outside of me, beyond me.

And when is there time to remember, to sift, to weigh, to estimate, to total? I will start and there will be an interruption and I will have to gather it all together again. Or I will become engulfed with all I did or did not do, with what should have been and what cannot be helped.

She was a beautiful baby. The first and only one of our five that was beautiful at birth. You do not guess how new and uneasy her tenancy in her now-loveliness. You did not know her all those years she was thought homely, or see her poring over her baby pictures, making me tell her over and over how beautiful she had been—and would be, I would tell her—and was now, to the seeing eye. But the seeing eyes were few or non-existent. Including mine.

I nursed her. They feel that's important nowadays. I nursed all the children, but with her, with all the fierce rigidity of first motherhood, I did like the books then said. Though her cries battered me to trembling and my breasts ached with swollenness, I waited till the clock decreed.

Why do I put that first? I do not even know if it matters, or if it explains anything.

She was a beautiful baby. She blew shining bubbles of sound. She loved motion, loved light, loved color and music and textures. She would lie on the floor in her blue overalls patting the surface so hard in ecstasy her hands and feet would blur. She was a miracle to me, but when she was eight months old I had to leave her daytimes with the woman downstairs to whom she was no miracle at all, for I worked or looked for work and for Emily's father, who "could no longer endure" (he wrote in his good-bye note) "sharing want with us."

I was nineteen. It was the pre-relief, pre-WPA world of the depression. I would start running as soon as I got off the streetcar, running up the stairs, the place smelling sour, and awake or asleep to startle awake, when she saw me she would break into a clogged weeping that could not be comforted, a weeping I can hear yet.

After a while I found a job hashing at night so I could be with her days, and it was better. But it came to where I had to bring her to his family and leave her.

It took a long time to raise the money for her fare back. Then she got chicken pox and I had to wait longer. When she finally came, I hardly knew her, walking quick and nervous like her father, looking like her father, thin, and dressed in a shoddy red that yellowed her skin and glared at the pockmarks. All the baby loveliness gone.

She was two. Old enough for nursery school they said, and I did not know then what I know now—the fatigue of the long day, and the lacerations of group life in the kinds of nurseries that are only parking places for children.

Except that it would have made no difference if I had known. It was the only place there was. It was the only way we could be together, the only way I could hold a job.

And even without knowing, I knew. I knew the teacher that was evil because all these years it has curdled into my memory, the little boy hunched in the corner, her rasp, "why aren't you outside, because Alvin hits you? that's no reason, go out, scaredy." I knew Emily hated it even if she did not clutch and implore "don't go Mommy" like the other children, mornings.

She always had a reason why we should stay home. Momma, you look sick, Momma. I feel sick. Momma, the teachers aren't there today, they're sick. Momma, we can't go, there was a fire there last night. Momma, it's a holiday today, no school, they told me.

But never a direct protest, never rebellion. I think of our others in their three-, four-year-oldness—the explosions, the tempers, the denunciations, the demands—and I feel suddenly ill. I put the iron down. What in me demanded that goodness in her? And what was the cost, the cost to her of such goodness?

The old man living in the back once said in his gentle way: "You should smile at Emily more when you look at her." What *was* in my face when I looked at her? I loved her. There were all the acts of love.

It was only with the others I remembered what he said, and it was the face of joy, and not of care or tightness or worry I turned to them—too late for Emily. She does not smile easily, let alone almost always as her brothers and sisters do. Her face is closed and sombre, but when she wants, how fluid. You must have seen it in her pantomimes, you spoke of her rare gift for comedy on the stage that rouses a laughter out of the audience so dear they applaud and applaud and do not want to let her go.

Where does it come from, that comedy? There was none of it in her when she came back to me that second time, after I had had to send her away again. She had a new daddy now to learn to love, and I think perhaps it was a better time.

Except when we left her alone nights, telling ourselves she was old enough.

"Can't you go some other time, Mommy, like tomorrow?" she would ask. "Will it be just a little while you'll be gone? Do you promise?"

The time we came back, the front door open, the clock on the floor in the hall. She rigid awake. "It wasn't just a little while. I didn't cry. Three times I called you, just three times, and then I ran downstairs to open the door so you could come faster. The clock talked loud. I threw it away, it scared me what it talked."

She said the clock talked loud again that night I went to the hospital to have Susan. She was delirious with the fever that comes before red measles, but she was fully conscious all the week I was gone and the week after we were home when she could not come near the new baby or me.

She did not get well. She stayed skeleton thin, not wanting to eat, and night after night she had nightmares. She would call for me, and I would rouse from exhaustion to sleepily call back: "You're all right, darling, go to sleep, it's just a dream," and if she still called, in a sterner voice, "now go to sleep, Emily, there's nothing to hurt you." Twice, only twice, when I had to get up for Susan anyhow, I went in to sit with her.

Now when it is too late (as if she would let me hold and comfort her like I do the others) I get up and go to her at once at her moan or restless stirring. "Are you awake, Emily? Can I get you something?" And the answer is always the same: "No, I'm all right, go back to sleep, Mother."

They persuaded me at the clinic to send her away to a convalescent home in the country where "she can have the kind of food and care you can't manage for her, and you'll be free to concentrate on the new baby." They still send children to that place. I see pictures on the society page of sleek young women planning affairs to raise money for it, or dancing at the affairs, or decorating Easter eggs or filling Christmas stockings for the children.

They never have a picture of the children so I do not know if the girls still wear those gigantic red bows and the ravaged looks on the every other Sunday when parents can come to visit "unless otherwise notified"—as we were notified the first six weeks.

Oh it is a handsome place, green lawns and tall trees and fluted flower beds. High up on the balconies of each cottage the children stand, the girls in their red bows and white dresses, the boys in white suits and giant red ties. The parents stand below shrieking up to be heard and the children shriek down to be heard, and between them the invisible wall "Not To Be Contaminated by Parental Germs or Physical Affection."

There was a tiny girl who always stood hand in hand with Emily. Her parents never came. One visit she was gone. "They moved her to Rose Cottage" Emily shouted in explanation. "They don't like you to love anybody here."

She wrote once a week, the labored writing of a seven-year-old. "I am fine. How is the baby. If I write my leter nicly I will have a star. Love." There never was a star. We wrote every other day, letters she could never hold or keep but only hear read—once. "We simply do not have room for children to keep any personal possessions," they patiently explained when we pieced one Sunday's shrieking together to plead how much it would mean to Emily, who loved so to keep things, to be allowed to keep her letters and cards.

Each visit she looked frailer. "She isn't eating," they told us.

(They had runny eggs for breakfast or mush with lumps, Emily said later, I'd hold it in my mouth and not swallow. Nothing ever tasted good, just when they had chicken.)

It took us eight months to get her released home, and only the fact that she gained back so little of her seven lost pounds convinced the social worker.

I used to try to hold and love her after she came back, but her body would stay stiff, and after a while she'd push away. She ate little. Food sickened her, and I think much of life too. Oh she had physical lightness and brightness, twinkling by on skates, bouncing like a ball up and down up and down over the jump rope, skimming over the hill; but these were momentary.

She fretted about her appearance, thin and dark and foreign-looking at a time when every little girl was supposed to look or thought she should look a chubby blonde replica of Shirley Temple. The doorbell sometimes rang for her, but no one seemed to come and play in the house or be a best friend. Maybe because we moved so much.

There was a boy she loved painfully through two school semesters. Months later she told me how she had taken pennies from my purse to buy him candy. "Licorice was his favorite and I brought him some every day, but he still liked Jennifer better'n me. Why, Mommy?" The kind of question for which there is no answer.

School was a worry to her. She was not glib or quick in a world where glibness and quickness were easily confused with ability to learn. To her overworked and exasperated teachers she was an overconscientious "slow learner" who kept trying to catch up and was absent entirely too often.

I let her be absent, though sometimes the illness was imaginary. How different from my now-strictness about attendance with the others. I wasn't working. We had a new baby, I was home anyhow. Sometimes, after Susan grew old enough, I would keep her home from school, too, to have them all together.

Mostly Emily had asthma, and her breathing, harsh and labored, would fill the house with a curiously tranquil sound. I would bring the two old dresser mirrors and her boxes of collections to her bed. She would select beads and single earrings, bottle tops and shells, dried flowers and pebbles, old postcards and scraps, all sorts of oddments; then she and Susan would play Kingdom, setting up landscapes and furniture, peopling them with action.

Those were the only times of peaceful companionship between her and Susan, no, Emily toward Susan that poisonous feeling between them, that terrible balancing of hurts and needs I had to do between the two, and did so badly, those earlier years.

Oh there are conflicts between the others too, each one human, needing, demanding, hurting, taking—but only between Emily and Susan. I have edged away from it, that no, Emily toward Susan that corroding resentment. It seems so obvious on the surface, yet it is not obvious. Susan, the second child, Susan, golden- and curly-haired and chubby, quick and articulate and assured, everything in appearance and manner Emily was not; Susan, not able to resist Emily's precious things, losing or sometimes clumsily breaking them; Susan telling jokes and riddles to company for applause while Emily sat silent (to say to me later: that was *my* riddle, Mother, I told it to Susan); Susan, who for all the five years' difference in age was just a year behind Emily in developing physically.

I am glad for that slow physical development that widened the difference between her and her contemporaries, though she suffered over it. She was too vulnerable for that terrible world of youthful competition, of preening and parading, of constant measuring of yourself against every other, of envy, "If I had that copper hair," "If I had that skin. . . ." She tormented herself enough about not looking like the others, there was enough of the unsureness, the having to be conscious of words before you speak, the constant caring—what are they thinking of me? without having it all magnified by the merciless physical drives.

Ronnie is calling. He is wet and I change him. It is rare there is such a cry now. That time of motherhood is almost behind me when the ear is not one's own but must always be racked and listening for the child cry, the child call. We sit for a while and I hold him, looking out over the city spread in charcoal with its soft aisles of light. *"Shoogily,"* he breathes and curls closer. I carry him back to bed, asleep. *Shoogily*. A funny word, a family word, inherited from Emily, invented by her to say: *comfort*.

In this and other ways she leaves her seal, I say aloud. And startle at my saying it. What do I mean? What did I start to gather together, to try and make coherent? I was at the terrible, growing years. War years. I do not remember them well. I was working, there were four smaller ones now, there was not time for her. She had to help be a mother, and housekeeper, and shopper. She had to set her seal. Mornings of crisis and near hysteria trying to get lunches packed, hair combed, coats and shoes found, everyone to school or Child Care on time, the baby ready for transportation. And always the paper scribbled on by a smaller one, the book looked at by Susan then mislaid, the homework not done. Running out to that huge school where she was one, she was lost, she was a drop; suffering over the unpreparedness, stammering and unsure in her classes.

There was so little time left at night after the kids were bedded down. She would struggle over books, always eating (it was in those years she developed her enormous appetite that is legendary in our family) and I would be ironing, or preparing food for the next day, or writing V-mail to Bill, or tending the baby. Sometimes, to make me laugh, or out of her despair, she would imitate happenings or types at school.

I think I said once: "Why don't you do something like this in the school amateur show?" One morning she phoned me at work, hardly understandable through the weeping:

"Mother, I did it. I won, I won; they gave me first prize; they clapped and clapped and wouldn't let me go."

Now suddenly she was Somebody, and as imprisoned in her difference as she had been in anonymity.

She began to be asked to perform at other high schools, even in colleges, then at city and statewide affairs. The first one we went to, I only recognized her that first moment when thin, shy, she almost drowned herself into the curtains. Then: Was this Emily? The control, the command, the convulsing and deadly clowning, the spell, then the roaring, stamping audience, unwilling to let this rare and precious laughter out of their lives.

Afterwards: You ought to do something about her with a gift like that—but without money or knowing how, what does one do? We have left it all to her, and the gift has as often eddied inside, clogged and clotted, as been used and growing.

She is coming. She runs up the stairs two at a time with her light graceful step, and I know she is happy tonight. Whatever it was that occasioned your call did not happen today.

"Aren't you ever going to finish the ironing, Mother? Whistler painted his mother in a rocker. I'd have to paint mine standing over an ironing board." This is one of her communicative nights and she tells me everything and nothing as she fixes herself a plate of food out of the icebox.

She is so lovely. Why did you want me to come in at all? Why were you concerned? She will find her way.

She starts up the stairs to bed. "Don't get me up with the rest in the morning." "But I thought you were having midterms." "Oh, those," she comes back in, kisses me, and says quite lightly, "in a couple of years when we'll all be atom-dead they won't matter a bit."

She has said it before. She *believes* it. But because I have been dredging the past, and all that compounds a human being is so heavy and meaningful in me, I cannot endure it tonight.

I will never total it all. I will never come in to say: She was a child seldom smiled at. Her father left me before she was a year old. I had to work her first six years when there was work, or I sent her home and to his relatives. There were years she had care she hated. She was dark and thin and foreign-looking in a world where the prestige went to blondeness and curly hair and dimples, she was slow where glibness was prized. She was a child of anxious, not proud, love. We were poor and could not afford for her the soil of easy growth. I was a young mother, I was a distracted mother. There were the other children pushing up, demanding. Her younger sister seemed all that she was not. There were years she did not want me to touch her. She kept too much in herself, her life was such she had to keep too much in herself. My wisdom came too late. She has much to her and probably little will come of it. She is a child of her age, of depression, of war, of fear.

Let her be. So all that is in her will not bloom—but in how many does it? There is still enough left to live by. Only help her to know—help make it so there is cause for her to know—that she is more than this dress on the ironing board, helpless before the iron.

MAEVE BRENNAN was born in Ireland in 1917 and moved to America with her family when she was seventeen. As a girl in convent school she secretly kept a journal and wrote poems until the nuns found them. Her first writing job was at *Harper's Bazaar. New Yorker* editor William Shawn hired her to write the Long-Winded Lady column in the magazine's "Talk of the Town" section. For twenty years now she has been writing about the city, getting up at dawn to people-watch and eavesdrop, with only an open book for camouflage. "Nobody has ever noticed," she says, "that I never turn the page." She loves New York "because the chances for being invisible are so much greater."

All along she has been writing short stories, which have their settings in Dublin as well as in New York and environs. Scribners published her first book of fiction, *In and Out of Never-Never Land*, in 1969 and five years later another collection of short stories entitled *Christmas Eve.* Most of these stories had appeared in *The New Yorker* between 1953 and 1973. Her story "Family Walls" was included in *The Best American Short Stories of 1973.*

It is difficult to exaggerate her mastery of the art of fiction. Her sense of the spirit underlying the tangible world is communicated so effectively that reading her stories is always an experience of seeing anew and feeling deeply. One must go carefully through her work in order not to miss the wit and the quick soundings of the hidden reserves of tenderness. Her story "Christmas Eve" is a celebration of family life performed with such utter simplicity and grace that it is quite unforgettable. Her story about a marriage, "The Springs of Affection," suggests an imagination rooted in rich and ancient soil. Like her Irish literary ancestors, Yeats and Joyce and John Millington Synge, she is able to bring to life the extraordinariness of the ordinary with a sureness that makes her art seem sacramental.

Maeve Brennan
(1917–   )

THE ELDEST CHILD

Mrs. Bagot had lived in the house for fifteen years, ever since her marriage. Her three children had been born there, in the upstairs front bedroom, and she was glad of that, because her first child, her son, was dead, and it comforted her to think that she was still familiar with what had been his one glimpse of earth—he had died at three days. At the time he died she said to herself that she would never get used to it, and what she meant by that was that as long as she lived she would never accept what had happened in the mechanical subdued way that the rest of them accepted it. They carried on, they talked and moved about her room as though when they tidied the baby away they had really tidied him away, and it seemed to her that more than anything else they expressed the hope that nothing more would be said about him. They behaved as though what had happened was finished, as though some ordinary event had taken place and come to an end in a natural way. There had not been an ordinary event, and it had not come to an end.

Lying in her bed, Mrs. Bagot thought her husband and the rest of them seemed very strange, or else, she thought fearfully, perhaps it was she herself who was strange, delirious, or even a bit unbalanced. If she was unbalanced she wasn't going to let them know about it—not even Martin, who kept looking at her with frightened eyes and telling her she must try to rest. It might be better not to talk, yet she was very anxious to explain how she felt. Words did no good. Either they did not want to hear her, or they were not able to hear her. What she was trying to tell them seemed very simple to her. What had happened could not come to an end, that was all. It could not come to an end. Without a memory, how was the baby going to find his way? Mrs. Bagot would have liked to ask that question, but she wanted to express it properly, and she thought if she could just be left alone for a while she would be able to find the right words, so that she could make herself clearly understood—but they wouldn't leave her alone. They kept trying to rouse her, and yet when she spoke for any length of time they always silenced her by telling her it was God's will. She had accepted God's will all her life without argument, and she was not arguing now, but she knew that what had happened was not finished, and she was sure it was not God's will that she be left in this bewilderment. All she wanted was to say how she felt, but they mentioned God's will as though they were slamming a door between her and some territory that was forbidden to her. But only to her; everybody else knew all about it. She alone must lie quiet and silent under this semblance of ignorance that they wrapped about her like a shroud. They wanted her to be silent and not speak of this knowledge she had now, the knowledge that made her afraid. It was the same knowledge they all had, of course, but they did not want it spoken of. Everything about her seemed false, and Mrs. Bagot was tired of everything. She was tired of being told that she must do this for her own good and that she must do that for her own good, and it annoyed her when they said she was being brave—she was being what she had to be, she had no alternative. She felt very uncomfortable and out of place, and as though she had failed, but she did not know whether to push her failure away or comfort it, and in any case it seemed to have drifted out of reach.

She was not making sense. She could not get her thoughts sorted out. Something was drifting away—that was as far as she could go in her mind. No wonder she couldn't talk properly. What she wanted to say was really quite simple. Two things. First, there was the failure that had emptied and darkened her mind until nothing remained now but a black wash. Second, there was something that drifted and dwindled, always dwindling, until it was now no more than a small shape, very small, not to be identified except as something lost. Mrs. Bagot thought she was the only one who could still identify that shape, and she was afraid to take her eyes off it, because it became constantly smaller, showing as it diminished the new horizons it was reaching, although it drifted so gently it seemed not to move at all. Mrs. Bagot would never have dreamed her mind could stretch so far, or that her thoughts could follow so faithfully, or that she could watch so steadily, without tears or sleep.

The fierce demands that had been made on her body and on her attention were finished. She could have met all those demands, and more. She could have moved mountains. She had found that the more the child demanded of her, the more she had to give. Her strength came up in waves that had their source in a sea of calm and unconquerable devotion. The child's holy trust made her open her eyes, and she took stock of herself and found that everything was all right, and that she could meet what challenges arose and meet them well, and that she had nothing to apologize for—on the contrary, she had every reason to rejoice. Her days took on an orderliness that introduced her to a sense of ease and confidence she had never been told about. The house became a kingdom, significant, private, and safe. She smiled often, a smile of innocent importance.

Perhaps she had let herself get too proud. She had seen at once that the child was unique. She had been thankful, but perhaps not thankful enough. The first minute she had held him in her arms, immediately after he was born, she had seen his friendliness. He was fine. There was nothing in the world the matter with him. She had remarked to herself that his tiny face had a very humorous expression, as though he already knew exactly what was going on. And he was determined to live. He was full of fight. She had felt him fight toward life with all her strength, and then again, with all her strength. In a little while, he would have recognized her.

What she watched now made no demands on anyone. There was no impatience there, and no impatience in her, either. She lay on her side, and her hand beat gently on the pillow in obedience to words, an old tune, that had been sounding in her head for some time, and that she now began to listen to. It was an old song, very slow, a tenor voice from long ago and far away. She listened idly.

> "Oft in the stilly night
> Ere slumber's chain hath bound me
> Fond memory brings the light
> Of other days around me."

Over and over and over again, the same words, the same kind, simple words. Mrs. Bagot thought she must have heard that song a hundred times or more.

"Oft in the stilly night
Ere slumber's chain hath bound me
Fond memory brings the light
Of other days around me.
The smiles, the tears, of boyhood's years
The words of love then spoken
The eyes that shone, now dimmed and gone
The cheerful hearts now broken."

It was a very kind song. She had never noticed the words before, even though she knew them well. Loving words, loving eyes, loving hearts. The faraway voice she listened to was joined by others, as the first bird of dawn is joined by other birds, all telling the same story, telling it over and over again, because it is the only story they know.

There was the song, and then, there was the small shape that drifted uncomplainingly from distant horizon to still more distant horizon. Mrs. Bagot closed her eyes. She felt herself being beckoned to a place where she could hide, for the time being.

For the past day or so, she had turned from everyone, even from Martin. He no longer attempted to touch her. He had not even touched her hand since the evening he knelt down beside the bed and tried to put his arms around her. She struggled so fiercely against him that he had to let her go, and he stood up and stepped away from her. It really seemed she might injure herself, fighting against him, and that she would rather injure herself than lie quietly against him, even for a minute. He could not understand her. It was his loss as much as hers, but she behaved as though it had to do only with her. She pushed him away, and then when she was free of him she turned her face away from him and began crying in a way that pleaded for attention and consolation from someone, but not from him—that was plain. But before that, when she was pushing him away, he had seen her face, and the expression on it was of hatred. She might have been a wild animal, for all the control he had over her then, but if so she was a wild animal in a trap, because she was too weak to go very far. He pitied her, and the thought sped through his mind that if she could get up and run, or fly, he would let her go as far as she wished, and hope she would come back to him in her own time, when her anger and grief were spent. But he forgot that thought immediately in his panic at her distress, and he called down to the woman who had come in to help around the house, and asked her to come up at once. She had heard the noise and was on her way up anyway, and she was in the room almost as soon as he called—Mrs. Knox, a small, red-faced, gray-haired woman who enjoyed the illusion that life had nothing to teach her.

"Oh, I've been afraid of this all day," she said confidently, and she began to lift Mrs. Bagot up so that she could straighten the pillows and prop her up for her tea. But Mrs. Bagot struck out at the woman and began crying, "Oh, leave me alone, leave me alone. Why can't the two of you leave me alone." Then she wailed, "Oh, leave me alone," in a high strange voice, an artificial voice, and at that moment Mr. Bagot became convinced that she was acting, and that the best thing to do was walk off and leave her there, whether that was what she really wanted or not. Oh, but he loved her. He stared at her, and said to himself that it would have given him the greatest joy to see her lying there with the baby in her arms, but although that was true, the reverse was not true—to see her lying there as she was did not cause him terrible grief or anything like it. He felt ashamed and lonely and impatient, and he longed to say to her, "Delia, stop all this nonsense and let me talk to you." He wanted to appear masterful and kind and understanding, but she drowned him out with her wails, and he made up his mind she was acting, because if she was not acting, and if the grief she felt was real, then it was excessive grief, and perhaps incurable. She was getting stronger every day, the doctor had said so, and she had better learn to control herself or she would be a nervous wreck. And it wasn't a bit like her, to have no thought for him, or for what he might be suffering. It wasn't like her at all. She was always kind. He began to fear she would never be the same. He would have liked to kneel down beside the bed and talk to her in a very quiet voice, and make her understand that he knew what she was going through, and that he was going through much the same thing himself, and to ask her not to shut him away from her. But he felt afraid of her, and in any case Mrs. Knox was in the room. He was helpless. He was trying to think of something to say, not to walk out in silence, when Mrs. Knox came around the end of the bed and touched his arm familiarly, as though they were conspirators.

"The poor child is upset," she said. "We'll leave her by

herself awhile, and then I'll bring her up something to eat. Now, you go along down. I have your own tea all ready."

Delia turned her head on the pillow and looked at him. "Martin," she said, "I am not angry with you."

He would have gone to her then, but Mrs. Knox spoke at once. "We know you're not angry, Mrs. Bagot," she said. "Now, you rest yourself, and I'll be back in a minute with your tray." She gave Martin a little push to start him out of the room, and since Delia was already turning her face away, he walked out and down the stairs.

There seemed to be no end to the damage—even the house looked bleak and the furniture looked poor and cheap. It was only a year since they moved into the house, and it had all seemed lovely then. Only a year. He was beginning to fear that Delia had turned against him. He had visions of awful scenes and strains in the future, a miserable life. He wished they could go back to the beginning and start all over again, but the place where they had stood together, where they had been happy, was all trampled over and so spoiled that it seemed impossible ever to make it smooth again. And how could they even begin to make it smooth with this one memory, which they should have shared, standing like an enemy between them and making enemies out of them. He would not let himself think of the baby. He might never be able to forget the shape of the poor little defeated bundle he had carried out of the bedroom in his arms, and that he had cried over down here in the hall, but he was not going to let his mind dwell on it, not for one minute. He wanted Delia as she used to be. He wanted the girl who would never have struck out at him, or spoken roughly to him. He was beginning to see there were things about her that he had never guessed at and that he did not want to know about. He thought, Better let her rest, and let this fit work itself out. Maybe tomorrow she'll be herself again. He had a fancy that when he next approached Delia it would be on tiptoe, going very quietly, hardly breathing, moving into her presence without a sound that might startle her, or surprise her, or even wake her up, so that he might find her again as she had been the first time he saw her, quiet, untroubled, hardly speaking, alone, altogether alone and all his.

Mrs. Bagot was telling the truth when she told Martin she was not angry with him. It irritated her that he thought all he had to do was put his arms around her and all her sorrow would go away, but she wasn't really angry with him. What it was—he held her so tightly that she was afraid she might lose sight of the baby, and the fear made her frantic. The baby must not drift out of sight, that was her only thought, and that is why she struck out at Martin and begged to be left alone. As he walked out of the room, she turned her face away so that he would not see the tears beginning to pour down her face again. Then she slept. When Martin came up to the room next time, she was asleep, and not, as he suspected, pretending to be asleep, but he was grateful for the pretense, if that is what it was, and he crept away, back downstairs to his book.

Mrs. Bagot slept for a long time. When she woke up, the room was dark and the house was silent. Outside was silent too; she could hear nothing. This was the front bedroom, where she and Martin slept together, and she lay in their big bed. The room was made irregular by its windows—a bow window, and then, in the flat section of wall that faced the door, French windows. The French windows were partly open, and the long white net curtains that covered them moved gently in a breeze Mrs. Bagot could not feel. She had washed all the curtains last week, and starched them, getting ready for the baby. In the dim light of the street lamp, she could see the dark roof line of the row of houses across the street, and beyond the houses a very soft blackness, the sky. She was much calmer than she had been, and she no longer feared that she would lose sight of the small shape that had drifted, she noticed, much further away while she slept. He was travelling a long way, but she would watch him. She was his mother, and it was all she could do for him now. She could do it. She was weak, and the world was very shaky, but the light of other days shone steadily and showed the truth. She was no longer bewildered, and the next time Martin came to stand hopefully beside her bed she smiled at him and spoke to him in her ordinary voice.

CARSON McCULLERS was born in Columbia, Georgia, in 1917. As a child, she practiced the piano five hours a day, planning to be a concert pianist. She raised money to come to New York and study at the Juilliard School of Music by giving lectures on music appreciation to her mother's friends. There is a legend, recounted by her good friend Tennessee Williams in his essay "Praise to Assenting Angels," that once in the city she unwittingly took a room in a house of prostitution, made friends with the tenants, and trusted one of them to show her the subway route to Juilliard. When her guide disappeared with her tuition money, Carson McCullers gave up her plans for a musical career and turned to writing. She studied it at night, with Sylvia Chatfield Bates at New York University, and with Whit Burnett at Columbia. Burnett was editor with Martha Foley of *Story* magazine, in which "Wunderkind" appeared as McCullers's first published story. Her first novel, *The Heart Is a Lonely Hunter,* was published when she was twenty-three, and from then on she was famous. In the opinion of Tennessee Williams she was the only great talent to appear in America since the generation of major writers that emerged in the twenties (Crane, Katherine Anne Porter, cummings, Faulkner, Hemingway, Fitzgerald, and Eliot).

Carson McCullers suffered from poor health all her life. At the age of thirty-one, a series of strokes left her paralyzed on the left side; subsequent strokes and operations led to her having to type her novels with one finger, then to write in longhand, and finally to dictate. Her life was also marked by the sorrow of two difficult marriages to the same man, as well as by the constant need for money to pay her medical bills. She kept writing until seven weeks before she died of a brain hemorrhage in 1967.

Like many writers, she has been most admired by other

writers, especially Europeans. Dame Edith Sitwell said that Carson McCullers "has a great poet's eye and mind and senses, together with a great prose writer's sense of construction and character. She is a transcendental writer." Asked to name the contemporary American writers she read most, Doris Lessing mentioned Malamud, Mailer, Algren, Heller, "and, of course, Carson McCullers." In the magazine journalism she often had to resort to in order to pay her medical bills she wrote with spirited disingenuousness about the writers she loved (Dostoevsky, Isak Dinesen, Faulkner) and the writer's art: "Above all, love is the main generator of all good writing. Love, passion, compassion are all welded together."

Carson McCullers
(1917–1967)

WUNDERKIND

She came into the living room, her music satchel plopping against her winter-stockinged legs and her other arm weighted down with school books, and stood for a moment listening to the sounds from the studio. A soft procession of piano chords and the tuning of a violin. Then Mister Bilderbach called out to her in his chunky, guttural tones: "That you, Bienchen?"

As she jerked off her mittens she saw that her fingers were twitching to the motions of the fugue she had practiced that morning. "Yes," she answered. "It's me."

"I," the voice corrected. "Just a moment."

She could hear Mister Lafkowitz talking—his words spun out in a silky, unintelligible hum. A voice almost like a woman's, she thought, compared to Mister Bilderbach's. Restlessness scattered her attention. She fumbled with her geometry book and *Le Voyage de Monsieur Perrichon* before putting them on the table. She sat down on the sofa and began to take her music from the satchel. Again she saw her hands—the quivering tendons that stretched down from her knuckles, the sore finger tip capped with curled, dingy tape. The sight sharpened the fear that had begun to torment her for the past few months.

Noiselessly she mumbled a few phrases of encouragement to herself. A good lesson—a good lesson—like it used to be— Her lips closed as she heard the stolid sound of Mister Bilderbach's footsteps across the floor of the studio and the creaking of the door as it slid open.

For a moment she had the peculiar feeling that during most of the fifteen years of her life she had been looking at the face and shoulders that jutted from behind the door, in a silence disturbed only by the muted, blank plucking of a violin string. Mister Bilderbach. Her teacher, Mister Bilderbach. The quick eyes behind the horn-rimmed glasses; the light, thin hair and the narrow face beneath; the lips full and loose shut and the lower one pink and shining from the bites of his teeth; the forked veins in his temples throbbing plainly enough to be observed across the room.

"Aren't you a little early?" he asked, glancing at the clock on the mantelpiece that had pointed to five minutes of twelve for a month. "Josel's in here. We're running over a little sonatina by someone he knows."

"Good," she said, trying to smile. "I'll listen." She could see her fingers sinking powerless into a blur of piano keys. She felt tired—felt that if he looked at her much longer her hands might tremble.

He stood uncertain, halfway in the room. Sharply his teeth pushed down on his bright, swollen lip. "Hungry, Bienchen?" he asked. "There's some apple cake Anna made, and milk."

"I'll wait till afterward," she said. "Thanks."

"After you finish with a very fine lesson—eh?" His smile seemed to crumble at the corners.

There was a sound from behind him in the studio and Mister Lafkowitz pushed at the other panel of the door and stood beside him.

"Frances?" he said, smiling. "And how is the work coming now?"

Without meaning to, Mister Lafkowitz always made her feel clumsy and overgrown. He was such a small man himself, with a weary look when he was not holding his violin. His eyebrows curved high above his sallow Jewish face as though asking a question, but the lids of his eyes drowsed languorous and indifferent. Today he seemed distracted. She watched him come into the room for no apparent purpose, holding his pearl-tipped bow in his still fingers, slowly gliding the white horsehair through a chalky piece of rosin. His eyes were sharp bright slits today and the linen handkerchief that flowed down from his collar darkened the shadows beneath them.

"I gather you're doing a lot now," smiled Mister Lafkowitz, although she had not yet answered the question.

She looked at Mister Bilderbach. He turned away. His heavy shoulders pushed the door open wide so that the late afternoon sun came through the window of the studio and shafted yellow over the dusty living room. Behind her teacher she could see the squat long piano, the window, and the bust of Brahms.

"No," she said to Mister Lafkowitz, "I'm doing terribly."

Her thin fingers flipped at the pages of her music. "I don't know what's the matter," she said, looking at Mister Bilderbach's stooped muscular back that stood tense and listening.

Mister Lafkowitz smiled. "There are times, I suppose, when one—"

A harsh chord sounded from the piano. "Don't you think we'd better get on with this?" asked Mister Bilderbach.

"Immediately," said Mister Lafkowitz, giving the bow one more scrape before starting toward the door. She could see him pick up his violin from the top of the piano. He caught her eye and lowered the instrument. "You've seen the picture of Heime?"

Her fingers curled tight over the sharp corner of the satchel. "What picture?"

"One of Heime in the *Musical Courier* there on the table. Inside the top cover."

The sonatina began. Discordant yet somehow simple. Empty but with a sharp-cut style of its own. She reached for the magazine and opened it.

There Heime was—in the left-hand corner. Holding his violin with his fingers hooked down over the strings for a pizzicato. With his dark serge knickers strapped neatly beneath his knees, a sweater and rolled collar. It was a bad picture. Although it was snapped in profile his eyes were cut around toward the photographer and his finger looked as though it would pluck the wrong string. He seemed suffering to turn around toward the picture-taking apparatus. He was thinner—his stomach did not poke out now—but he hadn't changed much in six months.

Heime Israelsky, talented young violinist, snapped while at work in his teacher's studio on Riverside Drive. Young Master Israelsky, who will soon celebrate his fifteenth birthday, has been invited to play the Beethoven Concerta with—

That morning, after she had practiced from six until eight, her dad had made her sit down at the table with the family for breakfast. She hated breakfast; it gave her a sick feeling afterward. She would rather wait and get four chocolate bars with her twenty cents lunch money and munch them during school—bringing up little morsels from her pocket under cover of her handkerchief, stopping dead when the silver paper rattled. But this morning her dad had put a fried egg on her plate and she had known that if it burst—so that the slimy yellow oozed over the white—she would cry. And that had happened. The same feeling was upon her now. Gingerly she laid the magazine back on the table and closed her eyes.

The music in the studio seemed to be urging violently and clumsily for something that was not to be had. After a moment her thoughts drew back from Heime and the concerta and the picture—and hovered around the lesson once more. She slid over on the sofa until she could see plainly into the studio—the two of them playing, peering at the notations on the piano, lustfully drawing out all that was there.

She could not forget the memory of Mister Bilderbach's face as he stared at her a moment ago. Her hands, still twitching unconsciously to the motions of the fugue, closed over her bony knees. Tired, she was. And with a circling, sinking away feeling like the one that often came to her just before she dropped off to sleep on the nights when she had over-practiced. Like those weary half-dreams that buzzed and carried her out into their own whirling space.

A *Wunderkind*—a *Wunderkind*—a *Wunderkind*. The syllables would come out rolling in the deep German way, roar against her ears and then fall to a murmur. Along with the faces circling, swelling out in distortion, diminishing to pale blobs—Mister Bilderbach, Mrs. Bilderbach, Heime, Mister Lafkowitz. Around and around in a circle revolving to the guttural *Wunderkind*. Mister Bilderbach looming large in the middle of the circle, his face urging—with the others around him.

Phrases of music seesawing crazily. Notes she had been practicing falling over each other like a handful of marbles dropped downstairs. Bach, Debussy, Prokofieff, Brahms—timed grotesquely to the far-off throb of her tired body and the buzzing circle.

Sometimes—when she had not worked more than three hours or had stayed out from high school—the dreams were not so confused. The music soared clearly in her mind and quick, precise little memories would come back—clear as the sissy "Age of Innocence" picture Heime had given her after their joint concert was over.

A *Wunderkind*—a *Wunderkind*. That was what Mister Bilderbach had called her when, at twelve, she first came to him. Older pupils had repeated the word.

Not that he had ever said the word to her. "Bienchen—" (She had a plain American name but he never used it except when her mistakes were enormous.) "Bienchen," he would say, "I know it must be terrible. Carrying around all the time a head that thick. Poor Bienchen—"

Mister Bilderbach's father had been a Dutch violinist. His mother was from Prague. He had been born in this country and had spent his youth in Germany. So many times she wished she had not been born and brought up in just Cincinnati. How do you say *cheese* in German? Mister Bilderbach, what is Dutch for *I don't understand you?*

The first day she came to the studio. After she played the whole Second Hungarian Rhapsody from memory. The room graying with twilight. His face as he leaned over the piano.

"Now we begin all over," he said that first day. "It—playing music—is more than cleverness. If a twelve-year-old girl's fingers cover so many keys to a second—that means nothing."

He tapped his broad chest and his forehead with his stubby hand. "Here and here. You are old enough to understand that." He lighted a cigarette and gently blew the first exhalation above her head. "And work—work—work—. We will start now with these Bach Inventions and these little Schumann pieces." His hands moved again—this time to jerk the cord of the lamp behind her and point to the music. "I will show you how I wish this practiced. Listen carefully now."

She had been at the piano for almost three hours and was very tired. His deep voice sounded as though it had been straying inside her for a long time. She wanted to reach out and touch his muscle-flexed finger that pointed out the phrases, wanted to feel the gleaming gold band ring and the strong hairy back of his hand.

She had lessons Tuesday after school and on Saturday afternoons. Often she stayed, when the Saturday lesson was finished, for dinner, and then spent the night and took the streetcar home the next morning. Mrs. Bilderbach liked her in her calm, almost dumb way. She was much different from her husband. She was quiet and fat and slow. When she wasn't in the kitchen, cooking the rich dishes that both of them loved, she seemed to spend all her time in their bed upstairs, reading magazines or just looking with a half-smile at nothing. When they had married in Germany she had been a *lieder* singer. She didn't sing any more (she said it was her throat). When he would call her in from the kitchen to listen to a pupil she would always smile and say that it was *gut*, very *gut*.

When Frances was thirteen it came to her one day that the Bilderbachs had no children. It seemed strange. Once she had been back in the kitchen with Mrs. Bilderbach when he had come striding in from the studio, tense with anger at some pupil who had annoyed him. His wife stood stirring the thick soup until his hand groped out and rested on her shoulder. Then she turned—stood placid—while he folded his arms about her and buried his sharp face in the white, nerveless flesh of her neck. They stood that way without moving. And then his face jerked back suddenly, the anger diminished to a quiet inexpressiveness, and he had returned to the studio.

After she had started with Mister Bilderbach and didn't have time to see anything of the people at high school, Heime had been the only friend of her own age. He was Mister Lafkowitz's pupil and would come with him to Mister Bilderbach's on evenings when she would be there. They would listen to their teachers' playing. And often they themselves went over chamber music together—Mozart sonatas or Bloch.

A *Wunderkind*—a *Wunderkind*.

Heime was a *Wunderkind*. He and she, then.

Heime had been playing the violin since he was four. He didn't have to go to school; Mister Lafkowitz's brother, who was crippled, used to teach him geometry and European history and French verbs in the afternoon. When he was thirteen he had as fine a technique as any violinist in Cincinnati—everyone said so. But playing the violin must be easier than the piano. She knew it must be.

Heime always seemed to smell of corduroy pants and the food he had eaten and rosin. Half the time, too, his hands were dirty around the knuckles and the cuffs of his shirts peeped out dingily from the sleeves of his sweater. She always watched his hands when he played—thin only at the joints with the hard little blobs of flesh bulging over the short-cut nails and the babyish-looking crease that showed so plainly in his bowing wrist.

In the dreams, as when she was awake, she could remember the concert only in a blur. She had not known it was unsuccessful for her until months after. True, the papers had praised Heime more than her. But he was much shorter than she. When they stood together on the stage he came only to her shoulders. And that made a difference with people, she knew. Also, there was the matter of the sonata they played together. The Bloch.

"No, no—I don't think that would be appropriate," Mister Bilderbach had said when the Bloch was suggested to end the programme. "Now that John Powell thing—the Sonate Virginianesque."

She hadn't understood then; she wanted it to be the Bloch as much as Mister Lafkowitz and Heime.

Mister Bilderbach had given in. Later, after the reviews had said she lacked the temperament for that type of music, after they called her playing thin and lacking in feeling, she felt cheated.

"That oie oie stuff," said Mister Bilderbach, crackling the newspapers at her. "Not for you, Bienchen. Leave all that to the Heimes and vitses and skys."

A *Wunderkind*. No matter what the papers said, that was what he had called her.

Why was it Heime had done so much better at the concert than she? At school sometimes, when she was supposed to be watching someone do a geometry problem on the blackboard, the question would twist knife-like inside her. She would worry about it in bed, and even sometimes when she was supposed to be concentrating at the piano. It wasn't just the Bloch and her not being Jewish—not entirely. It wasn't that Heime didn't have to go to school and had begun his training so early, either. It was—?

Once she thought she knew.

"Play the Fantasia and Fugue," Mister Bilderbach had demanded one evening a year ago—after he and Mister Lafkowitz had finished reading some music together.

The Bach, as she played, seemed to her well done. From the tail of her eye she could see the calm, pleased expression on Mister Bilderbach's face, see his hands rise climactically from the chair arms and then sink down loose and satisfied when the high points of the phrases had been passed successfully. She stood up from the piano when it was over, swallowing to loosen the bands that the music seemed to have drawn around her throat and chest. But—

"Frances—" Mister Lafkowitz had said then, suddenly, looking at her with his thin mouth curved and his eyes almost covered by their delicate lids. "Do you know how many children Bach had?"

She turned to him, puzzled. "A good many. Twenty some odd."

"Well then—" The corners of his smile etched themselves gently in his pale face. "He could not have been so cold—then."

Mister Bilderbach was not pleased; his guttural effulgence of German words had *Kind* in it somewhere. Mister Lafkowitz raised his eyebrows. She had caught the point easily enough, but she felt no deception in keeping her face blank and immature because that was the way Mister Bilderbach wanted her to look.

Yet such things had nothing to do with it. Nothing very much, at least, for she would grow older. Mister Bilderbach understood that, and even Mister Lafkowitz had not meant just what he said.

In the dreams Mister Bilderbach's face loomed out and contracted in the center of the whirling circle. The lip surging softly, the veins in his temples insisting.

But sometimes, before she slept, there were such clear memories; as when she pulled a hole in the heel of her stocking down, so that her shoe would hide it. "Bienchen, Bienchen!" And bringing Mrs. Bilderbach's workbasket in and showing her how it should be darned and not gathered together in a lumpy heap.

And the time she graduated from Junior High.

"What you wear?" asked Mrs. Bilderbach the Sunday morning at breakfast when she told them about how they had practiced to march into the auditorium.

"An evening dress my cousin had last year."

"Ah—Bienchen!" he said, circling his warm coffee cup with his heavy hands, looking up at her with wrinkles around his laughing eyes. "I bet I know what Bienchen wants—"

He insisted. He would not believe her when she explained that she honestly didn't care at all.

"Like this, Anna," he said, pushing his napkin across the table and mincing to the other side of the room, swishing his hips, rolling up his eyes behind his horn-rimmed glasses.

The next Saturday afternoon, after her lessons, he took her to the department stores downtown. His thick fingers smoothed over the filmy nets and crackling taffetas that the saleswomen unwound from their bolts. He held colors to her face, cocking his head to one side, and selected pink. Shoes, he remembered too. He liked best some white kid pumps. They seemed a little like old ladies' shoes to her and the Red Cross label in the instep had a charity look. But it really didn't matter at all. When Mrs. Bilderbach began to cut out the dress and fit it to her with pins, he interrupted his lessons to stand by and suggest ruffles around the hips and neck and a fancy rosette on the shoulder. The music was coming along nicely then. Dresses and commencement and such made no difference.

Nothing mattered much except playing the music as it must be played, bringing out the thing that must be in her, practicing, practicing, playing so that Mister Bilderbach's face lost some of its urging look. Putting the thing into her music that Myra Hess had, and Yehudi Menuhin—even Heime!

What had begun to happen to her four months ago? The notes began springing out with a glib, dead intonation. Adolescence, she thought. Some kids played with promise—and worked and worked until, like her, the least little thing would start them crying, and worn out with trying to get the thing across—the longing thing they felt—something queer began to happen— But not she! She was like Heime. She had to be. She—

Once it was there for sure. And you didn't lose things like that. A *Wunderkind* . . . . A *Wunderkind*. . . . Of her he said it, rolling the words in the sure, deep German way. And in the dreams even deeper, more certain than ever. With his face looming out at her, and the longing phrases of music mixed in with the zooming, circling round, round, round—A *Wunderkind*. A *Wunderkind*. . . .

This afternoon Mister Bilderbach did not show Mister Lafkowitz to the front door, as he usually did. He stayed at the piano, softly pressing a solitary note. Listening, Frances watched the violinist wind his scarf about his pale throat.

"A good picture of Heime," she said, picking up her music. "I got a letter from him a couple of months ago—telling about hearing Schnabel and Huberman and about Carnegie Hall and things to eat at the Russian Tea Room."

To put off going into the studio a moment longer she waited until Mister Lafkowitz was ready to leave and then stood behind him as he opened the door. The frosty cold outside cut into the room. It was growing late and the air was seeped with the pale yellow of winter twilight. When the door swung to on its hinges, the house seemed darker and more silent than ever before she had known it to be.

As she went into the studio Mister Bilderbach got up from the piano and silently watched her settle herself at the keyboard.

"Well, Bienchen," he said, "this afternoon we are going to begin all over. Start from scratch. Forget the last few months."

He looked as though he were trying to act a part in a movie. His solid body swayed from toe to heel, he rubbed his hands together, and even smiled in a satisfied, movie way. Then suddenly he thrust this manner brusquely aside. His heavy shoulders slouched and he began to run through the stack of music she had brought in. "The Bach—no, not yet," he murmured. "The Beethoven? Yes. The Variation Sonata. Opus 26."

The keys of the piano hemmed her in—stiff and white and dead-seeming.

"Wait a minute," he said. He stood in the curve of the piano, elbows propped, and looked at her. "Today I expect something from you. Now this sonata—it's the first Beethoven sonata you ever worked on. Every note is under control—technically—you have nothing to cope with but the music. Only music now. That's all you think about."

He rustled through the pages of her volume until he found the place. Then he pulled his teaching chair halfway across the room, turned it around and seated himself, straddling the back with his legs.

For some reason, she knew, this position of his usually had a good effect on her performance. But today she felt that she would notice him from the corner of her eye and be disturbed. His back was stiffly tilted, his legs looked tense. The heavy volume before him seemed to balance dangerously on the chair back. "Now we begin," he said with a peremptory dart of his eyes in her direction.

Her hands rounded over the keys and then sank down. The first notes were too loud, the other phrases followed dryly.

Arrestingly his hand rose from the score. "Wait! Think a minute what you're playing. How is this beginning marked?"

"An *andante*."

"All right. Don't drag it into an *adagio* then. And play

deeply into the keys. Don't snatch it off shallowly that way. A graceful, deep-toned *andante*—"

She tried again. Her hands seemed separate from the music that was in her.

"Listen," he interrupted. "Which of these varations dominates the whole?"

"The dirge," she answered.

"Then prepare for that. This is an *andante*—but it's not salon stuff as you just played it. Start out softly, *piano*, and make it swell out just before the arpeggio. Make it warm and dramatic. And down here—where it's marked *dolce* make the counter melody sing out. You know all that. We've gone over all that side of it before. Now play it. Feel it as Beethoven wrote it down. Feel that tragedy and restraint."

She could not stop looking at his hands. They seemed to rest tentatively on the music, ready to fly up as a stop signal as soon as she would begin, the gleaming flash of his ring calling her to halt. "Mister Bilderbach—maybe if I—if you let me play on through the first variation without stopping I could do better."

"I won't interrupt," he said.

Her pale face leaned over too close to the keys. She played through the first part, and, obeying a nod from him, began the second. There were no flaws that jarred on her, but the phrases shaped from her fingers before she had put into them the meaning that she felt.

When she had finished he looked up from the music and began to speak with dull bluntness: "I hardly heard those harmonic fillings in the right hand. And incidentally, this part was supposed to take on intensity, develop the fire-shadowings that were supposed to be inherent in the first part. Go on with the next one, though."

She wanted to start it with subdued viciousness and progress to a feeling of deep, swollen sorrow. Her mind told her that. But her hands seemed to gum in the keys like limp macaroni and she could not imagine the music as it should be.

When the last note had stopped vibrating, he closed the book and deliberately got up from the chair. He was moving his lower jaw from side to side—and between his open lips she could glimpse the pink healthy lane to his throat and his strong, smoke-yellowed teeth. He laid the Beethoven gingerly on top of the rest of her music and propped his elbows on the smooth, black piano top once more. "No," he said simply, looking at her.

Her mouth began to quiver. "I can't help it. I—"

Suddenly he strained his lips into a smile. "Listen, Bienchen," he began in a new, forced voice. "You still play the Harmonious Blacksmith, don't you? I told you not to drop it from your repertoire."

"Yes," she said, "I practice it now and then."

His voice was the one he used for children. "It was among the first things we worked on together—remember. So strongly you used to play it—like a real blacksmith's daughter. You see, Bienchen, I know you so well—as if you were my own girl. I know what you have—I've heard you play so many things beautifully. You used to—"

He stopped in confusion and inhaled from his pulpy stub of cigarette. The smoke drowsed out from his pink lips and clung in a gray mist around her lank hair and childish forehead.

"Make it happy and simple," he said, switching on the lamp behind her and stepping back from the piano.

For a moment he stood just inside the bright circle the light made. Then impulsively he squatted down to the floor. "Vigorous," he said.

She could not stop looking at him, sitting on one heel with the other foot resting squarely before him for balance, the muscles of his strong thighs straining under the cloth of his trousers, his back straight, his elbows staunchly propped on his knees. "Simply now," he repeated with a gesture of his fleshy hands. "Think of the blacksmith—working out in the sunshine all day. Working easily and undisturbed."

She could not look down at the piano. The light brightened the hairs on the backs of his outspread hands, made the lenses of his glasses glitter.

"All of it," he urged. "Now!"

She felt that the marrows of her bones were hollow and there was no blood left in her. Her heart that had been springing against her chest all afternoon felt suddenly dead. She saw it gray and limp and shriveled at the edges like an oyster.

His face seemed to throb out in space before her, come closer with the lurching motion in the veins of his temples. In retreat, she looked down at the piano. Her lips shook like jelly and a surge of noiseless tears made the white keys blur in a watery line. "I can't," she whispered. "I don't know why, but I just can't—can't any more."

His tense body slackened and, holding his hand to his side, he pulled himself up. She clutched her music and hurried past him.

Her coat. The mittens and galoshes. The schoolbooks and the satchel he had given her on her birthday. All from the silent room that was hers. Quickly—before he would have to speak.

As she passed through the vestibule she could not help but see his hands—held out from his body that leaned against the studio door, relaxed and purposeless. The door shut to firmly. Dragging her books and satchel she stumbled down the stone steps, turned in the wrong direction, and hurried down the street that had become confused with noise and bicycles and the games of other children.

DORIS LESSING was born in Kermanshah, Persia, in 1919, the daughter of an army captain and a mother who was a musician. In 1924 she moved with her parents and brother to a farm in Southern Rhodesia. She was educated at a Roman Catholic convent school in Salisbury, the capital of Southern Rhodesia. At the age of fourteen she left school to earn her living at various secretarial jobs. She started writing at the age of eighteen, and much of her work bears the imprint of her early exposure to the injustices of racial discrimination. In 1949, after a brief marriage which ended in divorce, she left South Africa for England, "the ideal country to live in because it is quiet and unstimulating and leaves you in peace." In *In Pursuit of the English,* an autobiographical narrative that comes close to being a novel, she describes her first year in England, on her own, with a young child and very little money. She is best known for her five-volume Martha Quest sequence, *Children of Violence,* and, of course, for *The Golden Notebook,* where, in the words of critic Dorothy Brewster, "she had things to say that required a departure from the formal novel and she tried to find a shape that would contain them." Now a popular document among students of Women's Liberation, *The Golden Notebook* has been called "a simply enormous book about writer's block." Doris Lessing says it is "about certain political and sexual attitudes that have force now; it is an attempt to explain them, to objectivize them, to set them in relation with each other."

She has expressed her faith in the future of the novel. Though the novel is born of the middle class, she says, it will not die with it, for the novelist has one advantage denied to other artists: the novel is the only popular art form where the artist speaks directly in clear words to his audience. "The novelist talks as one individual to individuals—in a small personal voice." She still rereads her first teachers in fiction, Tolstoy, Dostoevsky, Turgenev, Balzac, and Stendhal, because they radiate the warmth, the compassion, the humanity, and the love of people which make their novels statements of belief in man himself. Because she dislikes the "English attitude towards women," she has never felt close to the English novelists, except for Hardy, the Brontës—and Dickens, in spite of "the nonsense he writes about women."

Doris Lessing has published more than fifty short stories, collected in four volumes. "Some writers I know have stopped writing short stories because, as they say, 'there is no market for them.' Others like myself, the addicts, go on, and I suspect would go on even if there really wasn't any home for them but a private drawer." A compulsive eavesdropper, she picks up her stories at the laundry, on buses, at the market—as well as in police courts, for she has played an active part in political demonstrations.

Doris Lessing
(1919–   )

TO ROOM NINETEEN

This is a story, I suppose, about a failure in intelligence: the Rawlings' marriage was grounded in intelligence.

They were older when they married than most of their married friends: in their well-seasoned late twenties. Both had had a number of affairs, sweet rather than bitter; and when they fell in love—for they did fall in love—had known each other for some time. They joked that they had saved each other "for the real thing." That they had waited so long (but not too long) for this real thing was to them a proof of their sensible discrimination. A good many of their friends had married young, and now (they felt) probably regretted lost opportunities; while others, still unmarried, seemed to them arid, self-doubting, and likely to make desperate or romantic marriages.

Not only they, but others, felt they were well matched: their friends' delight was an additional proof of their happiness. They had played the same roles, male and female, in this group or set, if such a wide, loosely connected, constantly changing constellation of people could be called a set. They had both become, by virtue of their moderation, their humour, and their abstinence from painful experience people to whom others came for advice. They could be, and were, relied on. It was one of those cases of a man and a young woman linking themselves whom no one else had ever thought of linking, probably because of their similarities. But then everyone exclaimed: Of course! How right! How was it we never thought of it before!

And so they married amid general rejoicing, and because of their foresight and their sense for what was probable, nothing was a surprise to them.

Both had well-paid jobs. Matthew was a subeditor on a large London newspaper, and Susan worked in an advertising firm. He was not the stuff of which editors or publicized journalists are made, but he was much more than "a subeditor," being one of the essential background people who in fact steady, inspire and make possible the people in the limelight. He was content with this position. Susan had a talent for commercial drawing. She was humorous about the advertisements she was responsible for, but she did not feel strongly about them one way or the other.

Both, before they married, had had pleasant flats, but they felt it unwise to base a marriage on either flat, because it might seem like a submission of personality on the part of the one whose flat it was not. They moved into a new flat in South Kensington on the clear understanding that when their marriage had settled down (a process they knew would not take long, and was in fact more a humorous concession to popular wisdom than what was due to themselves) they would buy a house and start a family.

And this is what happened. They lived in their charming flat for two years, giving parties and going to them, being a popular young married couple, and then Susan became pregnant, she gave up her job, and they bought a house in Richmond. It was typical of this couple that they had a son first, then a daughter, then twins, son and daughter. Everything right, appropriate, and what everyone would wish for, if they could choose. But people did feel these two had chosen; this balanced and sensible family was no more than what was due to them because of their infallible sense for *choosing* right.

And so they lived with their four children in their gardened house in Richmond and were happy. They had everything they had wanted and had planned for.

And yet . . .

Well, even this was expected, that there must be a certain flatness. . . .

Yes, yes, of course, it was natural they sometimes felt like this. Like what?

Their life seemed to be like a snake biting its tail. Matthew's job for the sake of Susan, children, house, and garden—which caravanserai needed a well-paid job to maintain it. And Susan's practical intelligence for the sake of Matthew, the children, the house and the garden—which unit would have collapsed in a week without her.

But there was no point about which either could say: "For the sake of *this* is all the rest." Children? But children can't be a center of life and a reason for being. They can be a thousand things that are delightful, interesting, satisfying, but they can't be a wellspring to live from. Or they shouldn't be. Susan and Matthew knew that well enough.

Matthew's job? Ridiculous. It was an interesting job, but scarcely a reason for living. Matthew took pride in doing it well; but he could hardly be expected to be proud of the newspaper: the newspaper he read, *his* newspaper, was not the one he worked for.

Their love for each other? Well, that was nearest it. If this wasn't a centre, what was? Yes, it was around this point, their love, that the whole extraordinary structure revolved. For extraordinary it certainly was. Both Susan and Matthew had moments of thinking so, of looking in secret disbelief at this thing they had created: marriage, four children, big house, garden, charwomen, friends, cars . . . and this *thing*, this entity, all of it had come into existence, been blown into being out of nowhere, because Susan loved Matthew and Matthew loved Susan. Extraordinary. So that was the central point, the wellspring.

And if one felt that it simply was not strong enough, important enough, to support it all, well, whose fault was that? Certainly neither Susan's nor Matthew's. It was in the nature of things. And they sensibly blamed neither themselves nor each other.

On the contrary, they used their intelligence to preserve what they had created from a painful and explosive world: they looked around them, and took lessons. All around them, marriages collapsing, or breaking, or rubbing along (even worse, they felt). They must not make the same mistakes, they must not.

They had avoided the pitfall so many of their friends had fallen into—of buying a house in the country *for the sake of the children;* so that the husband became a weekend husband, a weekend father, and the wife always careful not to ask what went on in the town flat which they called (in joke) a bachelor flat. No, Matthew was a full-time husband, a full-time father, and at nights, in the big married bed in the big married bedroom (which had an attractive view of the river) they lay beside each other talking and he told her about his day, and what he had done, and whom he had met; and she told him about her day (not as interesting, but that was not her fault) for both knew of the hidden resentments and deprivations of the woman who has lived her own life—and above all, has earned her own living—and is now dependent on a husband for outside interests and money.

Nor did Susan make the mistake of taking a job for the sake of her independence, which she might very well have done, since her old firm, missing her qualities of humour, balance, and sense, invited her often to go back. Children needed their mother to a certain age, that both parents knew and agreed on; and when these four healthy wisely brought-up children were of the right age, Susan would work again, because she knew, and so did he, what happened to women of fifty at the height of their energy and ability, with grown-up children who no longer needed their full devotion.

So here was this couple, testing their marriage, looking after it, treating it like a small boat full of helpless people in a very stormy sea. Well, of course, so it was. . . . The storms of the world were bad, but not too close—which is not to say they were selfishly felt: Susan and Matthew were both well-informed and responsible people. And the inner storms and quicksands were understood and charted. So everything was all right. Everything was in order. Yes, things were under control.

So what did it matter if they felt dry, flat? People like themselves, fed on a hundred books (psychological, anthropological, sociological) could scarcely be unprepared for the dry, controlled wistfulness which is the distinguishing mark of the intelligent marriage. Two people, endowed with education, with discrimination, with judgment, linked together voluntarily from their will to be happy together and to be of use to others—one sees them everywhere, one knows them, one even is that thing oneself: sadness because so much is after all so little. These two, unsurprised, turned towards each other with even more courtesy and gentle love: this was life, that two people, no matter how carefully chosen, could not be everything to each other. In fact, even to say so, to think in such a way, was banal, they were ashamed to do it.

It was banal, too, when one night Matthew came home late and confessed he had been to a party, taken a girl home and slept with her. Susan forgave him, of course. Except that forgiveness is hardly the word. Understanding, yes. But if you understand something you don't forgive it, you are the thing itself: forgiveness is for what you *don't* understand. Nor had he *confessed*—what sort of word is that?

The whole thing was not important. After all, years ago they had joked: Of course I'm not going to be faithful to you, no one can be faithful to one person for a whole lifetime. (And there was the word *faithful*—stupid, all these words, stupid, belonging to a savage old world.) But the incident left both of them irritable. Strange, but they were both bad-tempered, annoyed. There was something unassimilable about it.

Making love splendidly after he had come home that night, both had felt that the idea that Myra Jenkins, a pretty girl met at a party, could be even relevant was ridiculous. They had loved each other for over a decade, would love each other for years more. Who, then, was Myra Jenkins?

Except, thought Susan, unaccountably bad-tempered, she was (is?) the first. In ten years. So either the ten years' fidelity was not important, or she isn't. (No, no, there is something wrong with this way of thinking, there must be.) But if she isn't important, presumably it wasn't important either when Matthew and I first went to bed with each other that afternoon whose delight even now (like a very long shadow at sundown) lays a long, wandlike finger over us. (Why did I say sundown?) Well, if what we felt that afternoon was not important, nothing is important, because if it hadn't been for what we felt, we wouldn't be Mr. and Mrs. Rawlings with four children, etc., etc. The whole thing is *absurd*—for him to have come home and told me was absurd. For him not to have told me was absurd. For me to care, or for that matter not to care, is absurd . . . and who is Myra Jenkins? Why, no one at all.

There was only one thing to do, and of course these sensible people did it: they put the thing behind them, and consciously, knowing what they were doing, moved forward into a different phase of their marriage, giving thanks for past good fortune as they did so.

For it was inevitable that the handsome, blond, attractive, manly man, Matthew Rawlings, should be at times tempted (oh, what a word!) by the attractive girls at parties she could not attend because of the four children; and that sometimes he would succumb (a word even more repulsive, if possible) and that she, a good-looking woman in the big well-tended garden at Richmond, would sometimes be pierced as by an arrow from the sky with bitterness. Except that bitterness was not in order, it was out of court. Did the casual girls touch the marriage? They did not. Rather it was they who knew defeat because of the handsome Matthew Rawlings' marriage body and soul to Susan Rawlings.

In that case why did Susan feel (though luckily not for longer than a few seconds at a time) as if life had become a desert, and that nothing mattered, and that her children were not her own?

Meanwhile her intelligence continued to assert that all was well. What if her Matthew did have an occasional sweet afternoon, the odd affair? For she knew quite well, except in her moments of aridity, that they were very happy, that the affairs were not important.

Perhaps that was the trouble? It was in the nature of things that the adventures and delights could no longer be hers, because of the four children and the big house that needed so much attention. But perhaps she was secretly wishing, and even knowing that she did, that the wildness and the beauty could be his. But he was married to her. She was married to him. They were married inextricably. And therefore the gods could not strike him with the real magic, not really. Well, was it Susan's fault that after he came home from an adventure he looked harassed rather than fulfilled? (In fact, that was how she knew he had been *unfaithful*, because of his sullen air, and his glances at her, similar to hers at him: What is that I share with this person that shields all delight from me?) But none of it by anybody's fault. (But what did they feel ought to be somebody's fault?) Nobody's fault, nothing to be at fault, no one to blame, no one to offer or to take it . . . and nothing wrong, either, except that Matthew never was really struck, as he wanted to be, by joy; and that Susan was more and more often threatened by emptiness. (It was usually in the garden that she was invaded by this feeling: she was coming to avoid the garden, unless the children or Matthew were with her.) There was no need to use the dramatic words, *unfaithful*, *forgive*, and the rest; intelligence forbade them. Intelligence barred, too, quarrelling, sulking, anger, silences of withdrawal, accusations and tears. Above all, intelligence forbids tears.

A high price has to be paid for the happy marriage with

the four healthy children in the large white gardened house.

And they were paying it willingly knowing what they were doing. When they lay side by side or breast to breast in the big civilized bedroom overlooking the wild sullied river, they laughed, often, for no particular reason; but they knew it was really because of these two small people, Susan and Matthew, supporting such an edifice on their intelligent love. The laugh comforted them; it saved them both, though from what, they did not know.

They were now both fortyish. The older children, boy and girl, were ten and eight, at school. The twins, six, were still at home. Susan did not have nurses or girls to help her: childhood is short; and she did not regret the hard work. Often enough she was bored, since small children can be boring; she was often very tired; but she regretted nothing. In another decade, she would turn herself back into being a woman with a life of her own.

Soon the twins would go to school, and they would be away from home from nine until four. These hours, so Susan saw it, would be the preparation for her own slow emancipation away from the role of hub-of-the-family into woman-with-her-own life. She was already planning for the hours of freedom when all the children would be "off her hands." That was the phrase used by Matthew and by Susan and by their friends, for the moment when the youngest child went off to school. "They'll be off your hands, darling Susan, and you'll have time to yourself." So said Matthew the intelligent husband who had often enough commended and consoled Susan, standing by her in spirit during the years when her soul was not her own, as she said, but her children's.

What it amounted to was that Susan saw herself as she had been at twenty-eight, unmarried; and then again somewhere about fifty, blossoming from the root of what she had been twenty years before. As if the essential Susan were in abeyance, as if she were in cold storage. Matthew said something like this to Susan one night: and she agreed that it was true—she did feel something like that. What, then, was this essential Susan? She did not know. Put like that it sounded ridiculous, and she did not really feel it. Anyway, they had a long discussion about the whole thing before going off to sleep in each other's arms.

So the twins went off to their school, two bright affectionate children who had no problems about it, since their older brother and sister had trodden this path so successfully before them. And now Susan was going to be alone in the big house, every day of the school term, except for the daily woman who came in to clean.

It was now, for the first time in this marriage, that something happened which neither of them had foreseen.

This is what happened. She returned, at nine-thirty, from taking the twins to the school by car, looking forward to seven blissful hours of freedom. On the first morning she was simply restless, worrying about the twins "naturally enough" since this was their first day away at school. She was hardly able to contain herself until they came back. Which they did happily, excited by the world of school, looking forward to the next day. And the next day Susan took them, dropped them, came back, and found herself reluctant to enter her big and beautiful home because it was as if something was waiting for her there that she did not wish to confront. Sensibly, however, she parked the car in the garage, entered the house, spoke to Mrs. Parkes the daily woman about her duties and went up to her bedroom. She was possessed by a fever which drove her out again, downstairs, into the kitchen, where Mrs. Parkes was making cake and did not need her, and into the garden. There she sat on a bench and tried to calm herself, looking at trees, at a brown glimpse of the river. But she was filled with tension, like a panic: as if an enemy was in the garden with her. She spoke to herself severely, thus: All this is quite natural. First, I spent twelve years of my adult life working, *living my own life*. Then I married, and from the moment I became pregnant for the first time I signed myself over, so to speak, to other people. To the children. Not for one moment in twelve years have I been alone, had time to myself. So now I have to learn to be myself again. That's all.

And she went indoors to help Mrs. Parkes cook and clean, and found some sewing to do for the children. She kept herself occupied every day. At the end of the first term she understood she felt two contrary emotions. First: secret astonishment and dismay that during those weeks when the house was empty of children she had in fact been more occupied (had been careful to keep herself occupied) than ever she had been when the children were around her needing her continual attention. Second: that now she knew the house would be full of them, and for five weeks, she resented the fact she would never be alone. She was already looking back at those hours of sewing, cooking (but by herself), as at a lost freedom which would not be hers for five long weeks. And the two months of term which would succeed the five weeks stretched alluringly open to her—freedom. But what freedom—when in fact she had been so careful *not* to be free of small duties during the last weeks? She looked at herself, Susan Rawlings, sitting in a big chair by the window in the bedroom, sewing shirts or dresses, which she might just as well have bought. She saw herself making cakes for hours at a time in the big family kitchen: yet usually she bought cakes. What she saw was a woman alone, that was true, but she had not felt alone. For instance, Mrs. Parkes was always somewhere in the house. And she did not like being in the garden at all, because of the closeness there of the enemy—irritation, restlessness, emptiness, whatever it was, which keeping her hands occupied made less dangerous for some reason.

Susan did not tell Matthew of these thoughts. They were not sensible. She did not recognize herself in them. What should she say to her dear friend and husband Matthew? "When I go into the garden, that is, if the children are not there, I feel as if there is an enemy there waiting to invade me." "What enemy, Susan darling?" "Well, I don't know, really. . . ." "Perhaps you should see a doctor?"

No, clearly this conversation should not take place. The holidays began and Susan welcomed them. Four children, lively, energetic, intelligent, demanding: she was never, not for a moment of her day, alone. If she was in a room, they would be in the next room, or waiting for her to do something for them; or it would soon be time for lunch or tea, or to take one of them to the dentist. Something to do: five weeks of it, thank goodness.

On the fourth day of these so welcome holidays, she found she was storming with anger at the twins, two shrinking beautiful children who (and this is what checked her) stood hand in hand looking at with sheer dismayed disbelief. This was their calm mother, shouting at them. And for what? They had come to her with some game, some bit of nonsense. They looked at each other, moved closer for support, and went off hand in hand, leaving Susan holding on to the windowsill of the living room, breathing deep, feeling sick. She went to lie down, telling the older children she had a headache. She heard the boy Harry telling the little ones: "It's all right, Mother's got a headache." She heard that *It's all right* with pain.

That night she said to her husband: "Today I shouted at the twins, quite unfairly." She sounded miserable, and he said gently: "Well, what of it?"

"It's more of an adjustment than I thought, their going to school."

"But Susie, Susie darling . . ." For she was crouched weeping on the bed. He comforted her: "Susan, what is all this about? You shouted at them? What of it? If you shouted at them fifty times a day it wouldn't be more than the little devils deserve." But she wouldn't laugh. She wept. Soon he comforted her with his body. She became calm. Calm, she wondered what was wrong with her, and why she should mind so much that she might, just once, have behaved unjustly with the children. What did it matter? They had forgotten it all long ago: Mother had a headache and everything was all right.

It was a long time later that Susan understood that that night, when she had wept and Matthew had driven the misery out of her with his big solid body, was the last time, ever in their married life, that they had been—to use their mutual language—with each other. And even that was a lie, because she had not told him of her real fears at all.

The five weeks passed, and Susan was in control of herself, and good and kind, and she looked forward to the holidays with a mixture of fear and longing. She did not know what to expect. She took the twins off to school (the elder children took themselves to school) and she returned to the house determined to face the enemy wherever he was, in the house, or the garden or—where?

She was again restless, she was possessed by restlessness. She cooked and sewed and worked as before, day after day, while Mrs. Parkes remonstrated: "Mrs. Rawlings, what's the need for it? I can do that, it's what you pay me for."

And it was so irrational that she checked herself. She would put the car into the garage, go up to her bedroom, and sit, hands in her lap, forcing herself to be quiet. She listened to Mrs. Parkes moving around the house. She looked out into the garden and saw the branches shake the trees. She sat defeating the enemy, restlessness. Emptiness.

She ought to be thinking about her life, about herself. But she did not. Or perhaps she could not. As soon as she forced her mind to think about Susan (for what else did she want to be alone for?) it skipped off to thoughts of butter or school clothes. Or it thought of Mrs. Parkes. She realized that she sat listening for the movements of the cleaning woman, following her every turn, bend, thought. She followed her in her mind from kitchen to bathroom, from table to oven, and it was as if the duster, the cleaning cloth, the saucepan, were in her own hand. She would hear herself saying: No, not like that, don't put that there. . . . Yet she did not give a damn what Mrs. Parkes did, or if she did it at all. Yet she could not prevent herself from being conscious of her, every minute. Yes, this was what was wrong with her: she needed, when she was alone, to be really alone, with no one near. She could not endure the knowledge that in ten minutes or in half an hour Mrs. Parkes would call up the stairs: "Mrs. Rawlings, there's no silver polish, Madam, we're out of flour."

So she left the house and went to sit in the garden where she was screened from the house by trees. She waited for the demon to appear and claim her, but he did not.

She was keeping him off, because she had not, after all, come to an end of arranging herself.

She was planning how to be somewhere where Mrs. Parkes would not come after her with a cup of tea, or a demand to be allowed to telephone (always irritating since Susan did not care who she telephoned or how often), or just a nice talk about something. Yes, she needed a place, or a state of affairs, where it would not be necessary to keep reminding herself: In ten minutes I must telephone Matthew about . . . and at half past three I must leave early for the children because the car needs cleaning. And at ten o'clock tomorrow I must remember. . . . she was possessed with resentment that the seven hours of freedom in every day (during weekdays in the school term) were not free, that never, not for one second, ever, was she free from the pressure of time, from having to remember this or that. She could never forget herself; never really let herself go into forgetfulness.

Resentment. It was poisoning her. (She looked at this emotion and thought it was absurd. Yet she felt it.) She was a prisoner. (She looked at this thought too, and it was no good telling herself it was a ridiculous one.) She must tell Matthew—but what? She as filled with emotions that were utterly ridiculous, that she despised, yet that nevertheless she was feeling so strongly she could not shake them off.

The school holidays came round, and this time they were for nearly two months, and she behaved with a conscious controlled decency that nearly drove her crazy. She would lock herself in the bathroom, and sit on the edge of the bath, breathing deep, trying to let go into some kind of calm. Or she went up into the spare room, usually empty, where no one would expect her to be. She heard the children calling "Mother, Mother," and kept silent, feeling guilty. Or she went to the very end of the garden, by herself, and looked at the slow-moving brown river; she looked at the river and closed her eyes and breathed slow and deep, taking it into her being, into her veins.

Then she returned to the family, wife and mother, smiling and responsible, feeling as if the pressure of these people—four lively children and her husband—were a painful pressure on the surface of her skin, a hand pressing on her brain. She did not once break down into irritation during these holidays, but it was like living out a prison sentence, and when the children went back to school, she sat on a white stone seat near the flowing river, and she thought: It is not even a year since the twins went to school, since *they were off my hands* (What on earth did I think I meant when I used that stupid phrase?) and yet I'm a different person. I'm simply not myself. I don't understand it.

Yet she had to understand it. For she knew that this structure—big white house, on which the mortgage still cost four hundred a year, a husband, so good and kind and insightful, four children, all doing so nicely, and the garden where she sat, and Mrs. Parkes the cleaning woman—all this depended on her, and yet she could not understand why, or even what it was she contributed to it.

She said to Matthew in their bedroom: "I think there must be something wrong with me."

And he said: "Surely not, Susan? You look marvellous —you're as lovely as ever."

She looked at the handsome blond man, with his clear, intelligent, blue-eyed face, and thought: Why is it I can't tell him? Why not? And she said: "I need to be alone more than I am."

At which he swung his slow blue gaze at her, and she saw what she had been dreading: Incredulity. Disbelief. And fear. An incredulous blue stare from a stranger who was her husband, as close to her as her own breath.

He said: "But the children are at school and off your hands."

She said to herself: I've got to force myself to say: Yes, but do you realize that I never feel free? There's never a moment I can say to myself: There's nothing I have to remind myself about, nothing I have to do in half an hour, or an hour, or two hours. . . .

But she said: "I don't feel well."

He said: "Perhaps you need a holiday."

She said, appalled: "But not without you, surely?" For she could not imagine herself going off without him. Yet that was what he meant. Seeing her face, he laughed, and opened his arms, and she went into them, thinking: Yes, yes, but why can't I say it? And what *is* it I have to say?

She tried to tell him, about never being free. And he listened and said: "But Susan, what sort of freedom can you possibly want—short of being dead! Am I ever free? I go to the office, and I have to be there at ten—all right, half past ten, sometimes. And I have to do this or that, don't I? Then I've got to come home at a certain time—I don't mean it, you know I don't—but if I'm not going to be back home at six I telephone you. When can I ever say to myself: I have nothing to be responsible for in the next six hours?"

Susan, hearing this, was remorseful. Because it was true. The good marriage, the house, the children, depended just as much on his voluntary bondage as it did on hers. But why did he not feel bound? Why didn't he chafe and become restless? No, there was something really wrong with her and this proved it.

And that word *bondage*—why had she used it? She had never felt marriage, or the children, as bondage. Neither had he, or surely they wouldn't be together lying in each other's arms content after twelve years of marriage.

No her state (whatever it was) was irrelevant nothing to do with her real good life with her family. She had to accept the fact that after all, she was an irrational person and to live with it. Some people had to live with crippled arms, or stammers, or being deaf. She would have to live knowing she was subject to a state of mind she could not own.

Nevertheless, as a result of this conversation with her husband, there was a new regime next holidays.

The spare room at the top of the house now had a cardboard sign saying: PRIVATE! DO NOT DISTURB! on it. (This sign had been drawn in colored chalks by the children, after a discussion between the parents in which it was decided this was psychologically the right thing.) The family and Mrs. Parkes knew this was "Mother's Room" and that she was entitled to her privacy. Many serious conversations took place between Matthew and the children about not taking Mother for granted. Susan overheard the first, between father and Harry, the older boy, and was surprised at her irritation over it. Surely she could have a room somewhere in that big house and retire into it without such a fuss being made? Without it being so solemnly discussed? Why couldn't she simply have announced: "I'm going to fit out the little top room for myself, and when I'm in it I'm not to be disturbed for anything short of fire"? Just that, and finished; instead of long earnest discussions. When she heard Harry and Matthew explaining it to the twins with Mrs. Parkes coming in—"Yes, well, a family sometimes gets on top of a woman"—she had to go right away to the bottom of the garden until the devils of exasperation had finished their dance in her blood.

But now there was a room, and she could go there when she liked, she used it seldom: she felt even more caged there than in her bedroom. One day she had gone up there after a lunch for ten children she had cooked and served because Mrs. Parkes was not there, and had sat alone for a while looking into the garden. She saw the children stream out from the kitchen and stand looking up at the window where she sat behind the curtains. They were all—her children and their friends—discussing Mother's Room. A few minutes later, the chase of children in some game came pounding up the stairs, but ended as abruptly as if they had fallen over a ravine, so sudden was the silence. They had remembered she was there, and had gone silent in a great gale of "Hush! Shhhhhh! Quiet, you'll disturb her. . . ." And they went tiptoeing downstairs like criminal conspirators. When she came down to make tea for them, they all apologized. The twins put their arms around her, from front and back, making a human cage of loving limbs, and promised it would never occur again. "We forgot, Mummy, we forgot all about it!"

What it amounted to was that Mother's Room, and her need for privacy, had become a valuable lesson in respect for other people's rights. Quite soon Susan was going up to the room only because it was a lesson it was a pity to drop. Then she took sewing up there, and the children and Mrs. Parkes came in and out: it had become another family room.

She sighed, and smiled, and resigned herself—she made jokes at her own expense with Matthew over the room. That is, she did from the self she liked, she respected. But at the same time, something inside her howled with impatience, with rage. . . . And she was frightened. One day she found herself kneeling by her bed and praying: "Dear God, keep it away from me, keep him away from me." She meant the devil, for she now thought of it, not caring if she were irrational, as some sort of demon. She imagined him, or it, as a youngish man, or perhaps a middle-aged man pretending to be young. Or a man young-looking from immaturity? At any rate, she saw the young-looking face which, when she drew closer, had dry lines about mouth and eyes. He was thinnish, meagre in build. And he had a reddish complexion, and ginger hair. That was he—a gingery, energetic man, and he wore a reddish hairy jacket, unpleasant to the touch.

Well, one day she saw him. She was standing at the bottom of the garden, watching the river ebb past, when she raised her eyes and saw this person, or being, sitting on the white stone bench. He was looking at her, and grinning. In his hand was a long crooked stick, which he had picked off the ground, or broken off the tree above him. He was absent-mindedly, out of an absent-minded or freakish impulse of spite, using the stick to stir around in the coils of a blindworm or a grass snake (or some kind of snakelike creature: it was whitish and unhealthy to look at, unpleasant). The snake was twisting about, flinging its coils from side to side in a kind of dance of protest against the teasing prodding stick.

Susan looked at him thinking: Who is the stranger? What is he doing in our garden? Then she recognized the man around whom her terrors had crystallized. As she did so, he vanished. She made herself walk over to the bench. A shadow from a branch lay across thin emerald grass, moving jerkily over its roughness, and she could see why she had taken it for a snake, lashing and twisting. She went back to the house thinking: Right, then, so I've seen him with my own eyes, so I'm not crazy after all—there *is* a danger because I've seen him. He is lurking in the garden and sometimes even in the house, and he wants *to get into me and to take me over.*

She dreamed of having a room or a place, anywhere, where she could go and sit, by herself, no one knowing where she was.

Once, near Victoria, she found herself outside a news agent that had Rooms to Let advertised. She decided to rent a room, telling no one. Sometimes she could take the the train in from Richmond and sit alone in it for an hour or two. Yet how could she? A room would cost three or four pounds a week, and she earned no money, and how could she explain to Matthew that she needed such a sum? What for? It did not occur to her that she was taking it for granted she wasn't going to tell him about the room.

Well, it was out of the question, having a room; yet she knew she must.

One day, when a school term was well established, and none of the children had measles or other ailments, and everything seemed in order, she did the shopping early, explained to Mrs. Parkes she was meeting an old school friend, took the train to Victoria, searched until she found a small quiet hotel, and asked for a room for the day. They did not let rooms by the day, the manageress said, looking doubtful, since Susan so obviously was not the kind of woman who needed a room for unrespectable reasons. Susan made a long explanation about not being well, being unable to shop without frequent rests for lying down. At last she was allowed to rent the room provided she paid a full night's price for it. She was taken up by the manageress and a maid, both concerned over the state of her health . . . which must be pretty bad if, living at Richmond (she had signed her name and address in the register), she needed a shelter at Victoria.

The room was ordinary and anonymous, and was just what Susan needed. She put a shilling in the gas fire, and sat, eyes shut, in a dingy armchair with her back to a dingy window. She was alone. She was alone. She was alone. She could feel pressures lifting off her. First the sounds of traffic came very loud; then they seemed to vanish; she might even have slept a little. A knock on the door: it was Miss Townsend the manageress, bringing her a cup of tea with her own hands, so concerned was she over Susan's long silence and possible illness.

Miss Townsend was a lonely woman of fifty, running this hotel with all the rectitude expected of her, and she sensed in Susan the possibility of understanding companionship. She stayed to talk. Susan found herself in the middle of a fantastic story about her illness, which got more and more improbable as she tried to make it tally with the large house at Richmond, well-off husband, and four children. Suppose she said instead: Miss Townsend, I'm here in your hotel because I need to be alone for a few hours, above all *alone and with no one knowing where I am.* She said it mentally, and saw, mentally, the look that would inevitably come on Miss Townsend's elderly maiden's face. "Miss Townsend, my four children and my husband are driving me insane, do you understand that? Yes, I can see from the gleam of hysteria in your eyes that comes from loneliness controlled but only just contained that I've got everything in the world you've ever longed for. Well, Miss Townsend, I don't want any of it. You can have it, Miss Townsend. I wish I was absolutely alone in the world, like you. Miss Townsend, I'm besieged by seven devils, Miss Townsend, Miss Townsend, let me stay here in your hotel where the devils can't get me. . . ." Instead of saying all this, she described her anemia, agreed to try Miss Townsend's remedy for it, which was raw liver, minced, between whole-meal bread, and said yes, perhaps it would be better if she stayed at home and let a friend do shopping for her. She paid her bill and left the hotel, defeated.

At home Mrs. Parkes said she didn't really like it, no, not really, when Mrs. Rawlings was away from nine in the morning until five. The teacher had telephoned from school to say Joan's teeth were paining her, and she hadn't known what to say; and what was she to make for the children's tea, Mrs. Rawlings hadn't said.

All this was nonsense, of course. Mrs. Parkes's complaint was that Susan had withdrawn herself spiritually, leaving the burden of the big house on her.

Susan looked back at her day of "freedom" which had resulted in her becoming a friend to the lonely Miss Townsend, and in Mrs. Parkes's remonstrances. Yet she remembered the short blissful hour of being alone, really alone.

She was determined to arrange her life, no matter what it cost, so that she could have that solitude more often. An absolute solitude, where no one knew her or cared about her.

But how? She thought of saying to her old employer: I want to back you up in a story with Matthew that I am doing part-time work for you. The truth is that . . . but she would have to tell him a lie too, and which lie? She could not say: I want to sit by myself three or four times a week in a rented room. And besides, he knew Matthew, and she could not really ask him to tell lies on her behalf, apart from his being bound to think it meant a lover.

Suppose she really took a part-time job, which she could get through fast and efficiently, leaving time for herself. What job? Addressing envelopes? Canvassing?

And there was Mrs. Parkes, working widow, who knew exactly what she was prepared to give to the house, who knew by instinct when her mistress withdrew in spirit from her responsibilities. Mrs. Parkes was one of the servers of this world, but she needed someone to serve. She had to have Mrs. Rawlings, her madam, at the top of the house or in the garden, so that she could come and get support from her: "Yes, the bread's not what it was when I was a girl. . . . Yes, Harry's got a wonderful appetite, I wonder where he puts it all. . . . Yes, it's lucky the twins are so much of a size, they can wear each other's shoes, that's a saving in these hard times. . . . Yes, the cherry jam from Switzerland is not a patch on the jam from Poland, and three times the price. . . ." And so on. That sort of talk Mrs. Parkes must have, every day, or she would leave, not knowing herself why she left.

Susan Rawlings, thinking these thoughts, found that she was prowling through the great thicketed garden like a wild cat: she was walking up the stairs, down the stairs, through the rooms, into the garden, along the brown running river, back, up through the house, down again. . . . It was a wonder Mrs. Parkes did not think it strange. But on the contrary, Mrs. Rawlings could do what she liked, she could stand on her head if she wanted, provided she was *there*. Susan Rawlings prowled and muttered through her house, hating Mrs. Parkes, hating poor Miss Townsend, dreaming of her hour of solitude in the dingy respectability of Miss Townsend's hotel bedroom, and she knew quite well she was mad. Yes, she was mad.

She said to Matthew that she must have a holiday. Matthew agreed with her. This was not as things had been once—how they had talked in each other's arms in the marriage bed. He had, she knew, diagnosed her finally as *unreasonable*. She had become someone outside himself that he had to manage. They were living side by side in this house like two tolerably friendly strangers.

Having told Mrs. Parkes, or rather, asked for her permission, she went off on a walking holiday in Wales. She chose the remotest place she knew of. Every morning the children telephoned her before they went off to school, to encourage and support her, just as they had over Mother's Room. Every evening she telephoned them, spoke to each child in turn, and then to Matthew. Mrs. Parkes, given permission to telephone for instructions or advice, did so every day at lunchtime. When, as happened three times, Mrs. Rawlings was out on the mountainside, Mrs. Parkes asked that she should ring back at such and such a time, for she would not be happy in what she was doing without Mrs. Rawlings' blessing.

Susan prowled over wild country with the telephone wire holding her to her duty like a leash. The next time she must telephone, or wait to be telephoned, nailed her to her cross. The mountains themselves seemed trammelled by her unfreedom. Everywhere on the mountains, where she met no one at all, from breakfast time to dusk, excepting sheep, or a shepherd, she came face to face with her own craziness which might attack her in the broadest valleys, so that they seemed too small; or on a mountain-top from which she could see a hundred other mountains and valleys, so that they seemed too low, too small, with the sky pressing down too close. She would stand gazing at a hillside brilliant with ferns and bracken, jewelled with running water, and see nothing but her devil, who lifted inhuman eyes at her from where he leaned negligently on a rock, switching at his ugly yellow boots with a leafy twig.

She returned to her home and family, with the Welsh emptiness at the back of her mind like a promise of freedom.

She told her husband she wanted to have an *au pair* girl.

They were in their bedroom, it was late at night, the children slept. He sat, shirted and slippered, in a chair by the window, looking out. She sat brushing her hair and watching him in the mirror. A time-hallowed scene in the connubial bedroom. He said nothing, while she heard the arguments coming into his mind, only to be rejected because every one was *reasonable.*

"It seems strange to get one now, after all, the children are in school most of the day. Surely the time for you to have help was when you were stuck with them day and night. Why don't you ask Mrs. Parkes to cook for you? She's even offered to—I can understand if you are tired of cooking for six people. But you know that an *au pair* girl means all kinds of problems, it's not like having an ordinary char in during the day. . . ."

Finally he said carefully: "Are you thinking of going back to work?"

"No," she said, "no, not really." She made herself sound vague, rather stupid. She went on brushing her black hair and peering at herself so as to be oblivious of the short uneasy glances her Matthew kept giving her. "Do you think we can't afford it?" she went on vaguely, not at all the old efficient Susan who knew exactly what they could afford.

"It's not that," he said, looking out of the window at dark trees, so as not to look at her. Meanwhile she examined a round, candid, pleasant face with clear dark brows and clear gray eyes. A sensible face. She brushed thick healthy black hair and thought: Yet that's the reflection of a madwoman. How very strange! Much more to the point if what looked back at me was the gingery green-eyed demon with his dry meagre smile. . . . Why wasn't Matthew agreeing? After all, what else could he do? She was breaking her part of the bargain and there was no way of forcing her to keep it: that her spirit, her soul, should live in this house, so that the people in it could grow like plants in water, and Mrs. Parkes remain content in their service. In return for this, he would be a good loving husband, and responsible towards the children. Well, nothing like this had been true of either of them for a long tme. He did his duty, perfunctorily; she did not even pretend to do hers. And he had become like other husbands, with his real life in his work and the people he met there, and very likely a serious affair. All this was her fault.

At last he drew heavy curtains, blotting out the trees, and turned to force her attention: "Susan, are you really sure we need a girl?" But she would not meet his appeal at all: She was running the brush over her hair again and again, lifting fine black clouds in a small hiss of electricity. She was peering in and smiling as if she were amused at the clinging hissing hair that followed the brush.

"Yes, I think it would be a good idea on the whole," she said, with the cunning of a madwoman evading the real point.

In the mirror she could see her Matthew lying on his back, his hands behind his head, staring upwards, his face sad and hard. She felt her heart (the old heart of Susan Rawlings) soften and call out to him. But she set it to be indifferent.

He said: "Susan, the children?" It was an appeal that *almost* reached her. He opened his arms, lifting them from where they had lain by his sides, palms up, empty. She had only to run across and fling herself into them, onto his hard, warm chest, and melt into herself, into Susan. But she could not. She would not see his lifted arms. She said vaguely: "Well, surely it'll be even better for them? We'll get a French or a German girl and they'll learn the language."

In the dark she lay beside him, feeling frozen, a stranger. She felt as if Susan had been spirited away. She disliked very much this woman who lay here, cold and indifferent beside a suffering man, but she could not change her.

Next morning she set about getting a girl, and very soon came Sophie Traub from Hamburg, a girl of twenty, laughing, healthy, blue-eyed, intending to learn English. Indeed, she already spoke a good deal. In return for a room—"Mother's Room"—and her food, she undertook to do some light cooking, and to be with the children when Mrs. Rawlings asked. She was an intelligent girl and understood perfectly what was needed. Susan said: "I go off sometimes, for the morning or for the day—well, sometimes the children run home from school, or they ring up, or a teacher rings up. I should be here, really. And there's the daily woman. . . ." And Sophie laughed her deep fruity *Fräulein's* laugh, showed her fine white teeth and her dimples, and said: "You want some person to play mistress of the house sometimes, not so?"

"Yes, that is just so," said Susan, a bit dry, despite herself, thinking in secret fear how easy it was, how much nearer to the end she was than she thought. Healthy Fräulein Traub's instant understanding of their position proved this to be true.

The *au pair* girl, because of her own common sense, or (as Susan said to herself with her new inward shudder) because she had been *chosen* so well by Susan, was a success with everyone, the children liking her, Mrs. Parkes forgetting almost at once that she was German, and Matthew finding her "nice to have around the house." For he was now taking things as they came, from the surface of life, withdrawn both as a husband and a father from the household.

One day Susan saw how Sophie and Mrs. Parkes were talking and laughing in the kitchen, and she announced that she would be away until teatime. She knew exactly where to go and what she must look for. She took the District Line to South Kensington, changed to the Circle, got off at Paddington, and walked around looking at the smaller hotels until she was satisfied with one which had FRED'S HOTEL painted on windowpanes that needed cleaning. The façade was a faded shiny yellow, like unhealthy skin. A door at the end of a passage said she must knock; she did, and Fred appeared. He was not at all attractive, not in any way, being fattish, and run-down, and wearing a tasteless striped suit. He had small sharp eyes in a white creased face, and was quite prepared to let Mrs. Jones (she chose the farcical name deliberately, staring him out) have a room three days a week from ten until six. Provided of course that she paid in advance each time she came? Susan produced fifteen shillings (no price had been set by him) and held it out, still fixing him with a bold unblinking challenge she had not known until then she could use at will. Looking at her still, he took up a ten-shilling note from her palm between thumb and forefinger, fingered it; then shuffled up two half crowns, held out his own palm with these bits of money displayed thereon, and let her gaze lower broodingly at them. They were standing in the passage, a red-shaded light above, bare boards beneath, and a strong smell of floor polish rising about them. He shot his gaze up at her over the still-extended palm, and smiled as if to say: What do you take me for? "I shan't," said Susan, "be using this room for the purposes of making money." He still waited. She added another five shillings, at which he nodded and said: "You pay, and I ask no questions." "Good," said Susan. He now went past her to the stairs, and there waited a moment: the light from the street door being in her eyes, she lost sight of him momentarily. Then she saw a sober-suited, white-faced, white-balding little man trotting up the stairs like a waiter, and she went after him. They proceeded in utter silence up the stairs of this house where no questions were asked—Fred's Hotel, which could afford the freedom for its visitors that poor Miss Townsend's hotel could not. The room was hideous. It had a single window, with thin green brocade curtains, a three-quarter bed that had a cheap green satin bedspread on it, a fireplace with a gas fire and a shilling meter by it, a chest of drawers, and a green wicker armchair.

"Thank you," said Susan, knowing that Fred (if this was Fred, and not George, or Herbert or Charlie) was looking at her, not so much with curiosity, an emotion he would not own to, for professional reasons, but with a philosophical sense of what was appropriate. Having taken her money and shown her up and agreed to everything, he was clearly disapproving of her for coming here. She did not belong here at all, so his look said. (But she knew, already, how very much she did belong: the room had been waiting for her to join it.) "Would you have me called at five o'clock, please?" and he nodded and went downstairs.

It was twelve in the morning. She was free. She sat in the armchair, she simply sat, she closed her eyes and sat and let herself be alone. She was alone and no one knew where she was. When a knock came on the door she was annoyed, and prepared to show it: but it was Fred himself, it was five o'clock and he was calling her as ordered. He flicked his sharp little eyes over the room—bed, first. It was undisturbed. She might never have been in the room at all. She thanked him, said she would be returning the day after tomorrow, and left. She was back home in time to cook supper, to put the children to bed, to cook a second supper for her husband and herself later. And to welcome Sophie back from the pictures where she had gone with a friend. All these things she did cheerfully, willingly. But she was thinking all the time of the hotel room, she was longing for it with her whole being.

Three times a week. She arrived promptly at ten, looked Fred in the eyes, gave him twenty shillings, followed him up the stairs, went into the room, and shut the door on him with gentle firmness. For Fred, disapproving of her being here at all, was quite ready to let friendship, or at least acquaintanceship, follow his disapproval, if only she would let him. But he was content to go off on her dismissing nod, with the twenty shillings in his hand.

She sat in the armchair and shut her eyes.

What did she *do* in the room? Why, nothing at all. From the chair, when it had rested her, she went to the window, stretching her arms, smiling, treasuring her anonymity, to look out. She was no longer Susan Rawlings, mother of four, wife of Matthew, employer of Mrs. Parkes and of Sophie Traub, with these and those relations with friends, schoolteachers, tradesmen. She no longer was mistress of the big white house and garden, owning clothes suitable for this and that activity or occasion. She was Mrs. Jones, and she was alone, and she had no past and no future. Here I am, she thought, after all these years of being married and having children and playing those roles of responsibility—and I'm just the same. Yet there have been times I thought that nothing existed of me except the roles that went with being Mrs. Matthew Rawlings. Yes, here I am, and if I never saw any of my family again, here I would still be . . . how very strange that is! And she leaned on the sill, and looked into the street, loving the men and women who passed, because she did not know them. She looked at the downtrodden buildings over the street, and at the sky, wet and dingy, or sometimes blue, and she felt she had never seen buildings or sky before. And then she went back to the chair, empty, her mind a blank. Sometimes she talked aloud, saying nothing—an exclamation, meaningless, followed by a comment about the floral pattern on the thin rug, or a stain on the green satin coverlet. For the most part, she wool-gathered—what word is there for it?—brooded, wandered, simply went dark, feeling emptiness run deliciously through her veins like the movement of her blood.

This room had become more her own than the house she lived in. One morning she found Fred taking her a flight higher than usual. She stopped, refusing to go up, and demanded her usual room, Number 19. "Well, you'll have to wait half an hour then," he said. Willingly she descended to the dark disinfectant-smelling hall, and sat waiting until the two, man and woman, came down the stairs, giving her swift indifferent glances before they hurried out into the street, separating at the door. She went up to the room, *her* room, which they had just vacated. It was no less hers, though the windows were set wide open, and a maid was straightening the bed as she came in.

After these days of solitude, it was both easy to play her part as mother and wife, and difficult—because it was so easy: she felt an imposter. She felt as if her shell moved here, with her family, answering to Mummy, Mother, Susan, Mrs. Rawlings. She was surprised no one saw through her, that she wasn't turned out of doors, as a fake. On the contrary, it seemed the children loved her more; Matthew and she "got on" pleasantly, and Mrs. Parkes was happy in her work under (for the most part, it must be confessed) Sophie Traub. At night she lay beside her husband, and they made love again, apparently just as they used to, when they were really married. But she, Susan, or the being who answered so readily and improbably to the name of Susan, was not there: she was in Fred's Hotel, in Paddington, waiting for the easing hours of solitude to begin.

Soon she made a new arrangement with Fred and with Sophie. It was for five days a week. As for the money, five pounds, she simply asked Matthew for it. She saw that she was not even frightened he might ask what for: he would give it to her, she knew that, and yet it was terrifying it could be so, for this close couple, these partners, had once known the destination of every shilling they must spend. He agreed to give her five pounds a week. She asked for just so much, not a penny more. He sounded indifferent about it. It was as if he were paying her, she thought: *paying her off*—yes, that was it. Terror came back for a moment, when she understood this, but she stilled it: things had gone too far for that. Now, every week, on Sunday nights, he gave her five pounds, turning away from her before their eyes could meet on the transaction. As for Sophie Traub, she was to be somewhere in or near the house until six at night, after which she was free. She was not to cook, or to clean, she was simply to be there. So she gardened or sewed, and asked friends in, being a person who was bound to have a lot of friends. If the children were sick, she nursed them. If teachers telephoned, she answered them sensibly. For the five daytimes in the school week, she was altogether the mistress of the house.

One night in the bedroom, Matthew asked: "Susan, I don't want to interfere—don't think that, please—but are you sure you are well?"

She was brushing her hair at the mirror. She made two more strokes on either side of her head, before she replied: "Yes, dear, I am sure I am well."

He was again lying on his back, his big blond head on his hands, his elbows angled up and part-concealing his face. He said: "Then, Susan, I have to ask you this question, though you must understand, I'm not putting any sort of pressure on you." (Susan heard the word "pressure" with dismay, because this was inevitable, of course she could not go on like this.) "Are things going to go on like this?"

"Well," she said, going vague and bright and idiotic again, so as to escape: "Well, I don't see why not."

He was jerking his elbows up and down, in annoyance or in pain, and, looking at him, she saw he had got thin, even gaunt; and restless angry movements were not what she remembered of him. He said: "Do you want a divorce, is that it?"

At this, Susan only with the greatest difficulty stopped herself from laughing: she could hear the bright bubbling laughter she *would* have emitted, had she let herself. He could only mean one thing: she had a lover, and that was why she spent her days in London, as lost to him as if she had vanished to another continent.

Then the small panic set in again: she understood that he hoped she did have a lover, he was begging her to say so, because otherwise it would be too terrifying.

She thought this out, as she brushed her hair, watching the fine black stuff fly up to make its little clouds of electricity, hiss, hiss, hiss. Behind her head, across the room, was a blue wall. She realized she was absorbed in watching the black hair making shapes against the blue. She should be answering him. "Do *you* want a divorce, Matthew?"

He said: "That surely isn't the point, is it?"

"You brought it up, I didn't," she said, brightly, suppressing meaningless tinkling laughter.

Next day she asked Fred: "Have enquiries been made for me?"

He hesitated, and she said: "I've been coming here a year now. I've made no trouble, and you've been paid every day. I have a right to be told."

"As a matter of fact, Mrs. Jones, a man did come asking."

"A man from a detective agency?"

"Well, he could have been, couldn't he?"

"I was asking you. . . . Well, what did you tell him?"

"I told him a Mrs. Jones came every weekday from ten until five or six and stayed in Number Nineteen by herself."

"Describing me?"

"Well, Mrs. Jones, I had no alternative. Put yourself in my place."

"By rights I should deduct what that man gave you for the information."

He raised shocked eyes: she was not the sort of person to make jokes like this! Then he chose to laugh: a pinkish wet slit appeared across his white wrinkled face: his eyes positively begged her to laugh, otherwise he might lose some money. She remained grave, looking at him.

He stopped laughing and said: "You want to go up now?"—returning to the familiarity, the comradeship, of the country where no questions are asked, on which (and he knew it) she depended completely.

She went up to sit in her wicker chair. But it was not the same. Her husband had searched her out. (The world had searched her out.) The pressures were on her. She was here with his connivance. He might walk in at any moment, here, into Room 19. She imagined the report from the detective agency: "A woman calling herself Mrs. Jones, fitting the description of your wife (etc., etc., etc.), stays alone all day in Room No. 19. She insists on this room, waits for it if it is engaged. As far as the proprietor knows, she receives no visitors there, male or female." A report something on these lines, Matthew must have received.

Well, of course he was right: things couldn't go on like this. He had put an end to it all simply by sending the detective after her.

She tried to shrink herself back into the shelter of the room, a snail pecked out of its shell and trying to squirm back. But the peace of the room had gone. She was trying consciously to revive it, trying to let go into the dark creative trance (or whatever it was) that she had found there. It was no use, yet she craved for it, she was as ill as a suddenly deprived addict.

Several times she returned to the room, to look for herself there, but instead she found the unnamed spirit of restlessness, a prickling fevered hunger for movement, an irritable self-consciousness that made her brain feel as if it had colored lights going on and off inside it. Instead of the soft dark that had been the room's air, were now waiting for her demons that made her dash blindly about, muttering words of hate; she was impelling herself from point to point like a moth dashing herself against a windowpane, sliding to the bottom, fluttering off on broken wings, then crashing into the invisible barrier again. And again and again. Soon she was exhausted, and she told Fred that for a while she would not be needing the room, she was going on holiday. Home she went, to the big white house by the river. The middle of a weekday, and she felt guilty at returning to her own home when not expected. She stood unseen, looking in at the kitchen window. Mrs. Parkes, wearing a discarded floral overall of Susan's, was stooping to slide something into the oven. Sophie, arms folded, was leaning her back against a cupboard and laughing at some joke made by a girl not seen before by Susan—a dark foreign girl, Sophie's visitor. In an armchair Molly, one of the twins, lay curled, sucking her thumb and watching the grownups. She must have some sickness, to be kept from school. The child's listless face, the dark circles under her eyes, hurt Susan: Molly was looking at the three grownups working and talking exactly the same way Susan looked at the four through the kitchen window: she was remote, shut off from them.

But then, just as Susan imagined herself going in, picking up the little girl, and sitting in an armchair with her, stroking her probably heated forehead, Sophie did just that: she had been standing on one leg, the other knee flexed, its foot set against the wall. Now she let her foot in its ribbon-tied red shoe slide down the wall, stood solid on two feet, clapping her hands before and behind her, and sang a couple of lines in German, so that the child lifted her heavy eyes at her and began to smile. Then she walked, or rather skipped, over to the child, swung her up, and let her fall into her lap at the same moment she sat herself. She said "Hopla! Hopla! Molly . . ." and began stroking the dark untidy young head that Molly laid on her shoulder for comfort.

Well. . . . Susan blinked the tears of farewell out of her eyes, and went quietly up the house to her bedroom. There she sat looking at the river through the trees. She felt at peace, but in a way that was new to her. She had no desire to move, to talk, to do anything at all. The devils that had haunted the house, the garden, were not there; but she knew it was because her soul was in Room 19 in Fred's Hotel; she was not really here at all. It was a sensation that should have been frightening: to sit at her own bedroom window, listening to Sophie's rich young voice sing German nursery songs to her child, listening to Mrs. Parkes clatter and move below, and to know that all this had nothing to do with her: she was already out of it.

Later, she made herself go down and say she was home: it was unfair to be here unannounced. She took lunch with Mrs. Parkes, Sophie, Sophie's Italian friend Maria, and her daughter Molly, and felt like a visitor.

A few days later, at bedtime, Matthew said: "Here's your five pounds," and pushed them over at her. Yet he must have known she had not been leaving the house at all.

She shook her head, gave it back to him, and said, in explanation, not in accusation: "As soon as you knew where I was, there was no point."

He nodded, not looking at her. He was turned away from her: thinking, she knew, how best to handle this wife who terrified him.

He said: "I wasn't trying to ... it's just that I was worried."

"Yes, I know."

"I must confess that I was beginning to wonder . . ."

"You thought I had a lover?"

"Yes, I am afraid I did."

She knew that he wished she had. She sat wondering how to say: "For a year now I've been spending all my days in a very sordid hotel room. It's the place where I'm happy. In fact, without it I don't exist." She heard herself saying this, and understood how terrified he was that she might. So instead she said: "Well, perhaps you're not far wrong."

Probably Matthew would think the hotel proprietor lied: he would want to think so.

"Well," he said, and she could hear his voice spring up, so to speak, with relief: "in that case I must confess I've got a bit of an affair on myself."

She said, detached and interested: "Really? Who is she?" and saw Matthew's startled look because of this reaction.

"It's Phil. Phil Hunt."

She had known Phil Hunt well in the old unmarried days. She was thinking: No, she won't do, she's too neurotic and difficult. She's never been happy yet. Sophie's much better: Well, Matthew will see that himself, as sensible as he is.

This line of thought went on in silence, while she said aloud: "It's no point telling you about mine, because you don't know him."

Quick, quick, invent, she thought. Remember how you invented all that nonsense for Miss Townsend.

She began slowly, careful not to contradict herself: "His name is Michael—(*Michael What?*)—"Michael Plant." (What a silly name!) "He's rather like you—in looks, I mean." And indeed, she could imagine herself being touched by no one but Matthew himself. "He's a publisher." (Really? Why?) "He's got a wife already and two children."

She brought out this fantasy, proud of herself.

Matthew said: "Are you two thinking of marrying?"

She said, before she could stop herself: "Good God, *no!*"

She realized, if Matthew wanted to marry Phil Hunt, that this was too emphatic, but apparently it was all right, for his voice sounded relieved as he said: "It is a bit impossible to imagine oneself married to anyone else, isn't it?" With which he pulled her to him, so that her head lay on his shoulder. She turned her face into the dark of his flesh, and listened to the blood pounding through her ears saying: I am alone, I am alone, I am alone.

In the morning Susan lay in bed while he dressed.

He had been thinking things out in the night, because now he said: "Susan, why don't we make a foursome?"

Of course, she said to herself, of course he would be bound to say that. If one is sensible, if one is reasonable, if one never allows oneself a base thought or an envious emotion, naturally one says: Let's make a foursome!

"Why not?" she said.

"We could all meet for lunch. I mean, it's ridiculous, you sneaking off to filthy hotels, and me staying late at the office, and all the lies everyone has to tell."

What on earth did I say his name was?—she panicked, then said: "I think it's a good idea, but Michael is away at the moment. When he comes back though—and I'm sure you two would like each other."

"He's away, is he? So that's why you've been . . ." Her husband put his hand to the knot of his tie in a gesture of male coquetry she would not have associated with him; and he bent to kiss her cheek with the expression that goes with the words: Oh you naughty little puss! And she felt its answering look, naughty and coy, come onto her face.

Inside she was dissolving in horror at them both, at how far they had both sunk from honesty to emotion.

So now she was saddled with a lover, and he had a mistress! How ordinary, how reassuring, how jolly! And now they would make a foursome of it, and go about to theatres and restaurants. After all, the Rawlings could well afford that sort of thing, and presumably the publisher Michael Plant could afford to do himself and his mistress quite well. No, there was nothing to stop the four of them developing the most intricate relationship of civilized tolerance, all enveloped in a charming afterglow of autumnal passion. Perhaps they would all go off on holidays together? She had known people who did. Or perhaps Matthew would draw the line there? Why should he, though, if he was capable of talking about "foursomes" at all?

She lay in the empty bedroom, listening to the car drive off with Matthew in it, off to work. Then she heard the children clattering off to school to the accompaniment of Sophie's cheerfully ringing voice. She slid down into the hollow of the bed, for shelter against her own irrelevance. And she stretched out her hand to the hollow where her husband's body had lain, but found no comfort there: he was not her husband. She curled herself up in a small tight ball under the clothes: she could stay here all day, all week, indeed, all her life.

But in a few days she must produce Michael Plant, and—but how? She must presumably find some agreeable man prepared to impersonate a publisher called Michael Plant. And in return for which she would—what? Well, for one thing they would make love. The idea made her want to cry with sheer exhaustion. Oh no, she had finished with all that—the proof of it was that the words "make love," or even imagining it, trying hard to revive no more than the pleasures of sensuality, let alone affection, or love, made her want to run away and hide from the sheer effort of the thing. . . . Good Lord, why make love at all? Why make love with anyone? Or if you are going to make love, what does it matter who with? Why shouldn't she simply walk into the street, pick up a man and have a roaring sexual affair with him? Why not? Or even with Fred? What difference did it make?

But she had let herself in for it—an interminable stretch of time with a lover, called Michael, as part of a gallant civilized foursome. Well, she could not, and she would not.

She got up, dressed, went down to find Mrs. Parkes, and asked for the loan of a pound, since Matthew, she said, had forgotten to leave her money. She exchanged with Mrs. Parkes variations on the theme that husbands are all the same, they don't think, and without saying a word to Sophie, whose voice could be heard upstairs from the telephone, walked to the underground, travelled to South Kensington, changed to the Inner Circle, got out at Paddington, and walked to Fred's Hotel. There she told Fred that she wasn't going on holiday after all, she needed the room. She would have to wait an hour, Fred said. She went to a busy tearoom-cum-restaurant around the corner, and sat watching the people flow in and out the door that kept swinging open and shut, watched them mingle and merge and separate, felt her being flow into them, into their movement. When the hour was up she left a half crown for her pot of tea, and left the place without looking back at it, just as she had left her house, the big, beautiful white house, without another look, but silently dedicating it to Sophie. She returned to Fred, received the key of No. 19, now free, and ascended the grimy stairs slowly, letting floor after floor fall away below her, keeping her eyes lifted, so that floor after floor descended jerkily to her level of vision, and fell away out of sight.

No. 19 was the same. She saw everything with an acute, narrow, checking glance: the cheap shine of the satin spread, which had been replaced carelessly after the two bodies had finished their convulsions under it; a trace of powder on the glass that topped the chest of drawers; an intense green shade in a fold of the curtain. She stood at the window, looking down, watching people pass and pass and pass until her mind went dark from the constant movement. Then she sat in the wicker chair, letting herself go slack. But she had to be careful, because she did not want, today, to be surprised by Fred's knock at five o'clock.

The demons were not here. They had gone forever, because she was buying her freedom from them. She was slipping already into the dark fructifying dreaming that seemed to caress her inwardly, like the movement of her blood . . . but she had to think about Matthew first. Should she write a letter for the coroner? But what should she say?

She would like to leave him with the look on his face she had seen this morning—banal, admittedly, but at least confidently healthy. Well, that was impossible, one did not look like that with a wife dead from suicide. But how to leave him believing she was dying because of a man—because of the fascinating publisher Michael Plant? Oh, how ridiculous! How absurd! How humiliating! But she decided not to trouble about it, simply not to think about the living. If he wanted to believe she had a lover, he would believe it. And he *did* want to believe it. Even when he had found out that there was no publisher in London called Michael Plant, he would think: Oh poor Susan, she was afraid to give me his real name.

And what did it matter whether he married Phil Hunt or Sophie? Though it ought to be Sophie, who was already the mother of those children . . . and what hypocrisy to sit here worrying about the children, when she was going to leave them because she had not got the energy to stay.

She had about four hours. She spent them delightfully, darkly, sweetly, letting herself slide gently, gently, to the edge of the river. Then, with hardly a break in her consciousness, she got up, pushed the thin rug against the door, made sure the windows were tight shut, put two shillings in the meter, and turned on the gas. For the first time since she had been in the room she lay on the hard bed that smelled stale, that smelled of sweat and sex.

She lay on her back on the green satin cover, but her legs were chilly. She got up, found a blanket folded in the bottom of the chest of drawers, and carefully covered her legs with it. She was quite content lying there, listening to the faint soft hiss of the gas that poured into the room, into her lungs, into her brain, as she drifted off into the dark river.

GRACE PALEY was born in the Bronx in 1922, the child of Jewish immigrants. She attended Hunter College and New York University. She has taught literature at Columbia, Syracuse University, and Sarah Lawrence College, served as secretary at the Greenwich Village Peace Center, and won two fellowships in fiction. Her first book of stories, *The Little Disturbances of Man* (1959), went out of print in 1965, but it stayed alive underground where it was loved and raved about; it was reissued by Viking in 1968.

Philip Roth has said, "Grace Paley has deep feelings, a wild imagination, and a style whose toughness and bumpiness arise not out of exasperation with the language, but the daring and heart of a genuine writer of prose." Donald Barthelme calls her "a wonderful writer and a troublemaker. We are fortunate to have her in this country." She is thought of as a troublemaker for her long and active commitment to ending the war in Vietnam. About her lives as a full-time peace activist and a part-time writer of short fiction she has said that she's spent "most of the last couple of years in radical, nonviolent antiwar organizations. Have curtailed my own writing. Have been in jail and will go again. This murdering of our young must end."

Throughout the sixties her stories were published in *Esquire, Atlantic,* and *New American Review,* and in 1974 seventeen of these stories were published in a collection, *Enormous Changes at the Last Minute.* Grace Paley says she only writes when she feels like it. Sometimes she writes on the subway. Writing about city life, she speaks with the diverse tongues of a scold, a poet, and a prophetic conscience.

Grace Paley
(1922–)

AN INTEREST IN LIFE

My husband gave me a broom one Christmas. This wasn't right. No one can tell me it was meant kindly.

"I don't want you not to have anything for Christmas while I'm away in the Army," he said. "Virginia, please look at it. It comes with this fancy dustpan. It hangs off a stick. Look at it, will you? Are you blind or crosseyed?"

"Thanks, chum," I said. I had always wanted a dustpan hooked up that way. It was a good one. My husband doesn't shop in bargain basements or January sales.

Still and all, in spite of the quality, it was a mean present to give a woman you planned on never seeing again, a person you had children with and got onto all the time, drunk or sober, even when everybody had to get up early in the morning.

I asked him if he could wait and join the Army in a half hour, as I had to get the groceries. I don't like to leave kids alone in a three-room apartment full of gas and electricity. Fire may break out from a nasty remark. Or the oldest decides to get even with the youngest.

"Just this once," he said. "But you better figure out how to get along without me."

"You're a handicapped person mentally," I said. "You should've been institutionalized years ago." I slammed the door. I didn't want to see him pack his underwear and ironed shirts.

I never got further than the front stoop, though, because there was Mrs. Raftery, wringing her hands, tears in her eyes as though she had a monopoly on all the good news.

"Mrs. Raftery!" I said, putting my arm around her. "Don't cry." She leaned on me because I am such a horsy build. "Don't cry, Mrs. Raftery, please!" I said.

"That's like you, Virginia. Always looking at the ugly side of things. 'Take in the wash. It's rainin'!' That's you.

You're the first one knows it when the dumb-waiter breaks."

"Oh, come on now, that's not so. It just isn't so," I said. "I'm the exact opposite."

"Did you see Mrs. Cullen yet?" she asked, paying no attention.

"Where?"

"Virginia!" she said, shocked. "She's passed away. The whole house knows it. They've got her in white like a bride and you never saw a beautiful creature like that. She must be eighty. Her husband's proud."

"She was never more than an acquaintance; she didn't have any children," I said.

"Well, I don't care about that. Now, Virginia, you do what I say now, you go downstairs and you say like this—listen to me—say, 'I hear, Mr. Cullen, your wife's passed away. I'm sorry.' Then ask him how he is. Then you ought to go around the corner and see her. She's in Witson & Wayde. Then you ought to go over to the church when they carry her over."

"It's not my church," I said.

"That's no reason, Virginia. You go up like this," she said, parting from me to do a prancy dance. "Up the big front steps, into the church you go. It's beautiful in there. You can't help kneeling only for a minute. Then round to the right. Then up the other stairway. Then you come to a great oak door that's arched above you, then," she said, seizing a deep, deep breath, for all the good it would do her, "and then turn the knob slo-owly and open the door and see for yourself: Our Blessed Mother is in charge. Beautiful. Beautiful. Beautiful."

I sighed in and I groaned out, so as to melt a certain pain around my heart. A steel ring like arthritis, at my age.

"You are a groaner," Mrs. Raftery said, gawking into my mouth.

"I am not," I said. I got a whiff of her, a terrible cheap wine lush.

My husband threw a penny at the door from the inside to take my notice from Mrs. Raftery. He rattled the glass door to make sure I looked at him. He had a fat duffel bag on each shoulder. Where did he acquire so much worldly possession? What was in them? My grandma's goose feathers from across the ocean? Or all the diaper-service diapers? To this day the truth is shrouded in mystery.

"What the hell are you doing, Virginia?" he said, dumping them at my feet. "Standing out here on your hind legs telling everybody your business? The Army gives you a certain time, for God's sakes, they're not kidding." Then he said, "I beg your pardon," to Mrs. Raftery. He took hold of me with his two arms as though in love and pressed his body hard against mine so that I could feel him for the last time and suffer my loss. Then he kissed me in a mean way to nearly split my lip. Then he winked and said, "That's all for now," and skipped off into the future, duffel bags full of rags.

He left me in an embarrassing situation, nearly fainting, in front of that old widow, who can't even remember the half of it. "He's a crook," said Mrs. Raftery. "Is he leaving for good or just temporarily, Virginia?"

"Oh, he's probably deserting me," I said, and sat down on the stoop, pulling my big knees up to my chin.

"If that's the case, tell the Welfare right away," she said. "He's a bum, leaving you just before Christmas. Tell the cops," she said. "They'll provide the toys for the little kids gladly. And don't forget to let the grocer in on it. He won't be so hard on you expecting payment."

She saw that sadness was stretched world-wide across my face. Mrs. Raftery isn't the worst person. She said, "Look around for comfort, dear." With a nervous finger she pointed to the truckers eating lunch on their haunches across the street, leaning on the loading platforms. She waved her hand to include in all the men marching up and down in search of a decent luncheonette. She didn't leave out the six longshoremen loafing under the fish-market marquee. "If their lungs and stomachs ain't crushed by overwork, they disappear somewhere in the world. Don't be disappointed, Virginia. I don't know a man living'd last you a lifetime."

Ten days later Girard asked, "Where's Daddy?"

"Ask me no questions, I'll tell you no lies." I didn't want the children to know the facts. Present or past, a child should have a father.

"Where *is* Daddy?" Girard asked the week after that.

"He joined the Army," I said.

"He made my bunk bed," said Phillip.

"The truth shall make ye free," I said.

Then I sat down with pencil and pad to get in control of my resources. The facts, when I added and subtracted them, were that my husband had left me with fourteen dollars, and the rent unpaid, in an emergency state. He'd claimed he was sorry to do this, but my opinion is, out of sight, out of mind. "The city won't let you starve," he'd said. "After all, you're half the population. You're keeping up the good work. Without you the race would die out. Who'd pay the taxes? Who'd keep the streets clean? There wouldn't be no Army. A man like me wouldn't have no place to go."

I sent Girard right down to Mrs. Raftery with a request about the whereabouts of Welfare. She responded RSVP with an extra comment in left-handed script: "Poor Girard . . . he's never the boy my John was!"

Who asked her?

I called on Welfare right after the new year. In no time I discovered that they're rigged up to deal with liars, and if you're truthful it's disappointing to them. They may even refuse to handle your case if you're too truthful.

They asked sensible questions at first. They asked where my husband had enlisted. I didn't know. They put some letter writers and agents after him. "He's not in the United States Army," they said. "Try the Brazilian Army," I suggested.

They have no sense of kidding around. They're not the least bit lighthearted and they tried. "Oh no," they said. "That was incorrect. He is not in the Brazilian Army."

"No?" I said. "How strange! He must be in the Mexican Navy."

By law, they had to hound his brothers. They wrote to his brother who has a first-class card in the Teamsters and owns an apartment house in California. They asked his two brothers in Jersey to help me. They have large families. Rightfully they laughed. Then they wrote to Thomas, the oldest, the smart one (the one they all worked so hard for years to keep him in college until his brains could pay off). He was the one who sent ten dollars immediately, saying, "What a bastard! I'll send something time to time, Ginny, but whatever you do, don't tell the authorities." Of course I never did. Soon they began to guess they were better people than me, that I was in trouble because I deserved it, and then they liked me better.

But they never fixed my refrigerator. Every time I called I said patiently, "The milk is sour . . ." I said, "Corn beef went bad." Sitting in that beer-stinking phone booth in Felan's for the sixth time (sixty cents) with the baby on my lap and Barbie tapping at the glass door with an American flag, I cried into the secretary's hardhearted ear, "I bought real butter for the holiday, and it's rancid . . ." They said, "You'll have to get a better bid on the repair job."

While I waited indoors for a man to bid, Girard took to swinging back and forth on top of the bathroom door, just to soothe himself, giving me the laugh, dreamy, nibbling calcimine off the ceiling. On first sight Mrs. Raftery said, "Whack the monkey, he'd be better off on arsenic."

But Girard is my son and I'm the judge. It means a terrible thing for the future, though I don't know what to call it.

It was from constantly thinking of my foreknowledge on this and other subjects, it was from observing when I put my lipstick on daily, how my face was just curling up to die, that John Raftery came from Jersey to rescue me.

On Thursdays, anyway, John Raftery took the tubes to visit his mother. The whole house knew it. She was cheerful even before breakfast. She sang out loud in a girlish brogue that only came to tongue for grand occasions. Hanging out the wash, she blushed to recall what a remarkable boy her John had been. "Ask the sisters around the corner," she said to the open kitchen windows. "They'll never forget John."

That particular night after supper Mrs. Raftery said to her son, "John, how come you don't say hello to your old friend Virginia? She's had hard luck and she's gloomy."

"Is that so, Mother?" he said, and immediately climbed two flights to knock at my door.

"Oh, John," I said at the sight of him, hat in hand in a white shirt and blue-striped tie, spick-and-span, a Sunday-school man. "Hello!"

"Welcome, John!" I said. "Sit down. Come right in. How are you? You look awfully good. You do. Tell me, how've you been all this time, John?"

"How've I been?" he asked thoughtfully. To answer within reason, he described his life with Margaret, marriage, work, and children up to the present day.

I had nothing good to report. Now that he had put the subject around before my very eyes, every burnt-up day of my life smoked in shame, and I couldn't even get a clear view of the good half hours.

"Of course," he said, "you do have lovely children. Noticeable-looking, Virginia. Good looks is always something to be thankful for."

"Thankful?" I said. "I don't have to thank anything but my own foolishness for four children when I'm twenty-six years old, deserted, and poverty-struck, regardless of looks. A man can't help it, but I could have behaved better."

"Don't be so cruel on yourself, Ginny," he said. "Children come from God."

"You're still great on holy subjects, aren't you? You know damn well where children come from."

He did know. His red face reddened further. John Raftery has had that color coming out on him boy and man from keeping his rages so inward.

Still he made more sense in his conversation after that, and I poured fresh tea to tell him how my husband used to like me because I was a passionate person. That was until he took a look around and saw how in the long run this life only meant more of the same thing. He tried to turn away from me once he came to this understanding, and make me hate him. His face changed. He gave up his brand of cigarettes, which we had in common. He threw out the two pairs of socks I knitted by hand. "If there's anything I hate in this world, it's navy blue," he said. Oh, I could have dyed them. I would have done anything for him, if he were only not too sorry to ask me.

"You were a nice kid in those days," said John, referring to certain Saturday nights. "A wild, nice kid."

"Aaah," I said, disgusted. Whatever I was then, was on the way to where I am now. "I was fresh. If I had a kid like me, I'd slap her cross-eyed."

The very next Thursday John gave me a beautiful radio with a record player. "Enjoy yourself," he said. That really made Welfare speechless. We didn't own any records, but the investigator saw my burden was lightened and he scribbled a dozen pages about it in his notebook.

On the third Thursday he brought a walking doll (twenty-four inches) for Linda and Barbie with a card inscribed, "A baby doll for a couple of dolls." He had also had a couple of drinks at his mother's, and this made him want to dance. "La-la-la, let yourself go . . ."

"You gotta give a little," he sang, "live a little . . ." He said, "Virginia, may I have this dance?"

"Sssh, we finally got them asleep. Please, turn the radio down. Quiet. Deathly silence, John Raftery."

"Let me do your dishes, Virginia."

"Don't be silly, you're a guest in my house," I said. "I still regard you as a guest."

"Tell me I'm the most gorgeous thing," I said, dipping my arm to the funny bone in dish soup.

He didn't answer. "I'm having a lot of trouble at work," was all he said. Then I heard him push the chair back. He came up behind me, put his arms around my waistline, and kissed my cheek. He whirled me around and took my hands. He said, "An old friend is better than rubies." He looked me in the eye. He held my attention by trying to be honest. And he kissed me a short sweet kiss on my mouth.

"Please sit down, Virginia," he said. He kneeled before me and put his head in my lap. I was stirred by so much activity. Then he looked up at me and, as though proposing marriage for life, he offered—because he was drunk—to place his immortal soul in peril to comfort me.

First I said, "Thank you." Then I said, "No."

I was sorry for him, but he's devout, a leader of the Fathers' Club at his church, active in all the lay groups for charities, orphans, etc. I knew that if he stayed late to love with me, he would not do it lightly but would in the end pay terrible penance and ruin his long life. The responsibility would be on me.

So I said no.

And Barbie is such a light sleeper. All she has to do, I thought, is wake up and wander in and see her mother and her new friend John with his pants around his knees, wrestling on the kitchen table. A vision like that could affect a kid for life.

I said no.

Everyone in this building is so goddamn nosy. That evening I had to say no.

But John came to visit, anyway, on the fourth Thursday. This time he brought the discarded dresses of Margaret's daughters, organdy party dresses and glazed cotton for every day. He gently admired Barbara and Linda, his blue eyes rolling to back up a couple of dozen oohs and ahs.

Even Phillip, who thinks God gave him just a certain number of hellos and he better save them for the final judgment, Phillip leaned on John and said, "Why don't you bring your boy to play with me? I don't have nobody who to play with." (Phillip's a liar. There must be at least seventy-one children in this house, pale pink to medium brown, English-talking and gibbering in Spanish, rough-and-tough boys, the Lone Ranger's bloody pals, or the exact picture of Supermouse. If a boy wanted a friend, he could pick the very one out of his neighbors.)

Also, Girard is a cold fish. He was in a lonesome despair. Sometimes he looked in the mirror and said, "How come I have such an ugly face? My nose is funny. Mostly people don't like me." He was a liar too. Girard has a face like his father's. His eyes are the color of those little blue plums in August. He looks like an advertisement in a magazine. He could be a child model and make a lot of money. He is my first child, and if he thinks he is ugly, I think I am ugly.

John said, "I can't stand to see a boy mope like that. . . . What do the sisters say in school?"

"He doesn't pay attention is all they say. You can't get much out of them."

"My middle boy was like that," said John. "Couldn't take an interest. Aaah, I wish I didn't have all that headache on the job. I'd grab Girard by the collar and make him take notice of the world. I wish I could ask him out to Jersey to play in all that space."

"Why not?" I said.

"Why, Virginia, I'm surprised you don't know why not. You know I can't take your children out to meet my children."

I felt a lot of strong arthritis in my ribs.

"My mother's the funny one, Virginia." He felt he had to continue with the subject matter. "I don't know. I guess she likes the idea of bugging Margaret. She says, 'You goin' up, John?' 'Yes, Mother,' I say. 'Behave yourself, John,' she says. 'That husband might come home and hack-saw you into hell. You're a Catholic man, John,' she says. But I figured it out. She likes to know I'm in the building. I swear, Virginia, she wishes me the best of luck."

"I do too, John," I said. We drank a last glass of beer to make sure of a peaceful sleep. "Good night, Virginia," he said, looping his muffler neatly under his chin. "Don't worry. I'll be thinking of what to do about Girard."

I got into the big bed that I share with the girls in the little room. For once I had no trouble falling asleep. I only had to worry about Linda and Barbara and Phillip. It was a great relief to me that John had taken over the thinking about Girard.

John was sincere. That's true. He paid a lot of attention to Girard, smoking out all his sneaky sorrows. He registered him into a wild pack of cub scouts that went up to the Bronx once a week to let off steam. He gave him a Junior Erector Set. And sometimes when his family wasn't listening he prayed at great length for him.

One Sunday, Sister Veronica said in her sweet voice from another life, "He's not worse. He might even be a little better. How are *you,* Virginia?" putting her hand on mine. Everybody around here acts like they know everything.

"Just fine," I said.

"We ought to start on Phillip," John said, "if it's true Girard's improving."

"You should've been a social worker, John."

"A lot of people have noticed that about me," said John.

"Your mother was always acting so crazy about you, how come she didn't knock herself out a little to see you in college? Like we did for Thomas?"

"Now, Virginia, be fair. She's a poor old woman. My father was a weak earner. She had to have my wages, and I'll tell you, Virginia, I'm not sorry. Look at Thomas. He's still in school. Drop him in this jungle and he'd be devoured. He hasn't had a touch of real life. And here I am with a good chunk of a family, a home of my own, a name in the building trades. One thing I have to tell you, the poor old woman is sorry. I said one day (oh, in passing—years ago) that I might marry you. She stuck a knife in herself. It's a fact. Not more than an eighth of an inch. You never saw such a gory Sunday. One thing—you would have been a better daughter-in-law to her than Margaret."

"Marry me?" I said.

"Well, yes. . . . aah—I always liked you, then . . . Why do you think I'd sit in the shade of this kitchen every Thursday night? For God's sakes, the only warm thing around here is this teacup. Yes, sir, I did want to marry you, Virginia."

"No kidding, John? Really?" It was nice to know. Better late than never, to learn you were desired in youth.

I didn't tell John, but the truth is, I would never have married him. Once I met my husband with his winking looks, he was my only interest. Wild as I had been with John and others, I turned all my wildness over to him and then there was no question in my mind.

Still, face facts, if my husband didn't budge on in life, it was my fault. On me, as they say, be it. I greeted the morn with a song. I had a hello for everyone but the landlord. Ask the people on the block, come or go—even the Spanish ones, with their sad dark faces—they have to smile when they see me.

But for his own comfort, he should have done better lifewise and moneywise. I was happy, but I am now in possession of knowledge that this is wrong. Happiness isn't so bad for a woman. She gets fatter, she gets older, she could lie down, nuzzling a regiment of men and little kids, she could just die of the pleasure. But men are different, they have to own money, or they have to be famous, or everybody on the block has to look up to them from the cellar stairs.

A woman counts her children and acts snotty, like she invented life, but men *must* do well in the world. I know that men are not fooled by being happy.

"A funny guy," said John, guessing where my thoughts had gone. "What stopped him up? He was nobody's fool. He had a funny thing about him, Virginia, if you don't mind my saying so. He wasn't much distance up, but he was all set and ready to be looking down on us all."

"He was very smart, John. You don't realize that. His hobby was crossword puzzles, and I said to him real often, as did others around here, that he ought to go out on the '$64 Question.' Why not? But he laughed. You know what he said? He said, 'That proves how dumb you are if you think I'm smart.' "

"A funny guy," said John. "Get it all off your chest," he said. "Talk it out, Virginia; it's the only way to kill the pain."

By and large, I was happy to oblige. Still I could not carry through about certain cruel remarks. It was like trying to move back into the dry mouth of a nightmare to remember that the last day I was happy was the middle of a week in March, when I told my husband I was going to have Linda. Barbara was five months old to the hour. The boys were three and four. I had to tell him. It was the last day with anything happy about it.

Later on he said, "Oh, you make me so sick, you're so goddamn big and fat, you look like a goddamn brownstone, the way you're squared off in front."

"Well, where are you going tonight?" I asked.

"How should I know?" he said. "Your big ass takes up the whole goddamn bed," he said. "There's no room for me." He bought a sleeping bag and slept on the floor.

I couldn't believe it. I would start every morning fresh. I couldn't believe that he would turn against me so, while I was still young and even his friends still liked me.

But he did, he turned absolutely against me and became no friend of mine. "All you ever think about is making babies. This place stinks like the men's room in the BMT. It's a fucking *pissoir.*" He was strong on truth all through the year. "That kid eats more than the five of us put together," he said. "Stop stuffing your face, you fat dumbbell," he said to Phillip.

Then he worked on the neighbors. "Get that nosy old bag out of here," he said. "If she comes on once more with 'my son in the building trades' I'll squash her for the cat."

Then he turned on Spielvogel, the checker, his oldest friend, who only visited on holidays and never spoke to me (shy, the way some bachelors are). "That sonofabitch, don't hand me that friendship crap, all he's after is your ass. That's what I need—a little shitmaker of his using up the air in this flat."

And then there was no one else to dispose of. We were left alone fair and square, facing each other.

"Now, Virginia," he said, "I come to the end of my rope. I see a black wall ahead of me. What the hell am I supposed to do? I only got one life. Should I lie down and die? I don't know what to do any more. I'll give it to you straight, Virginia, if I stick around, you can't help it, you'll hate me . . ."

"I hate you right now," I said. "So do whatever you like."

"This place drives me nuts," he mumbled. "I don't know what to do around here. I want to get you a present. Something."

"I told you, do whatever you like. Buy me a rattrap for rats."

That's when he went down to the House Appliance Store, and he brought back a new broom and a classy dustpan.

"A new broom sweeps clean," he said. "I got to get out of here," he said. "I'm going nuts." Then he began to stuff the duffel bags, and I went to the grocery store but was stopped by Mrs. Raftery, who had to tell me what she considered so beautiful—death—then he kissed and went to join some army somewhere.

I didn't tell John any of this, because I think it makes a woman look too bad to tell on how another man has treated her. He begins to see her through the other man's eyes, a sitting duck, a skinful of flaws. After all, I had come to depend on John. All my husband's friends were strangers now, though I had always said to them, "Feel welcome."

And the family men in the building looked too cunning, as though they had all personally deserted me. If they met me on the stairs, they carried the heaviest groceries up and helped bring Linda's stroller down, but they never asked me a question worth answering at all.

Besides that, Girard and Phillip taught the girls the days of the week: Monday, Tuesday, Wednesday, Johnday, Friday. They waited for him once a week, under the hallway lamp, half asleep like bugs in the sun, sitting in their little chairs with their names on in gold, a birth present from my mother-in-law. At fifteen after eight he punctually came, to read a story, pass out some kisses, and tuck them into bed.

But one night, after a long Johnday of them squealing my eardrum split, after a rainy afternoon with brother constantly raising up his hand against brother, with the girls near ready to go to court over the proper ownership of Melinda Lee, the twenty-four-inch walking doll, the doorbell rang three times. Not any of those times did John's face greet me.

I was too ashamed to call down to Mrs. Raftery, and she was too mean to knock on my door and explain.

He didn't come the following Thursday either. Girard said sadly, "He must've run away, John."

I had to give him up after two weeks' absence and no word. I didn't know how to tell the children: something about right and wrong, goodness and meanness, men and women. I had it all at my finger tips, ready to hand over. But I didn't think I ought to take mistakes and truth away from them. Who knows? They might make a truer friend in this world somewhere than I have ever made. So I just put them to bed and sat in the kitchen and cried.

In the middle of my third beer, searching in my mind for the next step, I found the decision to go on "Strike It Rich." I scrounged some paper and pencil from the toy box and I listed all my troubles, which must be done in order to qualify. The list when complete could have brought tears to the eye of God if He had a minute. At the sight of it my bitterness began to improve. All that is really necessary for survival of the fittest, it seems, is an interest in life, good, bad, or peculiar.

As always happens in these cases where you have begun to help yourself with plans, news comes from an opposite direction. The doorbell rang, two short and two long—meaning John.

My first thought was to wake the children and make them happy. "No! No!" he said. "Please don't put yourself to that trouble. Virginia, I'm dog-tired," he said. "Dog-tired. My job is a damn headache. It's too much. It's all day and it scuttles my mind at night, and in the end who does the credit go to?

"Virginia," he said, "I don't know if I can come any more. I've been wanting to tell you. I just don't know. What's it all about? Could you answer me if I asked you? I can't figure this whole thing out at all."

I started the tea steeping because his fingers when I touched them were cold. I didn't speak. I tried looking at it from his man point of view, and I thought he had to take a bus, the tubes, and a subway to see me; and then the subway, the tubes, and a bus to go back home at 1 A.M. It wouldn't be any trouble at all for him to part with us forever. I thought about my life, and I gave strongest consideration to my children. If given the choice, I decided to choose not to live without him.

"What's that?" he asked, pointing to my careful list of troubles. "Writing a letter?"

"Oh no," I said, "it's for 'Strike It Rich.' I hope to go on the program."

"Virginia, for goodness' sakes," he said, giving it a glance, "you don't have a ghost. They'd laugh you out of the studio. Those people really suffer."

"Are you sure, John?" I asked.

"No question in my mind at all," said John. "Have you ever seen that program? I mean, in addition to all of this—the little disturbances of man"—he waved a scornful hand at my list—"they *suffer*. They live in the forefront of tornadoes, their lives are washed off by floods—catastrophes of God. Oh, Virginia."

"Are you sure, John?"

"For goodness' sake . . ."

Sadly I put my list away. Still, if things got worse, I could always make use of it.

Once that was settled, I acted on an earlier decision. I pushed his cup of scalding tea aside. I wedged myself onto his lap between his hard belt buckle and the table. I put my arms around his neck and said, "How come you're so cold, John?" He has a kind face and he knew how to look astonished. He said, "Why, Virginia, I'm getting warmer." We laughed.

John became a lover to me that night.

Mrs. Raftery is sometimes silly and sick from her private source of cheap wine. She expects John often. "Honor your mother, what's the matter with you, John?" she complains. "Honor. Honor."

"Virginia dear," she says. "You never would've taken John away to Jersey like Margaret. I wish he'd've married you."

"You didn't like me much in those days."

"That's a lie," she says. I know she's a hypocrite, but no more than the rest of the world.

What is remarkable to me is that it doesn't seem to conscience John as I thought it might. It is still hard to believe that a man who sends out the Ten Commandments every year for a Christmas card can be so easy buttoning and unbuttoning.

Of course we must be very careful not to wake the children or disturb the neighbors who will enjoy another person's excitement just so far, and then the pleasure enrages them. We must be very careful for ourselves too, for when my husband comes back, realizing the babies are in school and everything easier, he won't forgive me if I've started it all up again—noisy signs of life that are so much trouble to a man.

We haven't seen him in two and a half years. Although people have suggested it, I do not want the police or Intelligence or a private eye or anyone to go after him to bring him back. I know that if he expected to stay away forever he would have written and said so. As it is, I just don't know what evening, any time, he may appear. Sometimes, stumbling over a blockbuster of a dream at midnight, I wake up to vision his soft arrival.

He comes in the door with his old key. He gives me a

strict look and says, "Well, you look older, Virginia." "So do you," I say, although he hasn't changed a bit.

He settles in the kitchen because the children are asleep all over the rest of the house. I unknot his tie and offer him a cold sandwich. He raps my backside, paying attention to the bounce. I walk around him as though he were a Maypole, kissing as I go.

"I didn't like the Army much," he says. "Next time I think I might go join the Merchant Marine."

"What army?" I say.

"It's pretty much the same everywhere," he says.

"I wouldn't be a bit surprised," I say.

"I lost my cuff link, goddamnit," he says, and drops to the floor to look for it. I go down too on my knees, but I know he never had a cuff link in his life. Still I would do a lot for him.

"Got you off your feet that time," he says, laughing. "Oh yes, I did." And before I can even make myself half comfortable on that polka-dotted linoleum, he got onto me right where we were and the truth is, we were so happy, we forgot the precautions.

FLANNERY O'CONNOR was born in Savannah, Georgia, in 1925 and moved to Milledgeville, Georgia, in 1938. She had her first story published at the age of twenty-one, while attending the Writers Workshop at the University of Iowa. In his introduction to her collection of stories, *Everything That Rises Must Converge*, the poet Robert Fitzgerald describes the period that O'Connor lived with him and his wife and children on their Connecticut farm, writing her first novel, *Wise Blood*. Before the book was finished, she suffered her first major attack of lupus on the way home to Georgia for the Christmas holidays. It took her five years to finish the novel and she fought the lupus (a disease of the blood vessels that had killed her father) for fourteen years, writing, lecturing, and traveling when she wasn't in the hospital. She died in August, 1964, at the age of thirty-nine. *The Complete Stories of Flannery O'Connor* received the National Book Award for fiction in 1971.

When asked the major influences on her life, Flannery O'Connor answered, "Probably being a Catholic, and a Southerner, and a writer." She wrote, she said, "because I'm good at it." She spoke of fiction-writing as a religious vocation and her own gift as rooted in and nourished by her very orthodox Catholicism. She once told an audience that "the Catholic sacramental view of life is one that maintains and supports at every turn the vision that the storyteller must have if he is going to write fiction of any depth."

Flannery O'Connor (*1925–1964*)

REVELATION

The doctor's waiting room, which was very small, was almost full when the Turpins entered and Mrs. Turpin, who was very large, made it look even smaller by her presence. She stood looming at the head of the magazine table set in the center of it, a living demonstration that the room was inadequate and ridiculous. Her little bright black eyes took in all the patients as she sized up the seating situation. There was one vacant chair and a place on the sofa occupied by a blond child in a dirty blue romper who should have been told to move over and make room for the lady. He was five or six, but Mrs. Turpin saw at once that no one was going to tell him to move over. He was slumped down in the seat, his arms idle at his sides and his eyes idle in his head; his nose ran unchecked.

Mrs. Turpin put a firm hand on Claud's shoulder and said in a voice that included anyone who wanted to listen, "Claud, you sit in that chair there," and gave him a push down into the vacant one. Claud was florid and bald and sturdy, somewhat shorter than Mrs. Turpin, but he sat down as if he were accustomed to doing what she told him to.

Mrs. Turpin remained standing. The only man in the room besides Claud was a lean stringy old fellow with a rusty hand spread out on each knee, whose eyes were closed as if he were asleep or dead or pretending to be so as not to get up and offer her his seat. Her gaze settled agreeably on a well-dressed grey-haired lady whose eyes met hers and whose expression said: if that child belonged to me, he would have some manners and move over—there's plenty of room there for you and him too.

Claud looked up with a sigh and made as if to rise.

"Sit down," Mrs. Turpin said. "You know you're not supposed to stand on that leg. He has an ulcer on his leg," she explained.

Claud lifted his foot onto the magazine table and rolled

his trouser leg up to reveal a purple swelling on a plump marble-white calf.

"My!" the pleasant lady said. "How did you do that?"

"A cow kicked him," Mrs. Turpin said.

"Goodness!" said the lady.

Claud rolled his trouser leg down.

"Maybe the little boy would move over," the lady suggested, but the child not stir.

"Somebody will be leaving in a minute," Mrs. Turpin said. She could not understand why a doctor—with as much money as they made charging five dollars a day to just stick their head in the hospital door and look at you—couldn't afford a decent-sized waiting room. This one was hardly bigger than a garage. The table was cluttered with limp-looking magazines and at one end of it there was a big green glass ash tray full of cigarette butts and cotton wads with little blood spots on them. If she had had anything to do with the running of the place, that would have been emptied every so often. There were no chairs against the wall at the head of the room. It had a rectangular-shaped panel in it that permitted a view of the office where the nurse came and went and the secretary listened to the radio. A plastic fern in a gold pot sat in the opening and trailed its fronds down almost to the floor. The radio was softly playing gospel music.

Just then the inner door opened and a nurse with the highest stack of yellow hair Mrs. Turpin had ever seen put her face in the crack and called for the next patient. The woman sitting beside Claud grasped the two arms of her chair and hoisted herself up; she pulled her dress free from her legs and lumbered through the door where the nurse had disappeared.

Mrs. Turpin eased into the vacant chair, which held her tight as a corset. "I wish I could reduce," she said, and rolled her eyes and gave a comic sigh.

"Oh, *you* aren't fat," the stylish lady said.

"Ooooo I am too," Mrs. Turpin said. "Claud he eats all he wants to and never weighs over one hundred and seventy-five pounds, but me I just look at something good to eat and I gain some weight," and her stomach and shoulders shook with laughter. "You can eat all you want to, can't you, Claud?" she asked, turning to him.

Claud only grinned.

"Well, as long as you have such a good disposition," the

stylish lady said, "I don't think it makes a bit of difference what size you are. You just can't beat a good disposition."

Next to her was a fat girl of eighteen or nineteen, scowling into a thick blue book which Mrs. Turpin saw was entitled *Human Development*. The girl raised her head and directed her scowl at Mrs. Turpin as if she did not like her looks. She appeared annoyed that anyone should speak while she tried to read. The poor girl's face was blue with acne and Mrs. Turpin thought how pitiful it was to have a face like that at that age. She gave the girl a friendly smile but the girl only scowled the harder. Mrs. Turpin herself was fat but she had always had good skin, and, though she was forty-seven years old, there was not a wrinkle in her face except around her eyes from laughing too much.

Next to the ugly girl was the child, still in exactly the same position, and next to him was a thin leathery old woman in a cotton print dress. She and Claud had three sacks of chicken feed in their pump house that was in the same print. She had seen from the first that the child belonged with the old woman. She could tell by the way they sat—kind of vacant and white-trashy, as if they would sit there until Doomsday if nobody called and told them to get up. And at right angles but next to the well-dressed pleasant lady was a lank-faced woman who was certainly the child's mother. She had on a yellow sweat shirt and wine-colored slacks, both gritty-looking, and the rims of her lips were stained with snuff. Her dirty yellow hair was tied behind with a little piece of red paper ribbon. Worse than niggers any day, Mrs. Turpin thought.

The gospel hymn playing was, "When I looked up and He looked down," and Mrs. Turpin, who knew it, supplied the last line mentally, "And wona these days I know I'll we-eara crown."

Without appearing to, Mrs. Turpin always noticed people's feet. The well-dressed lady had on red and grey suede shoes to match her dress. Mrs. Turpin had on her good black patent leather pumps. The ugly girl had on Girl Scout shoes and heavy socks. The old woman had on tennis shoes and the white-trashy mother had on what appeared to be bedroom slippers, black straw with gold braid threaded through them—exactly what you would have expected her to have on.

Sometimes at night when she couldn't go to sleep, Mrs. Turpin would occupy herself with the question of who she would have chosen to be if she couldn't have been herself. If Jesus had said to her before he made her, "There's only two places available for you. You can either be a nigger or white-trash," what would she have said? "Please, Jesus, please," she would have said, "just let me wait until there's another place available," and he would have said, "No, you have to go right now and I have only those two places so make up your mind." She would have wiggled and squirmed and begged and pleaded but it would have been no use and finally she would have said, "All right, make me a nigger then—but that don't mean a trashy one." And he would have made her a neat clean respectable Negro woman, herself but black.

Next to the child's mother was a red-headed youngish woman, reading one of the magazines and working a piece of chewing gum, hell for leather, as Claud would say. Mrs. Turpin could not see the woman's feet. She was not white-trash, just common. Sometimes Mrs. Turpin occupied herself at night naming the classes of people. On the bottom of the heap were most colored people, not the kind she would have been if she had been one, but most of them; then next to them—not above, just away from—were the white-trash; then above them were the home-owners, and above them the home-and-land owners, to which she and Claud belonged. Above she and Claud were people with a lot of money and much bigger houses and much more land. But here the complexity of it would begin to bear in on her, for some of the people with a lot of money were common and ought to be below she and Claud and some of the people who had good blood had lost their money and had to rent and then there were colored people who owned their homes and land as well. There was a colored dentist in town who had two red Lincolns and a swimming pool and a farm with registered white-face cattle on it. Usually by the time she had fallen asleep all the classes of people were moiling and roiling around in her head, and she would dream they were all crammed in together in a box car, being ridden off to be put in a gas oven.

"That's a beautiful clock," she said and nodded to her right. It was a big wall clock, the face encased in a brass sunburst.

"Yes, it's very pretty," the stylish lady said agreeably. "And right on the dot too," she added, glancing at her watch.

The ugly girl beside her cast an eye upward at the clock, smirked, then looked directly at Mrs. Turpin and smirked again. Then she returned her eyes to her book. She was obviously the lady's daughter because, although they didn't look anything alike as to disposition, they both had the same shape of face and the same blue eyes. On the lady they sparkled pleasantly but in the girl's seared face they appeared alternately to smolder and to blaze.

What if Jesus had said, "All right, you can be white-trash or a nigger or ugly"!

Mrs. Turpin felt an awful pity for the girl, though she thought it was one thing to be ugly and another to act ugly.

The woman with the snuff-stained lips turned around in her chair and looked up at the clock. Then she turned back and appeared to look a little to the side of Mrs. Turpin. There was a cast in one of her eyes. "You want to know wher you can get you one of themther clocks?" she asked in a loud voice.

"No. I already have a nice clock," Mrs. Turpin said. Once somebody like her got a leg in the conversation, she would be all over it.

"You can get you one with green stamps," the woman said. "That's most likely wher he got hisn. Save you up enough, you can get you most anythang. I got me some joo'ry."

Ought to have got you a wash rag and some soap, Mrs. Turpin thought.

"I get contour sheets with mine," the pleasant lady said.

The daughter slammed her book shut. She looked straight in front of her, directly through Mrs. Turpin and on through the yellow curtain and the plate glass window which made the wall behind her. The girl's eyes seemed lit all of a sudden with a peculiar light, an unnatural light like night road signs give. Mrs. Turpin turned her head to see if there was anything going on outside that she should see, but she could not see anything. Figures passing cast only a pale shadow through the curtain. There was no reason the girl should single her out for her ugly looks.

"Miss Finley," the nurse said, cracking the door. The gum-chewing woman got up and passed in front of her and Claud and went into the office. She had on red high-heeled shoes.

Directly across the table, the ugly girl's eyes were fixed

on Mrs. Turpin as if she had some very special reason for disliking her.

"This is wonderful weather, isn't it?" the girl's mother said.

"It's good weather for cotton if you can get the niggers to pick it," Mrs. Turpin said, "but niggers don't want to pick cotton any more. You can't get the white folks to pick it and now you can't get the niggers—because they got to be right up there with the white folks."

"They gonna *try* anyways," the white-trash woman said, leaning forward.

"Do you have one of those cotton-picking machines?" the pleasant lady asked.

"No," Mrs. Turpin said, "they leave half the cotton in the field. We don't have much cotton anyway. If you want to make it farming now, you have to have a little of everything. We got a couple of acres of cotton and a few hogs and chickens and just enough white-face that Claud can look after them himself."

"One thang I don't want," the white-trash woman said, wiping her mouth with the back of her hand. "Hogs. Nasty stinking things, a-gruntin and a-rootin all over the place."

Mrs. Turpin gave her the merest edge of her attention. "Our hogs are not dirty and they don't stink," she said. "They're cleaner than some children I've seen. Their feet never touch the ground. We have a pig-parlor—that's where you raise them on concrete," she explained to the pleasant lady, "and Claud scoots them down with the hose every afternoon and washes off the floor." Cleaner by far than that child right there, she thought. Poor nasty little thing. He had not moved except to put the thumb of his dirty hand into his mouth.

The woman turned her face away from Mrs. Turpin. "I know I wouldn't scoot down no hog with no hose," she said to the wall.

You wouldn't have no hog to scoot down, Mrs. Turpin said to herself.

"A-gruntin and a-rootin and a-groanin," the woman muttered.

"We got a little of everything," Mrs. Turpin said to the pleasant lady. "It's no use in having more than you can handle yourself with help like it is. We found enough niggers to pick our cotton this year but Claud he has to go after them and take them home again in the evening. They can't walk that half a mile. No they can't. I tell you," she said and laughed merrily, "I sure am tired of buttering up niggers, but you got to love em if you want em to work for you. When they come in the morning, I run out and I say, 'Hi yawl this morning?' and when Claud drives them off to the field I just wave to beat the band and they just wave back." And she waved her hand rapidly to illustrate.

"Like you read out of the same book," the lady said, showing she understood perfectly.

"Child, yes," Mrs. Turpin said. "And when they come in from the field, I run out with a bucket of icewater. That's the way it's going to be from now on," she said. "You may as well face it."

"One thang I know," the white-trash woman said. "Two thangs I ain't going to do: love no niggers or scoot down no hog with no hose." And she let out a bark of contempt.

The look that Mrs. Turpin and the pleasant lady exchanged indicated they both understood that you had to *have* certain things before you could *know* certain things. But every time Mrs. Turpin exchanged a look with the lady, she was aware that the ugly girl's peculiar eyes were still on her, and she had trouble bringing her attention back to the conversation.

"When you got something," she said, "you got to look after it." And when you ain't got a thing but breath and britches, she added to herself, you can afford to come to town every morning and just sit on the Court House coping and spit.

A grotesque revolving shadow passed across the curtain behind her and was thrown palely on the opposite wall. Then a bicycle clattered down against the outside of the building. The door opened and a colored boy glided in with a tray from the drug store. It had two large red and white paper cups on it with tops on them. He was a tall, very black boy in discolored white pants and a green nylon shirt. He was chewing gum slowly, as if to music. He set the tray down in the office opening next to the fern and stuck his head through to look for the secretary. She was not in there. He rested his arms on the ledge and waited, his narrow bottom stuck out, swaying slowly to the left and right. He raised a hand over his head and scratched the base of his skull.

"You see that button there, boy?" Mrs. Turpin said.

"You can punch that and she'll come. She's probably in the back somewhere."

"Is thas right?" the boy said agreeably, as if he had never seen the button before. He leaned to the right and put his finger on it. "She sometime out," he said and twisted around to face his audience, his elbows behind him on the counter. The nurse appeared and he twisted back again. She handed him a dollar and he rooted in his pocket and made the change and counted it out to her. She gave him fifteen cents for a tip and he went out with the empty tray. The heavy door swung to slowly and closed at length with the sound of suction. For a moment no one spoke.

"They ought to send all them niggers back to Africa," the white-trash woman said. "That's wher they come from in the first place."

"Oh, I couldn't do without my good colored friends," the pleasant lady said.

"There's a heap of things worse than a nigger," Mrs. Turpin agreed. "It's all kinds of them just like it's all kinds of us."

"Yes, and it takes all kinds to make the world go round," the lady said in her musical voice.

As she said it, the raw-complexioned girl snapped her teeth together. Her lower lip turned downwards and inside out, revealing the pale pink inside of her mouth. After a second it rolled back up. It was the ugliest face Mrs. Turpin had ever seen anyone make and for a moment she was certain that the girl had made it at her. She was looking at her as if she had known and disliked her all her life—all of Mrs. Turpin's life, it seemed too, not just all the girl's life. Why, girl, I don't even know you, Mrs. Turpin said silently.

She forced her attention back to the discussion. "It wouldn't be practical to send them back to Africa," she said. "They wouldn't want to go. They got it too good here."

"Wouldn't be what they wanted—if I had anythang to do with it," the woman said.

"It wouldn't be a way in the world you could get all the niggers back over there," Mrs. Turpin said. "They'd be hiding out and lying down and turning sick on you and wailing and hollering and raring and pitching. It wouldn't be a way in the world to get them over there."

"They got over here," the trashy woman said. "Get back like they got over."

"It wasn't so many of them then," Mrs. Turpin explained.

The woman looked at Mrs. Turpin as if here was an idiot indeed but Mrs. Turpin was not bothered by the look, considering where it came from.

"Nooo," she said, "they're going to stay here where they can go to New York and marry white folks and improve their color. That's what they all want to do, every one of them, improve their color."

"You know what comes of that, don't you?" Claud asked.

"No, Claud, what?" Mrs. Turpin said.

Claud's eyes twinkled. "White-faced niggers," he said with never a smile.

Everybody in the office laughed except the white-trash and the ugly girl. The girl gripped the book in her lap with white fingers. The trashy woman looked around her from face to face as if she thought they were all idiots. The old woman in the feed sack dress continued to gaze expressionless across the floor at the high-top shoes of the man opposite her, the one who had been pretending to be asleep when the Turpins came in. He was laughing heartily, his hands still spread out on his knees. The child had fallen to the side and was lying now almost face down in the old woman's lap.

While they recovered from their laughter, the nasal chorus on the radio kept the room from silence.

"You go to blank blank
And I'll go to mine
But we'll all blank along
To-geth-ther,
And all along the blank
We'll hep eachother out
Smile-ling in any kind of
Weath-ther!"

Mrs. Turpin didn't catch every word but she caught enough to agree with the spirit of the song and it turned her thoughts sober. To help anybody out that needed it was her philosophy of life. She never spared herself when she found somebody in need, whether they were white or black, trash or decent. And of all she had to be thankful for, she was most thankful that this was so. If Jesus had said, "You can be high society and have all the money you want and be thin and svelte-like, but you can't be a good woman with it," she would have had to say, "Well don't make me that then. Make me a good woman and it don't matter what else, how fat or how ugly or how poor!" Her heart rose. He had not made her a nigger or white-trash or ugly! He had made her herself and given her a little of everything. Jesus, thank you! she said. Thank you thank you thank you! Whenever she counted her blessings she felt as buoyant as if she weighed one hundred and twenty-five pounds instead of one hundred and eighty.

"What's wrong with your little boy?" the pleasant lady asked the white-trashy woman.

"He has a ulcer," the woman said proudly. "He ain't give me a minute's peace since he was born. Him and her are just alike," she said, nodding at the old woman, who was running her leathery fingers through the child's pale hair. "Look like I can't get nothing down them two but Co' Cola and candy."

That's all you try to get down em, Mrs. Turpin said to herself. Too lazy to light the fire. There was nothing you could tell her about people like them that she didn't know already. And it was not just that they didn't have anything. Because if you gave them everything, in two weeks it would all be broken or filthy or they would have chopped it up for lightwood. She knew all this from her own experience. Help them you must, but help them you couldn't.

All at once the ugly girl turned her lips inside out again. Her eyes were fixed like two drills on Mrs. Turpin. This time there was no mistaking that there was something urgent behind them.

Girl, Mrs. Turpin exclaimed silently, I haven't done a thing to you! The girl might be confusing her with somebody else. There was no need to sit by and let herself be intimidated. "You must be in college," she said boldly, looking directly at the girl. "I see you reading a book there."

The girl continued to stare and pointedly did not answer. Her mother blushed at this rudeness. "The lady asked you a question, Mary Grace," she said under her breath.

"I have ears," Mary Grace said.

The poor mother blushed again. "Mary Grace goes to

Wellesley College," she explained. She twisted one of the buttons on her dress. "In Massachusetts," she added with a grimace. "And in the summer she just keeps right on studying. Just reads all the time, a real book worm. She's done real well at Wellesley; she's taking English and Math and History and Psychology and Social Studies," she rattled on, "and I think it's too much. I think she ought to get out and have fun."

The girl looked as if she would like to hurl them all through the plate glass window.

"Way up north," Mrs. Turpin murmured and thought, well, it hasn't done much for her manners.

"I'd almost rather have him sick," the white-trash woman said, wrenching the attention back to herself. "He's so mean when he ain't. Look like some children just take natural to meanness. It's some gets bad when they get sick but he was the opposite. Took sick and turned good. He don't give me no trouble now. It's me waitin to see the doctor," she said.

If I was going to send anybody back to Africa, Mrs. Turpin thought, it would be your kind, woman. "Yes, indeed," she said aloud, but looking up at the ceiling, "it's a heap of things worse than a nigger." And dirtier than a hog, she added to herself.

"I think people with bad dispositions are more to be pitied than anyone on earth," the pleasant lady said in a voice that was decidedly thin.

"I thank the Lord he has blessed me with a good one," Mrs. Turpin said. "The day has never dawned that I couldn't find something to laugh at."

"Not since she married me anyways," Claud said with a comical straight face.

Everybody laughed except the girl and the white-trash.

Mrs. Turpin's stomach shook. "He's such a caution," she said, "that I can't help but laugh at him."

The girl made a loud ugly noise through her teeth.

Her mother's mouth grew thin and tight. "I think the worst thing in the world," she said, "is an ungrateful person. To have everything and not appreciate it. I know a girl," she said, "who has parents who would give her anything, a little brother who loves her dearly, who is getting a good education, who wears the best clothes, but who can never say a kind word to anyone, who never smiles, who just criticizes and complains all day long."

"Is she too old to paddle?" Claud asked.

The girl's face was almost purple.

"Yes," the lady said, "I'm afraid there's nothing to do but leave her to her folly. Some day she'll wake up and it'll be too late."

"It never hurt anyone to smile," Mrs. Turpin said. "It just makes you feel better all over."

"Of course," the lady said sadly, "but there are just some people you can't tell anything to. They can't take criticism."

"If it's one thing I am," Mrs. Turpin said with feeling, "it's grateful. When I think who all I could have been besides myself and what all I got, a little of everything, and a good disposition besides, I just feel like shouting, 'Thank you, Jesus, for making everything the way it is!' It could have been different!" For one thing, somebody else could have got Claud. At the thought of this, she was flooded with gratitude and a terrible pang of joy ran through her. "Oh thank you, Jesus, Jesus, thank you!" she cried aloud.

The book struck her directly over her left eye. It struck almost at the same instant that she realized the girl was about to hurl it. Before she could utter a sound, the raw face came crashing across the table toward her, howling. The girl's fingers sank like clamps into the soft flesh of her neck. She heard the mother cry out and Claud shout, "Whoa!" There was an instant when she was certain that she was about to be in an earthquake.

All at once her vision narrowed and she saw everything as if it were happening in a small room far away, or as if she were looking at it through the wrong end of a telescope. Claud's face crumpled and fell out of sight. The nurse ran in, then out, then in again. Then the gangling figure of the doctor rushed out of the inner door. Magazines flew this way and that as the table turned over. The girl fell with a thud and Mrs. Turpin's vision suddenly reversed itself and she saw everything large instead of small. The eyes of the white-trashy woman were staring hugely at the floor. There the girl, held down on one side by the nurse and on the other by her mother, was wrenching and turning in their grasp. The doctor was kneeling astride her, trying to hold her arm down. He managed after a second to sink a long needle into it.

Mrs. Turpin felt entirely hollow except for her heart

which swung from side to side as if it were agitated in a great empty drum of flesh.

"Somebody that's not busy call for the ambulance," the doctor said in the off-hand voice young doctors adopt for terrible occasions.

Mrs. Turpin could not have moved a finger. The old man who had been sitting next to her skipped nimbly into the office and made the call, for the secretary still seemed to be gone.

"Claud!" Mrs. Turpin called.

He was not in his chair. She knew she must jump up and find him but she felt like someone trying to catch a train in a dream, when everything moves in slow motion and the faster you try to run the slower you go.

"Here I am," a suffocated voice, very unlike Claud's, said.

He was doubled up in the corner on the floor, pale as paper, holding his leg. She wanted to get up and go to him but she could not move. Instead, her gaze was drawn slowly downward to the churning face on the floor, which she could see over the doctor's shoulder.

The girl's eyes stopped rolling and focused on her. They seemed a much lighter blue than before, as if a door that had been tightly closed behind them was now open to admit light and air.

Mrs. Turpin's head cleared and her power of motion returned. She leaned forward until she was looking directly into the fierce brilliant eyes. There was no doubt in her mind that the girl did know her, knew her in some intense and personal way, beyond time and place and condition. "What you got to say to me?" she asked hoarsely and held her breath, waiting, as for a revelation.

The girl raised her head. Her gaze locked with Mrs. Turpin's. "Go back to hell where you came from, you old wart hog," she whispered. Her voice was low but clear. Her eyes burned for a moment as if she saw with pleasure that her message had struck its target.

Mrs. Turpin sank back in her chair.

After a moment the girl's eyes closed and she turned her head wearily to the side.

The doctor rose and handed the nurse the empty syringe. He leaned over and put both hands for a moment on the mother's shoulders, which were shaking. She was sitting on the floor, her lips pressed together, holding Mary Grace's hand in her lap. The girl's fingers were gripped like a baby's around her thumb. "Go on to the hospital," he said. "I'll call and make the arrangements."

"Now let's see that neck," he said in a jovial voice to Mrs. Turpin. He began to inspect her neck with his first two fingers. Two little moon-shaped lines like pink fish bones were indented over her windpipe. There was the beginning of an angry red swelling above her eye. His fingers passed over this also.

"Lea' me be," she said thickly and shook him off. "See about Claud. She kicked him."

"I'll see about him in a minute," he said and felt her pulse. He was a thin grey-haired man, given to pleasantries. "Go home and have yourself a vacation the rest of the day," he said and patted her on the shoulder.

Quit your pattin me, Mrs. Turpin growled to herself.

"And put an ice pack over that eye," he said. Then he went and squatted down beside Claud and looked at his leg. After a moment he pulled him up and Claud limped after him into the office.

Until the ambulance came, the only sounds in the room were the tremulous moans of the girl's mother, who continued to sit on the floor. The white-trash woman did not take her eyes off the girl. Mrs. Turpin looked straight ahead at nothing. Presently the ambulance drew up, a long dark shadow, behind the curtain. The attendants came in and set the stretcher down beside the girl and lifted her expertly onto it and carried her out. The nurse helped the mother gather up her things. The shadow of the ambulance moved silently away and the nurse came back in the office.

"That ther girl is going to be a lunatic, ain't she?" the white-trash woman asked the nurse, but the nurse kept on to the back and never answered her.

"Yes, she's going to be a lunatic," the white-trash woman said to the rest of them.

"Po' critter," the old woman murmured. The child's face was still in her lap. His eyes looked idly out over her knees. He had not moved during the disturbance except to draw one leg up under him.

"I thank Gawd," the white-trash woman said fervently, "I ain't a lunatic."

Claud came limping out and the Turpins went home.

As their pick-up truck turned into their own dirt road and made the crest of the hill, Mrs. Turpin gripped the window ledge and looked out suspiciously. The land sloped gracefully down through a field dotted with lavender weeds and at the start of the rise their small yellow frame house, with its little flower beds spread out around it like a fancy apron, sat primly in its accustomed place between two giant hickory trees. She would not have been startled to see a burnt wound between two blackened chimneys.

Neither of them felt like eating so they put on their house clothes and lowered the shade in the bedroom and lay down, Claud with his leg on a pillow and herself with a damp washcloth over her eye. The instant she was flat on her back, the image of a razor-backed hog with warts on its face and horns coming out behind its ears snorted into her head. She moaned, a low quiet moan.

"I am not," she said tearfully, "a wart hog. From hell." But the denial had no force. The girl's eyes and her words, even the tone of her voice, low but clear, directed only to her, brooked no repudiation. She had been singled out for the message, though there was trash in the room to whom it might justly have been applied. The full force of this fact struck her only now. There was a woman there who was neglecting her own child but she had been overlooked. The message had been given to Ruby Turpin, a respectable, hard-working, church-going woman. The tears dried. Her eyes began to burn instead with wrath.

She rose on her elbow and the washcloth fell into her hand. Claud was lying on his back, snoring. She wanted to tell him what the girl had said. At the same time, she did not wish to put the image of herself as a wart hog from hell into his mind.

"Hey, Claud," she muttered and pushed his shoulder.

Claud opened one pale baby blue eye.

She looked into it warily. He did not think about anything. He just went his way.

"Wha, whasit?" he said and closed the eye again.

"Nothing," she said. "Does your leg pain you?"

"Hurts like hell," Claud said.

"It'll quit terreckly," she said and lay back down. In a moment Claud was snoring again. For the rest of the afternoon they lay there. Claud slept. She scowled at the ceiling. Occasionally she raised her fist and made a small stabbing motion over her chest as if she was defending her innocence to invisible guests who were like the comforters of Job, reasonable-seeming but wrong.

About five-thirty Claud stirred. "Got to go after those niggers," he sighed, not moving.

She was looking straight up as if there were unintelligible handwriting on the ceiling. The protuberance over her eye had turned a greenish-blue. "Listen here," she said.

"What?"

"Kiss me."

Claud leaned over and kissed her loudly on the mouth. He pinched her side and their hands interlocked. Her expression of ferocious concentration did not change. Claud got up, groaning and growling, and limped off. She continued to study the ceiling.

She did not get up until she heard the pick-up truck coming back with the Negroes. Then she rose and thrust her feet in her brown oxfords, which she did not bother to lace, and stumped out onto the back porch and got her red plastic bucket. She emptied a tray of ice cubes into it and filled it half full of water and went out into the back yard. Every afternoon after Claud had brought the hands in, one of the boys helped him put out hay and the rest waited in the back of the truck until he was ready to take them home. The truck was parked in the shade under one of the hickory trees.

"Hi yawl this evening?" Mrs. Turpin asked grimly, appearing with the bucket and the dipper. There were three women and a boy in the truck.

"Us doin nicely," the oldest woman said. "Hi you doin?" and her gaze stuck immediately on the dark lump on Mrs. Turpin's forehead. "You done fell down, ain't you?" she asked in a solicitous voice. The old woman was dark and almost toothless. She had on an old felt hat of Claud's set back on her head. The other two women were younger and lighter and they both had new bright green sun hats. One of them had hers on her head; the other had taken hers off and the boy was grinning beneath it.

Mrs. Turpin set the bucket down on the floor of the truck. "Yawl hep yourselves," she said. She looked around to make sure Claud had gone. "No. I didn't fall down," she said, folding her arms. "It was something worse than that."

"Ain't nothing bad happen to you!" the old woman said. She said it as if they all knew that Mrs. Turpin was protected in some special way by Divine Providence. "You just had you a little fall."

"We were in town at the doctor's office for where the

cow kicked Mr. Turpin," Mrs. Turpin said in a flat tone that indicated they could leave off their foolishness. "And there was this girl there. A big fat girl with her face all broke out. I could look at that girl and tell she was peculiar but I couldn't tell how. And me and her mama were just talking and going along and all of a sudden WHAM! She throws this big book she was reading at me and . . ."

"Naw!" the old woman cried out.

"And then she jumps over the table and commences to choke me."

"Naw!" they all exclaimed, "naw!"

"Hi come she do that?" the old woman asked. "What ail her?"

Mrs. Turpin only glared in front of her.

"Something ail her," the old woman said.

"They carried her off in an ambulance," Mrs. Turpin continued, "but before she went she was rolling on the floor and they were trying to hold her down to give her a shot and she said something to me." She paused. "You know what she said to me?"

"What she say?" they asked.

"She said," Mrs. Turpin began and stopped, her face very dark and heavy. The sun was getting whiter and whiter, blanching the sky overhead so that the leaves of the hickory tree were black in the face of it. She could not bring forth the words. "Something real ugly," she muttered.

"She sho shouldn't said nothin ugly to you," the old woman said. "You so sweet. You the sweetest lady I know."

"She pretty too," the one with the hat on said.

"And stout," the other one said. "I never knowed no sweeter white lady."

"That's the truth befo' Jesus," the old woman said. "Amen! You des as sweet and pretty as you can be."

Mrs. Turpin knew just exactly how much Negro flattery was worth and it added to her rage. "She said," she began again and finished this time with a fierce rush of breath, "that I was an old wart hog from hell."

There was an astounded silence.

"Where she at?" the youngest woman cried in a piercing voice.

"Lemme see her. I'll kill her!"

"I'll kill her with you!" the other one cried.

"She b'long in the sylum," the old woman said emphatically. "You the sweetest white lady I know."

"She pretty too," the other two said. "Stout as she can be and sweet. Jesus satisfied with her!"

"Deed he is," the old woman declared.

Idiots! Mrs. Turpin growled to herself. You could never say anything intelligent to a nigger. You could talk at them but not with them. "Yawl ain't drunk your water," she said shortly. "Leave the bucket in the truck when you're finished with it. I got more to do than just stand around and pass the time of day," and she moved off and into the house.

She stood for a moment in the middle of the kitchen. The dark protuberance over her eye looked like a miniature tornado cloud which might any moment sweep across the horizon of her brow. Her lower lip protruded dangerously. She squared her massive shoulders. Then she marched into the front of the house and out the side door and started down the road to the pig parlor. She had the look of a woman going single-handed, weaponless, into battle.

The sun was a deep yellow now like a harvest moon and was riding westward very fast over the far tree line as if it meant to reach the hogs before she did. The road was rutted and she kicked several good-sized stones out of her path as she strode along. The pig parlor was on a little knoll at the end of a lane that ran off from the side of the barn. It was a square of concrete as large as a small room, with a board fence about four feet high around it. The concrete floor sloped slightly so that the hog wash could drain off into a trench where it was carried to the field for fertilizer. Claud was standing on the outside, on the edge of the concrete, hanging onto the top board, hosing down the floor inside. The hose was connected to the faucet of a water trough nearby.

Mrs. Turpin climbed up beside him and glowered down at the hogs inside. There were seven long-snouted bristly shoats in it—tan with liver-colored spots—and an old sow a few weeks off from farrowing. She was lying on her side grunting. The shoats were running about shaking themselves like idiot children, their little slit pig eyes searching the floor for anything left. She had read that pigs were the most intelligent animal. She doubted it. They were supposed to be smarter than dogs. There had even been a pig astronaut. He had performed his assignment perfectly but died of a heart attack afterwards because they left him in his electric suit, sitting upright throughout his examination when naturally a hog should be on all fours.

A-gruntin and a-rootin and a-groanin.

"Gimme that hose," she said, yanking it away from Claud. "Go on and carry them niggers home and then get off that leg."

"You look like you might have swallowed a mad dog," Claud observed, but he got down and limped off. He paid no attention to her humors.

Until he was out of earshot, Mrs. Turpin stood on the side of the pen, holding the hose and pointing the stream of water at the hind quarters of any shoat that looked as if it might try to lie down. When he had had time to get over the hill, she turned her head slightly and her wrathful eyes scanned the path. He was nowhere in sight. She turned back again and seemed to gather herself up. Her shoulders rose and she drew in her breath.

"What do you send me a message like that for?" she said in a low fierce voice, barely above a whisper but with the force of a shout in its concentrated fury. "How am I a hog and me both? How am I saved and from hell too?" Her free fist was knotted and with the other she gripped the hose, blindly pointing the stream of water in and out of the eye of the old sow whose outraged squeal she did not hear.

The pig parlor commanded a view of the back pasture where their twenty beef cows were gathered around the hay-bales Claud and the boy had put out. The freshly cut pasture sloped down to the highway. Across it was their cotton field and beyond that a dark green dusty wood which they owned as well. The sun was behind the wood, very red, looking over the paling of trees like a farmer inspecting his own hogs.

"Why me?" she rumbled. "It's no trash around here, black or white, that I haven't given to. And break my back to the bone every day working. And do for the church."

She appeared to be the right size woman to command the arena before her. "How am I a hog?" she demanded. "Exactly how am I like them?" and she jabbed the stream of water at the shoats. "There was plenty of trash there. It didn't have to be me.

"If you like trash better, go get yourself some trash then," she railed. "You could have made me trash. Or a nigger. If trash is what you wanted why didn't you make me trash?" She shook her fist with the hose in it and a watery snake appeared momentarily in the air. "I could quit working and take it easy and be filthy," she growled. "Lounge about the sidewalks all day drinking root beer. Dip snuff and spit in every puddle and have it all over my face. I could be nasty.

"Or you could have made me a nigger. It's too late for me to be a nigger," she said with deep sarcasm, "but I could act like one. Lay down in the middle of the road and stop traffic. Roll on the ground."

In the deepening light everything was taking on a mysterious hue. The pasture was growing a peculiar glassy green and the streak of highway had turned lavender. She braced herself for a final assault and this time her voice rolled out over the pasture. "Go on," she yelled, "call me a hog! Call me a hog again. From hell. Call me a wart hog from hell. Put that bottom rail on top. There'll still be a top and bottom!"

A garbled echo returned to her.

A final surge of fury shook her and she roared, "Who do you think you are?"

The color of everything, field and crimson sky, burned for a moment with a transparent intensity. The question carried over the pasture and across the highway and the cotton field and returned to her clearly like an answer from beyond the wood.

She opened her mouth but no sound came out of it.

A tiny truck, Claud's, appeared on the highway, heading rapidly out of sight. Its gears scraped thinly. It looked like a child's toy. At any moment a bigger truck might smash into it and scatter Claud's and the niggers' brains all over the road.

Mrs. Turpin stood there, her gaze fixed on the highway, all her muscles rigid, until in five or six minutes the truck reappeared, returning. She waited until it had had time to turn into their own road. Then like a monumental statue coming to life, she bent her head slowly and gazed, as if through the very heart of mystery, down into the pig parlor at the hogs. They had settled all in one corner around the old sow who was grunting softly. A red glow suffused them. They appeared to pant with a secret life.

Until the sun slipped finally behind the tree line, Mrs. Turpin remained there with her gaze bent to them as if she were absorbing some abysmal life-giving knowledge. At last she lifted her head. There was only a purple streak in the sky, cutting through a field of crimson and leading, like an extension of the highway, into the descending dusk. She raised her hands from the side of the pen in a gesture hieratic and profound. A visionary light settled in her eyes. She saw the streak as a vast swinging bridge extending upward from the earth through a field of living fire. Upon it a vast horde of souls were rumbling toward heaven. There were whole companies of white-trash, clear for the first time in their lives, and bands of black niggers in white robes, and battalions of freaks and lunatics shouting and clapping and leaping like frogs. And bringing up the end of the procession was a tribe of people whom she recognized at once as those who, like herself and Claud, had always had a little of everything and the God-given wit to use it right. She leaned forward to observe them closer. They were marching behind the others with great dignity, accountable as they had always been for good order and common sense and respectable behavior. They alone were on key. Yet she could see by their shocked and altered faces that even their virtues were being burned away. She lowered her hands and gripped the rail of the hog pen, her eyes small but fixed unblinkingly on what lay ahead. In a moment the vision faded but she remained where she was, immobile.

At length she got down and turned off the faucet and made her slow way on the darkening path to the house. In the woods around her the invisible cricket choruses had struck up, but what she heard were the voices of the souls climbing upward into the starry field and shouting hallelujah.

JEAN STUBBS was born in 1926 in Lancashire, England, and studied art at the Manchester School of Art. She began writing short stories in 1962. They have been published widely in magazines and in collections such as Macmillan's *Winter's Tales* and the *Ghost Books*. In 1964 she won the Tom Gallon Trust Award for short story writing with "A Child's Four Seasons," originally published in *Winter's Tales 10*. She has also written ten novels, the best known of which is *Dear Laura*, a Book of the Month Club alternate choice and a nominee for the Edgar Award. She writes novels as well as short stories because, as she says, "I enjoy both forms."

Jean Stubbs
(1926–   )

COUSIN LEWIS

The last time Margery saw Cousin Lewis he was twenty-five and she only thirteen. But time, she felt, was on her side. She hung back, coping with love and puppy fat, and he stood resplendent in his Air Force uniform and talked of bombing raids over Germany in a suitably casual fashion. Outside, beyond the black-out curtains, searchlights picked out clouds and waited for something more important.

"Ah well, back to the circus!" said Cousin Lewis, and pulled his cap peak straight in the hall mirror.

"Best of luck, old chap," said Margery's father.

"Take care of yourself, Lewis," said Margery's mother. "Lovely to see you."

"Will the war last long enough for me to join the R.A.F.?" asked Benny, who was nearly nine.

"Good Lord, I hope not!" said Cousin Lewis. "Give me a kiss, Marjie!"

She put her lips to his cheek, which was cool and brown, and hoped no one would rag her afterwards. And because she was exalted by the kiss and afraid of the ridicule she said something in shocking bad taste.

"What happens if they shoot you down?" she asked.

But Cousin Lewis, having come to terms with that possibility, only laughed.

"I'll be washed up!" he said gaily, and lifted his hand to them in salute.

That was how she remembered him: young and brave, with the war before him and safety behind him. A laugh and a salute and footsteps treading jubilantly into the dark.

A week later his bomber poured from the night sky in one long flame, and seared a field in France. They were all much too worried about his mother to consider Margery, who was only a child and would forget.

She was, thought Benny, as good as a brother—and what

greater compliment could he pay a girl? She climbed trees, cooked potatoes in the hot ash of bonfires, and forgot to wash her neck. But gradually she betrayed him, her breasts rearing shyly beneath jerseys and dresses, her eyes looking for older boys. She did not marry as soon as they expected, being in her thirties before she met Hugh Jones, and already an aunt twice over.

Margery's father liked Hugh instantly, and they sat smoking identical pipes and discussing farming until midnight.

"Mind you, North Wales is very different from Suffolk," said Hugh defensively, thinking of his stone farmhouse like a fortress on the ridge. "You're very well-groomed down here, compared to Nant Uchaf. Life's easier in the south. But I'm not a poor man, and Marjie knows what to expect. She isn't a girl to hanker after the bright lights, now is she?"

"No-o," said her father, ruminating, "but she does enjoy a binge now and again."

"She can go to Bangor or Caernarvon," Hugh offered. "There's a lot of nice cafés there for morning coffee and afternoon tea and that. I'm not the sort of man who expects a woman to turn into a hermit. Cinemas, there are." He thought. "Dress shops," he said.

"Oh, she hardly ever buys clothes. She's not a great spender. Quite the contrary. Her mother has always had the greatest difficulty in getting her out of slacks and jerseys. She's no highbrow, either. No yearning for the Royal Festival Hall or a night at the Aldwych. Come to think of it," said Margery's father, sucking the stem of his pipe, "I don't know what she *does* do in London. She just walks round, I suppose, and looks up the odd school friend who has a flat in town. Girls' gossip. She was always a reserved child, used to sit in her room for hours, talking to herself. Got a gift for mimicry. We thought she might have wanted to go on the stage at one time, but she's a home bird—isn't she, my love?" as his wife came in.

Margery's mother said, at a tangent, "We've talked the wedding over until we're hoarse, and Margery's having her bath and we're both going to bed. There's a plate of chicken sandwiches on the kitchen table and coffee in the pot and beer in the fridge. Come when you like—only remember the alarm clock's set for five-thirty tomorrow morning!"

"I was telling Hugh that Margery likes a binge in town, now and again, but she's actually a home bird."

"Home bird?" cried Margery's mother, with the fatuous expression of one whose daughter has been a joy to her, "why, you can't drag that girl away from home. I'll be glad to have my kitchen to myself! She can do anything around the house and farm. Anything. Can't she, Ken?"

"Good as a man—and good as a woman, too. I'm surprised—we're both surprised—that she hasn't married earlier. Aren't we, love?"

An expression was born and despatched on the face of Margery's mother, but escaped the notice of both men.

"Oh—she had the good sense to wait until Hugh came along," she said, closing the subject.

"I'm very lucky," said Hugh.

They hastened to agree with him, and to add that their daughter was equally fortunate.

"There's been no other engagement," said her father quickly. "The odd boy-friend, here and there, but none of them seemed to suit her."

"She was wise enough to bide her time," said Margery's mother. "Girls seem to think that the right man comes along like a bar of chocolate, the day they're twenty-one. And that's silly. I always say that if they have a good home and plenty of interests they can wait, and choose well."

"I'm no chicken myself," said Hugh, being thirty-eight. "But with my dad dying when I was twenty, and my mother lingering on all those years, and the farm to pull up after the war—I had to wait too. And I'm glad I did."

"Just remember what I said, about Margery needing a day out now and then, and she'll be a wife in a million," said her father.

The expression hovered for a moment or two, puckering the forehead of Margery's mother, compressing her mouth, and was banished by a smile.

"Oh, you must let wives off the hook occasionally," she said. "We work all the better for a day out."

Margery made a graceful bride, wearing her mother's veil and a satin dress created by Miss Pierce who did all the village fine sewing. Her thin brown face and intent blue eyes looked out from the photograph in her parents' living room. She clasped her husband's arm as though she were drowning, and he stood straight by her side, an able life-saver. Her letters sounded happy.

She made a couple of expeditions in the first year they were married, and distressed Hugh by refusing to plan ahead.

"I don't *mind* you going out, love," he said three times over breakfast. "I mind that you didn't give me a bit more warning."

Her long face was obstinate, her eyes remote.

"I simply thought this morning, that I'd like a change," she said, and reminded him of her mother as she sped off on a domestic tangent. "I've put a stew in the oven and I've fed the hens, and you'll be out until this evening. Your sandwiches are ready and I've made a flask of tea. You'll get a drink at the pub—and I must run if I'm to catch that bus."

"But when will you be back?" he cried after her flying headscarf.

She waved, and called something about the bus time-table. He remembered then that she had not even said where she was going. All day he sought comfort in her father's advice, whistling up the dog, and saying sorrowfully, "But he never said how *sudden* she was!"

Margery returned decorously at six o'clock and was serving stew up on his mother's willow-pattern plates when he unlatched the door. He noted with pleasure that she had changed for him, and an air of refreshed serenity was evident in the folds of her dress. After tea she insisted on filling his pipe and sitting on his knee in the rocking-chair.

Soothed, he said, "Did you buy anything?" looking into the bright heart of the coal fire.

"I brought you a jar of *Gentleman's Relish* to try," she said, teasing, "and if you don't eat it—I shall!"

"Did you go to the pictures?"

"There was nothing I hadn't seen."

"Did you meet anyone we know?"

She shook her head, smiling.

"What *have* you done, then, all day? Where have you been?"

She was radiant.

"I went to Caernarvon. I looked at the shops, and the sea, and the castle. I was thinking. Can't you guess?"

"No, I can't," he said, too comfortable to be impatient, too loving to be suspicious.

"We're going to have a baby, Hughie!"

In his joy he connected her mysterious absence with a visit to the doctor, and forgot for a long time that their own doctor lived only three miles away in the opposite direction to Caernarvon.

The second trip, two months before David was born, occurred in his absence. Foreseeing the probability of an argument, she waited until he began his morning's work, and then left another stew and a message with Mrs. Griffiths who came in to help. This time, it appeared, she visited Bangor, went on to Llandudno, and missed her connection. He was beside himself when the telephone rang and she asked him to come and collect her. All the way he rehearsed accusations, which became dumb at the sight of her woeful face, her swollen body on a bench in the square.

"For God's sake," he cried, as she scrambled into the van, "what possessed you, Marjie?"

"I wanted something for the baby," she said, and her bottom lip trembled. "It was to be a surprise."

"I was surprised, by Gow! You've got three drawerfuls of clothes at home. And what's in that suitcase?"

"Dry-cleaning," she said. "With the winter coming on I might not be able to get out again. And I bought you a Paisley neck scarf. They're all the rage."

"Don't cry then, love," he said, wondering whenever he should wear it, and what clothes she found necessary to clean when they both lived in trousers and sweaters from morning to night. "Don't cry, love. I didn't know where you were, you see. I didn't know where in God's name to start looking."

Then their son arrived after a long bout in the nearest hospital, and he imagined her safely tethered. But once or twice in David's babyhood she packed a rucksack, put him in his sling, and disappeared unaccountably. She said she had been on the mountains.

"Which mountains?" Hugh asked, aghast to think of those two frail beings at the mercy of height and weather.

"I don't know all their names, yet," she said defensively. "But I showed David our farm from the top of one ridge, and I'm very careful where I go."

When he heard that a second child was expected his pleasure mingled with relief. Now at last she must settle down. Only once did he have to collect her, exhausted by late pregnancy, holding David's small hand and bearing the inevitable rucksack. And this time her condition did not avert his anger, because the child was weeping with cold and tiredness, nor would he unwrap the bribe of a gift.

"You have responsibilities," he cried, "for God's sake put them first. It's not as though you were seventeen."

"What's my age got to do with it?" she wept, struggling to push David's heavy limbs into his sleeping-suit.

"Everything," shouted Hugh. "Nobody minds a slip of a girl taking off when she feels like it. But a married woman of your age should have out grown all that nonsense. And what's in that rucksack, for the love of heaven?"

"Our food and his nappies and bottle," she sobbed, and stuffed it under the stairs cupboard without unpacking it, and said she wanted to go back to Suffolk.

The next day she was weary, white and submissive.

"I know I can't go out like I did," she said, stirring porridge and wiping her eyes. "I'll find some other way of amusing myself."

"What can I do for you, Marjie?" he asked, feeling brutish.

"Nothing," she said, moving away from his hand. "You're very good to me and I'm very lucky. I'll be all right."

"We'll get a telly," he said. "The Thomases have a telly."

"That will be nice for David too. I shall like that."

But he saw he had not plumbed the real depths of her grief. And when their daughter Mair was born, and summer came, he used every opportunity to take them out: sometimes a family day at the seaside, sometimes a working trip in which he left them to picnic while he walked his acres and talked sheep. The children thrived but Margery drooped, in spite of her thanks and her protestations of happiness. Several times she woke him by muttering and crying and turning in her sleep. Once, he tackled the problem of transferring his thoughts to paper without Margery knowing, and wrote to her parents. They drove up the following weekend and took Margery and the children back with them for a holiday. She returned, having spent two days in London, buoyant and transfigured.

Perhaps it's the climate, or the place, Hugh thought. But he could do nothing to alter either, since the farm was his life and Margery had taken on both of them for better or worse, and they loved each other. But as the children grew up and became communicative her interest quickened. She had been a conscientious and tender mother, now she was their amusement centre. No games were quite so good as the ones she made up, and the secret games were best of all. The sound of her voice would bring David even from the barn, and she could coax Mair out of a tantrum by whispering in her ear. Invisible strings bound them to their mother, and the strings grew into a web. They loved their father, but could manage without him. The absence of their mother, even though she was only sorting out rubbish in the loft, made them a little fearful.

They had been married six years when their third and last child was born, another boy whom they named Colm. The birth began as it should, in the bed where Hugh was born, and ended in an ambulance ride to Bangor hospital.

"No more now, Hughie lad," said the doctor privately. "Call it a day and be thankful that the ones you've got are sound and hearty. I don't think Margery will grieve, mind you. She's a good mother, but I get the impression she likes them more as they grow up. Not a great one for having a baby round all the time."

Remembering the laughter and flushed faces, the shining eyes, as he came home of an evening, Hugh agreed.

"She's a wonder at amusing them," he said. "I'm the daft one that likes a baby to nurse?" He added, with a dart of jealousy, "Sometimes I think I'm the odd one out, you know!"

"Oh, that's as it should be," said the doctor, getting into his car. "The child belongs to its mother at this age. Your turn will come soon enough. Then she'll be left to fill your stomachs while you show those two boys of yours how to run a farm. And time goes. By Gow, it goes. Is Mrs. Griffiths still coming in a few mornings a week? That's right, Hughie lad. Give Margery all the rest you can while she feeds this one."

Three-year-old Mair cherished her father and was content to sit in his lap and watch the flames change, and the shadows reach and recede on the white walls, that evening. But David, at five, demanded more sophisticated fare. They had been quietened by the promise of the baby brother, and Mamma home at the end of the week. But a week was a long time to spend with Mrs. Griffiths' admonitions and their father's loving silence.

"I want Cousin Lewis, dadda!" David cried, and Mair twisted her little brown head round to agree with him.

"Cousin Lewis," she repeated. "Cousin Lewis."

"Who's he?" asked Hugh, in honest bewilderment.

But they could not explain, only say that he made them laugh and told them stories.

"When does he come?" cried Hugh.

They could not cope with the mysteries of time, but said he sometimes came, not every time. All Hugh's old demons became one devil, and he stormed into the maternity ward at Bangor the following afternoon, determined to have this out.

"Who the hell's Cousin Lewis?" he shouted, before Margery could more than smile a welcome.

She flushed from neck to forehead, holding the flowers he had thrust at her in his terror.

"Hush, Hughie," she whispered, humiliated. "Don't shout so. Sister's looking at you!"

Sister's face expressed such a high degree of discontent that Hugh pulled out a chair and sat on it before repeating his question in a lower voice.

"Who is he, eh? Who is he? Is that who you've been meeting all these years? Running off without telling me."

Margery looked puzzled, then relieved, then laughed outright and caught his hand and kissed it.

"You frightened me to death for a minute," she said. "I couldn't think. Have the children been talking to you? What did they say?"

"They said they wanted Cousin Lewis because he told them stories and made them laugh, and he only came sometimes."

"Ah!" Serenity illumined even her maternity nightdress, designed more for practical than ornamental purposes. "It's only a game," she said. "My actual Cousin Lewis was killed in the war when I was thirteen, but he always made Benny and me laugh and told *us* stories. So when they're fratchy or bored I pretend to be him, to amuse them. Of course," she added, "most of the tales I tell them never happened. I make them up by this time, to their level, you know. But we play Cousin Lewis like—oh, Ludo or Snakes and Ladders. That's all. It's only play, my love. Only another game."

He could have wept with thankfulness. Suddenly they all

meant so much to him: Margery and David and Mair and now little Colm.

"Oh, God in heaven," he said on a long breath, "I was so bloody scared!"

"Why, Hughie, Hughie," she whispered, "you didn't think I had a fancy man, did you?'

"No, love. I did not."

"You *did!*" she said, smiling, "and I'm very flattered. You must be blind, Hughie, if you can't see that I'm not the type a man looks at twice. I'm just another housewife now, Hughie. Haven't you seen me lately?"

He stared at the thick brown hair pulled into a plait at the top of her head, at the brown face—not so thin these days, at her intent blue gaze and firm round arms, and found her wholly beautiful. But not, he admitted only to his secret male self, the sort to turn anybody's head.

"The man who didn't snatch you up and run off with you is a damn fool!" he declared. "And I'd knock him down if he didn't!"

And then they both laughed together and she put both arms round his neck. Sister looked approvingly in their direction and nodded a stately cap at Hugh as he prepared to leave. But before he went another, and happier, thought occurred to him.

"Why, you've settled down, girl!" he cried.

"Oh—the expeditions? Yes, Hughie. I've settled down."

Their farm was isolated. Visitors usually made sure of a welcome before they arrived, and casual callers were infrequent. Therefore David had celebrated his ninth birthday, Mair entered her second year at the local primary school, and Colm reached the chattering stage before Hugh found the first letter stuck in his windscreen. He thought it must be a parking ticket, though he was law-abiding and meticulous almost to the point of obsession. So he drew out the envelope with cold fingers and read it twice before he comprehended the meaning.

"Your wife has a visitor while you're away," read the printed letters.

He crumpled the paper in one big brown hand and stuffed it into a litter-basket. But the words danced in the rain against his windscreen all the way home from market, and loomed from the corners of strange dreams for a week afterwards. He took the message apart in his mind and disproved it a thousand times, without ridding himself of its implications. David and Mair were at school all day, but Colm was still with his mother. She would not, he knew, frighten the child with the presence of another man, would not lay the burden of secrecy on a three-year-old boy. But he began to ask her questions which fretted round the edges of her day.

"Been by yourselves?" he would ask, watching as he lit his pipe.

"Except for Mrs. Griffiths this morning."

"No one this afternoon?"

"Who would there be?" Margery asked amazed. "Unless you count the grocery van, of course."

"Who drives the van then?"

"Old Bob Williams still."

"Didn't you go out at all?"

"In *this* rain?" she cried. "We're not ducks, are we, Colm?"

"Not ducks," Colm chattered. "Not duck-duck-duckies."

"I just thought you might be feeling lonely."

She shrugged her shoulders, smiling at him.

"If I was frightened of being lonely," she said, "I'd have died of it before now—wouldn't I?"

His pipe held no consolation, nor the fire comfort.

"I can take you out tomorrow," he offered. "I can drop you in Portmadoc and pick you up at five."

"Oh no, Hughie—though it's sweet of you. The children will be home from school before five, and I like to be here when they come in. But if we could go on Saturday . . ."

"Why Saturday?" he cried, suddenly suspicious, sitting up in his chair.

"Because Colm needs new wellingtons," she said, astonished at him, "and Portmadoc has a better selection than the village."

"Oh, yes. Yes. All right, then. We'll go on Saturday."

The second letter came through the post, three months later.

"Your wife's friend can't cover all his tracks. I saw him through the window yesterday."

"What's wrong?" Margery asked.

Beside himself, he threw the note on her plate, and she set down the teapot before she opened it.

"Well?" he said.

She was very pale as she handed it back.

"Hughie," she said quietly. "I will swear on your mother's bible that no one was here yesterday but me and Colm."

"Then who do they mean?"

"For goodness sake don't shout, Hughie! The children."

Three heads turned from one parent to the other. Six pairs of childish eyes noted Margery's pallor and Hugh's shaking hands. Six pairs of childish ears heard fear in her voice and rage in his.

"I want to ask you children something," said Hugh deliberately.

"Hugh Jones!" Margery said, in shocked disbelief.

He waved her to silence and controlled his anger.

"Some nasty-minded . . ." he began, and then altered his approach and tried to bring it down to the level of their innocence. "Some people say that Mamma has too many visitors," he ended absurdly.

Before he could elaborate the children gave a combined shriek of laughter, so wildly in contrast with his own mood that he could have struck them to the ground.

"Listen to me, listen!" he cried.

But he had started a wave of protest.

"I can't bring even my very best friend Olwen to tea, except in the summer," said David. "Because he can't walk back alone in the dark."

"I can't bring my very best friend Dyllis unless her Dadda is going past in the milk van on his way home," cried Mair.

"And Colm has no school-friends anyway," said Margery quietly.

He looked at her and saw that he had grievously broken some cardinal rule in their relationship. He felt so sick and isolated in that hail of childish reproaches that he shouted "Silence, silence!" And then balled up the letter and flung it into the grate.

The children watched him curiously until Margery spoke, and he noticed how the sound of her voice brought them to attention at once.

"The person who wrote to Daddy thinks that *I* have too many visitors," she said calmly. "They weren't talking about you. So tell Dadda, all of you, which of my friends comes here."

"On Christmas Day?" Mair asked.

"No, not on Christmas Day because everyone comes

then. And Dadda," she said, looking full at him, "is here on Christmas Day."

The children bent to their porridge and considered obediently.

"There's Mrs. Griffiths," said Mair.

"And on a one Wednesday Mrs. Evans comes with Gwyn, and on another one Wednesday we go to Gwyn's house," said Colm, for this was his weekly treat and he could never bear the disappointment of bad weather or measles.

"Does Mrs. Morgan come, now that Olwen is at school with me?" asked David.

"Sometimes she does, but she has another baby now," said Margery.

"She came once on my birthday and brought her baby," said Colm.

"And there's Mrs. Griffiths," said Mair.

"We said Mrs. Griffiths already . . ."

"There are the men on the farm, of course," said Margery in that terrible calm voice. "Do any of them come while Dadda is away, Colm? Do you remember?"

He shook his head and made a road in his porridge and filled it with sugar, unobserved.

Hugh's sick fury dwelled on his few labourers, men mostly in late middle-age who had worked for his father, and seemed hewn from the mountains in which they were reared. He knew he would reject every one of them.

"But we *are* forgetting someone," said Margery, and he caught himself listening to her voice as the children did, because it said so much more than the words. She was lighthearted now, and funny, and dangerous. "We're forgetting Mamma's best boy-friend—Daffie Richards."

Cooling breakfasts and hurrying clocks were ignored in a whoop of delight, for poor Daffie was half-witted, less than five feet high, had a cleft palate that rendered him unintelligible and a hare-lip to complete his list of disfigurements. Margery lifted one capable hand and hushed them.

"We mustn't laugh at Daffie," she said, penitent. "Tell Dadda, Colm, why we are very kind to poor people like Daffie and don't make fun of them."

"Because-it-might-be-us-and-we're-lucky," said Colm obediently, and laughed incredulously.

"So Mamma makes a big fuss over Daffie, doesn't she,

Colm?" said Margery, comfortably in control of her own table once more. "And we bring him in and make him sit by the fire and give him cake and tea. I expect other people out in the rain and cold are very jealous when they see Daffie enjoying himself. Now if either of you are to get to school on time Dadda will have to run you down in the van, because the milk lorry will have gone by now."

Nothing had been said which could accuse Hugh, and yet his two elder children accused him with their eyes, and they kissed their mother more affectionately than usual. So he drove in wretched silence to school, and tormented himself all day with the scene at the breakfast table, and wondered who wished him so ill that they taunted his wife for loving-kindness.

"The one in uniform is back again," jeered the note.

"I thought you'd scared him off but he was here again the other day," shrieked another.

"This has been going on for years, you know," whispered a third.

Hugh picked the children up from school that afternoon and drove them into Portmadoc. They gaped at him as he marched them into a teashop.

"It'll cost you, Dadda!" said Mair, always practical.

"I don't care what it costs," said Hugh. "Do you like these cakes?"

"Not blooming half!" said David, and opened his eyes as Hugh ordered a child's dream of tea.

"Now," said Hugh, "I want you to listen carefully, and this is our secret because we don't want to upset Mamma."

They did not want to upset her, and would not. He saw that in the way their faces shut against him and their childish shoulders moved together for protection. He might or might not want to hurt her, but before he did they would be armed in her protection. His secret was nothing to them, except that they might learn from it and so shield her.

"Somebody is trying to make trouble between Mamma and me," he said, and his hands trembled as he pressed delicacies upon them. "Somebody says that a man comes to see her while I am out. They say he wears a uniform."

A curious closed look on their faces terrified him and he shouted, "It's not the truth, is it? Is it?"

"Dadda," Mair whispered, leaning over the table, "will

you not speak so loud, please? The ladies are looking at us."

He passed one hand over his face and started again.

"I'll kill the pair of you if you hide anything!" he whispered fiercely.

Their young eyes were proof against him. They exchanged silent messages.

"It's only a game, Dad," said David. "We couldn't think what you meant for a minute. It's only Mamma being Cousin Lewis."

"She dresses up, like at Christmas, in an old uniform," said Mair, "and tells us stories about Cousin Lewis. She always has done, hasn't she, Davie?"

"And not only Cousin Lewis, either," David joined in. "She does dozens of different people. She once frightened me by being Pew the blind man in *Treasure Island.*"

"She was the witch, and put us both in the oven in gingerbread people for Hansel and Gretel," cried Mair, her mouth joyful.

They tossed the conversation between them with a skill they had not inherited from their father, and he lost himself gloriously in the explanation.

"Eat up now," he cried, sweating with relief, "and remember—this is our secret. We won't tell Mamma in case it makes her upset."

"Like she was at breakfast, that other time?" asked David.

"Yes," said Hugh, discomfited. "Yes. Eat up, now. Eat up."

He bought a box of chocolates before they went home, puzzling over the expensive wrappers, clumsy in the smart little shop.

"That damned eagle's got another lamb, Mr. Jones," cried his shepherd.

Hugh stared down in anger at the eyeless toy in the grass, and whistled his dog to come away from it.

"I'll get him," he said, nodding. "I'll get him if I wait a week. John, I'm going home for my gun. When I get back I'll settle behind that wall, and you put a couple of lambs in the field by themselves, and keep well away with the rest of the herd. I'll shoot that bugger if it's the last thing I do."

He was in the farmyard, in his anger, before he heard the man's voice in the kitchen and held his breath to listen.

He could not catch what was said and the voice was unknown to him: a pleasant cultured baritone which raised his hackles, roused his temper, and roughened him. Perhaps, he thought, with a leap of heart, it was Margery fooling for the children. Then he remembered that Colm was spending the day at Aunt Morwen's house and the others were at school. Moving quietly to surprise them, he unlatched the door and flung it open in one movement, and slammed it behind him.

The man had just arrived, for he wore a dark blue felt trilby, pulled rakishly down over one eye, and a light grey mackintosh. No uniform. And now Hugh realised how far he and anyone else had been from the truth, with his fears of one man meeting her surreptitiously, at long intervals, over the last ten years. No love affair could flourish on such poor soil, against such odds of circumstance, for such a length of time. There had been many men, met by chance, taken lightly. And his wife, the stray-running bitch who sought out and drew them, had covered her tracks with little bribes and children's games.

So even as the stranger turned to face him he struck him to the floor, and then lifted his field gun from the rack over the fireplace and covered him.

"I'll kill the bloody pair of you," he said quietly. "Now where is she? Where is she?"

The empty farmhouse echoed *Margery, Margery,* and she did not answer. And then he saw that the hand warding him off was Margery's hand, and Margery's voice was weeping with hurt and fear and begging him to stop.

He stood agape as she raised herself to kneeling position, and clasped her bruised face and rocked to and fro in grief. For she had not, in fun, slipped on one of his mackintoshes and crowned it with a hat, she was fully and impeccably clothed in things he had never seen before: suit, shirt, tie, socks. Her shoes were polished, her cuff-links impeccably chosen. Even to his country eyes she seemed smarter as a man than she had ever done as a woman.

"For Christ's sake, Margery, what are you up to?" he whispered.

"Why did you come back?" she cried. "You should be on the mountain!"

"That damned eagle got another lamb," he said stiffly. He could not stop looking at her. He noticed that a three-pointed scarlet handkerchief tucked in her dark-blue breast pocket was the same shade as her tie.

She was still dizzy from the blow and he helped her, with distaste, to her feet. The muzzle of the gun indicated her clothing.

"Where did you get all that stuff?" he asked.

"I've had it for years," she sobbed. "It's out of fashion now. I look a freak walking round these days—like something from an old film. The trousers," she said distractedly, "are too wide in the leg. Men don't wear them like that any more. And I've seen—lovely ones—in Caernarvon. But they cost too much. I never had that sort of money. Everything else is out of fashion, too."

"You mean you've got some more?"

"Upstairs, in the loft, in a trunk. I've got a trunkful. Evening dress, sports clothes, an old R.A.F. uniform, slacks and sweaters and cravats. It's harmless enough," she added, seeing his face.

"Harmless? With the neighbourhood thinking you meet a lot of fancy men? Harmless? What about my children having a mother that dresses up like that?"

She wiped her mouth with her knuckles, where a tooth had cut her lip, and then with a wholly masculine gesture she reached for a handkerchief in her trouser pocket.

"They think it's all a game," she said. "They call me *Cousin Lewis.*"

"How long have you—been this way?" he asked, waving the gun at her outfit.

"I wish you'd stop pointing that thing at me," she said, weary. "Oh, years and years, Hugh. Years and years. It hasn't stopped me from making you happy, has it? It hasn't prevented me from being a good mother. It's my only weakness. I'm all right usually. Then, now and again, I just have to dress up. That's all."

He lowered himself into his armchair and stood the gun carefully against its side.

"All?" he said, at last. "Why—I don't know you. I've never known you."

"Just once in a while," she pleaded. "Once in a while. And I've been careful. Someone must have been watching with binoculars to see me at all."

"No," he shouted, shaking his head from side to side to free himself of her. "No. I don't know you. Oh Christ, I don't know you. I don't know you."

She filled the kettle and set it on the fire, brought out cups and saucers and measured tea into the warmed pot.

"I can't drink with you—like that," he said thickly.

She was upstairs a long time, and he looked about him as though the farmhouse was strange and his life an emptiness. When she came down again she had changed, out of deference, into a dress. He accepted his tea and stirred sugar round and round, thinking.

"What are you going to do?" Margery asked.

"I don't know," he said. "I don't know. But I can't—can't touch you again. Not now. I'd feel—I'd not know—who you were. I'd feel—dirty."

"But I'm a woman," she cried. "I love you. We've had children together, lived together, for ten years. It's only the clothes, now and again. I'm quite normal, otherwise. I'm a woman, I tell you. I'm a woman."

"Are you?" he said, not out of cruelty but because he no longer knew her.

She wept dreadfully, coughing and sobbing.

"Do your parents know?" he asked.

She shook her head, and said she thought perhaps they had been afraid to find out. It was easier, after all, to set her absences down as a whim.

"Oh my God," he said. "What a burden. Who shall I turn to? Who can I ask?"

"Listen," she said. "I can go to a doctor, a psychiatrist. I can have treatment. We'll be just the same as we always were. I'll have treatment."

"No," he said. "You must go home. I'll manage with the children. You must go home. Mrs. Griffiths will help me."

"I'm not leaving them, too!" she cried. "They love me, and I love them. They were always more mine than yours. If you asked them to choose between us they wouldn't choose you!"

They had reached a pitch of cruelty that could destroy them now.

"The court wouldn't choose you," he said slowly. "And I should go to court and get it done, legal and proper. Legal and proper."

She was silent, and began to prick sausages, to peel potatoes.

"It's a half-day at school," she said. "They'll be home for dinner. Are you stopping?"

"I couldn't eat it," he said simply. "I don't know what to do. I can't eat."

She drew herself up, embattled but not wholly lost.

"My parents will take us in," she said, with dignity. "And if the court finds out how much those children love and depend on me—and if I promise to have treatment—I'd stand a chance of keeping them. I would."

"Are you telling me that the law would let my sons and my daughter be brought up by a woman who dresses up as a man? Let them get into the way of not knowing one sex from the other?"

"If I had treatment. If they knew."

"This—man—they call Cousin Lewis—were you in love with him?"

"Yes," she said, "at thirteen. In love as one never is again, with someone who can never let you down, never be destroyed. At thirteen I was in love with him."

He measured the quality and breadth of the fabric she had woven round him and his children for ten years, and realised its value. He was close on fifty, and had never looked at another woman. He was bound, root and stock, to this heap of wind-driven stones, the wind-driven patch of earth and mountain. And three young lives could be wrecked in their leave-taking. He put his hand on hers, though the touch of her flesh was still unpleasant to him.

"We'll go to a specialist if we have to," he said. "We'll stick it out. For the children, for what we've made together. But I'm promising no miracles, Margery, because I can't. We might be like brother and sister for the rest of our days—not out of spite on my part, but because I couldn't help it."

"I—accept that," she said quietly. "I'll do my best."

"I'm not an educated man," Hugh said, tired. "I see life as a simple thing. It's hard for me to know more than that. But I'll try. Only, no more games, Margery. No more games."

"No," she said. "I promise. Hush now. I can hear the children."

"Then I'll be back at tea-time," he said, and picked up his gun. "I'll have my bread and cheese out there with John, and wait for that eagle."

"It's raining hard," she said. "Wrap up well."

She hesitated, and then put her lips to his hard brown cheek, but he moved away as though her touch burned him. She walked blindly into the scullery, and he, just as blindly, pulled on his mackintosh and drew the hat down over his eyes.

But the children, running round the corner of the farmhouse, freed from school, saw the grey mackintosh and dark blue hat as another extension of their lives, and called out with joy.

"It's Cousin Lewis!" cried Mair, running, bright with wind and rain, to greet him.

EDNA O'BRIEN was born in 1930 in Tuamgraney, County Clare, a tiny village in the West of Ireland, two miles south of Scarriff, the town where she attended the National School and which later became the setting for her story "Irish Revel," a West of Ireland version of Joyce's classic story "The Dead." Edna O'Brien left Clare at the age of sixteen to study pharmacy in Dublin. She married, had two children, and in 1959 moved to London where in the first three weeks she wrote her first novel, *The Country Girls*—"it wrote itself; my arm held the pen."

She writes about life in rural Ireland and urbane London, and about sex, in particular, with what has been called a "barnyard robustness," and this, perhaps, is one of the reasons why her books are banned in Ireland. But more likely she is the censor's target because many of the characters in her eight novels and more than thirty short stories reveal the bitter side of Irish life. Behavior that some Irish would deem pious and pure O'Brien perceives as a tangle of religious fanaticism and cruelty and prejudice. And the Irish people, though she finds them more imaginatively exciting than the English, "have a rather dreadful and historic habit of not brooking any other point of view or any contradiction."

She has told her many interviewers that she always wanted to be a writer. "I believe I wrote, in my head, before I talked." She says she writes because of an "ache or dissatisfaction which makes me go on. It's something terribly intangible—almost like seeing something superb in the sky, in behavior, or in the land, and seeing it is not enough. You have to somehow set it down for someone else to see, even though that sounds arrogant."

Edna O'Brien

(1930–)

A JOURNEY

February the twenty-second. Not far away was the honking of waterfowl from the pond in Battersea Park. The wrong side of London, some said, but she liked it, found it homely; the big power station was her landmark, as once upon a time a straggle of blue hills in Ireland had been.

The morning was cold, the ice had clawed at the window and left its telltale marks—long jagged lines, criss-cross lines, scrawls, lines at war with one another, lines bent on torment. It was still like twilight in the bedroom, and yet she wakened with alertness and her heart was as warm as a little ball of knitting wool. He was deep in a trough of sleep, impervious to nudging, to hitting, to pounding. He was beautiful. His hair like a halo was arced around his head—beautiful hair, not quite brown, not quite red, not quite gold, of the same darkness as gunmetal but with strands of brightness. Oh Christ, he'll think he's in his own house with his own woman, she thought as his eyelids flickered and he peered through. But he didn't. He knew where he was and said how glad he was to be there, and drawing her toward him he held her and squeezed her out like a bit of old washing.

They were off to Scotland, where he had to deliver a lecture to some students at a technical college, and later to a group of men—fellow-unionists who worked in the shipyards. "We're going a-travelling," she said, almost worried.

"Yes, pet," he said.

At any rate he hadn't changed his mind yet. He was a bit of a vacillator.

She made the coffee while he contemplated getting up, and from the kitchen she kept urging him, saying how they would be late, how he must please bestir himself. For some reason she was reminded of her wedding morning; both mornings had a feeling of unrealness, plus the same uncertainty and the same anxiety about being late. But that was a long time ago. That was over, and dry in the mouth like a pod or a desiccated seed. This was this.

Why do I love him, this man upstairs, this Boyce, she thought. A workingman, a man unaccustomed to a woman like her, a man shy and moody and inarticulate.

Not that speech was what mattered between people. She learned that the very day she had accosted him on a train a few weeks before. A young man. She saw him and simply had to touch the newspaper he was scanning, flick it delicately with her finger; and he stared across at her and very quietly received her into his being, but without a word, without even a face-saving hello.

"I can't say things," he had said, and then breathed out quickly and nervously as if it had cost him a lot to admit it. He was like a hound, a little whippet. To venture loving him was like crossing the Rubicon—also daft. Also dicey. A journey of pain. She had no idea then how extensive that journey would be. A good man? Maybe. Maybe not. She was looking for reasons to unlove him. When he came down to the kitchen, he almost but didn't smile. There was such a tentativeness about him. Is it always going to be like this, she thought, spilling the coffee, slopping it in the saucer, and then nervously dumping the brown granular mass from a strainer onto an ashtray, and for no reason.

"I have no composure," she said. From him a wan smile. Would her buying the tickets be all right, would he look away while she paid, would it be an auspicious trip? She took his hand and warmed it and said she never wanted to do aught else, and he said not to say such things, not to say them, but in fact they were only a skimming of the real things she was longing to say. Years divided them, class divided them, position divided them. He wanted to give her a present and couldn't in case it wasn't swish enough. He bought perfume off a hawker in Oxford Circus, offered it to her, and then took it back. Probably gave it to Madge, his woman, put it down on the table along with his pay packet. Or maybe left it on a dressing table, if they had one. A tender moment? All these unknowns divided them. The morning she was getting married he was pruning trees in an English park, earning a smallish sum and living with a woman who had four children. He had always lived with some woman or another but insisted that he wasn't a philanderer, wasn't. He lived with Madge now, drank two pints of beer every evening, cuddled his baby girl, and smoked forty cigarettes a day.

In the taxi, he whispered to her to please not look at him like that, and at the airport he spent the bulk of the waiting time in the gents'. She wondered if there was a barber's in there, or if perhaps he had done a disappearance act, like people on their wedding day who do not show up at the altar rails. In fact, he had bought a plastic hairbrush to straighten his hair for the journey because it had got tangled in the night. Afterward, he put it in her travel bag. Did she need a travel bag? How long were they to stay? No knowing. They were terribly near and they were not near. No outsider could guess the relationship. In the plane, the hostess tried hard to flirt with him, said she'd seen him on television, but he skirted the subject by asking for a light. He was very active in his union and often appeared in television debates; at private meetings, he exhorted the members to think hard for themselves, to forget race and creed but to be on the side of their fellow-workers and to rope in new ones. He had made quite a reputation for himself by reading them cases from history, clippings from old newspapers, making them realize how they had been ill-treated for hundreds of years. He was a scaffolder like his father before him, but he had left Belfast soon after his parents died. His brothers and sisters were scattered.

When they got to the city destination, he suddenly suggested that she dump her bag in a safety locker, and she knew then that she shouldn't have brought it, that possibly they would not be staying overnight. Walking up the street of Edinburgh with a bitter breeze in their faces, she pointed to a castle that looked like a dungeon and asked him what he thought of it. Not much. He didn't think much—that was his answer. What did he do? Dream, daydream, imagine, forget? The leaves in the municipal flower bed were blowing and shivered like tatters, but the soil was a beautiful flaky black. They happened to be passing a funeral parlor and she asked if he preferred burial or cremation, but about that, too, he was indifferent. It made no matter. They should still be in bed, under covers, drowsed. She linked him and he jerked his arm away, saying those who knew him knew the woman he lived with and he would not like to appear knavish. They were halfway up the hill, and there was between them now one of those little swords of silence that are always slicing love—that kind of love.

"If Madge knew about this, she'd be immeasurably hurt," he said.

But Madge will know, she thought but did not say. She said instead that it was colder up north, that they were not far from the sea, and didn't he detect bits of hail in the wind? He saw her sadness, traced it lightly with his finger, traced the near-tears and the little pouch under the lids. He said, "You're a terrible woman altogether," to which she replied, "You're not a bad bloke," and they laughed. He was supposed to have travelled by train the night before, the very night he slept with her and had his hair pulled from the roots, like a bush brought away from a hillside. How good a liar was he, and how strong a man? He had crossed the street ahead of her, and to make amends he waited for her by the lights and watched her, admiring, as she came toward him, watched her walk, her lovely legs, her long, incongruous skirt, and watched the effect she had on others—one of shock, as if she were undressed or carrying some sort of invisible torch. He spoke of it—her poise—and even referred to an ancient queen.

"It's not that it's not pleasant holding your arm," he said, and took her elbow, feeling the wobble of the funny bone. Then he had to make a phone call, and soon they were going somewhere in a taxi, and the back streets of Edinburgh were not unlike the back streets of any other town—a bit black, a bit decrepit, pub fronts being washed down.

He's afraid of me, she thought. And I'm afraid of him. Fear is corrosive, and she felt certain that the woman he lived with was much more adept at living and arguing than she was. Probably would insist that he bring in the coal or clean out the ashes or share his last cigarette, would put her cards on the table. For a moment she was seized with a desire to see them together, and had the terrible idea that she would call at their place as a door-to-door saleswoman with a little attaché case full of cleaning stuffs, so she would have to go in and show her wares. She would see their kitchen and their pram and the baby in it, she would see how disposed they were to one another. But that would not be necessary, because he was leaving, because he had told her that between him and the woman it was all over; it had all gone dry and flaccid. When Boyce looked at her then, it was a true felt look and laden with sweetness—white, mesmerizing, like the blossom that hangs from the cherry tree.

Before addressing the students, he called on some friends. Even that was furtive—he didn't knock; he whistled some sort of code through the letter box. In the big, sparsely furnished room there was a pregnant cat—marmalade—and the leftovers of a breakfast, and a man and a woman who had obviously just tumbled out of their bed. She thought, This is how it should be. When, through a crack in the door, catching a glimpse of their big tossed bed and the dented pillows without pillow slips, she ached to go in and lie there, she knew that the sight of it had permeated her consciousness and it was a longing she would always feel. That longing was replaced by a stitch in the chest, then a lot of stitches, and then something like a lump in the back of the mouth—something sad that would not dissolve. Would he live with her, as he had said? Would he do it? Would he forsake everything—fear, respectability, safeness, the woman, the child? The questions were like pendulums swinging this way and that. The answers would swing, too.

The woman she had just met was called Ita and the man was called Jim the Limb. He had some defect in his right arm. They were plump and radiant, what with their night and their big breakfast and now a fresh pot of tea. They were chain smokers. Ita said her fur coat and the marmalade cat were alike, and Boyce said that was a wrong thing to say. But there was no wrong thing so far as she was concerned. She just wanted them to welcome her in, to accept her. When they talked about the union and the various men and the weekly meetings, when they discussed a rally that was to take place in London, she thought, Let me be one of you, let me put aside my old stupid flitting life, let me take part, let me in. Her life was not exactly soignée and she, too, had lived in poor rooms and ridden a ridiculous bicycle and swapped old shoes for other old shoes, but she seemed not to belong, because she had bettered herself—had done it on her own, and now that she was a graphic designer she designed alone. Also, these people in the union were townspeople; they all had lived in small steep town houses, slept two or three or four to a bed, sparred, lived in and out of one another's pockets, knew familiarity well enough to know that it was tolerable.

Ita announced that she was not going to the factory that morning, said dammit, the bloody sweatshop, and told of two women who were fired because they had gone deaf from the machines and weren't able to hear proper.

Instantly Boyce said they must fight it. They were a clan. Yet when he winked at *her* he seemed to be saying something else, something ambiguous, like "I see you there, I am not forsaking you"—or was he saying "Look how influential I am, look at me"? A word he often used was "big shot." Maybe he had dreams of being a big shot? Just before the four of them left the house for the college, he went for the third time to the lavatory, and she believed he had gone to be sick. Yet when he stood on the small ladder platform, holding up a faulty loudspeaker, brandishing it, making jokes about it—calling it Big Brother—he seemed to be utterly in his element. He spoke without notes, he spoke freely, telling the crowd of his background in Belfast, his father's work at the shipyards, his having to emigrate, his job in London, the lads, the way this fellow or that fellow had got nabbed, and though what he had to say was about discrimination, he made it all funny. When questions were put after he had finished, it was clear that he had cajoled them all, except for one dissenter—an aristocratic-looking boy in a dress suit, a boy who seemed to be on the brink of a nervous breakdown. Even with him he dealt deftly. He replied without any venom, and when the dissenter was booed and told to belt up, he said "Aach" to his friends who were heckling. The hat was passed around—a navy college cap—into which coins were tossed from all corners of the room. She hesitated, not knowing whether to give a lot or a little and wanting only to do the right thing. She gave a pound note, and afterward in the refectory to which they had all repaired she saw a girl hand him ten pounds and thought how the collection must have been to foot his expenses.

Ita and Jim decided to accompany them to Glasgow, where he was conducting the same sort of meeting in the evening, in a public hall. Getting to the station late, as they did, he said, "Let's jump in here," and ushered them into a first-class carriage, though their tickets were for second. When the ticket-collector came, she paid the difference, knowing that he had chosen the first because he felt it was where she belonged. They couldn't hear one another for the rattle of the train, the shunting of other carriages, and a whipping wind that lashed through a broken window. He dozed; sometimes, coming awake, he nudged her with his shoe. The ladies sat on one side, the men opposite, and Ita was whispering to her in her ear, saying how when she met Jim they had gone to bed for an entire week. Boyce looked at the women whispering and tittering and he seemed to like that, and there was a satisfaction in the way he lolled.

By the time they got to the station they were all hungry. "Starving you I am," he said to her as he asked a porter for the name of a restaurant. "A French joint," he said. As they were settling down in the garish room, Ita tripped over the flex of the table lamp and Jim glowered with embarrassment, said this wasn't home—not by a long shot. They dived into the basket of bread, calling for butter, butter. Boyce made jokes about the wine, sniffed it, and asked if for sure it was the best vintage. She fed him with her fingers the little potato sticks on her plate. He accepted them as if they were matches, then gobbled them down, and the others knew what they had suspected—that this pair were lovers. Jim said they looked like two people in a snapshot, and they smiled as if they *were*, and their faces scanned one another as if in a beautiful daze.

At the meeting, he gave the same spiel, except that it had to be shortened, and this he did by omitting one anecdote about a man who was sent to jail for speaking Gaelic in the northern province of his own country. There was a collection here, too, and the amount was much higher, because the bulk of the audience were workingmen, and proud to contribute.

From the hall they went with a group to a big ramshackle room at the top of a large house in the north side of the city. In the front hall there were dozens of milk bottles, and in the back hall two or three bicycles jumbled together. He had bought a bottle of whiskey, and in the kitchen off the big room she heated a kettle to make a hot punch for him because his throat was sore. He came out to the kitchen and told her what a grand person she was, and he kissed her stealthily. The kitchen was a shambles, and although at first intending to tidy it a bit, all she did was scald two cups and a tumbler for his punch. Some had hot whiskey, some had cold; she had hers laced in a cup of tea. They all talked, interrupting one another, joking, having inside conversation about meetings they'd been to and other meetings to which they'd sent hecklers, and demonstrations that they were planning to have, and all their supporters in France, Italy, and throughout Europe.

She looked up at the light shade, wrinkled plastic as big as a beach ball, and decorated with a lot of fishes. She felt useless. The designs she made were simple and geometric and somewhat moving, but at that moment they seemed irrelevant. They had no relation to these people, to their conversation, to their curious kind of bantering anger. She remembered nights on end when she had striven to make a shape or a design that would go straight to the quick of someone's being, she had gruelled over it—but to these people it would be a piece of folly. The place was unkempt, but still it was a place. Above the window, several brass rings had come off their hooks and the heavy velvet curtain gaped. He was being witty. Someone had said that there were more ways than one of killing a cat, and he had intervened to say that the word was "skinning." That was the first flicker of cruelty she had seen in him. She was sitting next him on the divan bed, she leaning back against the wall slightly out of the melee, he pressing forward making the odd joke. He said that at forty he might find his true vocation in life, and feared it might be as a whiz kid. There was a rocking chair in which one of the men sat, and several easy chairs with stained and torn upholstery, their springs dipping down to variable degrees, depending on the weight and pranks of the sitters. Sometimes a girl with plaits would rush over and sit on her man's knee and pull his beard and then the springs dropped like the inside of a broken melodeon. If only he and she could be that unreserved.

Then he was missing—out on the landing, using the phone. She knew they had missed the last plane back to London, and long ago had missed the last train, and that they would have to kip down somewhere, and she thought how awful if it had to be in the center of town, in the freezing cold, on a bench. Ita asked her if they were perhaps going to make a touring holiday, and she said no but couldn't add to that, couldn't gloss the reply with some extra little piece of information. When he came back to the room, he told her that a taxi was on its way.

"I don't know where we're heading for—a wonderland," he said, shaking hands with Ita, and then he said cheers to the room at large.

The hotel was close to the airport—a modern building made of concrete cubes, like something built by a child, and with vertical slits for windows. They might be turned away. He went in whistling. She waited, one foot on the step of the taxi and one on the footpath, and said an involuntary prayer. She saw him handing over money, then beckoning for her to come in. He had signed the register, and in the lift, as he fondled her, he told her the false name that he had used. It was a nice name—Egan. In the bedroom they thought of whiskey, and then of milk, and then of milk and whiskey, but they were too tired, and shy all over again, and neither of them imperious enough to give an order while the other was listening.

"I know you better now," he said. She wondered at what precise moment in the day he had come to know her better. Had he crept in on her like a little invisible camera and knew that he knew her and would know her for all time? Maybe some non-moment, when she walked gauchely toward the ladies' room, or when asked her second name she hesitated, in case by giving a name she should compromise him. She apologized for not talking more, and he said that that was what was lovely about her, and he apologized for giving the same lecture twice, and for all the stupid things that got said. Then he trotted around naked, getting his tiny transistor from his overcoat pocket, studying the hotel clock—a square face set into the bedside table—fiddling with the various lights. He had never stayed in a hotel before, and it was then he told her that there would be a refund if in the morning they didn't eat breakfast. He had paid. His earnings for the day had been swallowed up by the payment.

"I'll refund you," she said, and he said what rot, and in the dark they were together again—together like spare limbs, like rag dolls or bits of motorcar tire, bits of themselves, together, effortless and full of harmony, as if they had grown that way, always were and always would be. But she couldn't ask for a pledge. It had to come from him. He was thinking of leaving London, changing jobs, going back home to Belfast. Well, wherever he went she was going too. He had brought everything to a head, everything she had wanted to feel—love and pity and softness and passion and patience and barefaced jealousy. They went to sleep talking, then half talking, voices trailing away like tendrils, sleepy voices, sleepy brains, sleepy bodies, talking, not talking, dumb.

"I love you, I love you." He said it the very moment that the hotel clock triggered off, and the doubts and the endless cups of coffee and the bulging ashtrays were all sweet reminds of a day in which the fates changed. He said he dearly wished that they could lie there for hours on end and have coffee and papers sent up, and lie there and let the bloody airplanes and the bloody world go by.

But why were they hurrying? It was a Saturday and he had no work.

"I'll say goodbye here," he said, and he kissed her and pulled the lapel of her fur coat up around her neck so that she wouldn't feel the cold.

"But we're going together," she said.

He said yes, but they would be in public places and they would not be able to say goodbye—not intimately. He kissed her.

"We will be together?" she said.

"It will take time," he said.

"How long?" she asked.

"Months, years . . ."

They were ready to go.

In the plane, they talked first about mushrooms, and she said how mushrooms were reputed to be magic, and then she asked him if he had wanted a son rather than a daughter, and he said no, a daughter, and smiled at the thought of his little one. He read four of the morning papers—read them, reread them, combed the small news items that were put in at the last minute, and got printing ink all over his hands. The edges of the paper sometimes jutted against her nose or her eyes or her forehead, and without turning he would say, "Sorry, love." To live with, he would be all right—silent at times, undemonstrative, then all of a sudden touching as an infant. Every slight gesture of his, every "Sorry, love" tore at some place in her gut.

In London, a bus was waiting on the tarmac, right next to the landed plane. He said they needn't bother rushing, and as a result they were very nearly not taken at all. The steward looked down the aisle of the bus, put up a finger to say that there was room for only one, and then in the end grumpily let them both enter. They had to sit separately, with an aisle between them, and she began to revert to her cursed superstitions, such as if they passed a white gate all would be well.

At the terminus, he had to make a phone call, and she could see him, although she had not meant to look, gesticulating fiercely in the glass booth. When he came out, he was biting his thumb. After a while he said he was late, that the woman had had to stay home from work, that he was in the wrong again. She saw it clearly, cruelly—as clear and as cruel as the lines of ice that had claimed the windowpane. Claims. Responsibility. "Be here, be here."

They walked up the street toward the Underground station. No matter how she carried it, the travel bag bumped against her, or, when she changed hands, against him. Boyce said she was never to tell anyone. She said she wasn't likely to go spouting it, and he said why the frown, why spoil everything with a frown like that? It went out like a shooting star—the sense of peace, the suffusion, the near-happiness. He asked her to hang on while he got cigarettes, and then, plunging into the dark passage that led to the Underground, he saw her hesitate and said did she always take taxis? They kissed. It was a dark, unpropitious passage but a real kiss. Their mouths clung, the skin of their lips would not be parted; she felt that they might fall into a trance in order not to terminate it. He was as helpless then as a schoolboy, and his eyes as pathetic as watered ink.

"If I must, if I must talk to you, may I?" she said.

He looked at her bitterly. He was like a chisel. "I can't promise anything," he said, and repeated it. Then he was gone, doing a little hop through the turnstile and omitting to get a ticket. She walked on, the bag bumping off the calf of her leg; soon, when she had enough composure, she would hail a taxi. Would he go? Would he come back? What would he do? It was like a door that had just come ajar and anything could happen to it; it could shut tight or open a fraction or fly wide in a burst. She thought of the bigness and wonder of destiny; meeting him had been a fluke, and this now was a fluke, and so was the future, and they would be together or not be together as life the gaffer thought fit.

ALICE MUNRO was born in Wingham, Ontario, in 1931. She was educated in Canada and London. She began publishing short stories in the early fifties in *The Canadian Forum, The Tamarack Review, Queen's Quarterly,* and *The Montrealer.* After her first collection of short stories, *Dance of the Happy Shades,* was published in 1968, she received the Governor General's Award for Literature. She is now referred to as "one of the most significant short story writers in Canada today." In her short fiction and her novel *Lives of Girls and Women,* Alice Munro, as one critic has commented, depicts changes taking place in rural and small-town Canada from a moral rather than a sociological point of view. The point of view of her usually female narrator is that moral chaos is everywhere—there is nothing tangible or lasting that will give our existence in the modern world meaning or security. The story that follows here, "The Office," reminds one of Tillie Olsen's remark that "any woman who writes is a survivor."

Alice Munro
(1931–   )

THE OFFICE

The solution to my life occurred to me one evening while I was ironing a shirt. It was simple but audacious. I went into the living room where my husband was watching television and I said, "I think I ought to have an office."

It sounded fantastic, even to me. What do I want an office for? I have a house; it is pleasant and roomy and has a view of the sea; it provides appropriate places for eating and sleeping, and having baths and conversations with one's friends. Also I have a garden; there is no lack of space.

No. But here comes the disclosure which is not easy for me: I am a writer. That does not sound right. Too presumptuous; phony, or at least unconvincing. Try again. I write. Is that better? I *try* to write. That makes it worse. Hypocritical humility. Well then?

It doesn't matter. However I put it, the words create their space of silence, the delicate moment of exposure. But people are kind, the silence is quickly absorbed by the solicitude of friendly voices, crying variously, how wonderful, and good for *you*, and well, that *is* intriguing. And what do you write, they inquire with spirit. Fiction, I reply, bearing my humiliation by this time with ease, even a suggestion of flippancy, which was not always mine, and again, again, the perceptible circles of dismay are smoothed out by such ready and tactful voices—which have however exhausted their stock of consolatory phrases, and can say only, "*Ah!*"

So this is what I want an office for (I said to my husband): to write in. I was at once aware that it sounded like a finicky requirement, a piece of rare self-indulgence. To write, as everyone knows, you need a typewriter, or at least a pencil, some paper, a table and chair; I have all these things in a corner of my bedroom. But now I want an office as well.

And I was not even sure that I was going to write in it, if we come down to that. Maybe I would sit and stare at the wall; even that prospect was not unpleasant to me. It was really the sound of the word "office" that I liked, its sound of dignity and peace. And purposefulness and importance. But I did not care to mention this to my husband, so I launched instead into a high-flown explanation which went, as I remember, like this:

A house is all right for a man to work in. He brings his work into the house, a place is cleared for it; the house rearranges itself as best it can around him. Everybody recognizes that his work *exists*. He is not expected to answer the telephone, to find things that are lost, to see why the children are crying, or feed the cat. He can shut his door. Imagine (I said) a mother shutting her door, and the children knowing she is behind it; why, the very thought of it is outrageous to them. A woman who sits staring into space, into a country that is not her husband's or her children's is likewise known to be an offence against nature. So a house is not the same for a woman. She is not someone who walks into the house, to make use of it, and will walk out again. She *is* the house; there is no separation possible.

(And this is true, though as usual when arguing for something I am afraid I do not deserve, I put it in too emphatic and emotional terms. At certain times, perhaps on long spring evenings, still rainy and sad, with the cold bulbs in bloom and a light too mild for promise drifting over the sea, I have opened the windows and felt the house shrink back into wood and plaster and those humble elements of which it is made, and the life in it subside, leaving me exposed, empty-handed, but feeling a fierce and lawless quiver of freedom, of loneliness too harsh and perfect for me now to bear. Then I know how the rest of the time I am sheltered and encumbered, how insistently I am warmed and bound.)

"Go ahead, if you can find one cheap enough," is all my husband had to say to this. He is not like me, he does not really want explanations. That the heart of another person is a closed book, is something you will hear him say frequently, and without regret.

Even then I did not think it was something that could be accomplished. Perhaps at bottom it seemed to me too improper a wish to be granted. I could almost more easily have wished for a mink coat, for a diamond necklace; these are things women do obtain. The children, learning of my plans, greeted them with the most dashing skepticism and unconcern. Nevertheless I went down to the shopping centre which is two blocks from where I live; there I had noticed for several months, and without thinking how they could pertain to me, a couple of For Rent signs in the upstairs windows of a building that housed a drugstore and a beauty parlour. As I went up the stairs I had a feeling of complete unreality; surely renting was a complicated business, in the case of offices; you did not simply knock on the door of the vacant premises and wait to be admitted; it would have to be done through channels. Also, they would want too much money.

As it turned out, I did not even have to knock. A woman came out of one of the empty offices, dragging a vacuum cleaner, and pushing it with her foot, towards the open door across the hall, which evidently led to an apartment in the rear of the building. She and her husband lived in this apartment; their name was Malley; and it was indeed they who owned the building and rented out the offices. The rooms she had just been vacuuming were, she told me, fitted out for a dentist's office, and so would not interest me, but she would show me the other place. She invited me into her apartment while she put away the vacuum and got her key. Her husband, she said with a sigh I could not interpret, was not at home.

Mrs. Malley was a black-haired delicate-looking woman, perhaps in her early forties, slatternly but still faintly appealing, with such arbitrary touches of femininity as the thin line of bright lipstick, the pink feather slippers on obviously tender and swollen feet. She had the swaying passivity, the air of exhaustion and muted apprehension, that speaks of a life spent in close attention on a man who is by turns vigorous, crotchety and dependent. How much of this I saw at first, how much decided on later is of course impossible to tell. But I did think that she would have no children, the stress of her life, whatever it was, did not allow it, and in this I was not mistaken.

The room where I waited was evidently a combination living room and office. The first things I noticed were models of ships—galleons, clippers, Queen Marys—sitting on the tables, the window sills, the television. Where there were no ships there were potted plants and a clutter of what are sometimes called "masculine" ornaments—china deer heads, bronze horses, huge ashtrays of heavy, veined, shiny material. On the walls were framed photographs and what might have been diplomas. One photo showed a poodle and a bulldog, dressed in masculine and feminine clothing, and assuming with dismal embarrassment a pose of affection. Written across it was "Old Friends." But the room was really dominated by a portrait, with its own light and a gilded frame; it was of a good-looking, fair-haired man in middle age, sitting behind a desk, wearing a business suit and looking preeminently prosperous, rosy and agreeable. Here again, it is probably hindsight on my part that points out that in the portrait there is evident also some uneasiness, some lack of faith the man has in this role, a tendency he has to spread himself too bountifully and insistently, which for all anyone knows may lead to disaster.

Never mind the Malleys. As soon as I saw that office, I wanted it. It was larger than I needed, being divided in such a way that it would be suitable for a doctor's office. (We had a chiropractor in here but he left, says Mrs. Malley in her regretful but uninformative way.) The walls were cold and bare, white with a little grey, to cut the glare for the eyes. Since there were no doctors in evidence, nor had been, as Mrs. Malley freely told me, for some time, I offered twenty-five dollars a month. She said she would have to speak to her husband.

The next time I came, my offer was agreed upon, and I met Mr. Malley in the flesh. I explained, as I had already done to his wife, that I did not want to make use of my office during regular business hours, but during the week-ends and sometimes in the evening. He asked me what I would use it for, and I told him, not without wondering first whether I ought to say I did stenography.

He absorbed the information with good humour. "Ah, you're a writer."

"Well yes. I write."

"Then we'll do our best to see you're comfortable here," he said expansively. "I'm a great man for hobbies myself. All these ship-models, I do them in my spare time, they're a blessing for the nerves. People need an occupation for their nerves. I daresay you're the same."

"Something the same," I said, resolutely agreeable, even relieved that he saw my behaviour in this hazy and tolerant light. At least he did not ask me, as I half-expected, who was looking after the children, and did my husband approve? Ten years, maybe fifteen, had greatly softened, spread and defeated the man in the picture. His hips and thighs had now a startling accumulation of fat, causing him to move with a sigh, a cushiony settling of flesh, a ponderous matriarchal discomfort. His hair and eyes had faded, his features blurred, and the affable, predatory expression had collapsed into one of troubling humility and chronic mistrust. I did not look at him. I had not planned, in taking an office, to take on the responsibility of knowing any more human beings.

On the weekend I moved in, without the help of my family, who would have been kind. I brought my typewriter and a card table and chair, also a little wooden table on which I set a hot plate, a kettle, a jar of instant coffee, a spoon and a yellow mug. That was all. I brooded with satisfaction on the bareness of my walls, the cheap dignity of my essential furnishings, the remarkable lack of things to dust, wash or polish.

The sight was not so pleasing to Mr. Malley. He knocked on my door soon after I was settled and said that he wanted to explain a few things to me—about unscrewing the light in the outer room, which I would not need, about the radiator and how to work the awning outside the window. He looked around at everything with gloom and mystification and said it was an awfully uncomfortable place for a lady.

"It's perfectly all right for me," I said, not as discouragingly as I would have liked to, because I always have a tendency to placate people whom I dislike for no good reason, or simply do not want to know. I make elaborate offerings of courtesy sometimes, in the foolish hope that they will go away and leave me alone.

"What you want is a nice easy chair to sit in, while you're waiting for inspiration to hit. I've got a chair down in the basement, all kinds of stuff down there since my mother passed on last year. There's a bit of carpet rolled up in a corner down there, it isn't doing anybody any good. We could get this place fixed up so it'd be a lot more homelike for you."

But really, I said, but really I like it as it is.

"If you wanted to run up some curtains, I'd pay you for

the material. Place needs a touch of colour, I'm afraid you'll get morbid sitting in here."

Oh, no, I said, and laughed, I'm sure I won't.

"It'd be a different story if you was a man. A woman wants things a bit cosier."

So I got up and went to the window and looked down into the empty Sunday street through the slats of the Venetian blind, to avoid the accusing vulnerability of his fat face and I tried out a cold voice that is to be heard frequently in my thoughts but has great difficulty getting out of my cowardly mouth. "Mr. Malley, please don't bother me about this any more. I said it suits me. I have everything I want. Thanks for showing me about the light."

The effect was devastating enough to shame me. "I certainly wouldn't dream of bothering you," he said, with precision of speech and aloof sadness. "I merely made these suggestions for your comfort. Had I realized I was in your way, I would of left some time ago." When he had gone I felt better, even a little exhilarated at my victory though still ashamed of how easy it had been. I told myself that he would have had to be discouraged sooner or later, it was better to have it over with at the beginning.

The following weekend he knocked on my door. His expression of humility was exaggerated, almost enough so to seem mocking, yet in another sense it was real and I felt unsure of myself.

"I won't take up a minute of your time," he said. "I never meant to be a nuisance. I just wanted to tell you I'm sorry I offended you last time and I apologize. Here's a little present if you will accept."

He was carrying a plant whose name I did not know; it had thick, glossy leaves and grew out of a pot wrapped lavishly in pink and silver foil.

"There," he said, arranging this plant in a corner of my room. "I don't want any bad feelings with you and me. I'll take the blame. And I thought, maybe she won't accept furnishings, but what's the matter with a nice little plant, that'll brighten things up for you."

It was not possible for me, at this moment, to tell him that I did not want a plant. I hate house plants. He told me how to take care of it, how often to water it and so on; I thanked him. There was nothing else I could do, and I had the unpleasant feeling that beneath his offering of apologies and gifts he was well aware of this and in some way gratified by it. He kept on talking, using the words *bad feelings, offended, apologize.* I tried once to interrupt, with the idea of explaining that I had made provision for an area of my life where good feelings, or bad, did not enter in, that between him and me, in fact, it was not necessary that there be any feelings at all; but this struck me as a hopeless task. How could I confront, in the open, this craving for intimacy? Besides, the plant in its shiny paper had confused me.

"How's the writing progressing?" he said, with an air of putting all our unfortunate differences behind him.

"Oh, about as usual."

"Well if you ever run out of things to write about, I got a barrelful." Pause. "But I guess I'm just eatin' into your time here," he said with a kind of painful buoyancy. This was a test, and I did not pass it. I smiled, my eyes held by that magnificent plant; I said it was all right.

"I was just thinking about the fellow was in here before you. Chiropractor. You could of wrote a book about him."

I assumed a listening position, my hands no longer hovering over the keys. If cowardice and insincerity are big vices of mine, curiosity is certainly another.

"He had a good practice built up here. The only trouble was, he gave more adjustments than was listed in the book of chiropractory. Oh, he was adjusting right and left. I came in here after he moved out, and what do you think I found? Soundproofing! This whole room was soundproofed, to enable him to make his adjustments without disturbing anybody. This very room you're sitting writing your stories in.

"First we knew of it was a lady knocked on my door one day, wanted me to provide her with a passkey to his office. He'd locked his door against her.

"I guess he just got tired of treating her particular case. I guess he figured he'd been knocking away at it long enough. Lady well on in years, you know, and him just a young man. He had a nice young wife too and a couple of the prettiest children you ever would want to see. Filthy some of the things that go on in this world."

It took me some time to realize that he told this story not simply as a piece of gossip, but as something a writer would be particularly interested to hear. Writing and lewdness had a vague delicious connection in his mind. Even this notion, however, seemed so wistful, so infantile, that it struck me as a waste of energy to attack it. I knew now I must avoid hurting him for my own sake, not for his. It had been a great mistake to think that a little roughness would settle things.

The next present was a teapot. I insisted that I drank only coffee and told him to give it to his wife. He said that tea was better for the nerves and that he had known right away I was a nervous person, like himself. The teapot was covered with gilt and roses and I knew that it was not cheap, in spite of its extreme hideousness. I kept it on my table. I also continued to care for the plant, which thrived obscenely in the corner of my room. I could not decide what else to do. He bought me a wastebasket, a fancy one with Chinese mandarins on all eight sides; he got a foam rubber cushion for my chair. I despised myself for submitting to this blackmail. I did not even really pity him; it was just that I could not turn away, I could not turn away from that obsequious hunger. And he knew himself my tolerance was bought; in a way he must have hated me for it.

When he lingered in my office now he told me stories of himself. It occurred to me that he was revealing his life to me in the hope that I would write it down. Of course he had probably revealed it to plenty of people for no particular reason, but in my case there seemed to be a special, even desperate necessity. His life was a series of calamities, as people's lives often are; he had been let down by people he had trusted, refused help by those he had depended on, betrayed by the very friends to whom he had given kindness and material help. Other people, mere strangers and passersby, had taken time to torment him gratuitously, in novel and inventive ways. On occasion, his very life had been threatened. Moreover his wife was a difficulty, her health being poor and her temperament unstable; what was he to do? You see how it is, he said, lifting his hands, but I live. He looked to me to say yes.

I took to coming up the stairs on tiptoe, trying to turn my key without making a noise; this was foolish of course because I could not muffle my typewriter. I actually considered writing in longhand, and wished repeatedly for the evil chiropractor's soundproofing. I told my husband my problem and he said it was not a problem at all. Tell him you're busy, he said. As a matter of fact I did tell him; every time he came to my door, always armed with a little gift or an errand, he asked me how I was and I said that today I was busy. Ah, then, he said, as he eased himself through the door, he would not keep me a minute. And all the time, as I have said, he knew what was going on in my mind, how I weakly longed to be rid of him. He knew but could not afford to care.

One evening after I had gone home I discovered that I had left at the office a letter I had intended to post, and so I went back to get it. I saw from the street that the light was on in the room where I worked. Then I saw him bending over the card table. Of course, he came in at night and read what I had written! He heard me at the door, and when I came in he was picking up my wastebasket, saying he thought he would just tidy things up for me. He went out at once. I did not say anything, but found myself trembling with anger and gratification. To have found a just cause was a wonder, an unbearable relief.

Next time he came to my door I had locked it on the inside. I knew his step, his chummy cajoling knock. I continued typing loudly, but not uninterruptedly, so he would know I heard. He called my name, as if I was playing a trick; I bit my lips together not to answer. Unreasonably as ever, guilt assailed me but I typed on. That day I saw the earth was dry around the roots of the plant; I let it alone.

I was not prepared for what happened next. I found a note taped to my door, which said that Mr. Malley would be obliged if I would step into his office. I went at once to get it over with. He sat at his desk surrounded by obscure evidences of his authority; he looked at me from a distance, as one who was now compelled to see me in a new and sadly unfavourable light; the embarrassment which he showed seemed not for himself, but me. He started off by saying, with a rather stagey reluctance, that he had known of course when he took me in that I was a writer.

"I didn't let that worry me, though I have heard things about writers and artists and that type of person that didn't strike me as very encouraging. You know the sort of thing I mean."

This was something new; I could not think what it might lead to.

"Now you came to me and said, Mr. Malley, I want a place to write in. I believed you. I gave it to you. I didn't ask any questions. That's the kind of person I am. But you know the more I think about it, well, the more I am inclined to wonder."

"Wonder what?" I said.

"And your own attitude, that hasn't helped to put my mind at ease. Locking yourself in and refusing to answer your door. That's not a normal way for a person to behave. Not if they got nothing to hide. No more than it's normal for a young woman, says she has a husband and kids, to spend her time rattling away on a typewriter."

"But I don't think that—"

He lifted his hand, a forgiving gesture. "Now all I ask is, that you be open and aboveboard with me, I think I deserve that much, and if you are using that office for any other purpose, or at any other times than you let on, and having your friends or whoever they are up to see you—"

"I don't know what you mean."

"And another thing, you claim to be a writer. Well I read quite a bit of material, and I never have seen your name in print. Now maybe you write under some other name?"

"No," I said.

"Well I don't doubt there are writers whose names I haven't heard," he said genially. "We'll let that pass. Just you give me your word of honour there won't be any more deceptions, or any carryings-on, et cetera, in that office you occupy—"

My anger was delayed somehow, blocked off by a stupid incredulity. I only knew enough to get up and walk down the hall, his voice trailing after me, and lock the door. I thought—I must go. But after I had sat down in my own room, my work in front of me, I thought again how much I liked this room, how well I worked in it, and I decided not to be forced out. After all, I felt, the struggle between us had reached a deadlock. I could refuse to open the door, refuse to look at his notes, refuse to speak to him when we met. My rent was paid in advance and if I left now it was unlikely that I would get any refund. I resolved not to care. I had been taking my manuscript home every night, to prevent his reading it, and now it seemed that even this precaution was beneath me. What did it matter if he read it, any more than if the mice scampered over it in the dark?

Several times after this I found notes on my door. I intended not to read them, but I always did. His accusations grew more specific. He had heard voices in my room. My behaviour was disturbing his wife when she tried to take her afternoon nap. (I never came in the afternoons, except on weekends.) He had found a whiskey bottle in the garbage.

I wondered a good deal about that chiropractor. It was not comfortable to see how the legends of Mr. Malley's life were built up.

As the notes grew more virulent our personal encounters ceased. Once or twice I saw his stooped, sweatered back disappearing as I came into the hall. Gradually our relationship passed into something that was entirely fantasy. He accused me now, by note, of being intimate with people from *Numero Cinq*. This was a coffee-house in the neighbourhood, which I imagine he invoked for symbolic purposes. I felt that nothing much more would happen now, the notes would go on, their contents becoming possibly more grotesque and so less likely to affect me.

He knocked on my door on a Sunday morning, about eleven o'clock. I had just come in and taken my coat off and put my kettle on the hot plate.

This time it was another face, remote and transfigured, that shone with the cold light of intense joy at discovering the proofs of sin.

"I wonder," he said with emotion, "if you would mind following me down the hall?"

I followed him. The light was on in the washroom. This washroom was mine and no one else used it, but he had not given me a key for it and it was always open. He stopped in front of it, pushed back the door and stood with his eyes cast down, expelling his breath discreetly.

"Now who done that?" he said, in a voice of pure sorrow.

The walls above the toilet and above the washbasin were covered with drawings and comments of the sort you see sometimes in public washrooms on the beach, and in town hall lavatories in the little decaying towns where I grew up. They were done with a lipstick, as they usually are. Someone must have got up here the night before, I thought, possibly some of the gang who always loafed and cruised around the shopping centre on Saturday nights.

"It should have been locked," I said, coolly and firmly as if thus to remove myself from the scene. "It's quite a mess."

"It sure is. It's pretty filthy language, in my book. Maybe it's just a joke to your friends, but it isn't to me. Not to mention the art work. That's a nice thing to see when you open a door on your own premises in the morning."

I said, "I believe lipstick will wash off."

"I'm just glad I didn't have my wife see a thing like this. Upsets a woman that's had a nice bringing up. Now why don't you ask your friends up here to have a party with their pails and brushes? I'd like to have a look at the people with that kind of a sense of humour."

I turned to walk away and he turned heavily in front of me.

"I don't think there's any question how these decorations found their way onto my walls."

"If you're trying to say I had anything to do with it," I said, quite flatly and wearily, "you must be crazy."

"How did they get there then? Whose lavatory is this? Eh, whose?"

"There isn't any key to it. Anybody can come up here and walk in. Maybe some kids off the street came up here and did it last night after I went home, how do I know?"

"It's a shame the way the kids gets blamed for everything, when it's the elders that corrupts them. That's a thing you might do some thinking about, you know. There's laws. Obscenity laws. Applies to this sort of thing and literature too as I believe."

This is the first time I ever remember taking deep breaths, consciously, for purposes of self-control. I really wanted to murder him. I remember how soft and loathsome his face looked, with the eyes almost closed, nostrils extended to the soothing odour of righteousness, the odour of triumph. If this stupid thing had not happened, he would never have won. But he had. Perhaps he saw something in my face that unnerved him, even in this victorious moment, for he drew back to the wall, and began to say that actually, as a matter of fact, he had not really felt it was the sort of thing I personally would do, more the sort of thing that perhaps certain friends of mine—I got into my own room, shut the door.

The kettle was making a fearsome noise, having almost boiled dry. I snatched it off the hot plate, pulled out the plug and stood for a moment choking on rage. This spasm passed and I did what I had to do. I put my typewriter and paper on the chair and folded the card table. I screwed the top tightly on the instant coffee and put it and the yellow mug and the teaspoon into the bag in which I had brought them; it was still lying folded on the shelf. I wished childishly to take some vengeance on the potted plant, which sat in the corner with the flowery teapot, the waste-basket, the cushion, and—I forgot—a little plastic pencil sharpener behind it.

When I was taking things down to the car Mrs. Malley came. I had seen little of her since that first day. She did not seem upset, but practical and resigned.

"He is lying down," she said. "He is not himself."

She carried the bag with the coffee and the mug in it. She was so still I felt my anger leave me, to be replaced by an absorbing depression.

I have not yet found another office. I think that I will try again some day, but not yet. I have to wait at least until that picture fades that I see so clearly in my mind, though I never saw it in reality—Mr. Malley with his rags and brushes and a pail of soapy water, scrubbing in his clumsy way, his deliberately clumsy way, at the toilet walls, stooping with difficulty, breathing sorrowfully, arranging in his mind the bizarre but somehow never quite satisfactory narrative of yet another betrayal of trust. While I arrange words, and think it is my right to be rid of him.

JOYCE CAROL OATES was born in Lockport, New York, in 1938. She graduated Phi Beta Kappa from Syracuse University and received an M.A. in English from the University of Wisconsin. She has been Instructor and Assistant Professor of English at the University of Detroit and the University of Windsor, Ontario, respectively, a recipient of a National Endowment of the Arts grant, a Guggenheim, an O. Henry short story award, and the National Book Award for fiction in 1970. At the age of thirty-five she had published ten volumes, including short stories, poetry, novels, and literary criticism. Critics and reviewers have called her "one of the most promising American writers," "the best young novelist in the United States today," possessing "Tolstoy's sense of history as it overwhelms the individual," a writer of "the best of contemporary fiction." The story that follows here appeared in her collection *The Wheel of Love*, reviewed as "one of the finest collections of short fiction ever written by an American." "In a Region of Ice," which won first prize in the O. Henry short stories awards for 1967, substantiates her remarks to an interviewer that her theme is love: "it takes many different forms, many different social levels. . . . I think I write about love in an unconscious way. I look back upon the novels I've written, and I say, yes, this was my subject. But at the time I'm writing I'm not really conscious of that. I'm writing about a certain person who does this and that and comes to a certain end." "Where Are You Going, Where Have You Been?", her widely anthologized story and another masterpiece of short fiction, is one of the best examples of her ability to show the connection between social and psychological ugliness, between physical waste and lovelessness. Showing this connection is, in her view, what literature is all about. She wrote in a book review: "It seems to me that the greatest works of literature deal with the human soul caught in the stampede of time, unable to gauge the profundity of what passes over it, like the characters of Yeats who live through terrifying events but who cannot understand them; in this way history passes over most of us. Society is caught in a convulsion, whether of growth or of death, and ordinary people are destroyed. They do not, however, understand that they are destroyed."

Joyce Carol Oates
(1938–   )

IN THE REGION OF ICE

Sister Irene was a tall, deft woman in her early thirties. What one could see of her face made a striking impression—serious, hard gray eyes, a long slender nose, a face waxen with thought. Seen at the right time, from the right angle, she was almost handsome. In her past teaching positions she had drawn a little upon the fact of her being young and brilliant and also a nun, but she was beginning to grow out of that.

This was a new university and an entirely new world. She had heard—of course it was true—that the Jesuit administration of this school had hired her at the last moment to save money and to head off the appointment of a man of dubious religious commitment. She had prayed for the necessary energy to get her through this first semester. She had no trouble with teaching itself; once she stood before a classroom she felt herself capable of anything. It was the world immediately outside the classroom that confused and alarmed her, though she let none of this show—the cynicism of her colleagues, the indifference of many of the students, and, above all, the looks she got that told her nothing much would be expected of her because she was a nun. This took energy, strength. At times she had the idea that she was on trial and that the excuses she made to herself about her discomfort were only the common excuses made by guilty people. But in front of a class she had no time to worry about herself or the conflicts in her mind. She became, once and for all, a figure existing only for the benefit of others, an instrument by which facts were communicated.

About two weeks after the semester began, Sister Irene noticed a new student in her class. He was slight, and fair-haired, and his face was blank, but not blank by accident, blank on purpose, suppressed and restricted into a dumbness that looked hysterical. She was prepared for him before he raised his hand, and when she saw his arm jerk, as if he had at last lost control of it, she nodded to him without hesitation.

"Sister, how can this be reconciled with Shakespeare's vision in *Hamlet?* How can these opposing views be in the same mind?"

Students glanced at him, mildly surprised. He did not belong in the class, and this was mysterious, but his manner was urgent and blind.

"There is no need to reconcile opposing views," Sister Irene said, leaning forward against the podium. "In one play Shakespeare suggests one vision, in another play another; the plays are not simultaneous creations, and even if they were, we never demand a logical—"

"We must demand a logical consistency," the young man said. "The idea of education is itself predicated upon consistency, order, sanity—"

He had interrupted her, and she hardened her face against him—for his sake, not her own, since she did not really care. But he noticed nothing. "Please see me after class," she said.

After class the young man hurried up to her.

"Sister Irene, I hope you didn't mind my visiting today. I'd heard some things, interesting things," he said. He stared at her, and something in her face allowed him to smile. "I . . . could we talk in your office? Do you have time?"

They walked down to her office. Sister Irene sat at her desk, and the young man sat facing her; for a moment they were self-conscious and silent.

"Well I suppose you know—I'm a Jew," he said.

Sister Irene stared at him. "Yes?" she said.

"What am I doing at a Catholic University, huh?" He grinned. "That's what you want to know."

She made a vague movement of her hand to show that she had no thoughts on this, nothing at all, but he seemed not to catch it. He was sitting on the edge of the straight-backed chair. She saw that he was young but did not really look young. There were harsh lines on either side of his mouth, as if he had misused that youthful mouth somehow. His skin was almost as pale as hers, his eyes were dark and not quite in focus. He looked at her and through her and around her, as his voice surrounded them both. His voice was a little shrill at times.

"Listen, I did the right thing today—visiting your class! God, what a lucky accident it was; some jerk mentioned you, said you were a good teacher—I thought, what a laugh! These people know about good teachers here? But yes, listen, yes, I'm not kidding—you are good. I mean that."

Sister Irene frowned. "I don't quite understand what all this means."

He smiled and waved aside her formality, as if he knew better. "Listen, I got my B.A. at Columbia, then I came back here to this crappy city. I mean, I did it on purpose, I wanted to come back. I wanted to. I have my reasons for doing things. I'm on a three-thousand-dollar fellowship," he said, and waited for that to impress her. "You know, I could have gone almost anywhere with that fellowship, and I came back home here—my home's in the city—and enrolled here. This was last year. This is my second year. I'm working on a thesis. I mean I was, my master's thesis—but the hell with that. What I want to ask you is this: Can I enroll in your class, is it too late? We have to get special permission if we're late."

Sister Irene felt something nudging her, some uneasiness in him that was pleading with her not to be offended by his abrupt, familiar manner. He seemed to be promising another self, a better self, as if his fair, childish, almost cherubic face were doing tricks to distract her from what his words said.

"Are you in English studies?" she asked.

"I was in history. Listen," he said, and his mouth did something odd, drawing itself down into a smile that made the lines about it deepen like knives, "listen, they kicked me out."

He sat back, watching her. He crossed his legs. He took out a package of cigarettes and offered her one. Sister Irene shook her head, staring at his hands. They were small and stubby and might have belonged to a ten-year-old, and the nails were a strange near-violet color. It took him awhile to extract a cigarette.

"Yeah, kicked me out. What do you think of that?"

"I don't understand."

"My master's thesis was coming along beautifully, and then this bastard—I mean, excuse me, this professor, I won't pollute your office with his name—he started making criticisms, he said some things were unacceptable, he—"

The boy leaned forward and hunched his narrow shoulders in a parody of secrecy. "We had an argument. I told him some frank things, things only a broad-minded person could hear about himself. That takes courage, right? He didn't have it! He kicked me out of the master's program, so now I'm coming into English. Literature is greater than history; European history is one big pile of garbage. Sky-high. Filth and rotting corpses, right? Aristotle says that poetry is higher than history; he's right; in your class today I suddenly realized that this is my field, Shakespeare, only Shakespeare is—"

Sister Irene guessed that he was going to say that only Shakespeare was equal to him, and she caught the moment of recognition and hesitation, the half-raised arm, the keen, frowning forehead, the narrowed eyes; then he thought better of it and did not end the sentence. "The students in your class are mainly negligible, I can tell you that. You're new here, and I've been here a year—I would have finished my studies last year but my father got sick, he was hospitalized, I couldn't take exams and it was a mess—but I'll make it through English in one year or drop dead. I can do it, I can do anything. I'll take six courses at once—" He broke off, breathless. Sister Irene tried to smile. "All right then, it's settled? You'll let me in? Have I missed anything so far?"

He had no idea of the rudeness of his question. Sister Irene, feeling suddenly exhausted, said, "I'll give you a syllabus of the course."

"Fine! Wonderful!"

He got to his feet eagerly. He looked through the schedule, muttering to himself, making favorable noises. It struck Sister Irene that she was making a mistake to let him in. There were these moments when one had to make an intelligent decision. . . . But she was sympathetic with him, yes. She was sympathetic with something about him.

She found out his name the next day: Allen Weinstein.

After this she came to her Shakespeare class with a sense of excitement. It became clear to her at once that Weinstein was the most intelligent student in the class. Until he had enrolled, she had not understood what was lacking, a mind that could appreciate her own. Within a week his jagged, protean mind had alienated the other students, and though he sat in the center of the class, he seemed totally alone, encased by a miniature world of his own. When he spoke of the "frenetic humanism of the High Renaissance," Sister Irene dreaded the raised eyebrows and mocking smiles of the other students, who no longer bothered to look at Weinstein. She wanted to defend him, but she never did, because there was something rude and dismal about his knowledge; he used it like a weapon, talking passionately of Nietzsche and Goethe and Freud until Sister Irene would be forced to close discussion.

In meditation, alone, she often thought of him. When she tried to talk about him to a young nun, Sister Carlotta, everything sounded gross. "But no, he's an excellent student," she insisted. "I'm very grateful to have him in class. It's just that . . . he thinks ideas are real." Sister Carlotta, who loved literature also, had been forced to teach grade-school arithmetic for the last four years. That might have been why she said, a little sharply, "You don't think ideas are real?"

Sister Irene acquiesced with a smile, but of course she did not think so: only reality is real.

When Weinstein did not show up for class on the day the first paper was due, Sister Irene's heart sank, and the sensation was somehow a familiar one. She began her lecture and kept waiting for the door to open and for him to hurry noisily back to his seat, grinning an apology toward her—but nothing happened.

If she had been deceived by him, she made herself think angrily, it was as a teacher and not as a woman. He had promised her nothing.

Weinstein appeared the next day near the steps of the liberal arts building. She heard someone running behind her, a breathless exclamation: "Sister Irene!" She turned and saw him, panting and grinning in embarrassment. He wore a dark-blue suit with a necktie, and he looked, despite his childish face, like a little old man; there was something oddly precarious and fragile about him. "Sister Irene, I owe you an apology, right?" He raised his eyebrows and smiled a sad, forlorn, yet irritatingly conspiratorial smile. "The first paper—not in on time, and I know what your rules are. . . . You won't accept late papers. I know—that's good discipline, I'll do that when I teach too. But, unavoidably, I was unable to come to school yesterday. There are many—many—" He gulped for breath, and Sister Irene had the startling sense of seeing the real Weinstein stare out at her, a terrified prisoner behind the confident voice. "There are many complications in family life. Perhaps you are unaware—I mean—"

She did not like him, but she felt this sympathy, something tugging and nagging at her the way her parents had competed for her love so many years before. They had been whining, weak people, and out of their wet need for affection, the girl she had been (her name was Yvonne) had emerged stronger than either of them, contemptuous of tears because she had seen so many. But Weinstein was different; he was not simply weak—perhaps he was not weak at all—but his strength was confused and hysterical. She felt her customary rigidity as a teacher begin to falter. "You may turn your paper in today if you have it," she said, frowning.

Weinstein's mouth jerked into an incredulous grin. "Wonderful! Marvelous!" he said. "You are very understanding, Sister Irene, I must say. I must say . . . I didn't expect, really . . ." He was fumbling in a shabby old briefcase for the paper. Sister Irene waited. She was prepared for another of his excuses, certain that he did not have the paper, when he suddenly straightened up and handed her something. "Here! I took the liberty of writing thirty pages instead of just fifteen," he said. He was obviously quite excited; his cheeks were mottled pink and white. "You may disagree violently with my interpretation—I expect you to, in fact I'm counting on it—but let me warn you, I have the exact proof, right here in the play itself!" He was thumping at a book, his voice growing louder and shriller. Sister Irene, startled, wanted to put her hand over his mouth and soothe him.

"Look," he said breathlessly, "may I talk with you? I have a class now I hate, I loathe, I can't bear to sit through! Can I talk with you instead?"

Because she was nervous, she stared at the title page of the paper: " 'Erotic Melodies in *Romeo and Juliet*' by Allen Weinstein, Jr."

"All right?" he said. "Can we walk around here? Is it all right? I've been anxious to talk with you about some things you said in class."

She was reluctant, but he seemed not to notice. They walked slowly along the shaded campus paths. Weinstein did all the talking, of course, and Sister Irene recognized nothing in his cascade of words that she had mentioned in class. "The humanist must be committed to the totality of life," he said passionately. "This is the failing one finds everywhere in the academic world! I found it in New York and I found it here and I'm no ingénu, I don't go around with my mouth hanging open—I'm experienced, look, I've been to Europe, I've lived in Rome! I went everywhere in Europe except Germany, I don't talk about Germany . . . Sister Irene, think of the significant men in the last century, the men who've changed the world. Jews, right? Marx, Freud, Einstein! Not that I believe Marx, Marx is a madman . . . and Freud, no, my sympathies are with spiritual humanism. I believe that the Jewish race is the exclusive . . . the exclusive, what's the word, the exclusive means by which humanism will be extended. . . . Humanism begins by excluding the Jew, and now," he said with a high, surprised laugh, "the Jew will perfect it. After the Nazis, only the Jew is authorized to understand humanism, its limitations and its possibilities. So, I say that the humanist is committed to life in its totality and not just to his profession! The religious person is totally religious, he is his religion! What else? I recognize in you a humanist and a religious person—"

But he did not seem to be talking to her or even looking at her.

"Here, read this," he said. "I wrote it last night." It was a long free-verse poem, typed on a typewriter whose ribbon was worn out.

"There's this trouble with my father, a wonderful man, a lovely man, but his health—his strength is fading, do you see? What must it be to him to see his son growing up? I mean, I'm a man now, he's getting old, weak, his health is bad—it's hell, right? I sympathize with him. I'd do anything for him, I'd cut open my veins, anything for a father—right? That's why I wasn't in school yesterday," he said, and his voice dropped for the last sentence, as if he had been dragged back to earth by a fact.

Sister Irene tried to read the poem, then pretended to read it. A jumble of words dealing with "life" and "death" and "darkness" and "love." What do you think?" Weinstein said nervously, trying to read it over her shoulder and crowding against her.

"It's very . . . passionate," Sister Irene said.

This was the right comment; he took the poem back from her in silence, his face flushed with excitement. "Here, at this school, I have few people to talk with. I haven't shown anyone else that poem." He looked at her with his dark, intense eyes and Sister Irene felt them focus upon her. She was terrified at what he was trying to do—he was trying to force her into a human relationship.

"Thank you for your paper," she said, turning away.

When he came the next day, ten minutes late, he was haughty and disdainful. He had nothing to say and sat with his arms folded. Sister Irene took back with her to the convent a feeling of betrayal and confusion. She had been hurt. It was absurd and yet— She spent too much time thinking about him, as if he were somehow a kind of crystallization of her own loneliness; but she had no right to think so much of him. She did not want to think of him or of her loneliness. But Weinstein did so much more than think of his predicament: he embodied it, he acted it out, and that was perhaps why he fascinated her. It was as if he were doing a dance for her, a dance of shame and agony and delight, and so long as he did it, she was safe. She felt embarrassment for him, but also anxiety; she wanted to protect him. When the dean of the graduate school questioned her about Weinstein's work, she insisted that he was an "excellent" student, though she knew the dean had not wanted to hear that.

She prayed for guidance, she spent hours on her devotions, she was closer to her vocation than she had been for some years. Life at the convent became tinged with unreality, a misty distortion that took its tone from the glowering skies of the city at night, identical smokestacks ranged against the clouds and giving to the sky the excrement of the populated and successful earth. This city was not her city, this world was not her world. She felt no pride in knowing this, it was a fact. The little convent was not like an island in the center of this noisy world, but rather a kind of hole or crevice the world did not bother with, something of no interest. The convent's rhythm of life had nothing to do with the world's rhythm, it did not violate or alarm it in any way. Sister Irene tried to draw together the fragments of her life and synthesize them somehow in her vocation as a nun: she was a nun, she was recognized as a nun and had given herself happily to that life, she had a name, a place, she had dedicated her superior intelligence to the Church, she worked without pay and without expecting gratitude, she had given up pride, she did not think of herself but only of her work and her vocation, she did not think of anything external to these, she saturated herself daily in the knowledge that she was involved in the mystery of Christianity.

A daily terror attended this knowledge, however, for she sensed herself being drawn by that student, that Jewish boy, into a relationship she was not ready for. She wanted to cry out in fear that she was being forced into the role of a Christian, and what did that mean? What could her studies tell her? What could the other nuns tell her? She was alone, no one could help; he was making her into a Christian, and to her that was a mystery, a thing of terror, something others slipped on the way they slipped on their clothes, casually and thoughtlessly, but to her a magnificent and terrifying wonder.

For days she carried Weinstein's paper, marked A, around with her; he did not come to class. One day she checked with the graduate office and was told that Weinstein had called in to say his father was ill and he would not be able to attend classes for a while. "He's strange, I remember him," the secretary said. "He missed all his exams last spring and made a lot of trouble. He was in and out of here every day."

So there was no more of Weinstein for a while, and Sister Irene stopped expecting him to hurry into class. Then, one morning, she found a letter from him in her mailbox.

He had printed it in black ink, very carefully, as if he had not trusted handwriting. The return address was in bold letters that, like his voice, tried to grab onto her: Birchcrest Manor. Somewhere north of the city. "Dear Sister Irene," the block letters said, "I am doing well here and have time for reading and relaxing. The Manor is delightful. My doctor here is an excellent, intelligent man who has time for me, unlike my former doctor. If you have time, you might drop in on my father, who worries about me too much, I think, and explain to him what my condition is. He doesn't seem to understand. I feel about this new life the way that boy, what's his name, in *Measure for Measure*, feels about the prospects of a different life; you remember what he says to his sister when she visits him in prison, how he is looking forward to an escape into another world. Perhaps you could *explain* this to my father and he would stop worrying." The letter ended with the father's name and address, in letters that were just a little too big. Sister Irene, walking slowly down the corridor as she read the letter, felt her eyes cloud over with tears. She was cold with fear, it was something she had never experienced before. She knew what Weinstein was trying to tell her, and the desperation of his attempt made it all the more pathetic; he did not deserve this, why did God allow him to suffer so?

She read through Claudio's speech to his sister, in *Measure for Measure:*

> *Ay, but to die, and go we know not where;*
> *To lie in cold obstruction and to rot;*
> *This sensible warm motion to become*
> *A kneaded clod; and the delighted spirit*
> *To bathe in fiery floods, or to reside*
> *In thrilling region of thick-ribbed ice,*
> *To be imprison'd in the viewless winds*
> *And blown with restless violence round about*
> *The pendent world; or to be worse than worst*
> *Of those that lawless and incertain thought*
> *Imagines howling! 'Tis too horrible!*
> *The weariest and most loathed worldly life*
> *That age, ache, penury, and imprisonment*
> *Can lay on nature is a paradise*
> *To what we fear of death.*

Sister Irene called the father's number that day. "Allen Weinstein residence, who may I say is calling?" a woman said, bored. "May I speak to Mr. Weinstein? It's urgent—about his son," Sister Irene said. There was a pause at the other end. "You want to talk to his mother, maybe?" the woman said. "His mother? Yes, his mother, then. Please. It's very important."

She talked with this strange, unsuspected woman, a disembodied voice that suggested absolutely no face, and insisted upon going over that afternoon. The woman was nervous, but Sister Irene, who was a university professor, after all, knew enough to hide her own nervousness. She kept waiting for the woman to say, "Yes, Allen has mentioned you . . ." but nothing happened.

She persuaded Sister Carlotta to ride over with her. This urgency of hers was something they were all amazed by. They hadn't suspected that the set of her gray eyes could change to this blurred, distracted alarm, this sense of mission that seemed to have come to her from nowhere. Sister Irene drove across the city in the late afternoon traffic, with the high whining noises from residential streets where trees were being sawed down in pieces. She understood now the secret, sweet wildness that Christ must have felt, giving himself for man, dying for the billions of men who would never know of him and never understand the sacrifice. For the first time she approached the realization of that great act. In her troubled mind the city traffic was jumbled and yet oddly coherent, an image of the world that was always out of joint with what was happening in it, its inner history struggling with its external spectacle. This sacrifice of Christ's, so mysterious and legendary now, almost lost in time—it was that by which Christ transcended both God and man at one moment, more than man because of his fate to do what no other man could do, and more than God because no god could suffer as he did. She felt a flicker of something close to madness.

She drove nervously, uncertainly, afraid of missing the street and afraid of finding it too, for while one part of her rushed forward to confront these people who had betrayed their son, another part of her would have liked nothing so much as to be waiting as usual for the summons to dinner, safe in her room. . . . When she found the street and turned onto it, she was in a state of breathless excitement. Here lawns were bright green and marred with only a few leaves, magically clean, and the houses were enormous and pompous, a mixture of styles: ranch houses, colonial houses, French country houses, white-bricked wonders with curving glass and clumps of birch trees somehow encircled by white concrete. Sister Irene stared as if she had blundered into another world. This was a kind of heaven, and she was too shabby for it.

The Weinstein's house was the strangest one of all: it looked like a small Alpine lodge, with an inverted-V-shaped front entrance. Sister Irene drove up the black-topped driveway and let the car slow to a stop; she told Sister Carlotta she would not be long.

At the door she was met by Weinstein's mother, a small, nervous woman with hands like her son's. "Come in, come in," the woman said. She had once been beautiful, that was clear, but now in missing beauty she was not handsome, or even attractive but looked ruined and perplexed, the misshapen swelling of her white-blond professionally set hair like a cap lifting up from her surprised face. "He'll be right in. Allen?" she called, "our visitor is here." They went into the living room. There was a grand piano at one end and an organ at the other. In between were scatterings of brilliant modern furniture in conversational groups, and several puffed-up white rugs on the polished floor. Sister Irene could not stop shivering.

"Professor, it's so strange, but let me say when the phone rang I had a feeling—I had a feeling," the woman said, with damp eyes. Sister Irene sat, and the woman hovered about her. "Should I call you Professor? We don't . . . you know . . . we don't understand the technicalities that go with—Allen, my son, wanted to go here to the Catholic school; I told my husband why not? Why fight? It's the thing these days, they do anything they want for knowledge. And he had to come home, you know. He couldn't take care of himself in New York, that was the beginning of the trouble. . . . Should I call you Professor?"

"You can call me Sister Irene."

"Sister Irene?" the woman said, touching her throat in awe, as if something intimate and unexpected had happened.

Then Weinstein's father appeared, hurrying. He took long, impatient strides. Sister Irene stared at him and in that instant doubted everything—he was in his fifties, a tall, sharply handsome man, heavy but not fat, holding his shoulders back with what looked like an effort, but holding them back just the same. He wore a dark suit and his face was flushed, as if he had run a long distance.

"Now," he said, coming to Sister Irene and with a precise wave of his hand motioning his wife off, "now, let's straighten this out. A lot of confusion over that kid, eh?" He pulled a chair over, scraping it across a rug and pulling one corner over, so that its brown underside was exposed. "I came home early just for this, Libby phoned me. Sister, you got a letter from him, right?"

The wife looked at Sister Irene over her husband's head as if trying somehow to coach her, knowing that this man was so loud and impatient that no one could remember anything in his presence.

"A letter—yes—today—"

"He says what in it? You got the letter, eh? Can I see it?"

She gave it to him and wanted to explain, but he

silenced her with a flick of his hand. He read through the letter so quickly that Sister Irene thought perhaps he was trying to impress her with his skill at reading. "So?" he said, raising his eyes, smiling, "so what is this? He's happy out there, he says. He doesn't communicate with us any more, but he writes to you and says he's happy—what's that? I mean, what the hell is that?"

"But he isn't happy. He wants to come home," Sister Irene said. It was so important that she made him understand that she could not trust her voice; goaded by this man, it might suddenly turn shrill, as his son's did. "Someone must read their letters before they're mailed, so he tried to tell me something by making an allusion to—"

"What?"

"—an allusion to a play, so that I would know. He may be thinking suicide, he must be very unhappy—"

She ran out of breath. Weinstein's mother had begun to cry, but the father was shaking his head jerkily back and forth. "Forgive me, Sister, but it's a lot of crap, he needs the hospital, he needs help—right? It costs me fifty a day out there, and they've got the best place in the state, I figure it's worth it. He needs help, that kid, what do I care if he's unhappy? He's unbalanced!" he said angrily. "You want us to get him out again? We argued with the judge for two hours to get him in, an acquaintance of mine. Look, he can't control himself—he was smashing things here, he was hysterical. They need help, lady, and you do something about it fast! You do something! We made up our minds to do something and we did it! This letter—what the hell is this letter? He never talked like that to us!"

"But he means the opposite of what he says—"

"Then he's crazy! I'm the first to admit it." He was perspiring, and his face had darkened. "I've got no pride left this late. He's a little bastard, you want to know? He calls me names, he's filthy, got a filthy mouth—that's being smart, huh? They give him a big scholarship for his filthy mouth? I went to college, too, and I got out and knew something and I for Christ's sake did something with it; my wife is an intelligent woman, a learned woman, would you guess she does book reviews for the little newspaper out here? Intelligent isn't crazy—crazy isn't intelligent. Maybe for you at the school he writes nice papers and gets an A, but out here, around the house, he can't control himself, and we got him committed!"

"But—"

"We're fixing him up, don't worry about it!" He turned to his wife. "Libby, get out of here, I mean it. I'm sorry, but get out of here, you're making a fool of yourself, go stand in the kitchen or something, you and the goddamn maid can cry on each other's shoulders. That one in the kitchen is nuts too, they're all nuts. Sister," he said, his voice lowering, "I thank you immensely for coming out here. This is wonderful, your interest in my son. And I see he admires you—that letter there. But what about that letter? If he did want to get out, which I don't admit—he was willing to be committed, in the end he said okay himself—if he wanted out I wouldn't do it. Why? So what if he wants to come back? The next day he wants something else, what then? He's a sick kid, and I'm the first to admit it."

Sister Irene felt that sickness spread to her. She stood. The room was so big it seemed it must be a public place; there had been nothing personal or private about their conversation. Weinstein's mother was standing by the fireplace, sobbing. The father jumped to his feet and wiped his forehead in a gesture that was meant to help Sister Irene on her way out. "God what a day" he said, his eyes snatching at hers for understanding, "you know—one of those days all day long? Sister, I thank you a lot. There should be more people in the world who care about others, like you. I mean that."

On the way back to the convent, the man's words returned to her, and she could not get control of them; she could not even feel anger. She had been pressed down, forced back, what could she do? Weinstein might have been watching her somehow from a barred window, and he surely would have understood. The strange idea she had had on the way over, something about understanding Christ, came back to her now and sickened her. But the sickness was small. It could be contained.

About a month after her visit to his father, Weinstein himself showed up. He was dressed in a suit as before, even the necktie was the same. He came right into her office as if he had been pushed and could not stop.

"Sister," he said, and shook her hand. He must have seen fear in her because he smiled ironically. "Look, I'm released. I'm let out of the nut house. Can I sit down?"

He sat. Sister Irene was breathing quickly, as if in the presence of an enemy who does not know he is an enemy.

"So, they finally let me out. I heard what you did. You talked with him, that was all I wanted. You're the only one who gave a damn. Because you're a humanist and a religious person, you respect . . . the individual. Listen," he said, whispering, "it was hell out there! Hell Birchcrest Manor! All fixed up with fancy chairs and *Life* magazines lying around—and what do they do to you? They locked me up, they gave me shock treatments! Shock treatments, how do you like that, it's discredited by everybody now—they're crazy out there themselves, sadists. They locked me up, gave me hypodermic shots, they didn't treat me like a human being! Do you know what that is," Weinstein demanded savagely, "not to be treated like a human being? They made me an animal—for fifty dollars a day! Dirty filthy swine! Now I'm an outpatient because I stopped swearing at them. I found somebody's bobby pin, and when I wanted to scream I pressed it under my fingernail and it stopped me—the screaming went inside and not out—so they gave me good reports, those sick bastards. Now I'm an outpatient and I can walk along the street and breathe in the same filthy exhaust from the buses like all you normal people! Christ," he said, and threw himself back against the chair.

Sister Irene stared at him. She wanted to take his hand, to make some gesture that would close the aching distance between them. "Mr. Weinstein—"

"Call me Allen!" he said sharply.

"I'm very sorry—I'm terribly sorry—"

"My own parents committed me, but of course they didn't know what it was like. It was hell," he said thickly, "and there isn't any hell except what other people do to you. The psychiatrist out there, the main shrink, he hates Jews too, some of us were positive of that, and he's got a bigger nose than I do, a real beak." He made a noise of disgust. "A dirty bastard, a sick, dirty, pathetic bastard—all of them. Anyway, I'm getting out of here, and I came to ask you a favor."

"What do you mean?"

"I'm getting out. I'm leaving. I'm going up to Canada and lose myself. I'll get a job. I'll forget everything, I'll kill myself maybe—what's the difference? Look, can you lend me some money?"

"Money?"

"Just a little! I have to get to the border. I'm going to take a bus."

"But I don't have any money—"

"No money?" He stared at her. "You mean—you don't have any? Sure you have some!"

She stared at him as if he had asked her to do something obscene. Everything was splotched and uncertain before her eyes.

"You must . . . you must go back," she said, "you're making a—"

"I'll pay it back. Look, I'll pay it back, can you go to where you live or something and get it? I'm in a hurry. My friends are sons of bitches: one of them pretended he didn't see me yesterday—I stood right in the middle of the sidewalk and yelled at him, I called him some appropriate names! So he didn't see me, huh? You're the only one who understands me, you understand me like a poet, you—"

"I can't help you, I'm sorry—I . . ."

He looked to one side of her and flashed his gaze back, as if he could control it. He seemed to be trying to clear his vision.

"You have the soul of a poet," he whispered, "you're the only one. Everybody else is rotten! Can't you lend me some money, ten dollars maybe? I have three thousand in the bank, and I can't touch it! They take everything away from me, they make me into an animal. . . . You know I'm not an animal, don't you? Don't you?"

"Of course," Sister Irene whispered.

"You could get money. Help me. Give me your hand or something, touch me, help me—please. . . ." He reached for her hand and she drew back. He stared at her and his face seemed about to crumble, like a child's. "I want something from you, but I don't know what—I want something!" he cried. "Something real! I want you to look at me like I was a human being, is that too much to ask? I have a brain, I'm alive, I'm suffering—what does that mean? Does that mean nothing? I want something real and not this phony Christian love garbage—it's all in the books, it isn't personal—I want something real—look. . . ."

He tried to take her hand again, and this time she jerked away. She got to her feet. "Mr. Weinstein," she said, "please—"

"You! You nun!" he said scornfully, his mouth twisted

into a mock grin. "You nun! There's nothing under that ugly outfit, right? And you're not particularly smart even though you think you are; my father has more brains in his foot than you—"

He got to his feet and kicked the chair.

"You bitch!" he cried.

She shrank back against her desk as if she thought he might hit her, but he only ran out of the office.

Weinstein: the name was to become disembodied from the figure, as time went on. The semester passed, the autumn drizzle turned into snow, Sister Irene rode to school in the morning and left in the afternoon, four days a week, anonymous in her black winter cloak, quiet and stunned. University teaching was an anonymous task, each day dissociated from the rest, with no necessary sense of unity among the teachers: they came and went separately and might for a year just miss a colleague who left his office five minutes before they arrived, and it did not matter.

She heard of Weinstein's death, his suicide by drowning, from the English Department secretary, a handsome white-haired woman who kept a transistor radio on her desk. Sister Irene was not surprised; she had been thinking of him as dead for months. "They identified him by some special television way they have now," the secretary said. "They're shipping the body back. It was up in Quebec. . . ."

Sister Irene could feel a part of herself drifting off, lured by the plains of white snow to the north, the quiet, the emptiness, the sweep of the Great Lakes up to the silence of Canada. But she called that part of herself back. She could only be one person in her lifetime. That was the ugly truth, she thought, that she could not really regret Weinstein's suffering and death; she had only one life and had already given it to someone else. He had come too late to her. Fifteen years ago, perhaps, but not now.

She was only one person, she thought, walking down the corridor in a dream. Was she safe in this single person, or was she trapped? She had only one identity. She could make only one choice. What she had done or hadn't done was the result of that choice, and how was she guilty? If she could have felt guilt, she thought, she might at least have been able to feel something.

MARGARET DRABBLE was born in Yorkshire, England, in 1939. She was educated at the Mount School in York. Her first novel, *A Summer Bird-Cage*, was published in 1963 after a brilliant undergraduate career at Cambridge. Joyce Carol Oates has written about her six novels, uncollected short stories, and recent biography of novelist Arnold Bennett: "To know what London and England are like, one can do no better than to read Margaret Drabble. It is doubtful that there is any single American writer who represents the diversity and near-chaos of our culture as Drabble represents the tone of contemporary English culture." She is a great democrat. In Oates's words, "like her own fictional characters, [she] would declare the daily experience of life itself something extraordinary." Her originality, in the opinion of another critic, lies in having created a genuinely new kind of character. "There are, of course, innumerable women novelists who write from a feminine viewpoint, but Margaret Drabble differs from them in writing about young women who are not merely intelligent, educated, more or less attractive, and sharply observant. They are also mothers, and their involvement with their children cuts sharply across their concern with a career, and their desire for emotional freedom. For many novelists the emancipated woman and the mother are two sharply different types; Margaret Drabble has shown that in the modern world the two roles are often combined in the same person." The story that follows, "The Gifts of War" from *Winter's Tales 16,* is a beautiful example of her ability to make the reader feel the power of the maternal instinct. The story also reflects her ideas about her writing. She has said: "My books are I think mainly concerned with privilege and justice. Equality and egalitarianism preoccupy me constantly, and not very hopefully. None of my books is about feminism, because my belief in the necessity for justice for women (which they don't get at the moment) is so basic that I never think of using it as a subject. It is part of a whole."

Margaret Drabble (1939–)

THE GIFTS OF WAR

*Timeo Danaos et dona ferentes.** Aeneid II I 49

When she woke in the morning, she could tell at once, as soon as she reached consciousness, that she had some reason to feel pleased with herself, some rare cause for satisfaction. She lay there quietly for a time, enjoying the unfamiliar sensation, not bothering to place it, grateful for its vague comfortable warmth. It protected her from the disagreeable noise of her husband's snores, from the thought of getting breakfast, from the coldness of the linoleum when she finally dragged herself out of bed. She had to wake Kevin: he always overslept these days, and he took so long to get dressed and get his breakfast, she was surprised he wasn't always late for school. She never thought of making him go to bed earlier; she hadn't the heart to stop him watching the telly, and anyway she enjoyed his company, she liked having him around in the evenings, laughing in his silly seven-year-old way at jokes he didn't understand—jokes she didn't always understand herself, and which she couldn't explain when he asked her to. "You don't know *anything,* Mum," he would groan, but she didn't mind his condemnations: she didn't expect to know anything, it amused her to see him behaving like a man already, affecting superiority, harmlessly, helplessly, in an ignorance that was as yet so much greater than her own—though she would have died rather than have allowed him to suspect her amusement, her permissiveness. She grumbled at him constantly, even while wanting to keep him there: she snapped at his endless questions, she snubbed him, she repressed him, she provoked him. And she did not suffer from doing this, because she knew that they could not hurt each other: he was a child, he wasn't a proper man yet, he couldn't inflict true pain, any more

*I fear the Greeks, even when they bring gifts.

than she could truly repress him, and his teasing, obligatory conventional schoolboy complaints about her cooking and her stupidity seemed to exorcise, in a way, those other crueller onslaughts. It was as though she said to herself: if my little boy doesn't mean it when he shouts at me, perhaps my husband doesn't either: perhaps there's no more serious offence in my bruises and my greying hair than there is in those harmless childish moans. In the child, she found a way of accepting the man: she found a way of accepting, without too much submission, her lot.

She loved the child: she loved him with so much passion that a little of it spilled over generously onto the man who had misused her: in forgiving the child his dirty blazer and shirts and his dinner-covered tie, she forgave the man for his Friday nights and the childish vomit on the stairs and the bedroom floor. It never occurred to her that a grown man might resent more than hatred such second-hand forgiveness. She never thought of the man's emotions: she thought of her own, and her feelings for the child redeemed her from bitterness, and shed some light on the dark industrial terraces and the waste lands of the city's rubble. Her single-minded commitment was a wonder of the neighbourhood: she's a sour piece, the neighbours said, she keeps herself to herself a bit too much, but you've got to hand it to her, she's been a wonderful mother to that boy, she's had a hard life, but she's been a wonderful mother to that boy. And she, tightening her woolly headscarf over her aching ears as she walked down the cold steep windy street to join the queue at the post office or the butcher's, would stiffen proudly, her hard lips secretly smiling as she claimed and accepted and nodded to her role, her place, her social dignity.

This morning, as she woke Kevin, he reminded her instantly of her cause for satisfaction, bringing to the surface the pleasant knowledge that had underlain her wakening.

"Hi, Mum," he said, as he opened his eyes to her, "how old am I today?"

"Seven, of course," she said, staring dourly at him, pretending to conceal her instant knowledge of the question's meaning, assuming scorn and dismissal. "Come on, get up, child, you're going to be late as usual."

"And how old am I tomorrow, Mum?" he asked, watching her like a hawk, waiting for that delayed, inevitable break.

"Come on, come on," she said crossly, affecting impatience, stripping the blankets off him, watching him writhe in the cold air, small and bony in his striped pyjamas.

"Oh, go on, Mum," he said.

"What d'you mean, 'go on,'" she said, "don't be so cheeky, come on, get a move on, you'll get no breakfast if you don't get a move on."

"Just think, Mum," he said, "how old am I tomorrow?"

"I don't know what you're talking about," she said, ripping his pyjama jacket off him, wondering how long to give the game, secure in her sense of her own thing.

"Yes you do, yes you do," he yelled, his nerve beginning, very slightly, to falter. "You know what day it is tomorrow."

"Why, my goodness me," she said, judging that the moment had come, "I'd quite forgotten. Eight tomorrow. My goodness me."

And she watched him grin and wriggle, too big now for embraces, his affection clumsy and knobbly; she avoided the touch of him these days, pushing him irritably away when he leant on her chair-arm, twitching when he banged into her in the corridor or the kitchen, pulling her skirt or overall away from him when he tugged at it for attention, regretting sometimes the soft and round docile baby that he had once been, and yet proud at the same time of his gawky growing, happier, more familiar with the hostilities between them (a better cover for love) than she had been with the tender wide smiles of adoring infancy.

"What you got me for my birthday?" he asked, as he struggled out of his pyjama trousers: and she turned at the door and looked back at him, and said,

"What d'you mean, what've I got you? I've not got you anything. Only good boys get presents."

"I *am* good," he said: "I've been ever so good all week."

"Not that I noticed, you weren't," she said, knowing that too prompt an acquiescence would ruin the dangerous pleasure of doubtful anticipation.

"Go on, tell me," he said, and she could tell from his whining plea that he was almost sure that she had got what he wanted, almost sure but not quite sure, that he was, in fact, in the grip of an exactly manipulated degree of uncertainty, a torment of hope that would last him for a whole twenty-four hours, until the next birthday morning.

"I'm telling you," she said, her hand on the door, staring

at him sternly, "I'm telling you, I've not got you anything." And then, magically, delightfully, she allowed herself and him that lovely moment of grace: "I've not got you anything—*yet*," she said: portentous, conspiratorial, yet very very faintly threatening.

"You're going to get it today," he shrieked, unable to restrain himself, unable to keep the rules: and as though annoyed by his exuberance she marched smartly out of the small back room, and down the narrow stairs to the kitchen, shouting at him in an excessive parade of rigour, "Come on, get moving, get your things on, you'll be late for school, you're always late—": and she stood over him while he ate his flakes, watching each spoonful disappear, heaving a great sigh of resigned fury when he spilled on the oilcloth, catching his guilty glance as he wiped it with his sleeve, not letting him off, unwilling, unable to relax into a suspect tenderness.

He went out the back way to school: she saw him through the yard and stood in the doorway watching him disappear, as she always watched him, down the narrow alley separating the two rows of back-to-back cottages, along the ancient industrial cobbles, relics of another age: as he reached the Stephensons' door she called out to him, "Eight tomorrow, then," and smiled, and waved, and he smiled back, excited, affectionate, over the ten yards' gap, grinning, his grey knee socks pulled smartly up, his short cropped hair already standing earnestly on end, resisting the violent flattening of the brush with which she thumped him each morning: he reminded her of a bird, she didn't know why, she couldn't have said why, a bird, vulnerable, clumsy, tenacious, touching. Then Bill Stephenson emerged from his back door and joined him, and they went down the alley together, excluding her, leaving her behind, kicking at pebbles and fag packets with their scuffed much-polished shoes.

She went back through the yard and into the house, and made a pot of tea, and took it up to the man in bed. She dumped it down on the corner of the dressing-table beside him, her lips tight, as though she dared not loosen them: her face had only one expression, and she used it to conceal the two major emotions of her life, resentment and love. They were so violently opposed, these passions, that she could not move from one to the other: she lacked flexibility; so she inhabited a grim inexpressive no-man's-land between them, feeling in some way that she thus achieved a kind of justice.

"I'm going up town today," she said, as the man on the bed rolled over and stared at her.

He wheezed and stared.

"I'm going to get our Kevin his birthday present," she said, her voice cold and neutral, offering justice and no more.

"What'll I do about me dinner?" he said.

"I'll be back," she said. "And if I'm not, you can get your own. It won't kill you."

He mumbled and coughed, and she left the room. When she got downstairs, she began, at last, to enter upon the day's true enjoyment: slowly she took possession of it, this day that she had waited for, and which could not now be taken from her. She'd left herself a cup of tea on the table, but before she sat down to drink it she got her zip plastic purse from behind the clock on the dresser, and opened it, and got the money out. There it was, all of it: thirty shillings, three ten-bob notes, folded tightly up in a brown envelope: twenty-nine and eleven, she needed, and a penny over. Thirty shillings, saved, unspoken for, to spend. She'd wondered, from time to time, if she ought to use it to buy him something useful, but she knew now that she wasn't going to: she was going to get him what he wanted—a grotesque, unjustifiable luxury, a pointless gift. It never occurred to her that the pleasure she took in doing things for Kevin was anything other than selfish: she felt vaguely guilty about it, she would have started furtively, like a miser, had anyone knocked on the door and interrupted her contemplation, she would bitterly have denied the intensity of her anticipation.

And when she put her overcoat on, and tied on her headsquare, and set off down the road, she tried to appear to the neighbours as though she wasn't going anywhere in particular: she nodded calmly, she stopped to gape at Mrs. Phillips' new baby (all frilled up, poor mite, in ribbons and pink crochet, a dreadful sight poor little innocent like something off an iced cake, people should know better than to do such things to their own children); she even called in at the shop for a quarter of tea as a cover for her excursion, so reluctant was she to let anyone know that she was going to town, thus unusually, on a Wednesday morning. And as she walked down the steep hillside, where the abandoned tram-lines still ran, to the next fare stage of the bus, she could not have said whether she was making the extra walk to save two pence, or whether she was, more deviously, concealing her destination until the last moment from both herself and the neighbourhood.

Because she hardly ever went into town these days. In the old days she had come this way quite often, going down the hill on the tram with her girl friends, with nothing better in mind than a bit of window-shopping and a bit of a laugh and a cup of tea: penniless then as now, but still hopeful, still endowed with a touching faith that if by some miracle she could buy a pair of nylons or a particular blue lace blouse or a new brand of lipstick, then deliverance would be granted to her in the form of money, marriage, romance, the visiting prince who would glimpse her in the crowd, glorified by that seductive blouse, and carry her off to a better world. She could remember so well how hopeful they had been: even Betty Jones, fat, monstrous, ludicrous Betty Jones had cherished such rosy illusions, had gazed with them in longing at garments many sizes too small and far too expensive, somehow convinced that if she could by chance or good fortune acquire one all her flesh would melt away and reveal the lovely girl within. Time had taught Betty Jones: she shuffled now in shoes cracked and splitting beneath her own weight. Time had taught them all. The visiting prince, whom need and desire had once truly transfigured in her eyes, now lay there at home in bed, stubbly, disgusting, ill, malingering, unkind: she remembered the girl who had seen such other things in him with a contemptuous yet pitying wonder. What fools they all had been, to laugh, to giggle and point and whisper, to spend their small wages to deck themselves for such a sacrifice. When she saw the young girls today, of the age she had been then, still pointing and giggling with the same knowing ignorance, she was filled with a bitterness so acute that her teeth set against it, and the set lines of her face stiffened to resist and endure and conceal it. Sometimes she was possessed by a rash desire to warn them, to lean forward and tap on their shoulders, to see their astonished vacant faces, topped with their mad over-perfumed mounds of sticky hair, turn upon her in alarm and disbelief. What do you think you're playing at, she would say to them, what do you think you're at? Where do you think it leads you, what do you think you're asking for? And they would blink at her, uncomprehending, like condemned cattle, the sacrificial virgins, not yet made restless by the smell of blood. I could tell you a thing or two, she wanted to say, I could tell you enough to wipe those silly grins off your faces: but she said nothing, and she could not have said that it was envy or a true charitable pity that most possessed and disturbed her when she saw such innocents.

What withheld her most from envy, pure and straight and voracious, was a sense of her own salvation. Because, amazingly, she had been saved, against all probability: her life which had seemed after that bridal day of white nylon net and roses to sink deeply and almost instantly into a mire of penury and beer and butchery, had been so redeemed for her by her child that she could afford to smile with a kind of superior wisdom, a higher order of knowledge, at those who had not known her trials and her comforts. They would never attain, the silly teenagers, her own level of consolation; they would never know what it was like to find in an object which had at first appeared to her as a yet more lasting sentence, a death blow to the panic notions of despair and flight—to find in such a thing love, and identity, and human warmth. When she thought of this—which she did, often, though not clearly, having little else to think of—she felt as though she alone, or she one of the elected few, had been permitted to glimpse something of the very nature of the harsh, mysterious processes of human survival; and she could induce in herself a state of recognition that was almost visionary. It was all she had: and being isolated by pride from more neighbourly and everyday and diminishing attempts at commiseration, she knew it. She fed off it: her maternal role, her joy, her sorrow. She gazed out of the bus window now, as the bus approached the town centre and the shops, and as she thought of the gift she was going to buy him, her eyes lit on the bombed sites, and the rubble and decay of decades, and the exposed walls where dirty fading wallpapers had flapped in the wind for years, and she saw where the willowherb grew, green and purple, fields of it amongst the brick, on such thin soil, on the dust of broken bricks and stones, growing so tall in tenacious aspiration out of such shallow infertile ground. It was significant: she knew, as she looked at it, that it was significant. She herself had grown out of this landscape, she had nourished herself and her child upon it. She knew what it meant.

Frances Janet Ashton Hall also knew what it meant, for she too had been born and bred there; although, being younger, she had not lived there for so long, and, having been born into a different class of society, she knew that she was not sentenced to it for life, and was indeed upon the verge of escape, for the next autumn she was to embark upon a degree in economics at a southern University. Nevertheless, she knew what it meant. She was a post-war child, but it was not for nothing that she had witnessed since infancy the red and smoking skies of the steel-works (making arms for the Arabs, for the South Africans, for all those wicked countries)—it was not for nothing that she had seen the deep scars in the city's centre, not all disguised quite comfortably as car parks. In fact, she could even claim the distinction of having lost a relative in the air-raids: her great-aunt Susan, who had refused to allow herself to be evacuated to the Lake District, had perished from a stray bomb in the midst of a highly residential suburban area. Frances was not yet old enough to speculate upon the effect that this tale, oft-repeated, and with lurid details, had had upon the development of her sensibility; naturally she ascribed her ardent pacifism and her strong political convictions to her own innate radical virtue, and when she did look for ulterior motives for her faith she was far more likely to relate them to her recent passion for a newfound friend, one Michael Swaines, than to any childhood neurosis.

She admired Michael. She also liked him for reasons that had nothing to do with admiration, and being an intelligent and scrupulous girl she would spend fruitless, anxious and enjoyable hours trying to disentangle and isolate her various emotions, and to assess their respective values. Being very young, she set a high value on disinterest: standing now, for his sake, on a windy street corner in a conspicuous position outside the biggest department store in town, carrying a banner and wearing (no less) a sandwich-board, proclaiming the necessity for Peace in Vietnam, and calling for the banning of all armaments, nuclear or otherwise, she was carrying on a highly articulate dialogue with her own conscience, by means of which she was attempting to discover whether she was truly standing there for Michael's sake alone, or whether she would have stood there anyway, for the sake of the cause itself. What, she asked herself, if she had been solicited to make a fool of herself in this way merely by that disagreeable Nicholas, son of the Head of the Adult Education Centre? Would she have been prepared to oblige? No, she certainly would not, she would have laughed the idea of sandwich-boards to scorn, and would have found all sorts of convincing arguments against the kind of public display that she was now engaged in. But, on the other hand, this did not exactly invalidate her actions, for she *did* believe, with Michael, that demonstrations were necessary and useful: it was just that her natural reluctance to expose herself would have conquered her, had not Michael himself set about persuading her. So she was doing the right thing but for the wrong reason, like that man in *Murder in the Cathedral.* And perhaps it was for a *very* wrong reason, because she could not deny that she even found a sort of corrupt pleasure in doing things she didn't like doing—accosting strangers, shaking collection-boxes, being stared at—when she knew that it was being appreciated by other people: a kind of yearning for disgrace and martyrdom. Like stripping in public. Though not, surely, *quite* the same, because stripping didn't do any good, whereas telling people about the dangers of total war was a useful occupation. So doing the right thing for the wrong reason could at least be said to be better than doing the wrong thing for the wrong reason, couldn't it? Though her parents, of course, said it was the wrong thing anyway, and that one shouldn't molest innocent shoppers: Oh Lord, she thought with sudden gloom, perhaps my *only* reason for doing this is to annoy my parents: and bravely, to distract herself from the dreadful suspicion, she stepped forward and asked a scraggy thin woman in an old red velvet coat what she thought of the American policy in Vietnam.

"What's that?" said the woman, crossly, annoyed at being stopped in mid-stride, and when Frances repeated her question she gazed at her as though she were an idiot and walked on without replying. Frances, who was becoming used to such responses, was not as hurt as she had been at the beginning of the morning: she was even beginning to think it was quite funny. She wondered if she might knock off for a bit and go and look for Michael: he had gone into the store, to try to persuade the manager of the Toy Department not to sell toy machine-guns and toy bombs and toy battleships. She thought she would go and join him; and when a horrid man in a cloth cap spat on the pavement very near her left shoe and muttered something about bloody students bugger off ruining the city for decent folk, she made up her mind. So she ditched her sandwich-board and rolled her banner up, and set off through the swing doors into the cosy warmth: although it was Easter the weather was bitterly cold, spring seemed to reach them two months later than anywhere else in England. It was a pity, she thought, that there weren't any more Easter marches: she would have liked marching, it would have been more sociable; but Michael believed in isolated pockets of resistance. Really, what he meant was, he didn't like things that he wasn't organising himself. She didn't blame him for that, he was a marvellous organiser, it was amazing the amount of enthusiasm he'd got up in the Students' Union for what was after all rather a dud project: no, not dud, she hadn't meant that, what she meant was that it was no fun, and anyone with a lower sense of social responsibility than herself couldn't have been expected to find it very interesting. Very nice green stockings on the stocking counter, she wondered if she could afford a pair. This thing that Michael had about children and violence, it really was very odd: he had a brother who was writing a thesis on violence on the television and she supposed it must have affected him. She admired his faith. Although at the same time she couldn't help remembering a short story by Saki that she had read years ago, called "The Toys of Peace," which had been about the impossibility of making children play with anything but soldiers, or something to that effect.

When she reached the toy department, she located Michael immediately, because she could hear his voice raised in altercation. In fact, as she approached, she could see that quite a scene was going on, and if Michael hadn't looked quite so impressive when he was making a scene she would have lost nerve and fled: but as it was she approached, discreetly, and hovered on the outskirts of the centre of activity. Michael was arguing with a man in a black suit, some kind of manager figure she guessed (though what managers were or did she had no idea) and a woman in an overall: the man, she could see, was beginning to lose his patience, and was saying things like:

"Now look here, young man, we're not here to tell our customers what they ought to do, we're here to sell them what they want," and Michael was producing his usual arguments about responsibility and education and having to make a start somewhere and why not here and now; he'd already flashed around his leaflets on violence and delinquency, and was now offering his catalogue of harmless constructive wooden playthings.

"Look," he was saying, "look how much more attractive these wooden animals are, I'm sure you'd find they'd sell just as well, and they're far more durable"—whereat the woman in an overall sniffed and said since when had salesmen dressed themselves up as University students, if he wanted to sell them toys he ought to do it in the proper way; an interjection which Michael ignored, as he proceeded to pick up off the counter in front of him a peculiarly nasty piece of clockwork, a kind of car-cum-aeroplane thing with real bullets and knives in the wheels and hidden bomb-carriers and God knows what, she rather thought it was a model from some television puppet programme, it was called The Desperado Destruction Machine. "I mean to say, look at this horrible thing," Michael said to the manager, pressing a knob and nearly slicing off his own finger as an extra bit of machinery jumped out at him, "whatever do you think can happen to the minds of children who play with things like this?"

"That's a very nice model," said the manager, managing to sound personally grieved and hurt, "it's a very nice model, and you've no idea how popular it's been for the price. It's not a cheap foreign thing, that, you know, it's a really well-made toy. Look—" and he grabbed it back off Michael and pulled another lever, to display the ejector-seat mechanism. The driver figure was promptly ejected with such violence that he shot right across the room, and Michael, who was quite well brought up really, dashed off to retrieve it: and by the time he got back the situation had been increasingly complicated by the arrival of a real live customer who had turned up to buy that very object. Though if it really was as popular as the manager had said, perhaps that wasn't such a coincidence. Anyway, this customer seemed very set on purchasing one, and the overalled woman detached herself from Michael's scene and started to demonstrate one for her, trying to pretend as she did so that there was no scene in progress and that nothing had been going on at all: the manager too tried to hush Michael up by engaging him in conversation and backing him away from the counter and the transaction, but Michael wasn't so easy to silence: he continued to argue in a loud voice, and stood his ground. Frances wished that he would abandon this clearly pointless attempt, and all the more as he had by now noticed her presence, and she knew that at any moment he would appeal for her support. And finally the worst happened, as she had known it might; he turned to the woman who was trying to buy the Desperado Destruction Machine, and started to appeal to her, asking her if she wouldn't like to buy something less dangerous and destructive. The woman seemed confused at first, and when he asked her for whom she was buying it, she said that it was for her little boy's birthday, and she hadn't realised it was a dangerous toy, it was just something he'd set his heart on, he'd break his heart if he didn't get it, he'd seen it on the telly and he wanted one just like that: whereupon the manager, who had quite lost his grip, intervened and started to explain to her that there was nothing dangerous about the toy at all, on the contrary it was a well-made pure British product, with no lead paint or sharp edges, and that if Michael didn't shut up he'd call the police: whereupon Michael said that there was no law to stop customers discussing products in shops with one another, and he was himself a bona-fide customer, because look, he'd got a newly-purchased pair of socks in his pocket in a Will Baines bag. The woman continued to look confused, so Frances thought that she herself ought to intervene to support Michael, who had momentarily run out of aggression: and she said to the woman, in what she thought was a very friendly and reasonable tone, that nobody was trying to stop her buying her little boy a birthday present, they just wanted to point out that with all the violence in the world today anyway it was silly to add to it by encouraging children to play at killing and exterminating and things like that, and hadn't everyone seen enough bombing, particularly here (one of Michael's favourite points, this), and why didn't she buy her boy something constructive like Meccano or a farmyard set: and as she was saying all this she glanced from time to time to the woman's face, and there was something in it, she later acknowledged, that should have warned her. She stood there, the woman, her woollen headscarf so tight round her head that it seemed to clamp her jaws together into a violently imposed silence; her face unnaturally drawn, prematurely aged; her thickly-veined hands clutching a zip plastic purse and that stupid piece of clockwork machinery: and as she listened to

Frances's voice droning quietly and soothingly and placatingly away her face began to gather a glimmering of expression, from some depths of reaction too obscure to guess at: and as Frances finally ran down to a polite and only very faintly hopeful enquiring standstill, she opened her mouth and spoke. She said only one word, and it was a word that Frances had never heard before, though she had seen it in print in a once-banned book; and by some flash of insight, crossing the immeasurable gap of quality that separated their two lives, she knew that the woman herself had never before allowed it to pass her lips, that to her too it was a shocking syllable, portentous, unforgettable, not a familiar word casually dropped into the dividing spaces. Then the woman, having spoken, started to cry: incredibly, horribly, she started to cry. She dropped the clockwork toy on to the floor, and it fell so heavily that she could almost have been said to have thrown it down, and she stood there, staring at it, as the tears rolled down her face. Then she looked at them, and walked off. Nobody followed her: they stood there and let her go. They did not know how to follow her, nor what appeasement to offer for her unknown wound. So they did nothing. But Frances knew that in their innocence they had done something dreadful to her, in the light of which those long-since ended air raids and even distant Vietnam itself were an irrelevance, a triviality: but she did not know what it was, she could not know. At their feet, the Destruction Machine buzzed and whirred its way to a broken immobility, achieving a mild sensation in its death-throes by shooting a large spring coil out of its complex guts; she and Michael, after lengthy apologies, had to pay for it before they were allowed to leave the store.

JULIE HAYDEN was born in New York City in 1939. She graduated from Radcliffe and since 1971 has had five stories published in *The New Yorker.*

Julie Hayden
(1939–)

DAY-OLD BABY RATS

Down near the river a door slams; somebody wakes up, immediately flips over onto her back. She dreamt she went fishing, which is odd because she's never fished in her life. She thought someone was calling her "baby."

There's a lot of January light crawling from beneath room-darkener shades, casting mobile shadows on walls and ceiling. The mobile is composed of hundreds of white plastic circles the size of Communion wafers. As they spin they wax and wane, swell and vanish like little moons. Their shadows are like summer, like leaves, the leaves of the plane tree at the window, which hasn't any, right now, being in hibernation.

Through the crack between window and sill, air that tomorrow's papers will designate Unsatisfactory flows over one exposed arm, making the hairs stand up like sentries. Long trailer trucks continue to grind along the one-way street, tag end of a procession that began at 4 A.M. with the clank and whistle of trains on dead-end sidings, as melancholy as though they were the victims they had carried across the Hudson. The trucks carry meat for the Village butcher shops, the city's restaurants—pink sides of prime beef that you cannot purchase at the supermarket, U.S.D.A. choice, or commercial, pigs, lambs, chickens, rabbits, helped off the trucks by shivering men who warm their hands over trash-basket fires.

In the apartment across the hall the baby is bawling, "I want my milk."

It's cold and bloody in the refrigerated warehouses where the meat is stored prior to distribution. It's pretty cold in here, too. On her feet now, naked, she looks under the shade, which snaps smartly to the top of the window, disclosing a day: very clear for January. And colorful: stained-glass sky over a row of nineteenth-century houses painted pink and lime and lilac and beige, topped by clusters of chimney stacks, one of which emits a tornado of oily black smoke, fast dispersing. She ought to report it.

"I am sorry. The Office of Air Resources is closed till Monday. Please state the nature of the offense and the name and address of the violator and we will take action upon it when the office is open. This is a recording."

A pair of eyes on the fire escape, the golden gaze of the fat seven-toed tom from the next apartment; she hasn't a stitch on, backs away. Next thing, she's in the middle of the kitchen, bare and green as a guppy, trembling from head to toe, so much that it is difficult to open the door to the lower cabinet, which turns out to house a sizable bottle collection. On her knees she pours into a glass an ounce of Scotch, part of which sloshes over the linoleum in an amber puddle, fast dispersing. She gets the glass between her teeth. One, two, three, wait—the tremor peaks, subsides. She yawns and wipes the sleep from her eyes.

Getting dressed now, the radio going, the listener-sponsored radio. *Don't speak his name. He is everywhere, like spring. His eyes are leaves.*

She can find only one shoe and digs desperately in the welter of footwear like a retreat of mercenaries in the bottom of the closet; how did she get so many shoes? She tends to lose things that go in pairs. "Where's my other glove? My new earring—who took it?" she will wonder helplessly, too old to pray to St. Anthony, patron of lost objects.

His eyes are leaves, the birds his messengers.

Certainly somebody took her wallet last week while she was shopping for pants on Eighth Street. It *was* lifted, rather than absentmindedly abandoned in a restaurant, or on top of a cigarette machine. Later that evening a thin, limping man showed up on the doorstep with one half of her driver's license. He explained he had found it in a litter basket in Washington Square.

Look, flickering in the thicket, at the heart of the thorn tree. Cold as wind— Half shod, she switches to an all-news program: It is after ten o'clock; utilities are unchanged. The other shoe is in the bathroom; she spies it—spitting out a mouthful of toothpaste—under the radiator.

The shadow of a black man, the ripple of a war.

She wraps herself in a white rabbit-fur coat and goes out without locking the door, fumbling for her huge polarized sunglasses in her leather shoulder pouch, down two flights of stairs and onto the sidewalk. Now, here is the big brown United Parcel Service truck lumbering illegally up onto the curb and halting just short of the plane tree, which bears two deep gouges where the same truck wounded it last Monday morning. The driver hustles out and starts up the steps with a brown parcel, whistling.

In the vestibule he rings her bell, which of course nobody answers, since the apartment occupant is beside the truck, copying the license-plate and other relevant numbers into a little spiral notebook.

Still whistling, the young man with the brown uniform and small brown mustache comes back out with his parcel. The woman in the furry coat leans against the tree, glaring through her dark lenses.

"Lady." He stops in mid-trill. "Be nice. I can't go through this again. Just sign the little slip, I give you the package, and everybody's happy."

Through clenched teeth she says, "This time I am really going to report you. Really. Do you know that tree cost one hundred dollars to plant? And people like you, people like you—" But the last words emerge with difficulty, and tears fuzz the sharp outlines, her polarized vision of the sunny world. He cannot see the tears.

She's dying to know what is in the package. With rage the driver throws it back into the truck, THIS SIDE UP down. "You're bad news, lady," he yells, hurtling into the driver's seat; revs the motor. Afraid he's going to take out his temper on the tree, she gets in front of it, and now he cannot move the truck. "If you Don't. Get. Out. Of my. Way. I'm. Going. To Run. You. Down." His voice changes. "What do you want from me, lady?" he implores, unanswerably.

He gets his truck away without a mishap after all.

On the next block the drunk man starts out of the doorway where he has lain all night, stumbling toward her, clawing at his stained clothes. "Hey, don't I know you from somewheres?" His eyes look like pebbles, yellow and veined. "I know you. I know you a nice lady. Won'tcha gimme something, please? Fourteen cents, all I need's like fourteen cents." Smiling brilliantly, dancing around her: "I know you, I watches you comings and you goings."

Finally she digs up from the depths of her pocketbook some change, which falls to the sidewalk; he goes after it, fumbling and muttering in the gutter. All fall he was a worry to her, sleeping so still in his doorway, a crumpled overcoat, and a bottle still in its paper bag at his head like a candle. He has lost the overcoat but acquired some mittens. How does he know her? How has he managed to fight the cold this long, into January?

Back in the apartment with the newspapers and their interesting headlines:

4 CHAIN-STORES
FIRE-BOMBED

7 L.I. CHILDREN
DIE IN BUS CRASH

FEAR TEN SLAIN
IN RACKETS WAR

GRAVEDIGGERS
CALL STRIKE

Drug Girl, 12, Tells of Freakout

A HUNGRY BABY
DIES: JAIL MOM

Army Dismisses Charge of
War Crimes by General

FOE ATTACKS . . .

POPE BLESSES . . .

Actual Tests Used to Perpare
Pupils for Reading Exams

At the table, with a cup of tea and a cigarette, she gets the gist of the day's news and what the department stores are featuring, since she has errands to run, things to buy. Fidgeting, tongue between her teeth. ("Don't *do* that," her mother used to say watchfully, "you'll ruin your occlusion.") Reaching the weather report (occluded front), she looks warily around, as though she were being watched. But there is nobody in the house, which is suddenly so quiet the only sound is her own, her heartbeat.

There are no clocks in the apartment. What time has it gotten to be? She rushes to the telephone to dial the time, and when she lifts the receiver a voice is immediately in her ear. "Washington operator here. I have a person-to-person call for Mmm. Blur. Hello, New York, will you accept the call, please, New York?" Superimposed on the operator's voice is another, tinny and distant—a woman's?—but she cannot make out the words.

Who does she know in Washington?

No, she will not accept the call, she will not accept the charges. It must be past noon; the sun will be setting before too long. Before 4:37, according to the newspaper.

She has not lost her wristwatch, but she cannot seem to extricate it from the repair shop; it's been there for three weeks with a shattered crystal and a broken hand that she suspects they're keeping in traction. She turns her own hands palms up; the creases gleam with sweat—snail tracks.

Steadier now, tongue emergent, she's refilling a pocket flask from the kitchen liquor supply. It's a four-ounce hip-hugger model with a cute red leather jacket that can be unbuttoned for cleaning; she carries it everywhere in case of emergency, of entrapment in subway or elevator. Its predecessor fell on the floor of the ladies' room at the Art Students League, where she was waiting for a perennial art student to finish his life-studies class so they could go out to dinner and drinks or vice versa; how sorry she was to lose it! But she quickly replaced it with an identical model from Hoffritz.

With him she went to an island remote from the city and from everything else. Ten miles out in the Atlantic, off the coast of Maine, where the foghorn cries all night long, once a minute, "It *hurts,*" warning ships off the rocks where lobsters lie low (skittering anyway into the baited traps) and the brightest thing by night is the eye of the lighthouse, since the island is without community electricity. The wind blew constantly on the headlands several hundred feet over the sea. When the fog lifted, the ocean was the color of melted blue wax. Way down on the rocks, seals grazed, polychromatic as pigeons: blue, grey, brown, and spotted. Once, they thought they saw far out the spout of a whale.

Some sportsmen that week harpooned a small whale, a blackfish, and towed it into the harbor, stranding it on Fish Beach. All afternoon they worked to extract their three spearheads, up to the arms in blubber, till the sand was red and sticky and thick with flies.

She and he walked in the woods, when he wasn't painting, watched birds and the sunset, ate lobster with slippery fingers. Then she had an appetite, and used to collect leftover oranges or bananas from other tables to devour thoughtfully at night while the light house spun and the foghorn ached. Having gone through her fruit and her library books, she got into bed at last; he sighed, set on by his own bad dreams. It wasn't a success, that holiday. Making love in a blueberry patch, they reached up for berries and ate them where they lay. The days seemed very long. On the rocky cliffs they fought, wind whipping their barbed words out to sea. Back on the mainland, at the bus terminal, early in the morning: "You'll be all right?" he asked, peering into her face as though it were a steamed-up mirror.

On the river, a ship leaving for Valparaiso when the shipping page said it would sounds its plangent departure whistle—music for bones. Three times, as if it would never end, then ends for that particular voyage. It makes her eyes water.

Tropical fish in the living room move around in their tank, weaving gaudily through the underwater foliage, striped golden angelfish, jewel-like neon tetras, gouramis, a fat black molly. The one-eyed catfish oozes along the bottom of the aquarium as though vacuuming a rug. As she bends over them they rise, expecting a shower of ant eggs, frantically kissing the surface. She has forgotten to feed them. Again.

Somebody leaves the house for the second and final time that day. A fire siren evokes the noise of every dog on the block. There has been a fire in the Chinese laundry. An old Italian lady in a greasy black dress giggles at the snakes in the pet-shop window, her week's groceries piled in her grocery cart, and her cat on top of them. *He spreads like fire—don't smile.*

The Goodwill Exterminators have a new exhibit: among the pickled bugs and childishly hand-lettered signs, a jar of milk-white shrimps with tails, labelled "Day old baby Rats, caught in a Volkswagon on Perry Street by Myron." She digs her nails into her gloveless palms. *Don't smile; he hates it. Pretend not to tremble.* She checks her left wrist to see what time it is.

The sign over the bank spells out time and temperature in yellow dots:

12:57
79°

Very warm for January.

Near the subway entrance she buys the afternoon paper, and a man pushes her change over the papers with his hook.

The train stops just outside of the Fourteenth Street station and refuses to budge for several minutes. At Twenty-third Street, for some reason, a mob storms the cars, hustling for seats. A very small woman gets jammed in the half-open door—a midget, really, but still an ordinary-looking middle-aged woman in an out-of-style tweed coat and an out-of-town hat with a little veil, which is looped rakishly, accidentally, over one ear. She appears so helpless that somebody offers her a seat. "Hurry up, Daddy! Over here!" The other half of the door shuts, and she screams. The door opens. Her husband, who is taller, but only by an inch, rushes in, swinging a tiny child over the edge of the platform. They plop him onto the seat she gave up and stand guard, protectively.

"I need a lollipop," the baby shouts over the shriek of the train; no larger than a year-old infant, an achondroplastic dwarf without his parents' good proportions, with very short plump baby arms and no legs to speak of. His forehead bulges above a big, perplexed face, mouth turned down at the corners. Like any child he squirms petulantly in his seat, under a sign which reads "Little enough to ride for free? Little enough to ride your knee!" Daddy midget gives him a lemon lollipop.

She has to cook dinner for eight people next Thursday. She pickes out a five-quart casserole in Macy's basement, tries to charge it, discovers that all her credit cards are missing, buys it anyway, orders it sent. "Jeez, Miss, didn't you inform Credit yet?" The elevator to Credit is suffocatingly hot and reeks of fur and perfume. It stops at every floor, and by the eighth she has recalled that she has no charge account with Macy's.

(The U.P.S. man will make a real effort to deliver the dish in time, nicking off more of the bark of the plane tree; ringing and ringing but nobody's home.)

Sweating in her fur coat, she proceeds down the maze that leads to the subway platform, through a crowd of people eating ice-cream cones and asking which way to the Port Authority Bus Terminal; nearly bumps into a soldier who has taken a post by a gum machine. Not an ordinary

G.I. but someone on his way to a revolution. Leaf-patterned trousers tucked into combat boots, combat jacket of a different green, green beret pulled down nearly over his eyebrows—even his canteen is in camouflage. Only, his gun is not. He holds his rifle butt end down between his boots like a walking stick. He stares impassively over the crowd, as though he thinks he is invisible. And perhaps he is.

She has reached the last staircase when there is a voice at her back, a whisper: "Hey lady, you need help with your packages?" But her hands are empty.

She is holding very tightly to the railing. Another voice: Middle-aged lady who inquires kindly, "Are you sick, Miss? Do you need some help!"

She shakes her head no, but the lady helps her down anyway, talking cozily. "You know, I had a friend once who was so scared of the subway she'd get nauseous when the train came in. It's called claustrophobia? Well, finally the husband made her see the doctor. Well, it turned out that her brother had locked her in a closet once when she was a bitty thing, and she'd forgotten all about it. But her heart remembered." A leap of the heart. "You know, it was a funny thing. After she got well and rode subways without thinking twice about it, she had one of those freak accidents and almost lost an arm on a Flushing train. I bet the operations cost her more than the psychiatrist did. Well, honey, here's your train."

Tottering onto the lit car, she supports herself against a post, breathes easier until the doors have closed and the train starts down the dark passage. With a felt-tip pen, someone has lettered on the L&M ad, "God is a Sadist."

Quickly tiring of her own reflection in the dressing-room mirrors, she buys the first dress she tried on, a silky blue Ban-Lon number that makes her look thin as a doll. There is a delay when she tries to charge it. Shifting from foot to foot with impatience, says yes, she will report the loss.

(She will be extremely surprised when next tenth of the month a bill arrives from this department store for $600 worth of merchandise she never purchased. But perhaps she will have notified Credit Service in time to avoid the liability.)

A very young girl with a face like an angel's sits in an armchair in the ladies' lounge, breast bare to her infant daughter; the baby nurses with an expression of concentration, pink palm closing and unclosing rhythmically like a sea anemone. The mother's knees are spread in fatigue. Assorted clothes, diapers, bottles, and magazines are falling out of the department-store shopping bags beside her chair. She looks as though she has been travelling a long time. She has just gone to sleep; eyelashes hover like black spiders over her cheekbones. She snores.

Baby loses the soda fountain and wails angrily. Her mother automatically readjusts the small head and closes her eyes upon the world once more, breathing onto it the syllables, like prayer, "Goddamn son of a bitch bastards."

"Breathe in," the nurse instructed. "Pant. Harder." She tried to, like a good girl, sobbing obediently. "It won't hurt so much this way." Actually it hurt very little. "It works like a vacuum cleaner." Nature, she said, abhors a vacuum. "I usually have a cleaning woman," she told the fluorescent ceiling lights.

A sip from the red flask in the toilet, followed by a rush of acid.

Outside on Fifth Avenue, asbestos flakes eddy in spiral air currents like snow, the carcinogenic emission from a new skyscraper. Something blows into her eye before she can get out her dark glasses. She blinks to tear it away.

Bells jangle. The saffron robes, the shaven-head Buddhists chanting "Hare Krishna" surround her, offering their literature with gentle words. Under their sleazy peach-tinted rayon saris they wear sweaters and sweatshirts, and sneakers instead of sandals. Surely they're in the wrong climate. They sing, "Hare Krishna, Hare Krishna, Krishna Krishna, Hare Hare," snapping their belled fingers and jouncing to ward off the cold.

The literature is called "Back to Godhead," and shows a circle of girls with pleated skirts like fans dancing beneath stylized Indian flowers, a round moon. "Hare Rama, Hare Rama, Rama Rama, Hare Hare," the hectic singers chant.

"Oh my God, isn't that Al Silberstang from Fire Island?" says a passerby, nudging her companion to a halt. Al Silberstang does not cease from his dance. His eyes dwell on inner secrets. She searches for money so she can escape their circle. "Peace, peace, lady," says Al Silberstang, whirling away with her money. But there is no peace from the Buddhists, no peace from the chestnut and pretzel sellers, one at each corner, warming their hands over the braziers and reiterating their spiel.

Escaping across the street, she looks up to see where she is—a mistake; her head begins to spin. What did she eat for breakfast?

Here she is, the rival sect's headquarters, St. Patrick's Cathedral. A man on the steps brandishes a sign, "ANNOYING SICK H-BOMB DICTATOR WILL BE PUNISHED," at an old lady in an old mink, in a walker, going up the steps with the aid of a younger female, daughter or niece, who looks put-upon and cold in her short cloth coat. The old lady's arm is grasped on the other side by a nun. You can tell it is a nun from the navy-blue tailored outfit, like an airline stewardess's, and the truncated veil, revealing a steel-grey curly bang. Nuns never used to have grey hair. Or calves. The nuns of her youth floated like blackbirds. Step. By step. By step, the old lady is guided through a small door set into the heavily ornamented bronze ones. Around the corner is the aftermath of a Filipino wedding, the small white bride shivering and smiling for the photographers.

The nuns with their pale faces taught them myths about eternity and how to walk in processions. " 'Tis the month of our Mother, the blessed and beautiful days," the parochial school-children sang in May, carrying their sheaves of wheat down suburban sidewalks, under the magnolias. A pretty sight. Though *she'd* never really cottoned to Our Lady; she much preferred the Holy Ghost, perhaps because he was a bird.

Heaven, hell, purgatory, limbo, where little unbaptized children lived pleasantly in a garden, crawling on the green grass, and it never snowed. Purgatory was where they melted your sins away; hell was very hot. (A little boy died and a saint revived him. "Oh Mother," he cried, "I have been in such a terrible place!") She is cold. And hungry: the smell of burning chestnuts rises like incense. "Getcha hot chestnuts! Getcha pretzels!"

He scatters a handful of raw nuts over the coals, extends a bagful with a hand that is like a burnt pretzel, grins brilliantly. "I bet your hungry, pretty lady; I know you—"

Tugging at the door to the Cathedral, where she's never been. *He eats terror, gulps tears, and spits catastrophes.* The smell of incense, dazzling banks of red votive candles, the purple light from high stained-glass windows decorated with suffering saints. Tourists move chattily around the gloom of the nave; in the side aisles kneel the reverent few. She looks dizzily at the vaulted ceiling, light-years away. She steadies herself on a granite basin. Then, to show she's all right, dabbles holy water from the font and blesses herself like the tourists just ahead. The basin has specks floating in it and a layer of silt.

Her heart beats as though it were trying to get out. Looking for a place to sit down, she travels along an enormous aisle, toward where she sees people as at the small end of the telescope her father gave her once when she was thirteen and infatuated with science. It has been years since she was in church. And what a church! Are you supposed to cover your head these days? She has no cover, not even a handkerchief to pin to her hair.

At a side pew occupied mostly by women her knees signal *no farther*, and she slides in. Her uncovered scalp prickles dangerously. She thinks, with longing, of her flask.

As she plans about getting back down the aisle, or at least behind a stone pillar, the women begin trickling out the other side of the pew. An elbow in the ribs: it is the niece or daughter of the woman in the walker. "Miss, could you please move along, or are you asleep, dope?"

Unable to reply, she shies into the aisle, abandoning (she will remember later, in a crowded room) a brown-and-white box from Saks Fifth Avenue to the niece or the H-bomb man or St. Patrick. Or him, the god of fear. There's a convenient pillar, and—what is this?—a curtained cubicle behind a brass gate, private, hidden, a good place to take stock and think her way out, back to the right door. Sneaking a backward glance, she parts the white curtain, ducks in, groping for familiar leathery corners. Just as she has the cap off and is tilting the flask back, there is a hair-raising creak. Somebody else is only a breath away. And listening. And murmuring, through a grille, *"Ja, mein Kind?"* Fallen into the hands of the Nazis. "Yes, my child," he says impatiently.

Good heavens, somebody is answering. It is her own high parochial-school voice, her very tongue snapping out the appropriate response. "Bless me, Father, for I have sinned. It has been fifteen years since my last confession." At last she gets the bottleneck in her mouth. Alcohol is instantly absorbed through the stomach lining into the bloodstream. At once the molecules are joined up, spreading the cheerful news.

Anticipatory silence. Perhaps he only understands German. She racks her brain—she has no wish to go spilling the secrets of her life to a stranger. First you confessed sins against the Church, then against God. She remembers a sin against the Church: "I have missed Mass."

"How many times?"

"Every time." Quick swallow. A rush of confidence. "I used God's name in vain five times. I disobeyed my parents three times. I was rude to a nun once. I slapped my little sister. I was untruthful—" Running out of sins, she adds, desperately, "I smoked marijuana."

"On how many occasions?"

"I don't remember."

He clears his throat, beginning to sound like a Viennese psychiatrist. "So, is that all that you wish to tell me?"

"Well, not quite," she stalls (once more should do the trick). Then she realizes that now there are three of them in the confessional; someone else is waiting on the other side, behind the priest, making a priest sandwich, getting restless. She shifts heavily to assert her presence—probably the niece woman who called her "dope."

"Oh no, Father," she says, tilting the flask back for another round. Not all of it reaches her mouth, there's spillage; the booth fills with the odor of alcohol in addition to that of Listerine. She is tempted to offer him a nip through the grille, for his stomach's sake. "But it's been such a long time." A weak giggle. Her time, and the jig, is up.

The Big Ear is no longer fooled. "My daughter, I suspect you are spoofing me. There are penitents waiting; you are wasting my time. Why are you here? What do you want?" No answer. "Do you want absolution? If you are in some kind of trouble, we shall discuss it in the rectory at two-forty next Wednesday. Father Kleinhardt is the name."

"Father Kleinhardt, I am frightened."

"For your penance say three Hail Marys. Now make an Act of Contrition." Switching tongues, he begins to absolve her in Latin.

"I am frightened to death, Father." But he chooses not to hear.

She begins, "Oh my God, I am heartily sorry," and slips out, leaving him committed to the end of his Latin prayer, noticing a sign taped to the side altar: "Father Kleinhardt:

English-Deutsch." At the altar of St. Anthony a prayer is posted in mock parchment, promising the reciter forty days' indulgence. She has got away with it, she is outside, she is free.

The morning she left the northern island a young deer escaped from it, the only one of the herd imported from Boothbay Harbor who couldn't settle down but rampaged through the woods like a crazy thing and ate roses out of village gardens. After they found hoofprints on the beach, they put out salt for him in the woods. He passed her boat swimming like a small horned seal in a mainland direction; it was too late and too foggy for the lobster smacks to find him. By the time she reached the city he was fathoms deep, and the fish were grazing off his antlers. "Taxi, lady?" said a cabdriver outside the Port Authority Bus Terminal. The man drove demoniacally, hunched like a jockey over the wheel; only when they reached her apartment did she observe that it was because he couldn't straighten his back. In the full glare of the street lamp his features leapt at her: the thrust chin, the snub nose, the furrowed forehead with its huge wen, the maimed, cleft, two-fingered hoof of a congenitally deformed right hand. Smiling hilariously, he scratched at the wen. "Take it easy now, lady," he told her.

(The dead deer lies among the rocks, nibbled bare by sea worms and crustaceans, far from home; barnacles have attached themselves to his skeleton; when spring comes a fisherman will draw up with his catch its alien skull, and think it is something new.)

Once you have seen him he will never let you get away with anything.

Now it is time, definitely time, to start uptown, taking it easy and crossing with the lights. The sun has gone down, leaving a stain in the west. At a store window she acknowledges with a slight smile her reflection: a thin woman in a white coat and big black glasses, soon to be middle-aged, puzzled because the years went so fast and the days so slowly. And, someday, old.

Killing time, she stops to light a cigarette and is nearly swept over by an energetic group of tiny children, chattering in the half-light by Central Park. There are about eight of them, fat as chickadees in their snowsuits. Isn't it late for them to be out? "I'm *cold,*" complains one grumpy mite with thick glasses and a circle of mustard around his mouth to one of the two teachers, long-haired girls in furry coats like her own. They seem to have lassoed her. Then she realizes it's a rope; they're clinging to a rope, with a teacher at each end, and she has got in the middle. What a good idea; little children will hold on if you tell them to.

The teachers untangle her and say, "Come along now," jerking the children briskly down the sidewalk. A small spectacled girl has a pink balloon floating from the end of her little finger. There are a lot of pairs of spectacles for such a small group of kindergarten-aged children.

The children are blind. These are blind children, with their teachers, sightless among the seeing, though she can't see any too well herself, in her dark glasses with the sun gone down, hurrying toward an uptown appointment.

The hot light. An egg, a shiny egg dancing in a glass. (Sunday morning she will burn the bacon and spill the scrambled eggs on the floor trying to stamp out the fire in her bedroom slippers.) Lying on a table, somebody cried, "Hey that hurts, it hurts," and yet it didn't hurt that much.

"Relax. Don't fight it," said the nurse. "Would you care for a cigarette? I'm afraid all I've got is Salems"—putting it between dry lips.

An involvement of the inner space, a truly savage pain. Slurp, water whizzing in the basin. Will it travel down the sewers like an abandoned pet, eyeless, lost to the gene pool, never to breed?

Doctor having left the room, his assistant matter-of-factly sprinkled water over what was in the basin, saying, "I baptize thee in the name of the Father and of the Son and of the Holy Ghost."

"You are baptizing a newt," she said reproachfully.

The nurse looked ashamed. "Sorry, but I just have to do this. Say, you know, I keep newts?"

"I have tropical fish, myself."

Let's go to bed and tell lies—almost there now. *Committing our murders decently in private.* Punching the moon-white elevator button. The elevator boxes her into a private space; she rises with it, shaking in silence. *I don't know the enemy's you. You haven't heard he is me.*

He greets her at the door, waving a Martini glass, reeling her into the party. "Oh my God, am I glad to see you," she says.

ALICE WALKER was born in 1944 in Eatonton, Georgia. She attended Spelman College and received her degree from Sarah Lawrence College in 1965. She has been lecturer in literature and writing at numerous colleges and universities and the recipient of many awards and fellowships. Her published works include one novel, one collection of short stories, two books of poetry, and a biography of Langston Hughes for children. She is now at work on a book about black women writers. One of her first pieces of published writing, an essay entitled "The Civil Rights Movement: What Good Was It?" which won first prize in *The American Scholar*'s essay contest of 1966, shows her capacity to see the old woman who is her subject in her beautiful singularity as well as in her historical context and to communicate her sense of that many-leveled significance with intelligence and warmth. That early essay promised the imaginative prose and poetry she has now delivered. It promised, too, her intense relationship with the theme of the mystery and beauty of ordinary lives which gives the story that follows here its special radiance. "Everyday Use" was included in Martha Foley's *Best American Short Stories of 1973*. It is a product of the deep convictions Alice Walker expressed in an interview about her novel, *The Third Life of Grange Copeland*: "I was curious to know why people in families (specifically black families) are often cruel to each other and how much of this cruelty is caused by outside forces; such as various social injustices, segregation, unemployment, etc. . . . Family relationships are sacred. No amount of outside pressure and injustice must make us lose sight of that fact. . . . In the black family, love, cohesion, support, and concern are crucial since the racist society constantly acts to destroy the black individual, the black family unit, the black child. In America black people have only themselves and each other."

Alice Walker
(1944–   )

EVERYDAY USE

for your grandmama

I will wait for her in the yard that Maggie and I made so clean and wavy yesterday afternoon. A yard like this is more comfortable than most people know. It is not just a yard. It is like an extended living room. When the hard clay is swept clean as a floor and the fine sand around the edges lined with tiny, irregular grooves anyone can come and sit and look up into the elm tree and wait for the breezes that never come inside the house.

Maggie will be nervous until after her sister goes: she will stand hopelessly in corners homely and ashamed of the burn scars down her arms and legs, eyeing her sister with a mixture of envy and awe. She thinks her sister has held life always in the palm of one hand, that "no" is a word the world never learned to say to her.

You've no doubt seen those TV shows where the child who has "made it" is confronted, as a surprise, by her own mother and father, tottering in weakly from backstage. (A pleasant surprise, of course: What would they do if parent and child came on the show only to curse out and insult each other?) On TV mother and child embrace and smile into each other's faces. Sometimes the mother and father weep, the child wraps them in her arms and leans across the table to tell how she would not have made it without their help. I have seen these programs.

Sometimes I dream a dream in which Dee and I are suddenly brought together on a TV program of this sort. Out of a dark and soft-seated limousine I am ushered into a bright room filled with many people. There I meet a smiling, gray, sporty man like Johnny Carson who shakes my hand and tells me what a fine girl I have. Then we are on the stage and Dee is embracing me with tears in her eyes. She pins on my dress a large orchid, even though she has told me once that she thinks orchids are tacky flowers.

In real life I am a large, big-boned woman with rough, man-working hands. In the winter I wear flannel nightgowns to bed and overalls during the day. I can kill and clean a hog as mercilessly as a man. My fat keeps me hot in zero weather. I can work outside all day, breaking ice to get water for washing; I can eat pork liver cooked over the open fire minutes after it comes steaming from the hog. One winter I knocked a bull calf straight in the brain between the eyes with a sledge hammer and had the meat hung up to chill before nightfall. But of course all this does not show on television. I am the way my daughter would want me to be: a hundred pounds lighter, my skin like an uncooked barley pancake. My hair glistens in the hot bright lights. Johnny Carson has much to do to keep up with my quick and witty tongue.

But that is a mistake. I know even before I wake up. Who ever knew a Johnson with a quick tongue? Who can even imagine me looking a strange white man in the eye? It seems to me I have talked to them always with one foot raised in flight, with my head turned in whichever way is farthest from them. Dee, though. She would always look anyone in the eye. Hesitation was no part of her nature.

"How do I look, Mama?" Maggie says, showing just enough of her thin body enveloped in pink skirt and red blouse for me to know she's there, almost hidden by the door.

"Come out into the yard," I say.

Have you ever seen a lame animal, perhaps a dog run over by some careless person rich enough to own a car, sidle up to someone who is ignorant enough to be kind to him? That is the way my Maggie walks. She has been like this, chin on chest, eyes on ground, feet in shuffle, ever since the fire that burned the other house to the ground.

Dee is lighter than Maggie, with nicer hair and a fuller figure. She's a woman now, though sometimes I forget. How long ago was it that the other house burned? Ten, twelve years? Sometimes I can still hear the flames and feel Maggie's arms sticking to me, her hair smoking and her dress falling off her in little black papery flakes. Her eyes seemed stretched open, blazed open by the flames reflected in them. And Dee. I see her standing off under the sweet gum tree she used to dig gum out of; a look of concentration on her face as she watched the last dingy gray board of the house fall in toward the red-hot brick chimney. Why don't you do a dance around the ashes? I'd wanted to ask her. She had hated the house that much.

I used to think she hated Maggie, too. But that was before we raised the money, the church and me, to send her to Augusta to school. She used to read to us without pity; forcing words, lies, other folks' habits, whole lives upon us two, sitting trapped and ignorant underneath her voice. She washed us in a river of make-believe, burned us with a lot of knowledge we didn't necessarily need to know. Pressed us to her with the serious way she read, to shove us away at just the moment, like dimwits, we seemed about to understand.

Dee wanted nice things. A yellow organdy dress to wear to her graduation from high school; black pumps to match a green suit she'd made from an old suit somebody gave me. She was determined to stare down any disaster in her efforts. Her eyelids would not flicker for minutes at a time. Often I fought off the temptation to shake her. At sixteen she had a style of her own: and knew what style was.

I never had an education myself. After second grade the school was closed down. Don't ask me why: in 1927 colored asked fewer questions than they do now. Sometimes Maggie reads to me. She stumbles along goodnaturedly but can't see well. She knows she is not bright. Like good looks and money, quickness passed her by. She will marry John Thomas (who has mossy teeth in an earnest face) and then I'll be free to sit here and I guess just sing church songs to myself. Although I never was a good singer. Never could carry a tune. I was always better at a man's job. I used to love to milk till I was hooked in the side in '49. Cows are soothing and slow and don't bother you, unless you try to milk them the wrong way.

I have deliberately turned my back on the house. It is three rooms, just like the one that burned, except the roof is tin; they don't make shingle roofs any more. There are no real windows, just some holes cut in the sides, like the portholes in a ship, but not round and not square, with rawhide holding the shutters up on the outside. This house is in a pasture, too, like the other one. No doubt when Dee sees it she will want to tear it down. She wrote me once that no matter where we "choose" to live, she will manage to come see us. But she will never bring her friends. Maggie and I thought about this and Maggie asked me, "Mama, when did Dee ever *have* any friends?"

She had a few. Furtive boys in pink shirts hanging about on washday after school. Nervous girls who never laughed. Impressed with her they worshiped the well-turned phrase, the cute shape, the scalding humor that erupted like bubbles in lye. She read to them.

When she was courting Jimmy T she didn't have much time to pay to us, but turned all her faultfinding power on him. He *flew* to marry a cheap gal from a family of ignorant flashy people. She hardly had time to recompose herself.

When she comes I will meet—but there they are!

Maggie attempts to make a dash for the house, in her shuffling way, but I stay her with my hand. "Come back here," I say. And she stops and tries to dig a well in the sand with her toe.

It is hard to see them clearly through the strong sun. But even the first glimpse of leg out of the car tells me it is Dee. Her feet were always neat-looking, as if God himself had shaped them with a certain style. From the other side of the car comes a short, stocky man. Hair is all over his head a foot long and hanging from his chin like a kinky mule tail. I hear Maggie suck in her breath. "Uhnnnh," is what it sounds like. Like when you see the wriggling end of a snake just in front of your foot on the road. "Uhnnnh."

Dee next. A dress down to the ground, in this hot weather. A dress so loud it hurts my eyes. There are yellows and oranges enough to throw back the light of the sun. I feel my whole face warming from the heat waves it throws out. Earrings gold, too, and hanging down to her shoulders. Bracelets dangling and making noises when she moves her arm up to shake the folds of the dress out of her armpits. The dress is loose and flows, and as she walks closer, I like it. I hear Maggie go "Uhnnnh" again. It is her sister's hair. It stands straight up like the wool on a sheep. It is black as night and around the edges are two long pigtails that rope about like small lizards disappearing behind her ears.

"Wa-su-zo-Tean-o!" she says, coming on in that gliding way the dress makes her move. The short stocky fellow with the hair to his navel is all grinning and he follows up with "Asalamalakim, my mother and sister!" He moves to hug Maggie but she falls back, right up against the back of my chair. I feel her trembling there and when I look up I see the perspiration falling off her chin.

"Don't get up," says Dee. Since I am stout it takes something of a push. You can see me trying to move a second or two before I make it. She turns, showing white heels through her sandals, and goes back to the car. Out she peeks next with a Polaroid. She stoops down quickly and lines up picture after picture of me sitting there in front of the house with Maggie cowering behind me. She never takes a shot without making sure the house is included. When a cow comes nibbling around the edge of the yard she snaps it and me and Maggie *and* the house. Then she puts the Polaroid in the back seat of the car, and comes up and kisses me on the forehead.

Meanwhile Asalamalakim is going through the motions with Maggie's hand. Maggie's hand is as limp as a fish, and probably as cold, despite the sweat, and she keeps trying to pull it back. It looks like Asalamalakim wants to shake hands but wants to do it fancy. Or maybe he don't know how people shake hands. Anyhow, he soon gives up on Maggie.

"Well," I say. "Dee."

"No, Mama," she says. "Not 'Dee,' Wangero Leewanika Kemanjo!"

"What happened to 'Dee'?" I wanted to know.

"She's dead," Wangero said. "I couldn't bear it any longer being named after the people who oppress me."

"You know as well as me you was named after your aunt Dicie," I said. Dicie is my sister. She named Dee. We called her "Big Dee" after Dee was born.

"But who was *she* named after?" asked Wangero.

"I guess after Grandma Dee," I said.

"And who was she named after?" asked Wangero.

"Her mother," I said, and saw Wangero was getting tired. "That's about as far back as I can trace it," I said. Though, in fact, I probably could have carried it back beyond the Civil War through the branches.

"Well," said Asalamalakim, "there you are."

"Uhnnnh," I heard Maggie say.

"There I was not," I said, "before 'Dicie' cropped up in our family, so why should I try to trace it that far back?"

He just stood there grinning, looking down on me like

somebody inspecting a Model A car. Every once in a while he and Wangero sent eye signals over my head.

"How do you pronounce this name?" I asked.

"You don't have to call me by it if you don't want to," said Wangero.

"Why shouldn't I?" I asked. "If that's what you want us to call you, we'll call you."

"I know it might sound awkward at first," said Wangero.

"I'll get used to it," I said. "Ream it out again."

Well, soon we got the name out of the way. Asalamalakim had a name twice as long and three times as hard. After I tripped over it two or three times he told me to just call him Hakim-a-barber. I wanted to ask him was he a barber, but I didn't really think he was, so I didn't ask.

"You must belong to those beef-cattle peoples down the road," I said. They said "Asalamalakim" when they met you, too, but they didn't shake hands. Always too busy: feeding the cattle, fixing the fences, putting up salt-lick shelters, throwing down hay. When the white folks poisoned some of the herd the men stayed up all night with rifles in their hands. I walked a mile and a half just to see the sight.

Hakim-a-barber said, "I accept some of their doctrines, but farming and raising cattle is not my style." (They didn't tell me, and I didn't ask, whether Wangero [Dee] had really gone and married him.)

We sat down to eat and right away he said he didn't eat collards and pork was unclean. Wangero, though, went on through the chitlins and corn bread, the greens and everything else. She talked a blue streak over the sweet potatoes. Everything delighted her. Even the fact that we still used the benches her daddy made for the table when we couldn't afford to buy chairs.

"Oh, Mama!" she cried. Then turned to Hakim-a-barber. "I never knew how lovely these benches are. You can feel the rump prints," she said, running her hands underneath her and along the bench. Then she gave a sigh and her hand closed over Grandma Dee's butter dish. "That's it!" she said. "I knew there was something I wanted to ask you if I could have." She jumped up from the table and went over in the corner where the churn stood, the milk in it clabber by now. She looked at the churn and looked at it.

"This churn top is what I need," she said. "Didn't Uncle Buddy whittle it out of a tree you all used to have?"

"Yes," I said.

"Uh huh," she said happily. "And I want the dasher, too."

"Uncle Buddy whittle that, too?" asked the barber.

Dee (Wangero) looked up at me.

"Aunt Dee's first husband whittled the dash," said Maggie so low you almost couldn't hear her. "His name was Henry, but they called him Stash."

"Maggie's brain is like an elephant's," Wangero said, laughing. "I can use the churn top as a centerpiece for the alcove table," she said, sliding a plate over the churn, "and I'll think of something artistic to do with the dasher."

When she finished wrapping the dasher the handle stuck out. I took it for a moment in my hands. You didn't even have to look close to see where hands pushing the dasher up and down to make butter had left a kind of sink in the wood. In fact, there were a lot of small sinks; you could see where thumbs and fingers had sunk into the wood. It was beautiful light yellow wood, from a tree that grew in the yard where Big Dee and Stash had lived.

After dinner Dee (Wangero) went to the trunk at the foot of my bed and started rifling through it. Maggie hung back in the kitchen over the dishpan. Out came Wangero with two quilts. They had been pieced by Grandma Dee and then Big Dee and me had hung them on the quilt frames on the front porch and quilted them. One was in the Lone Star pattern. The other was Walk Around the Mountain. In both of them were scraps of dresses Grandma Dee had worn fifty and more years ago. Bits and pieces of Grandpa Jarrell's Paisley shirts. And one teeny faded blue piece, about the piece of a penny matchbox, that was from Great Grandpa Ezra's uniform that he wore in the Civil War.

"Mama," Wangero said sweet as a bird. "Can I have these old quilts?"

I heard something fall in the kitchen, and a minute later the kitchen door slammed.

"Why don't you take one or two of the others?" I asked. "These old things was just done by me and Big Dee from some tops your grandma pieced before she died."

"No," said Wangero. "I don't want those. They are stitched around the borders by machine."

"That'll make them last better," I said.

"That's not the point," said Wangero. "These are all

pieces of dresses Grandma used to wear. She did all this stitching by hand. Imagine!" She held the quilts securely in her arms, stroking them.

"Some of the pieces, like those lavender ones, come from old clothes her mother handed down to her," I said, moving up to touch the quilts. Dee (Wangero) moved back just enough so that I couldn't reach the quilts. They already belonged to her.

"Imagine!" she breathed again, clutching them closely to her bosom.

"The truth is," I said, "I promised to give them quilts to Maggie, for when she marries John Thomas."

She gasped like a bee had stung her.

"Maggie can't appreciate these quilts!" she said. "She'd probably be backward enough to put them to everyday use."

"I reckon she would," I said. "God knows I been saving 'em for long enough with nobody using 'em. I hope she will!" I didn't want to bring up how I had offered Dee (Wangero) a quilt when she went away to college. Then she had told me they were old-fashioned, out of style.

"But they're *priceless!*" she was saying now, furiously; for she has a temper. "Maggie would put them on the bed and in five years they'd be in rags. Less than that!"

"She can always make some more," I said. "Maggie knows how to quilt."

Dee (Wangero) looked at me with hatred. "You just will not understand. The point is these quilts, *these* quilts!"

"Well," I said, stumped. "What would *you* do with them?"

"Hang them," she said. As if that was the only thing you *could* do with quilts.

Maggie by now was standing in the door. I could almost hear the sound her feet made as they scraped over each other.

"She can have them, Mama," she said, like somebody used to never winning anything, or having anything reserved for her. "I can 'member Grandma Dee without the quilts."

I looked at her hard. She had filled her bottom lip with checkerberry snuff and it gave her face a kind of dopey, hangdog look. It was Grandma Dee and Big Dee who taught her how to quilt herself. She stood there with her scarred hands hidden in the folds of her skirt. She looked at her sister with something like fear but she wasn't mad at her. This was Maggie's portion. This was the way she knew God to work.

When I looked at her like that something hit me in the top of my head and ran down to the soles of my feet. Just like when I'm in church and the spirit of God touches me and I get happy and shout. I did something I never had done before: hugged Maggie to me, then dragged her on into the room, snatched the quilts out of Miss Wangero's hands and dumped them into Maggie's lap. Maggie just sat there on my bed with her mouth open.

"Take one or two of the others," I said to Dee.

But she turned without a word and went out to Hakim-a-barber.

"You just don't understand," she said, as Maggie and I came out to the car.

"What don't I understand?" I wanted to know.

"Your heritage," she said. And then she turned to Maggie, kissed her, and said, "You ought to try to make something of yourself, too, Maggie. It's really a new day for us. But from the way you and Mama still live you'd never know it."

She put on some sunglasses that hid everything above the tip of her nose and her chin.

Maggie smiled; maybe at the sunglasses. But a real smile, not scared. After we watched the car dust settle I asked Maggie to bring me a dip of snuff. And then the two of us sat there just enjoying, until it was time to go in the house and go to bed.

Bibliography

KATE CHOPIN (1851–1904)

At Fault (1890); *Bayou Folk* (1894); *A Night in Acadie* (1897); *The Awakening* (1899).

EDITH WHARTON (1862–1937)

The Greater Inclination (1899); *The Touchstone* (1900); *Crucial Instances* (1901); *The Valley of Decision* (1902); *Sanctuary* (1903); *Italian Villas* (1904); *Italian Backgrounds* (1905); *The House of Mirth* (1905); *The Fruit of the Tree* (1907); *The Hermit and the Wild Woman* (short stories) (1908); *Tales of Men and Ghosts* (1910); *Ethan Frome* (1911); *The Reef* (1912); *The Custom of the Country* (1913); *Fighting France* (1915); *Xingu and Other Stories* (1916); *Summer* (1917); *The Marne* (1918); *French Ways and Their Meaning* (1919); *The Age of Innocence* (1920); *In Morocco* (1920); *The Glimpses of the Moon* (1922); *A Son at the Front* (1923); *Old New York* (1924); *The Writing of Fiction* (1925); *Twilight Sleep* (1927); *The Children* (1928); *Hudson River Bracketed* (1929); *Certain People* (1930); *A Backward Glance* (1937); *Ghosts* (1937); *The Buccaneers* (1938).

WILLA CATHER (1873–1947)

The Troll Garden (short stories) (1905); *Alexander's Bridge* (1912); *O Pioneers!* (1913); *The Song of the Lark* (1915); *My Antonia* (1918); *Youth and the Bright Medusa* (short stories) (1920); *One of Ours* (1922); *A Lost Lady* (1923); *The Professor's House* (1925); *My Mortal Enemy* (1926); *Death Comes to the Archbishop* (1927); *Shadows on the Rock* (1931); *Obscure Destinies* (short stories) (1932); *Lucy Gayheart* (1935);

Not Under Forty (essays) (1936); *Sapphira and the Slave Girl* (1940).

SIDONIE-GABRIELLE COLETTE (1873–1954)

In Print in the United States:
A Thousand and One Mornings (1973); *Break of Day and the Blue Lantern* (1966); *Cheri and the Last of Cheri* (1974); *Earthly Paradise* (1966); *Gigi and Selected Writings* (1973); *Journey for Myself* (1972); *Places* (1970); *The Other Woman* (short stories) (1972); *The Pure and the Impure* (1967). Scheduled to appear: *Retreat From Love; The Cat; The Evening Star.*

GERTRUDE STEIN (1874–1946)

Three Lives (1908); *Tender Buttons* (1915); *Geography and Plays* (1922); *The Making of Americans* (1925); *Useful Knowledge* (1928); *Acquaintance with Description* (1929); *Ten Portraits* (1930); *Lucy Church Amiably* (1930); *Before the Flower of Friendship Faded Friendship Faded* (1931); *How to Write* (1931); *Operas and Plays* (1932); *Matisse, Picasso, and Gertrude Stein* (1932); *The Autobiography of Alice B. Toklas* (1933); *Four Saints in Three Acts* (1934); *Portraits and Prayers* (1934); *Lectures in America* (1935); *Narration* (1935); *The Geographical History of America: or, The Relation of Human Nature to the Human Mind* (1936); *Everybody's Autobiography* (1937); *Picasso* (1938); *The World is Round* (1939); *Paris France* (1940); *Ida* (1941).

VIRGINIA WOOLF (1882–1941)

Novels:
The Voyage Out (1915); *Night and Day* (1919); *Jacob's Room* (1922); *Mrs. Dalloway* (1925); *To the Lighthouse* (1927); *Orlando* (1928); *The Waves* (1931); *The Years* (1937); *Between the Acts* (1941).
Essays:
The Common Reader (1925, 1932); *A Room of One's Own* (1929); *Collected Essays* (4 vols., 1966–1967).
Biographies:
Flush (1933); *Roger Fry* (1940); *A Writer's Diary* (1953).

Short Stories:
A Haunted House and Other Stories (1944).

KATHERINE MANSFIELD (1888–1923)

Short Stories:
In a German Pension (1911); *Prelude* (1918); *Je ne parle pas français* (1919); *Bliss* (1920); *The Garden Party* (1922); *The Dove's Nest* (1923); *Something Childish* (1924); *The Aloe* (1930); *Collected Stories* (1945).
Various:
Poems (ed. J. M. Murry, 1923); *Maata* (novel; juvenile work). *Journal* (ed. J. M. Murry, 1927, definitive edition, 1954); *Letters* (1928); *The Scrapbook* (1946); *Letters to John Middleton Murry,* 1913–1922 (1951).

KATHERINE ANNE PORTER (1894–)

Stories:
Hacienda (1934); *Flowering Judas and Other Stories* (1935); *Noon Wine* (1937); *Pale Horse, Pale Rider* (1939); *The Leaning Tower and Other Stories* (1944).
Novel:
Ship of Fools (1962).
Essays:
The Days Before (1952). *The Collected Essays and Occasional Writings of Katherine Anne Porter* (1970).

KAY BOYLE (1903–)

Short Stories:
Short Stories (1929); *Wedding Day and Other Stories* (1930); *The First Lover and Other Stories* (1933); *The White Horses of Vienna and Other Stories* (1936); *The Crazy Hunter: Three Short Novels* (1940); *Thirty Stories* (1946); *The Smoking Mountain: Stories of Post War Germany* (1951); *Three Short Novels* (1958); *Nothing Ever Breaks Except the Heart* (1966).
Novels:
Plagued by the Nightingale (1931); *Year Before Last* (1932); *Gentlemen, I Address You Privately* (1933); *My Next Bride* (1934); *Death of a Man* (1936); *Monday Night* (1938); *Primer for Combat* (1942); *Avalanche* (1944); *A Frenchman Must Die* (1946); *1939*

(1948); *His Human Majesty* (1949); *The Seagull on the Step* (1955); *Generation Without Farewell* (1960); *The Underground Woman* (1975).

EUDORA WELTY (1909–)

Short Stories:
A Curtain of Green (1941); *The Wide Net and Other Stories* (1943); *The Golden Apples* (1949); *Selected Stories* (1954); *The Bride of the Innisfallen and Other Stories* (1955); *Thirteen Stories* (1965).
Novels:
The Robber Bridegroom (1942); *Delta Wedding* (1946); *The Ponder Heart* (1954); *Losing Battles* (1970).

HORTENSE CALISHER (1911–)

Short Stories:
In the Absence of Angels: Stories (1952); *Tale for the Mirror: A Novella and Other Stories* (1963); *Extreme Magic: A Novella and Other Stories* (1964).
Novels:
False Entry (1962); *Textures of Life* (1963); *Journal from Ellipsia* (1965); *The Railway Police and The Last Trolley Ride* (two novellas) (1966); *The New Yorkers* (1969); *Queenie* (1971).

ANN PETRY (1912–)

Short Stories:
Miss Muriel and Other Stories (1971);
Novels:
The Street (1946); *Country Place* (1947); *The Narrows* (1953).

MARY LAVIN (1912–)

Short Stories:
Tales from Bective Bridge (1942); *The Long Ago and Other Stories* (1944); *The Becker Wives and Other Stories* (1946); *A Single Lady and Other Stories* (1951); *The Patriot Son and Other Stories* (1957); *A Likely Story* (1957); *Selected Stories* (1959); *The Great Wave and Other Stories* (1961); *The Stories of*

Mary Lavin (2 vols., 1964, 1972); *In the Middle of the Fields and Other Stories* (1967); *Happiness and Other Stories* (1969); *A Memory and Other Stories* (1974).
Novels:
The House in Clewe Street (1945); *Mary O'Grady* (1950).

TILLIE OLSEN (1913–)

Short Stories:
Tell Me a Riddle (1961).
Novels:
Yonnondio from the Thirties (1974).

MAEVE BRENNAN (1917–)

Short Stories:
In and Out of Never-Never Land (1969); *Christmas Eve* (1973).

CARSON McCULLERS (1917–1967)

Novels:
The Heart Is a Lonely Hunter (1940); *Reflections in a Golden Eye* (1941); *The Member of the Wedding* (1946); *The Square Root of Wonderful* (1958); *Clock Without Hands* (1961).
Short Stories:
The Ballad of the Sad Café and Other Stories (1951).

DORIS LESSING (1919–)

Short Stories:
This Was the Old Chief's Country: Stories (1951); *Five: Short Novels* (1953); *The Habit of Loving* (1957); *A Man and Two Women: Stories* (1963); *African Stories* (1964); *Nine African Stories* (1968).
Novels:
The Grass Is Singing (1950); *Children of Violence: Martha Quest* (1952); *A Proper Marriage* (1954); *A Ripple from the Storm* (1958); *Landlocked* (1965); *The Four-Gated City* (1969); *Retreat to Innocence* (1953); *The Golden Notebook* (1962); *Briefing for a Descent into Hell* (1971); *The Summer Before Dark* (1973).

GRACE PALEY (1922–)

Short Stories:
The Little Disturbances of Man (1959); *Enormous Changes at the Last Minute* (1974).

FLANNERY O'CONNOR (1925–1964)

Short Stories:
A Good Man Is Hard to Find and Other Stories (1955); *Everything That Rises Must Converge* (1965); *The Complete Stories of Flannery O'Connor* (1971).
Novels:
Wise Blood (1952); *The Violent Bear It Away* (1960).

JEAN STUBBS (1926–)

The Rose-Grower (1962); *The Travelers* (1963); *Hanrahan's Colony* (1964); *The Straw Crown* (1966); *My Grand Enemy* (1967); *Dear Laura* (1973).

EDNA O'BRIEN (1930–)

Short Stories:
The Love Object (1968); *A Scandalous Woman and Other Stories* (1974).
Novels: *The Country Girls* (1960); *The Lonely Girl* (1962); *Girls in Their Married Bliss* (1964); *August Is A Wicked Month* (1965); *Casualties of Peace* (1966); *A Pagan Place* (1970); *Night* (1973).

ALICE MUNRO (1931–)

Short Stories:
Dance of the Happy Shades (1968); *Something I've Been Meaning To Tell You* (1974).
Novel:
The Lives of Girls and Women (1971).

JOYCE CAROL OATES (1938–)

Short Stories:
By The North Gate (1963); *Upon the Sweeping Flood* (1966); *The Wheel of Love* (1970); *Marriages & Infidelities* (1972); *The Seduction & Other Stories* (1975).
Novels:

With Shuddering Fall (1964); *A Garden of Earthly Delights* (1970); *Expensive People* (1968); *Them* (1969); *Wonderland* (1971); *Do with Me What You Will* (1973).

MARGARET DRABBLE (1939–)

Uncollected Short Stories:
"Hassan's Tower" in *Winter's Tales 12* (1966); "The Reunion" in *Winter's Tales 14* (1968); "The Gifts of War" in *Winter's Tales 16* (1970).
Novels:
A Summer Bird-Cage (1964); *The Garrick Year* (1964);
The Millstone (1965); *Jerusalem the Golden* (1967); *The Waterfall* (1969); *The Needle's Eye* (1972).

ALICE WALKER (1944–)

Short Stories:
In Love and Trouble (1973).
Novels:
The Third Life of Grange Copeland (1970).